Advance praise for *Leaving Co*

"Powerful and moving, *Leaving Coy's Hill* deftly examines the lifelong ambitions and friendships of abolitionist and suffragist Lucy Stone as she balances family and work, personal pain and public responsibilities, the strong pull of home and the prohibitive demands of the road. With an acute sense of place and an assured hand, Sherbrooke gives Lucy Stone the exposition and recognition she deeply deserves while bringing to light buried truths about the underbelly of the women's rights movement in the United States. A beautiful meditation on advocacy and courage with a heroine who is impossible to forget."

—Marjan Kamali, author of *The Stationery Shop* and *Together Tea*

"What could be more timely than Sherbrooke's gorgeously fictionalized and page-turning account of Lucy Stone, the first woman in Massachusetts to earn a college degree, to keep her maiden name, and to fight for women's rights? A stunning look at timeless issues—how we navigate motherhood and career, marriage or staying single, and how we create change in a world that seems to have gone crazy, all told through the lens of one extraordinary heroine."

—Caroline Leavitt, *New York Times* bestselling author of *Pictures of You* and *With or Without You*

"Sherbrooke taps into the current moment with authenticity and vulnerability, outrage and heartbreak. You'll shake your head and raise your fist as Lucy Stone, suffragist and abolitionist, fights maddeningly familiar battles—for pay and property, for physical safety and bodily autonomy, for universal rights and freedoms, and to etch her own name into the history books and prove she is no one's relic. *Leaving Coy's Hill* is deeply moving and profoundly relevant."

—Susan Bernhard, author of *Winter Loon*

"This propulsive and astonishing story transported me to another era while compelling me to think deeply about questions that are as relevant today as they were in the 1800s: *What is equality? What will we sacrifice for our principles? What makes a person whole?* Immersed in stunning detail and evocative voices from the past, I came to deeply respect Lucy Stone's tenacity, admire her passion and eloquence—and love her for her humility and her lasting power. A beautiful story that shines a powerful light on values we still struggle to realize and uphold."

—Katrin Schumann, author of *This Terrible Beauty* and *The Forgotten Hours*

"A powerful and stirring portrait of one of the most influential women in the equal rights movement. Thanks to Sherbrooke's skillful storytelling, Lucy Stone is no less inspiring today than she was 170 years ago. Don't be surprised if you find yourself ready to march!"

—Isla Morley, author of *The Last Blue* and *Come Sunday*

"With incredible elegance and insight, *Leaving Coy's Hill* strikes a perfect balance between historical setting and a rendering of the inner woman. I delighted in Lucy's character, her quirks, ambition, loves, as well as her friendships and connectedness to important figures of the time. While *Leaving Coy's Hill* illuminates the timeless female struggle for equality, tight roping career and motherhood, and achieving financial independence, its crowning achievement is an authentic, poetic voice. Sherbrooke's language set the clocks back a hundred and fifty years with its soothing, measured cadence. Clear your calendar for this one, it's an impossible-to-put-down, must read."

—Jeanne McWilliams Blasberg, author of *Eden* and *The Nine*

"*Leaving Coy's Hill* is both an intimate, urgent confession by a mother to a daughter and a powerful corrective to the biography of one of our country's most consequential yet under appreciated reformers. Katherine Sherbrooke has brought the daring, dauntless, silver-throated Lucy Stone to vivid life, giving us a thoroughly modern heroine whose bold vision has still yet to be fully realized more than a hundred years after her passing. An inspiring, provocative read."

—Christopher Castellani, author of *Leading Men*

"Lucy Stone is the heroine we all need right now. Author Katherine Sherbrooke brings the real historical figure of Lucy Stone to life as a stubborn and fierce defender of women's rights and the rights of Black Americans in an 1800's United States not quite ready for her message. Through her poignant and beautiful story about one woman's fight for justice two hundred years ago, Sherbrooke quietly reminds us all that the battle still isn't over."

—Julie Carrick Dalton, author of *Waiting for the Night Song*

LEAVING COY'S HILL

a novel

KATHERINE A. SHERBROOKE

PEGASUS BOOKS
NEW YORK LONDON

LEAVING COY'S HILL

Pegasus Books, Ltd.
148 West 37th Street, 13th Floor
New York, NY 10018

First Pegasus Books paperback edition August 2022
First Pegasus Books cloth edition May 2021

Interior design by Maria Fernandez

Library of Congress Cataloging-in-Publication Data is available.

ISBN: 978-1-63936-218-9

10 9 8 7 6 5 4 3 2 1

Printed in the United States of America
Distributed by Simon & Schuster
www.pegasusbooks.com

For all the women and men

who continue to fight for equality

I think, with never-ending gratitude, that the young women of today do not and can never know at what price their right to free speech and to speak at all in public has been earned.

—Lucy Stone, 1893

The root of oppression is the loss of memory.

—Paula Gunn Allen, 1986

LEAVING COY'S HILL

PART I

1
CHICAGO WORLD'S FAIR
1893

It has been years since I last spoke in front of such a large crowd. I remove my notes from the credenza, the pages fluttering in my hand. It's not nervousness that makes my hands tremble but rather a familiar excitement. The chance to inspire a crowd of young people is a gift for an old woman like me.

Alice rushes about our rooms, collecting my hat and coat, seeing to everything I need. I haven't told her that the pain in my abdomen is almost unbearable this morning, that I fear I might never recover my full energy again—there's no use worrying her when we are so far from home with little to be done about it. But it makes today's announcement all the more important. I should have promoted her to editor in chief of *The Women's Journal* months ago. The rigor of the job has been too much for me for some time, and she has certainly proven herself. At thirty-six, she's a smart and capable woman, a persuasive writer, thoughtful in her assessments and never hesitant to share a well-considered opinion. She's never had to bend her beliefs to please a husband. Not that she ever would. I was the same at that age. My convictions were all I had.

I can already picture her delight when she hears the news, how her hand will fly up to her mouth to cover the toothy grin she's never liked, how the tears will stream from her eyes. I can hear the enthusiastic applause of the audience and envision the nodding heads of thousands of subscribers across the country when they read of the change. They know our reliable assistant editor is more than ready to take the helm from me. I've dared to imagine this day for years, and I can't deny an overwhelming sense of pride that it has finally arrived.

A knock rattles our door, and Alice dutifully goes to see who might be calling so early in the day. She returns with a telegram in hand, her face pale.

"What is it?" I ask, pushing myself up from my chair, my spine gone cold.

"Johannes." She lowers herself onto a window seat, her eyes fixed on the paper in her lap.

It's always bad news that travels fast. I wait for her to put words to it.

"He says he needs to set sail earlier than planned," she says, looking up at me. "He wants me to come with him."

"To Armenia?" The words tumble out before I can control the panic in my voice.

"This is a proposal." She smiles into her hand as her cheeks turn pink.

I had no idea it was so serious. Alice and I work together every day, and yet she has said little to me about this man. Perhaps she thinks I'm too old to have useful insights. Or does she simply not value my counsel?

"Is it what you want?" I try this time to keep judgment out of my voice.

"I don't know. How does one know such a thing?"

Time presses in on me. I had hoped to present her with her future today, and I will admit I was anticipating the relief of putting the paper into such capable hands. The room wobbles on a wave of nausea. She looks toward the clock on the mantle.

"We'd best be off, or you'll be late for your speech." She snatches her coat from the rack by the door and takes my arm as we head for our carriage. She shortens her gate to match mine.

We find the Women's Pavilion among the acres of exhibits, canals, and attractions of the fair and enter the auditorium through the door behind the stage. When Alice parts the curtain, the applause rushes at us, and I wonder for a moment if we have interrupted someone else's remarks. She cups my elbow and guides me to the dais. Hundreds of people fill the seats, their smooth faces looking up at me. This is what will make the 1,000 rattling miles from Boston to Chicago worth it. My body is too much of a burden for that kind of travel anymore.

I scan the audience until I find my touchstone. I've always done this, picked out one person in the room to use as a bellwether for how my message is being received. I'm not used to having so many friendly faces to choose from. In the early days, I would often have to utilize a snarling bearded man as my measuring stick. But even that would suffice. Today I find a young woman about ten rows back who looks quite a bit like I did in my youth. She is petite, with thick brown hair pulled neatly off her face, and her smile accentuates pleasantly rounded cheeks. She even has my bright gray eyes. I decide to name her Hope.

I look down at my prepared remarks, entitled "The Progress of Fifty Years," and wonder if I should use this time to deliver an entirely different speech. Perhaps I should raise the question of whether what we've achieved can be called progress at all if women are forced to decide between professional opportunity and love. Which will Alice choose?

Hope unfolds and refolds a handkerchief in her lap. She is anxious for me to begin, is perhaps even worried that I will falter. I owe her the talk she came to hear. I grip the podium, scan my notes, and speak:

"Three years even before the last fifty marks the beginning of true progress—with the opening of a door, the door to education. When the first college in this country decided to allow women, it finally gave our sex access to the tree of knowledge, to a root system that could nourish our starving minds."

I remind Hope that once the spread of truth and knowledge began, it could not be stopped. Professional barriers were the next to fall. I tell her of my great friend Nette, who was the first female to be ordained as a Protestant minister, and Elizabeth Blackwell, the first female doctor licensed in the country. Hope is smiling and nodding; she is with me now.

I note the many guilds and organizations available to women and, perhaps most importantly, how the right for us to speak in public at all was won. Rows of shoulders relax into my words as they pour forth. Heads bob up and down with satisfaction.

That's when I see her, sitting in the front row of the balcony. How did I not notice her bright red shawl and wire-rimmed glasses earlier? Susan B. Anthony, as thin and prim as ever, her power undiminished by her years. Once my dear friend and most trusted ally, here she is, listening to me speak of our shared history, of the accomplishments we worked so hard together to achieve. It's kind of her to be here, but I cannot deny that the old anger still rankles, and I work hard to keep it out of my voice. I do not want her to know that I see her. I understood from the beginning that fighting for women's rights would not be easy work, that my own version of right and wrong would cost me friends. But never did I expect to lose this friend.

Over breakfast, I read in the morning paper an article entitled "Ms. Anthony Charms in Chicago." According to the article, Susan was well received here yesterday and gracious in her remarks. She passed the credit for the founding of our great women's movement onto four women, putting my name on a list that didn't include her own. We've learned to be good to each other in public. And yet we've been unable to forgive each other.

And how extraordinary, really, that neither of us is likely to survive long enough to walk into a booth and cast a proper vote. That will be a bitter pill for her. It is everything to her.

Hope's gaze implores me to go on. I summon my thoughts into a stream of words, coaxing them to flow through the auditorium. I will admit that I was blessed with a voice for this work. With a little practice, it's easy to speak loudly enough so those in the back row don't have to strain to hear. Doing so while not overwhelming the front row is the trick. No one likes a woman who yells. But they say I was born with a voice like a babbling brook, soothing to hear even as it cuts a new path into the silt of an unsuspecting mind.

I try not to grimace as I gather in my breath, the pain in my side thrumming.

I glance at my prepared remarks again and hesitate. I've arrived at the moment when I was planning to share the example of progress nearest to my heart, the success of *The Women's Journal* as one of the longest running papers in our country and the only one devoted entirely to women's rights, the moment when I had planned to introduce Alice as its new editor in chief.

But I can't do that now. She might think I'm trying to force a decision on her that's not mine to make. How ironic that such a hard-won opportunity might now be seen as a burden, an obligation she no longer wants because of the pull of a more traditional life. Why is it that her potential husband—any husband—never has to make that choice?

I turn over the papers in front of me and close my remarks instead with my most deeply held belief, that what we need most of all to continue our progress is to speak the truth fearlessly. Where I found that courage at so young an age, I don't know. But as Susan once said, "It is not bravery when you know you're right."

I look up to her before I can stop myself, and she tips her head at me—an entreaty to mend what divides us?

Alice is at my side then, steadying me against the sudden explosion of applause. Hope is on her feet, as is everyone around her. Tears rush down her cheeks and drip into her bright smile. A familiar joy swells in my heart, the sense that maybe I have changed one mind, moved one detractor, made one woman's place at her own dining table a more respected seat. That is all I have ever wanted.

I look into the balcony again to share the moment with Susan, but she is already gone.

❧

Back in our rooms, I lean into a soft pillow and drag my aching feet onto the settee. I am exhausted and unsettled in equal measure.

"What do you plan to do?" I ask, trying to find a gentle way back to our earlier conversation.

"I was thinking I should call on that fellow Harding this afternoon and finally grant him an interview with you," Alice says. "You must have seen Susan in the balcony today. Wouldn't it be the perfect time to set the record straight?"

"You know where I stand on that issue."

"It still makes no sense to me. Why should she be unfettered in writing history in the way that best suits her?"

Alice and I have been having this debate for years, ever since Susan and Elizabeth Cady Stanton published the first volume of the *History of Woman Suffrage* more than a decade ago, a book that essentially removed me from the story.

"I meant about Johannes," I say.

"Oh." She gazes out the tall window, which is closed against the soft drizzle outside and the throngs of carriages and umbrellas clattering below. "I do adore him. But I don't know how we could manage. He has his work, and I have mine."

"Work isn't always the best substitute for companionship. That I know from experience."

"So, you think I should go?" She speaks with surprise and something like excitement in her voice. "What about the *Journal*?"

I'm unsure how best to answer that. Pretending I could readily find a replacement would dramatically underestimate her value. I don't know of another woman in the country with the skills and experience she has. But telling her the truth—that I can't imagine the paper surviving without her after I'm gone—might limit her freedom to make the best choice for her.

"Would Johannes ever consider moving here?"

"His work is in Armenia. He feels responsible for helping to keep their culture alive. It would be hard for him to be anywhere else."

"It's difficult to compete with a passion like that. You might always feel second to his work." The pull of my own work has tested my priorities more than I'm sometimes willing to admit.

"I knew you'd be against it," she says.

"That's not what I said. But you have to weigh whatever you want right now against what you might have to give up. Sacrifice can put enormous strain on a relationship."

She pulls a chair close to mine. "You had to make the same choice once. Tell me how you decided."

I lean back, trying not to grimace. It's such a personal question.

"This isn't about me. This is about your life," I say.

"You said in your speech today that women can't truly move forward unless we understand the hurdles of the past, the limits that were put on us, the breakthroughs, the consequences borne. Why do you refuse to speak of your own?"

Her tone pains me. It isn't argumentative so much as the plea of a thirsty traveler wondering if a small sip of water is too much to ask of someone holding an overflowing jug.

My good friend Frederick Douglass taught me that personal stories have the greatest impact. He encouraged me when I was new to the speakers' circuit to include human stories in my anti-slavery speeches, like the story of the escaped slave I met in Cincinnati who broke her own daughter's neck rather than hand her over to the slave hunters who had caught them. He said I must also speak aloud of the nursemaid in Alabama who was repeatedly raped while her babe slept nearby. No one wants to hear these things, which is exactly the point. Mr. Douglass understood that laws ending slavery would not erase the premise that a negro's life, free or not, was considered inferior. Only by revealing individual hardships and triumphs do we come to truly care about one another. I've tried to infuse every lecture I've ever given with this idea, and yet my own stories have always felt too personal, or too specific, or both.

And how would Alice judge the choices I've made? Am I ready to admit to my mistakes, tell her how some of my most important relationships were damaged along the way? I couldn't bear to have her think less of me. And would those stories turn her away from our work? From attempting a life with Johannes? Which would I wish for her? My stomach churns again, and I shift my weight to my left side, trying to quell the spark of pain shooting through my abdomen.

"You don't really want to hear about all that," I finally say.

"I do," she says. "Now more than ever."

She takes off her shoes and tucks her feet beneath her skirts, the way she always does before diving into a favorite book of poetry. She is both relaxed and eager, attentive and entirely patient, a mixture of attributes I have long envied. I glance at the clock as it ticks relentlessly on. I know there are other speeches she plans to attend, scores of exhibits she wants to see.

"We have time," she says. "Tell me."

2

It's not easy to know where to start, Alice. This is new territory for me. What fragment of my life is worthy of note as a stepping-stone to a larger decision? Which decision won't make sense unless you know all that came before?

You already know that growing up under a staunch abolitionist played a central role in my childhood—it wasn't fashionable at the time, even in the North, and my father was as firm in his hatred of slavery as he was in his love of whiskey. And watching my eldest brothers head off to college before I turned ten sparked in me a burning desire to follow that path, even though no colleges accepted women at the time. But you asked about the choices I made regarding marriage, why I avoided it at all costs for so long, why I even considered it, and that story can only begin in one place—on the day my cousin Abigail got married. Up until then I was just a girl on a farm.

How I loved that farm! The morning was my favorite time, driving out the cows with Old Bogue wagging by my side. My brother Luther was supposed to share this chore with me, but he was afraid of the dark. So I often rose before dawn to enjoy the solace of the last star in the brightening sky. The climb up Coy's Hill invigorated my senses, and once at the top, I could see from our sheep pasture all the way to the apple orchard. Our acreage was an eternity to me, the rocky outcroppings of Coy's Hill my own personal castle. Anything was possible standing atop the edge of the world while everyone else was still asleep.

Abigail's wedding day rolled in on a wave of gray. The drizzle pecked at my cheeks and clung to Old Bogue's fur, but it could not dampen my excitement. I'd never been to a wedding before. I wondered how Abigail would feel putting on the dress she'd shown me—fashioned by her mother from a bolt of pale silk the color of the sky in winter, wispy white with only a hint of blue. I had never seen such fine fabric.

When I asked Abigail if she was nervous, she told me Jeb seemed nice enough and that her mother had said she would grow fond of him over time. Besides, not much would be changing. They were going to build their own cottage at Plum Tree Farm so Jeb could help Abigail's father. She would still be able to ride her horse, Willow, on their favorite trails every day, and I could still visit whenever I pleased. I didn't understand the point of it all, but at only twelve, I figured there was a lot about marriage I didn't understand.

Despite my anticipation, the wedding ceremony was unremarkable, with three hymns, a reading from the minister, and the speaking of the vows. Mama and all the older women in the congregation dabbed at their eyes as promises were made. I kept my eyes on the groom, hoping he might smile. Above all, I wanted Abigail to be marrying a kind man.

Father drove us back to Plum Tree Farm, the ropey veins in his forearms protruding as he whipped and steered the horses. Despite the overcast skies, the breeze was blowing from the direction of summer, and the grass soon dried. Five or six families came to Plum Tree to enjoy a rare afternoon of leisure. After Luther and I had our fill of rhubarb pie, I wandered down to the barn to visit Willow. He would have missed his daily ride that day, and I was sure he would appreciate some company.

Abigail had taken care of him entirely for the past ten years, from the time she was nine years old and he was a newborn colt. She named him after her favorite tree on account of his skinny legs. No one thought he would amount to much, but she'd seen strength in those tiny legs, like branches that can bend in on themselves without snapping. Sure enough, Willow had grown into a fine young horse. The way she rode him, they were two parts of the same body. They'd been inseparable for as long as I could remember.

Just before I reached the entrance of the barn, I heard a sputtering sound, the unmistakable gulps of someone trying to breathe through sobs. The pitch of the weeping told me it was Abigail. I ran the remaining distance to the door, but at first I didn't see her when I peered inside. I followed the sounds to Willow's stall and found her curled up on a pile of hay in the corner, her dress crumpled around her.

"What is it?" I asked, kneeling beside her.

It was some time before she could speak.

"He's gone," she said, and broke into a fresh set of sobs.

"Jeb?" I asked. But I had just seen him up by the house, celebrating.

She shook her head and whispered his name, grimacing with the pain of it. "Willow."

"Willow?" I suddenly realized that Willow wasn't in the stall with us and that I hadn't seen him out grazing. Had he taken ill? Had there been some kind of accident?

Abigail was crying too hard to say more. I stroked her back and waited, trying to swallow what felt like a clump of hay lodged in my throat.

Finally, Abigail sat up and rubbed her face, blotchy and wet. She exhaled a great breath of air and swept her hand over her tangled hair before she spoke.

"Jeb sold him," she said.

"What? How can that be?"

"I guess Jeb had some debts. He promised my father he would settle them right away, so we could start fresh." Abigail's words were slurred with fatigue. "A man came while we were at church. I didn't even get to say good-bye."

She broke down again, and I pulled her to me, trying to make sense of it.

"Did you tell your father? Surely he can fix this." While Uncle Joseph teased Abigail for her attachment to Willow—"Horses are for pulling things," he'd say—I knew he had his own favorites in the barn. He always said that Banshee and Vulcan knew what field to dig into before he even hitched them to the plow. He wouldn't let his daughter's horse be sold for some cluster of coins.

"Father said it is my husband's right to do what he thinks is best with his property, and it is my duty to support him," she said, clearly reciting his words.

"But Willow is *your* property."

"Not anymore." She looked small then, as if the hay might swallow her.

None of it made any sense. Question upon question piled up in my mind.

"Mother says once I have children, I won't have time for horses anyway, and my heart will be full again." A new rush of tears brimmed over her lashes. "But I don't know what I'll do without him."

How could her parents have known about this and allowed it to happen? And how could Abigail possibly live with Jeb now? I clutched Abigail tighter, overwhelmed by the sense that until that moment I had been seeing the world around me through a mist as thick as the low-lying fog that accompanies a summer storm. I hadn't tried hard enough to see the details for what they were: the animal-like grunts that came from Mama's bed some nights, her helpless whimpers seeping through my wall; Father's refusal to allow Mama the smallest sum of money, even though she had earned a significant share of it herself.

I pulled my right hand into a fist and tapped it against my thigh, something Mama had taught me to help control my temper. Abigail shook as she wept. I knew there were no words of comfort I could offer, but something had to be done to get Willow back.

After a long time, Abigail's weeping slowed. She lifted her head off my shoulder and settled back down into Willow's sleeping corner. I covered her with a riding blanket and kissed her forehead, the way Mama always did when putting me to bed. I backed out of the stall as quietly as I could.

I ran home through the woods that separated Plum Tree Farm from ours. I hadn't let my own sobs escape me when I was with Abigail, but now I allowed the fury to explode out of my throat in a high-pitched mix of fear and resolution, like a fox warning off prey. My pace quickened the more I thought about what had just happened. Father said our country was intended to put everyone on equal footing. Surely there were laws to protect against a cruel act like Jeb's.

Abigail needed to understand her rights. And I knew just who to ask.

❧

Mr. Merrill was the local judge, or at least he used to be. He'd stopped going to the courthouse a few years back and was lonely for conversation, I think. I walked by his house every afternoon on my way home from school, and he would often call out to me and invite me up to his porch for a glass of lemonade and ask me what I was studying in class. He told me stories about the cases he'd tried and especially liked it when I asked questions.

"Now, you're a smart one, aren't you?" he'd say, before adding, "It's a shame you weren't born a boy. You could have made a fine lawyer."

Mr. Merrill wasn't in his favorite rocking chair on the porch that afternoon. I strolled slowly past the kitchen window, twice, but even that didn't raise a call from within. I'd never stepped onto the front stoop uninvited but decided my questions couldn't wait. I knocked.

Mrs. Merrill opened the door.

"Hello, Lucy. How nice to see you," she said, wiping floured hands on her apron.

"I'm sorry to disturb, but is the judge home?"

When Mr. Merrill finally appeared, he smiled at me while trying to smooth an unruly patch of gray hair atop his head. His wool pants were slightly wrinkled, and I suspected I might have interrupted him in the middle of an afternoon nap.

"What brings you here on this fine day?" he asked, sitting in the rocking chair beside me and pulling out a pouch of tobacco for his pipe.

"I was wondering," I started, unsure how to begin. I decided to get right to the point. "What are the laws of marriage? Specifically, as they apply to the rights of the wife."

He raised his eyebrows as the flame from his match bobbed above the pipe.

"You're a bit young to be worried about that, aren't you?"

"This isn't for me. It's just—" I wasn't sure how much to say. My parents warned us all against telling stories that were not ours to tell. Gossip could be like a worm that, when multiplied, destroys a whole crop. "Something happened that I'm trying to understand, is all. And I was wondering what your ruling would be if the problem came before you as a judge."

"Ah," he said, nodding. "I heard about the Lamberton trouble. Upsetting business. I'm sorry you had to hear about it."

I didn't know what he meant. The Lambertons lived farther out of town than we did. Mr. Lamberton had a reputation for taking too hard to the bottle and neglecting the farm. My mother sometimes gave Mrs. Lamberton a brick of cheese for free when her pantry was empty, and we'd hosted all the children for supper more than once. She always seemed intensely grateful for the kindness and equally ashamed by the reality of needing it to feed her own family. As awful as that all was, I had the feeling he was talking about something else.

"And you, Miss Lucy, would like to know what the repercussion would be in court for Mr. Lamberton."

No one else called me Miss Lucy. It made me feel grown-up and capable of understanding his detailed legal explanations, which was important, because he rarely substituted small words for complicated ones just because I was twelve.

"Most of the laws of the Union, not to mention our customs, are based on the common laws of England, and I'm afraid that a husband has long had the right to beat his wife with an instrument of reasonable size."

Beat his wife? I couldn't control the look of surprise that must have jumped onto my face. My stomach clenched as something threatened to rise from my memory, but I pushed it aside. I couldn't allow myself to be distracted from the conversation at hand.

"The use of the word 'reasonable' is ludicrous, I know. There is a famous case, in 1782, where a Judge Buller determined that any whip, switch, or even piece of wood, as long as it is not much thicker than his thumb, could be considered reasonable." He chuckled. "That caused quite an uproar, every woman within a stone's throw of the courthouse demanding to see the size of his thumb. Can you imagine?"

Mrs. Merrill placed two glasses of lemonade and a small plate of sugar cookies on the table between our chairs, then stepped back and put her hands on her hips.

"Are you upsetting the child, William?" she asked.

"She came for the facts, dear. I will continue to give her the facts." He took another long pull off his pipe. Mrs. Merrill shook her head and went back inside.

"As I was saying," he continued, "we have these same laws here in our Union, except, I am pleased to say, in this fine commonwealth. Judge Sewall of Salem, back in 1696, I think it was, declared that married women should be free from bodily harm. So according to Massachusetts law anyway, corporal punishment of a wife is not permitted."

Hope blossomed in my chest.

"So, Mrs. Lamberton has a case against her husband, then?"

"I'm afraid this is where practical matters require great caution, Miss Lucy. Mrs. Lamberton would likely be no better off even if she did prosecute the case. I had a similar case come to me, back in 1821, *Mrs. Granger v. Mr. Granger*, with an allegation of wife-beating and a request for legal divorce. The wife-beating portion was easy to prove—her sister lived with her and had witnessed countless episodes. But Blackstone's law would ensure that were she to separate from her husband, she would lose everything."

"Blackstone's law?" I put the glass of lemonade I'd been clutching back on the table.

"Feme covert, it's called. As soon as a woman is married, everything she owns becomes her husband's possession. She has no right to land or income. Mrs. Granger came into her marriage with more than two hundred acres of inherited land and a small fortune her father had made in the spice trade. It all belonged to Mr. Granger by law. I had to counsel her that separating from him would have made her destitute."

"Everything becomes his?"

"It's what the law stipulates."

"So, if Mrs. Granger owned, hypothetically, a herd of cattle before she was married, her husband would have the right to sell them once they got married?"

"I suppose if he wanted to do that, yes, he could."

"And if she hadn't married?"

"Feme sole, that's called. As long as a woman is an adult, she can inherit her family's possessions and they are hers to keep."

My hope for Abigail shriveled. Willow wouldn't be coming back, and there was nothing I could do. By marrying Jeb, she'd essentially given Willow away. I gripped the arms of the rocker with both hands. And what about Mrs. Lamberton? Surely she couldn't be forced to live with a man who beat her? Massachusetts law at least said that wasn't legal. And in her case, there wasn't much in the way of possessions to leave behind. Besides, worldly goods are no measure of a person's soul, Mama always says.

"If Mrs. Lamberton were willing to start over, to find a new home, she could plead her case and get away from her husband?" I asked.

"Technically, but then we come to the children. Again, the laws do not complement each other well. She would have to be willing to leave her children behind."

"Why would she have to do that?"

"Women have no claim to their children, I'm afraid," he said gently.

The Merrills' porch blurred. The Lamberton children belonged to their father more than to their own mother? We belonged more to Father than Mama? But she had birthed us, nursed us, made our clothes, fed us, tended to us when we were sick. How could that be? No wife was ever free to leave if she couldn't take her children with her. Something again pricked at the surface of my memory, but I tamped it down.

Judge Merrill let out a sigh. "Mrs. Merrill is right. I am upsetting you. You have no need to worry about this, Miss Lucy. All you need to do is be sure to find a good man of your own. Then you won't have to worry about any of these problems."

The black tendril of an oncoming headache unfolded from my spine and began to wind its way around the back of my skull.

"I have to get home. Thank you for seeing me," I said, and hurried off the porch.

❧

By the time I arrived back at our farm, all the laundry had already been hung out to dry, and Mama was cleaving a chicken in two in the kitchen.

"There you are, Lucy. I've been wondering when you might turn up." Her voice was cheerful despite how tired she looked, the patches below her eyes the color of pond water.

We all worked hard, but no one as hard as my mother. She was barely five feet tall, and fiercely strong from all the churning, straining, molding, and pressing that occupied much of her day. When she wasn't making or selling cheese, she was weaving, mending, washing, and cooking. I don't recall ever seeing her sit down with the sun high in the sky outside of church, not until we'd all finished the evening meal and gathered around the hearth to listen to Father read aloud. Even then she toiled, a pile of mending in her lap, her needles flashing in the firelight.

And with all of Mama's hard work, she had nothing to keep for herself. She was forced to ask for coins to buy fabric for our clothes or yarn for the loom, permission Father rarely granted. He was king in our house, my mother treated like a peasant. I wanted to tell her to fight back. I wanted to pound my father's chest and tell him to change the rules. But I also understood for the first time how much the rules benefitted him. Even he said that those whom laws and custom benefit are the slowest to opt for change, regardless of harm to others. He had taught us that the seeds of moral depravity were born from the instinct to cling to power. Slavery not only imprisoned negroes, he said, but also shackled the hearts of slave owners to a power they never should have been granted, and one they would never willingly give up. Was marriage any different?

"You don't look well," Mama said as I leaned against the butcher block. "Do you feel ill?"

"I've decided something, Mama." I steadied myself, determined to keep any hint of hysteria or drama out of my voice.

She waited.

"I am never going to get married." The words felt good in my mouth.

"Oh dear, I know you're upset about Abigail, but good things come of making a family together. You'll see." She reached out to stroke my hair.

"No, Mama. I mean it. Not ever. I promise."

In our house, promises were not taken lightly. Your word was all you had in the end, Father would say.

"Oh, my dear girl," she said, and hugged me to her. She knew I meant it.

3

I can tell you now that my life took on a lonely tone after my declaration not to wed. There were no more visits to Willow's stall with apples for his feed bag. I tucked notes inside the saddle that still hung in the barn, Abigail's strained replies a reminder of how little of her life belonged to her anymore. While I once happily filled my days with school, helping Mama in the cheese cellar, exploring the rocky nooks of Coy's Hill with Luther, working the loom with my older sisters, and listening to Father read aloud at night from the abolitionist newspaper, *The Liberator*, my waking hours were now dominated by a determination to create a life free from dependence on any man. I knew this meant furthering my education so I could earn my own way, and I even dared to dream of working on behalf of anti-slavery activities. Perhaps more than anything, I dreamed of one day making my father proud. I yearned to show him that a daughter could have as much worth as a son, that I could further the cause most important to him if given the chance. Ironically, this required defying him at every turn. He believed there was no reason for a girl to be educated beyond reading, writing, and simple arithmetic. A woman's place was in the domestic sphere, raising children and keeping house. Anything else was unthinkable, and both of my older sisters were willing to oblige. I wasn't surprised when Eliza, with her kind nature and pleasant countenance, accepted the first proposal she received. But even Rhoda, who shared my love of reading and encouraged me in my schoolwork, married before turning twenty. They both assured me that their husbands-to-be were fine men, nothing like Jeb. But what had my mother thought of my father before she was confined beneath his roof? As the number of women in our house dwindled, I announced my intention to go to college. Father asked Mama if I had gone mad.

Suitors came but were turned away, each one causing my mother further distress as she watched my marrying years come and go. And the tension in the house increased with each of my efforts to further my future, my father somehow blaming my mother for her inability to inspire in me the desire for a more traditional life. It pains me now to think of the burden I must have been to her, but I was not willing to sign up for a life of servitude simply to appease them. I sometimes wondered if my mother didn't want more for me, hadn't wanted more for herself, but I knew that was a bit like wondering if a tree questions its value as a provider of shade and fruit. She was selfless in every way, and I could not fault her for that.

At a starting teaching salary of a dollar fifty per week, it took me until the age of twenty-five to save enough to enter college. And the hard-earned difficulties of Oberlin were no match for the long years afterward spent on the road lecturing on my own. While I made the acquaintance of some dear friends and colleagues along the way, it was a mostly solitary life. I never really questioned if it should be otherwise. Until I met Harry.

But I'm getting ahead of myself. What I'm trying to help you understand, Alice, is that as lonely as I may have been all those years, my views on marriage, which began to form the day of Abigail's wedding, only hardened as I grew older. The more I achieved on my own, the more I was determined not to risk losing any of it. You see, I had diligently forged the armor of my solitary fight, a battle wholly unsupported by my parents, a lone struggle against the many institutions bent on holding me back.

You need to understand what it was like if you are to fully appreciate my reluctance to link my future to any institution that would constrain me, marriage among them. Even Oberlin, one of the first colleges to throw open its doors to nurture young women, proved to be unfertile ground for much change. They were determined to prune all wild roots lest a unique flower be allowed to blossom.

I remember a morning during my junior year as clearly as I see you now. I was taking breakfast with John Langston, a newer student from Pennsylvania whose company I enjoyed and whose schedule was as demanding as my own. Most of the ladies in my dorm had their tuition fully funded, giving them hours of leisure time on campus, and most were six or eight years my junior. Needless to say, we didn't have much in common. But Mr. Langston, the son of a free blacksmith from the West Indies, shared my love of philosophy and my distaste for the religious requirements on campus. Our political views were also aligned, which was rarer at Oberlin than I had hoped. For such a progressive institution—also the first in the country to accept negroes—most students were decidedly moderate when it came to the kind of social change required not only to force the end of slavery but to remake society in its aftermath.

"Bacon this morning, Mr. Langston? Is it your birthday?" I sat down with my bowl of oatmeal. The smell coming from his plate was divine.

"I told you I've been saving for something special. I have an oral examination in chemistry today, so I reckon it's as good a time as any. May I offer you half?"

"I couldn't possibly." I felt a bit like Old Bogue, begging scraps. I had no idea before leaving home how lucky we'd been to have meat every day, and more fresh produce than we could possibly consume. "Unless you insist on teasing me by leaving it uneaten."

"I think I just lost my appetite," he said quietly, glancing over my shoulder.

I turned to see Mrs. Mahan shuffling our way, the broomstick of her neck teetering above her tight corset. She walked as if the mummifying accessory continued below her knees. Her face might have been quite lovely were it not so often pinched in an expression of one trying to determine the source of an unpalatable odor.

"Miss Stone," Mrs. Mahan said, coming to a halt at our table. "It has come to my attention that you failed to attend Sunday services. Please explain yourself."

"I was heeding your decision from last week, ma'am." I was careful to maintain eye contact with her. "You said women cannot attend services without their bonnet."

"I see. You insist on continuing this debate? Please report to the Ladies' Board at four P.M."

"I have a grammar class to teach from four to five."

"Perhaps you should have considered that before defying regulations. Find a substitute. We will see you at four." She carefully spun herself around and shuffled out of the dining hall.

I bit down on the inside of my cheek, wondering why it was always the women who were hardest on other women? President Mahan seemed a lovely and fair-minded man who kept in high regard the best interests of his students. His wife, on the other hand, seemed only interested in her own place in things, especially anything that involved sitting atop the pecking order of college wives.

"Her eye is never far from you, it seems," John said. "As my father always says, 'The rule makers stay closest to the rule breakers.'"

"And as you and I have discussed many times, the truth of the human condition must be prioritized above all, including the rules."

"And what human condition ails you, other than risk of death due to boredom from the insufferable length of Sunday services?"

"I'm certain the bonnet I'm forced to wear brings on my migraines. I petitioned them last week to allow me to attend without one, and before I could explain, Mrs. Mahan banged her gavel and said, 'No lady is allowed to attend services who doesn't wear a bonnet.' So I took her literally and didn't attend." I allowed a smile to creep onto my face.

"Clever," he said, his smile matching my own, "but risky."

"The trouble is that the cause of the migraines is real. I looked it up in the library. The temporal lobe is located right where the edge of a bonnet touches my head. In order to keep it on, the tightness is too much. But the Five Wives will never believe that."

We all called the women who ran the Ladies' Board the Five Wives, as they were the betrothed of the president, the provost, the reverend, and two head professors. The board approached with gusto their task of ensuring proper decorum among the ladies of the school. One such effort came in the form of mandatory weekly lectures on comportment, topics such as how much time was proper to spend with male students, under what circumstances specifically we should and should not fraternize, and how to interact in a classroom environment while maintaining the demeanor of a lady. I preferred my dish-washing duties.

"Bring the text with you to explain the science and bring the bonnet in question. Proof is a powerful thing," John said.

"And if they tell me to buy a bigger bonnet?"

"Then the truth will suffice."

"Good thinking," I said. We both knew I couldn't afford one.

To my delight, John's advice proved excellent. The Five Wives found that while they could not under any circumstances excuse me from church, they could make an exception to the covered head rule, with the understanding that I would always enter the church last and sit in the back. This meant that I would be last into the church, first out, and had escaped with no detention. I almost couldn't believe my good fortune.

Mrs. Mahan then added with a flourish, "Mind your place, Miss Stone. You would be wise not to have cause to reappear in front of this board. Consider yourself duly warned." And then she banged her silver-rimmed gavel, as if there were a large crowd to dismiss.

After my hearing, I had a few minutes to spare and headed down the long hall toward the postmaster's window.

"Good afternoon, Mr. Morgan," I said to the man whose jolly face peered out from the window every day of the week. He did not seem to mind the confines of his tight quarters, made tighter by his large belly.

"You're in a fine spirit, Miss Stone. I wish I had something for you today. But I'm certain the Massachusetts mail train will come through soon, my lady."

My moment's elation at the board's decision evaporated with the look of pity I saw in his eyes, a reminder that I had no one to share it with. Loneliness followed me like an invisible dog I could neither shoo away nor turn to for company. I hugged my stack of books and walked on. Crossing Tappan Square, a bare stretch of dirt with not one tree, it was hard not to miss the majestic oaks of our farm, surely bright orange by now. I pictured the view from atop Coy's Hill, so different from Ohio's endlessly flat landscape.

Despite the cost of postage, I penned a letter home every Friday, and yet I hadn't had a letter back in over six months. In my missives I shared my successes in trigonometry, Latin, and Greek as humbly as possible, wanting to assure my parents that the sacrifice of the great distance between us was proving valuable. I also tried to describe my surroundings and daily life on campus, hoping these details would somehow make our separation less acute. Classwork was of course the top priority, but my studies had to fit around dish-washing duties, teaching underclassmen two hours a day, mending clothes for fellow students—some had endless funds for such luxuries—and tutoring in the village. I sometimes had to rise at three in the morning to complete my homework. But I was careful not to complain in my letters and left out altogether news of my worsening migraines. There was no need to cause Mama worry. I recommended various texts I thought Father might enjoy and included my estimation of speakers who had visited campus, much in the style of William Lloyd Garrison's news from afar in *The Liberator*. I knew Father would be impressed to hear that Stephen Foster had recently visited, his abolitionist lecture causing a stir among students and faculty alike.

My self-pity at being forgotten was increasingly overshadowed by a growing dread. Perhaps the silence was an attempt to shield me from some kind of tragedy at home. The constant state of not knowing crystallized into a sharp ache that pressed upon my heart. We had lost my sister Rhoda to childbirth during my last year at home and Eliza to influenza the following summer. Could my younger sister Sarah have fallen ill? Had the press of years and so much heartache caught up with Mama?

By November I was growing increasingly concerned about my family and began to wonder if I should plan a trip home, my only way to know for sure what had befallen them. But it would cost me dearly. Not just the money, but I feared that if I left Ohio, I might never return.

Standing at the postmaster's window, I once again accepted his apologies for my lack of mail from afar, but he did have something for me. It was a note from Professor Thome, inviting me to his office the next day to discuss my petition to enroll in his rhetoric class.

The idea of being allowed to study rhetoric filled me with such a rush of excitement that I was up most of the night imagining what might be possible. This was my ultimate dream, the skill I had most hoped to learn in college. Of all the news Father read to us from *The Liberator*, the stories of public oratory influencing the country's perspective on abolition struck me the most. I had long imagined the thrill of standing up in front of an audience and inspiring women and men alike with powerful new ideas.

When the rooster crow finally came, I jumped out of bed and set to my toilet. I wasn't certain if the professor would be in his office before morning prayers but decided to skip breakfast in case I might have the chance to see him before the relentless rhythm of the day began in earnest.

The faculty offices were located on the top floor of Colonial Hall, a four-story rectangular building with one huge chimney in the middle. I watched my breath crystallize before me as I climbed the wooden stairwell, noting the sharpness of the indoor chill. Unlike the arctic wind outside, it had no clear source, but it was no less piercing, and my frayed coat was a pathetic defense. It had long ago stopped keeping me warm, but I had no funds to replace it. When I arrived at the professor's door, I was pleased to find him sitting in front of a real fireplace, not one of the potbelly stoves that warmed the classrooms below.

"Ah, Miss Stone," he said, looking up from the volume on his lap. "Do come in."

I sat on a fine, spindled armchair positioned next to shelves that brimmed with more books than even the judge's den in West Brookfield. The fire's warmth began to immediately thaw my outer layers.

"We have been discussing at length your desire to participate in my class," he began, skipping over usual small talk and niceties. "As I'm sure you know, most on the faculty are against the idea of a lady studying rhetoric, at best a waste of time, and at worst an enticement or endorsement of unsavory behavior. But before I say more, I realize that I have failed to ask you what has made you so intent on taking this course to begin with. Might you share that with me?"

I considered how best to answer his question. I was quite sure I shouldn't admit to the anger I felt listening to the infamous Pastoral Letter when it was read aloud in my church, the missive signed by all the ministers in Massachusetts denouncing the Grimké sisters for speaking in front of the state legislature, how motivated I became by the idea of speaking in public one day because of it. No, outright defiance was not something that would move him in my favor. I could have reminded him that my brother Bo was a preacher and had always been an inspiration to me. But I didn't care for the church and didn't want to give him a false sense of my intentions. I settled on the experience that had compelled me most of all, and one he might truly appreciate. I knew he was an abolitionist.

"I assume you know of Abby Kelley, Professor?" I asked.

"Yes, of course."

"And you find her to do important work even though she is a woman?"

"I appreciate that she tries to change the minds of the fairer sex in favor of abolition. Despite what men might admit to in public, many of us are swayed by the opinions of our wives, and in any case, we prefer a house when our philosophies are in harmony. So, I do believe her lectures to women have value, yes." He lit his pipe despite the early hour.

"I had the opportunity to see her speak in my hometown four years ago. She gave the most eloquent oration I have ever heard." I left out the fact that she had actually spoken to a crowd of both women and men.

To our surprise, Father had agreed to take Sarah and me to see her speak at our town hall in the summer of 1842. While he detested the idea of a woman speaking in public, he had never missed an anti-slavery meeting and wasn't prepared to start.

As I listened to her that night, my body felt like a river in spring, finally freed from winter's frozen grasp, the cool water rushing through my veins. A woman was actually speaking to a crowd of mostly men, and they were listening! I practically floated above my chair with the exhilaration of it, my emotions running wild. I was somehow nervous for her at every pause in her lecture, worried she might forget her next thought or that an unsuspecting naysayer would rush the stage. But whenever a moment's hesitation threatened to stretch too far, she would release a torrent of perfectly articulated ideas that built on her previous thoughts. With each stanza, the thrill of it hit me anew and caused a tremor in my limbs.

I watched her carefully: how she referenced her notes but managed to keep most of her focus on those seated before her; how she stood very erect, her spine straight with pride; how her feet, poking out beneath her skirts, suggested a wide stance, as if bracing herself for a charging dog. And she was anything but demure. She was unafraid to let her anger at the current state of the country show. She didn't hold back on expressing her scorn for slaveholders and those who upheld slavery as the law. I could see the disgust on her face, and I could hear it in her voice. When she concluded her remarks, I jumped to my feet and applauded, which earned me a glare from my father.

"Ever since, I have wanted to learn rhetoric, Professor, so that I might aid in the same cause and change hearts and minds like she has."

I also omitted the fact that she didn't change my father's mind about the propriety of women speaking in public in the least. After her speech, when a pack of dogs began to bark, he said, "Even the dogs know when the sluts are out." His words cut deeply, filling me with shock and shame. Father never used profane language near us, so he clearly wanted Sarah and me to understand the level of his disdain, that as far as he was concerned, what we had just witnessed was akin to Abby Kelley baring her breasts in public. Had he even listened to her impassioned plea, had he absorbed any of her powerful words? I remember the devastation of realizing that my father would never approve of my goals in life. But the good professor certainly didn't need to know that. Abby Kelley had moved others in the audience toward her ideas. All he needed to know was that I wanted to do the same.

"I see," Professor Thome said, and took a long pull off his pipe. "You should know that you have an admirer in President Mahan."

I tried not to look surprised given my recent interactions with his wife.

"That's lovely to hear," I offered, as casually as I could muster.

"He told me he has met your brother Bo and thinks highly of the family that has raised two such clear thinkers. He has also been impressed by your achievement in the college-degree program thus far. He has agreed to let me take you on if I am agreeable to it."

It took all my will to stay in my chair. I wanted to leap up and clap my hands.

"However, the administration is reluctant to make this decision without the consent of your parents."

Despair stomped on the small sprout of joy in my heart. I told myself to remain calm and sensible. This opportunity could not slip away.

"As my enrollment papers show, Professor, I am twenty-eight, and a full adult. Much older than most of the girls now enrolled."

"Indeed, but the payor of your tuition—your father, I presume?—must agree to this course."

"I pay my own tuition."

"I am aware that you work very hard outside mandatory service hours to earn extra pay." I heard praise in his voice. "But I assume it is to pay back a loan of some sort given to you by your father? That is quite the same."

"There is no loan, sir. I taught school for many years before coming in order to earn enough to enroll. The money is entirely mine."

I put my hand below my lace collar to quell the pounding in my chest. Working from the age of sixteen had been a practical reality to afford college, but it had never occurred to me that each dollar I had earned myself might carry more value than one provided by my father.

"Indeed. Well, I see," Professor Thome said. "In that case, I expect we can proceed. My next class is in the spring term. When the time comes, bring your enrollment card for me to sign. Otherwise the registrar won't know what to make of it."

"You won't be disappointed, Professor." I floated off my seat, as if propelled by magic. "I promise."

Lost in my happy thoughts about the expanse of learning awaiting me in the spring term, I almost didn't hear Mr. Morgan call my name from his little window.

I returned his greeting and stopped moving when I saw the expression on his face. He wore a peculiar grin, almost like Old Bogue's toothy smile when anticipating a link of sausage. He held a large package in his hands.

"I have been waiting for you, Miss Stone," he said. "This came last evening. I knew you would be eager to have it."

I gasped at the sight of the parcel. They hadn't forgotten me after all.

"Thank you so much, Mr. Morgan," I said, and immediately rushed back to the dorm with my prize.

As soon as I closed the door to my little room, I sat on the bed and tore open the package. A waterfall of letters gushed out, and I was unsure which I should look at first, the item under the tissue paper or the news of my family scattered on the floor. I reasoned that words were not to be rushed through, and my curiosity about what they had sent burned brightly.

Ripping open the tissue paper, I lifted out the most glorious woolen coat I had ever seen. The wool had clearly been boiled, making it especially thick and warm, and I could see my mother's handiwork in the rounded collar and perfect edging. I let my old coat fall to the floor and donned the new one, the weight of it immediately dissolving the icy layer of air encrusting the bodice of my dress. The hemline fell perfectly to my ankles. I hugged myself and burst into tears, feeling wildly grateful for a mother who would make me such a magnificent coat, and equally sorry for ever having doubted her. I was sure this coat had taken no small amount of time or expense to make, and she had done it just for me. Never had I enjoyed such a beautiful gift.

Gathering up the envelopes from the floor, I counted eight in all. From the handwriting I could tell there were at least three from my mother, a very thick one from Sarah, one from my brother Bo, and one from Father. Father had never written to me directly before, preferring to send his greetings through my mother, and I was immediately nervous about what might have caused him to take up his pen. But one envelope was clearly marked with the words "number one," so I opened it first.

My Dearest Lucy,

I hope this package finds you well and your studies successful. I am dreadfully sorry this took so long to get to you. Sarah and I decided quite some time ago to fashion a coat for you, but it took much longer than expected to find just the right wool, and your father was quite ill for a spell (not to worry, he is fine now) and so tending to him meant the coat was neglected for a time.

Please know we were thinking of you and writing to you in the meantime. We thought it made good sense to include all our letters with the package, having no foresight to such a long stretch before we could send it all off to you. You will find news in these envelopes that is quite old now but will let you know nonetheless how we get on at home.

With all my love, Your,
Mother

Laughter mingled with my tears as I read, grateful all over again that they had remembered me so well. I was sure Father had been the one to insist on saving the postage on the letters, but I could not begrudge him even that today.

I opened my father's letter next, certain it would be some kind of written reprimand. I tried to remember the countless details I had shared with them in my many letters to discern which one might have upset him. His reproach held power even at this distance.

The letter was neatly written, suggesting great care had been put into each word.

Dear Lucy,

You know I have long been opposed to your attendance at college as I do not feel advanced studies fit within the woman's sphere. I had hoped my lack of financial support would dissuade you from this folly, but I now see that your determination is not to falter.

When I worked in my father's tannery as a young man, I often had to rise in the pitch of night to begin work. I decided then to work as hard as possible so my own family would have a better life. Never did I think any of my children would have to suffer the same toil, perhaps not the same tasks, but something equally hard. It brought me distress to hear that you were working jobs at 8 cents an hour, then waking at 2 A.M. to study in secret as you do not have enough time to complete your work before lights out.

From here forward, money will be no issue for you. Let me know what the forthcoming terms will require for tuition, room, and board and I will forward the funds. You can repay me at some future time.

Father

I lay back on my bed, a tempest of emotion flowing over me. Had I actually changed my father's mind? Had I actually bored a hole into the impenetrable granite of his convictions? I put my hands on my face and let the tears flow once again. This is what I had dreamed of for more years than I cared to count. Father was finally able to recognize the value of my education, or at least the hard work I was putting in to achieve it. He was willing to fully support my endeavors. Had I really won him over?

And how carefree life at Oberlin would be without having to constantly worry after funds for the next semester. I could perhaps work only one job and use my pay to afford small comforts such as bacon with breakfast or a pair of socks not yet darned past recognition. And the extra time! I would have hours to spare for additional reading and quiet contemplation.

But I allowed myself to picture such things for only a moment or two, the truth not far from the surface. I wouldn't accept this offer. I had just assured Professor Thome that the tuition money was my own. I could not think of going against my word, and my father would never approve of me studying rhetoric. Denying myself the opportunity was out of the question. A combination of anger and self-pity caused a momentary catch in my breath, but I could not allow such thoughts to interfere on this happy day. I would simply continue to earn my own way, as it had always been.

I jolted upright. I had spent far too long enjoying the package from home. My algebra students were surely already assembling. The remaining letters would have to wait for a time when I could linger over them. Just knowing that everyone at home was safe, their news awaiting me on my nightstand, was enough for now.

I wiped my eyes and fastened my beautiful coat—taking a moment to appreciate the work of each buttonhole, picturing my mother's hands touching the very same fabric. In that moment, I had almost everything I could desire: a chance to learn rhetoric, love from home, an opening in the door to Father's heart. The only thing missing was a friend to share it with. I hadn't had many friends in my life, relying instead on my three sisters and Luther for entertainment or comfort in my early days, but it was hard not to notice the other girls on campus walking arm in arm, giggling together while I walked on alone. It wasn't that I didn't get along with my classmates, quite to the contrary. Mr. Langston, for one, was wonderful company, but the Five Wives would never hear of us socializing outside the cafeteria. And the mother of one of my students in the village welcomed me into her home like a daughter, but she was busy with her own brood. There was no one to whom I could confess my deepest fears and share my loftiest dreams with. That is, of course, until Nette arrived.

❧

One afternoon during the midday meal the following January, I was deep in conversation with several students from my Roman studies class when I noticed her standing not ten feet from me and staring conspicuously. I excused myself from the table.

"May I be of help to you somehow?" I asked.

"You must be Lucy Stone."

"Yes, I am." I had no idea how a complete stranger would know me by name.

"I am Antoinette Brown." She held out her hand and shook mine vigorously. "Please call me Nette. I saw you so comfortably holding forth at your table in mixed company, I knew it had to be you."

I appraised her. We could have passed for sisters had I the money for finer things. Nette's simple black dress was made of silk, the delicate lace collar fastened with a lovely brooch, and her leather boots had recently been buffed and polished. She wore her smooth brown hair tied up in a loose bun and, given her slight build, she could possibly be mistaken for me from behind. The difference was in Nette's large eyes, doe-like and positioned to suggest she had lately been surprised or frightened. But something in her demeanor suggested just the opposite. She was ready to observe the world around her and take what she could from it.

"Shall we sit?" I asked, leading her to a nearby table.

"You must tell me. Is it true you petitioned President Mahan to let you teach preparatory classes without first being here for a year? And then demanded the same pay as male students for the same work?"

"How do you know that?"

"Mr. Halifax. Do you know him?" I shook my head. "He is a trustee here and an old family friend. He accompanied me on the last stage and told me all about it."

I was stunned anew that a trustee of the college would not only know my name but find me an interesting enough subject to discuss with someone else.

"He said you are a staunch Garrisonian and he feels you speak much too freely on women's topics," Nette said. "He warned me to avoid you altogether. And so, I knew I must meet you at once."

Over the next several weeks, I was surprised to discover the level of affection I could hold for someone not my mother or a sister. I began to seek out Nette for walks in the sunset hours after evening prayers. We shared stories of our childhoods and compared life on a hardworking farm to a more refined urban existence. As little as Nette knew about the habits of cows, I knew less about calling cards for a proper tea. The common thread between our households was a refusal to accept our country's inequitable treatment of its inhabitants simply because of color and a belief that education and action could help mold a better future—at least for men.

Some nights, Nette would sneak into my room after curfew to seek my company and more conversation. I happily forewent additional reading on those nights given the chance to further deepen our bond. I had never had a friend so dear and found its cheering effects a powerful antidote for hours of lost sleep.

Nette's initial homesickness allowed me to confess my own. I wished I could tell my friend that more than two years away had made it easier to live without my mother's soft touch or the comfort of the rocky outcropping of Coy's Hill I loved so well, but my longing for home remained a dull ache. With Nette, I found I could express my inner longings without fear of having her hear them as complaint or self-pity. And we saw so much of the world through similar eyes, she and I. We were able to snicker behind our closed door at the matrons, who discouraged interacting with male students for academic purposes but who looked the other way if a courtship was deemed to be headed toward marriage. We poured through texts together, discussing Emerson's dense essays and Wordsworth's poetry. I told her everything about my brothers and sisters, and she confided in me her difficult relationship with her mother. We covered every topic under the great expanse of the sky. After talking deep into the night, holding off sleep for one more thought, one more exchange of ideas, sleep would inevitably sneak in and carry us away.

On one of these nights I confessed my truest desire to her.

"I wish to follow in Abby Kelley's footsteps one day. I want to become a public speaker on behalf of abolition." I hoped she might believe it possible.

"That is a dangerous life for a woman," Nette said, reaching for my hand. "I've heard that mobs sometimes come to her speeches and threaten her. How can you be so brave?"

I had read countless reports of crowds rushing the stage where she spoke, pulling on her skirts, throwing rotten apples at her face. More than once she had to be whisked away by a male colleague before being spirited out into the angry mob. Even so, she never missed a speaking engagement. She never chose silence over danger. I wanted to be like that.

"I don't think I could forgive myself were I not to use my freedom to help those denied it," I said.

"Do you think her words are working? Do you think a woman can influence such things?"

"When Miss Kelley came to my town, half of the crowd turned out simply for the spectacle of seeing a woman speak in public. What an opportunity to turn an unsuspecting mind around toward abolition. Even if it was only one!"

Nette was very quiet then, not her usual flurry of questions and comments, and I prayed this new friend would not try to dissuade me of my dream.

Finally, she spoke. "Can I tell you my hope for myself? I have yet to tell another soul."

I waited, watching the lamplight flicker on the wall of my room.

"I want to be ordained as a minister." Her tone suggested she had practiced those words before, perhaps whispered them to herself on solitary walks or to her own image in the looking glass.

I smiled.

"There has never been a female minister ordained," I said.

"I know. Do you think me foolish?"

"Here you think my desire requires bravery, but I have Abby Kelley and the Grimké sisters before me. You would be the very first!" I was delighted to hear she had dreams as big as mine, although I could not deny my concerns. "But the church is such rubbish. Do you have to waste your talents on its behalf? Why not join me in fighting for the negroes?"

"Your brother does good work in his congregation. You said yourself he is bringing understanding to his parishioners."

"I'm proud that Bo continues to hold his ground against the men in cloth who think church is no place to discuss abolition. But Nette, thirty or more ministers censured the Grimké sisters simply because they dared speak in public!"

I would never forget that day in church. I elbowed my sister until her ribs turned purple as we listened to our minister, haughty in his robes, read the Pastoral Letter that banned Sarah and Angelina Grimké from the Protestant church simply because they had spoken at a congressional hearing, the first and last time they would speak in public. The letter's words were forever seared into my mind: *The power of woman is in her dependence. . . . When she assumes the place and tone of man as a public reformer . . . she yields the power which God has given her for protection, and her character becomes unnatural.*

"The scripture is used as a bludgeon to hold down so many of our sex. How can you support it?" I asked.

"I know you question it, but my faith is dear to me, and I know I can do important work from a pulpit. Please do not try to talk me out of it."

"Well, one thing is for sure," I said, my excitement building. "We are both going to be orators. Won't Mr. Halifax be horrified! You must take Professor Thome's rhetoric class with me next term. We have to go see him at once and convince him to enroll you as well. Will your father protest?"

"My father has never questioned the goals of my education even if he doesn't know exactly what they are."

I wondered what it would feel like to have such unconditional support, and if it had something to do with her unrushed manner and her belief that God could be trusted to work his mysteries in her favor. I was glad at least to have her on my side.

"It is settled, then. Let's get to sleep now so we can present well to him tomorrow," I said, turning out the lantern.

Like so many nights before, we curled up together and drifted off into our separate dreams.

From then on, Nette and I worked furiously on our rhetorical skills. We ran a secret society of women who wanted to learn, housed in the living room of one of my negro reading students in town. We never wrote down our speeches for fear of being caught with evidence in hand—composing arguments in my head and reciting them from memory would serve me well later. The constant danger of being discovered heightened the urgency with which we honed our words, and our work together further increased the bond between Nette and me. Having a true friend who would fight beside me for what was rightly ours, one who would do anything for me as I would for her, brought a warmth to my heart quite unlike any I had previously known. She loved me for who I was and who I wanted to be.

The month before graduation, all the studying and toil was rewarded when I was chosen to prepare an essay for commencement. It was considered the highest honor bestowed upon a student, reserved only for those in the top 10 percent of the class, with the five graduation speakers ultimately selected by a panel of senior professors. Before my delight at achieving this high honor could register, Mrs. Mahan had more to say.

"You have the opportunity to select the male classmate of your choosing to read it for you at graduation."

"I beg your pardon?"

"Obviously, we cannot allow a lady to speak in public to a mixed crowd. Another classmate will deliver your remarks for you. They are due for review in two weeks' time," she said, and swiveled.

Anger rose in me like steam in a tightly covered kettle. I had wondered why Mrs. Mahan of all people had been picked to deliver such exciting news to me. Now I knew why.

"May I speak to your husband about this?" I struggled to keep my tone civil.

"That won't be necessary," she said over her shoulder before shuffling away.

I petitioned the administration to reconsider the policy and allow me to read my own essay. It was Professor Thome who delivered me their decision.

"I'm afraid that the college will simply not allow the spectacle of a woman speaking in public to dominate the proceedings. Your essay will be read by a classmate." He looked over his desk at me. His office struck me on that day as smaller than I had originally remembered.

"It will not." I folded my hands neatly on my lap. I had prepared myself for this.

"Miss Stone," he said, exasperation flooding his words. "This decision is final."

"There will be no essay," I clarified. "If I cannot read it myself, no one else will read my words."

He blinked at me and took a moment before responding. I fought back the tears threatening to push above my throat. What a triumph being chosen could have been. To be recognized publicly as one of the top students in the entire college and hand selected by the faculty to represent our class would have silenced all detractors: all the men who thought I had no right to be in advanced classes; all the women who wondered why I spent so much time bent over my books; my own parents who still questioned why I had gone to college at all. And now no one, including my father, would know of the honor. But I could not participate in an activity that suppressed me more than it elevated me.

"The opportunity to write an essay is a great honor," he finally said. "A woman has never before been chosen. It's a mark of progress. You shouldn't throw the opportunity away so easily."

So easily? Had he no idea how much the situation devastated me? But I would not indulge him with ranting or wailing.

"I will not allow this school to pat itself on the back for having done my sex the great favor of choosing me to write for graduation when you silence my voice in the very same moment. That is not progress at all."

I stood and held out my hand to him. Looking puzzled, he stood and shook it.

"I thank you for having me in your class. It meant the world to me. And I will use what I learned well. You can count on it."

Little did I know that my refusal to speak at graduation would earn me the notice of two men who would change my life. Without even trying, I had pulled back the bow string of my life, and my career was about to fly.

4

There are not sufficient words to describe my elation at being home again after four long years. As soon as the top of Coy's Hill appeared above the ears of my horse, my heart settled back into a spot in my chest that had been worn hollow. I knew much would be changed at home. Like his brothers before him, Luther hadn't returned after college. All of my beloved sisters were gone, Eliza and Rhoda buried too young, and Sarah married and moved away. Despite her desire to attend college like me, Sarah's equal desire for children had raised the louder call, sending her to the home of an older man I hoped treated her kindly. Would those losses be etched into Mama's face? And what of the changes within me these four long years? Would I seem a stranger to my own parents? Would Father see me as an educated person, ready to take on real work, to make a difference in the cause we both held most dear?

The minute I threw open the door of the porch, I was once again a babe in my mother's arms, the deep recognition of our souls unchanged by our separation. Mama embraced me fiercely before pulling back to stroke my hair and examine my face, finally allowing her mouth to stretch into a broad smile. She called Father in from the barn. He stood on the threshold and examined me for a moment.

"About time you're back," he said.

Little had changed in the house. The hurricane candle on the dining table had been replaced with an oil lantern, and the loom held a new pattern I hadn't seen Mama work before, but all else was in its place.

"It's so good to have you home," Mama said, her cheeks wet.

"Your mother will be grateful for the help, Lucy. She has been toiling alone for too long."

"I'm happy to do whatever I can. But I trust you've received my letters? You know I plan to lecture?"

By some grace of God, William Lloyd Garrison had attended Oberlin's graduation and, upon hearing about my refusal to submit an essay, had asked to meet me. He was standing next to Frederick Douglass when we were introduced. The overwhelm at meeting those two men, let alone at the same time, was almost too much to take in. I felt like a hawk circling the scene from above, seeing it all without fully participating.

"Professor Thome tells me you have a way with words," Garrison said, and then asked if I would be interested in lecturing for the Anti-Slavery Society. I remember nodding my head vigorously and finding myself at a loss for words for the first time in my life.

"Mrs. Hennesy is ready to retire as head teacher," Mama said, glancing at Father. "I'm sure she could put in a word for you. What an honor that would be."

I examined my father's expression. I had foolishly allowed myself to picture him wrapping me in his arms, giddy with the idea that Garrison—his personal hero, the man whose words he'd read to us from *The Liberator* every night of my youth—had chosen his very own daughter to help with the fight. But I saw no happiness there, no pride. I knew Mama was afraid for me. She had read too many accounts of the dangerous conditions faced by abolitionist speakers. But what was Father's excuse?

"What could be a higher honor than being asked by Mr. Garrison to lecture on the cause we all love so dearly? Someone has to stand up and do the work of change," I said, echoing something I had heard Father say countless times.

Father turned and walked back out the door, letting it slam behind him. My mother's gaze fell to the dishrag twisted in her hands.

When I left for my first lecture assignment six days later, my father barely said good-bye.

❧

My train arrived in Northampton near suppertime, and by the time I located the address of the local Anti-Slavery office, the sun had dipped behind the trees. I circled the brick building until I spotted a small block of wood with an etching of the Anti-Slavery Society symbol nailed above an iron latch. It looked to be a cellar door. I knocked. A heavyset woman flung the door wide, her apron dotted with grease, her hands smudged with an unfamiliar black substance.

"There you are, Miss Stone. I had almost given up on you." She turned away from the door as quickly as she had opened it.

The room reminded me of our own cellar, which housed my mother's cheese-making operation—the well-worn dirt floor, the large farmer's table in the middle of the room, the walls covered by wooden shelves. But each surface here held not cream and cornmeal and wheels of cheese, but leaflets, tracts, and posters. She pointed to a particular stack on the table.

"I've had these printed up for you. Titles of the lecture, your name. You can fill in the date and location of your talks when you get to each stop."

I touched my name. I'd never seen it in print before. Some of the black came off on my hand.

"There is a tavern up the hill. Mrs. Mulligan can get you a meal, and she should have a bed for you for tonight. I have to finish getting my own supper on, so I'm glad you caught me when you did. Good luck."

Flyers in hand, I was back out on the street before I had even gotten her name.

I trudged up the steep hill to Mulligan's Tavern, my bag pulling at my shoulder on the incline. The door to the tavern was open to the mild evening breeze, and I heard the men inside before I saw them, laughing and banging their mugs on a table. There were four of them, deep into cider and conversation. Mrs. Mulligan saw me standing at the door and waved me over to her station behind the bar. As I approached, she ducked behind another door and led me into a small kitchen. A bubbling pot took up the entire stove. I breathed in the steamy aroma, a stew of some kind.

"I thought you might prefer to take your meal in here, Miss Stone," she said, and held out her hand. "I'm Rosemary Mulligan."

"Thank you for having me."

"Helps feed the kids."

"Yes, of course. How much do I owe you?"

"Fifty cents covers your bed, supper, hot coffee, and a biscuit before you set out in the morning."

I pulled my money pouch from my bag and counted out the sum, already worried how I would manage if every night of lodging cost me this dearly. I was only paid six dollars a week.

She tucked the coins into her apron and filled a bowl with three ladles full of her concoction.

"Onion, carrot, and potato soup. You might find a few bites of rabbit if there's any left. I have to go mind the front, but when you're done, I'll take you upstairs to your room. Best that you get settled ahead of the others." She placed the bowl in front of me and disappeared again behind the door.

I leaned my face into the steam, taking in the smells before diving into the tastes. It was a good stock. I could tell by the grease lily pads floating across the surface. The potatoes carried the flavor of the rabbit, and the warm broth settled over my hunger, reducing it to a murmur.

Just as I tipped my bowl up to retrieve the last drops of soup, Mrs. Mulligan reappeared with a lantern and a small towel draped over her arm.

"Let's get you upstairs. Come with me." She headed up a steep stairway tucked behind the kitchen.

She opened a door into a cramped room with four beds lined up on one side and a washbasin on the other. A clothesline stretched across the far end, two quilts draped over it to make a kind of curtain. She pushed them aside to reveal a small mattress, tucked into the eaves of the house.

"This is yours," she said, putting the candle on the floor next to the makeshift bed. "I've made this nice and private, so once you settle yourself in here, the men won't even know you're here."

"Men?" I was expected to share a room with men?

"Don't you worry. I know the type. A few more mugs of cider and they won't barely find their own beds. They'll never find you. The privy is right out the back. I'll have coffee on by six. I know you have an early day tomorrow."

She was down the stairs again before I could fully absorb the reality of the situation. I was expecting life on the road to be difficult—avoiding the curious stares of passengers on trains wondering why a woman would be traveling alone, finding my way in a new town every day or two, eating with strangers—and I knew I faced danger in my public appearances. But it never occurred to me I would find danger during my sleeping hours as well. I picked up my bag and turned back toward the stairs, as if I had options, as if I had anywhere else to go. It was almost dark; I knew nothing about the town and might face even more danger out on the street. I put my bag back down. At least Mrs. Mulligan knew I was here, under her roof, in her care.

I pulled at the hanging quilts to make sure there was no gap that would reveal me behind them. Kneeling on the bed, I took the money pouch out of my bag again and wrapped the tie string around my wrist. I left everything else packed, making an escape in the dark easier if that became necessary. The privy would have to wait until morning if I was sure not to be discovered by the others, and changing into my nightclothes was out of the question. I blew out the candle and tucked my skirts around me before pulling the thin blanket up to my chin. I practiced laying as still as possible so as not to make any noise.

When the men finally began to lumber upstairs, they walked with my father's dragging boots, reminding me of those dreaded nights when he came home late from the tavern. The remains of a conversation came out in garbled bits, the men pushing each other, jockeying for the bed closest to the window. I held my breath, and then began to worry that the gulp of air I needed to make up for it would give me away. Clutching my money pouch, I let out a long, thin stream of air as delicately as possible, and then carefully filled my lungs again.

Gruff commentary and appreciative snorts slowly gave way to deep breathing and eventually rumbling snores. Listening carefully for the creak of a bedspring or the footfall of a standing man, I prayed for morning to come without trouble. To keep myself occupied, I moved my lips without making a sound, practicing my lecture scheduled for the next day in Waterford, the first I would ever give on my own. If I dozed off, my fists never lost their grip on my money pouch or the sheet at my chin. As soon as the sun rose, I limped stiffly out of the room and past the lumpy row of bunkmates who were none the wiser that I had ever been there.

The Unitarian church in Waterford sat on a hill about one mile from the train station, its white steeple a ready beacon for me. As I walked, I hoped the humidity would work the awful wrinkles out of my dress. Sleeping in my clothes and then sharing a bench on the train with a man twice my size had made a mockery of my skirts.

My eyes stung from lack of sleep, and my stomach rumbled, the cold biscuit I had eaten for breakfast rolling about my belly like a stone. I had only been away from Coy's Hill for two days and missed my mother's warm bread and fresh jam all over again.

I paused in front of the church to consider the enormity of what was before me. After all my years of saving for college, after all the hard work at Oberlin, I was out on my own. Free. The Anti-Slavery Society was counting on me, Lucy Stone, to sway hearts and minds, to influence change that would save lives, the kind of change needed to set our country on a truer course. I was terrified I'd let them down. I did not hold the church in much esteem, but I found myself saying a little prayer, nevertheless.

The enormous door groaned at my arrival, but the building was otherwise completely silent. I put my bag on the floor and called out to announce my presence. When no one answered, I walked down the aisle toward the nave. The pews were finely wrought pine, the walls covered in a patchwork of light from tall windows of clear glass, not the lead and dark-colored designs of my church in West Brookfield. I noticed a small door built into the paneling to the right of the pulpit. My knuckles had barely grazed the wooden surface when the door lurched toward me, a lean man with gray hair and a kind face standing in the opening, his tall frame unburdened by his robes. He struck me as what Father might have looked like without a lifetime of farm labor and too much drink.

"May I help you?"

I introduced myself and inquired about that night's lecture.

"Ah, yes. They told me you would be coming. I had to see it for myself to believe it." He held his prayer book to his chest and did not invite me inside his study or even suggest we take a seat in one of the pews.

"I am looking forward to speaking with the parish. What time am I expected to start?"

"That is entirely up to you."

"Thank you, but I assume you announced a start time to your congregation?"

The Anti-Slavery Society scheduled talks in churches as often as possible, not only because the venue was free, but the minister's Sunday announcements of upcoming lectures made for an instant crowd.

"I didn't tell them anything." He attempted a smile, but his lips had no curve in them.

"But you were expecting me today?" Perhaps he was further on in his years than I had originally suspected.

"Miss Stone, I made perfectly clear to the gentleman who proceeded you here. I want nothing to do with your organization or its message. I cannot prohibit you from using the space, as it belongs not to me but to the people of this parish, and if any of them are interested, so be it. But it is not up to me to create interest on your behalf. If no one comes, you have the town's answer." He put his hand on the door, suggesting our interview was over.

"Thank you for letting me know, sir, but please be assured: there will be a meeting here tonight." My fingers tensed into a ball, but I kept my voice calm and inviting. "I do hope you will attend."

I tapped my fist against my hip as I walked back up the aisle, opening my hand only to snatch up my bag and push out the door. I paused on the steps of the church, alone and unwelcome in this strange town. I had never before lectured to a crowd, had no idea how to find one to speak to, and had nothing but a stack of flyers and worn-out shoes for company. I admonished myself for not hanging a flyer outside the general store when I was in town—I would have to remember to do that next time. I wondered for a moment if Mr. Garrison hadn't made a terrible mistake putting his faith in me, a sob threatening to jump from my throat.

"No," I said out loud, albeit to myself. I would not fail. I gathered my skirts, took a deep breath, and formulated a plan. I had passed at least eight homes on my walk to the church and had noticed several lanes veering from the main street leading to more. I would simply have to knock on every door I could find and invite whoever answered to my lecture. Of course, if the minister was any indication, I might not find much of a welcome, but I knew that the prospect of seeing a woman speak in public was often enough to spark interest, even a groundswell of curiosity. I just had to spread the word.

The closest house to the church was a tiny shingled cottage, tucked behind an oak tree that shared much of its shade with the road. A young woman opened the door, and I counted three small children peeking out at me from behind her skirt. I explained the purpose of my visit, and she looked confused.

"I don't have time for any ladies' meeting," she said. "Plus, that's bedtime for the children."

I held back the urge to grab her hands and beg her to come, to bring me to her neighbors' houses and convince them to do the same. I fought to maintain my composure.

"Perhaps your husband would be interested in attending," I said. "I'd be grateful if you would let him know."

"Why would he go to a ladies' meeting?" She looked over her shoulder. "Now, Anna, don't knock your brother down."

"I have been asked to speak to everyone. Men and women are both invited."

"At Pastor Green's church? I would have heard about that."

"I assure you it will be taking place," I said for the second time in less than five minutes, doing my best to keep my rising doubts at bay. "I hope you will let your husband know."

She pushed a puff of air out her nose before shutting the door.

I closed my eyes and leaned my head against the door, trying to steel myself against the growing worry in my heart.

The next two hours were full of nearly identical conversations at similar doors, each woman displaying a slightly different mixture of disbelief and disapproval at my invitation. They greeted me while wiping their hands on an apron, bouncing a baby on a hip, coming out from a chicken coop, or trying to smooth a loose lock that had escaped a frazzled bun. Their ages and shapes and the number of children in their care varied house to house, but I couldn't help but notice that they all looked equally exhausted, a bone-weary exhaustion I had always associated with my mother. And none of them welcomed the distraction of my visit, instead seeing my presence as an intrusion on their limited time.

After my nineteenth or twentieth house, I began to feel a different kind of fatigue. The miles I had walked, even the effort of carrying my bag down long paths in search of houses, didn't weigh on me nearly as much as the idea that it might all be for naught, the prevailing winds so strong against me that I would fail in the most basic part of my task. The effectiveness of my oration could not be judged if I was left to speak to an empty room. And my wage certainly would not be justified. I had done my best to ready myself for facing the kind of hostility Abby Kelley had so long endured, but I had not considered the idea of speaking into silence, a significantly more daunting assignment.

I came next upon a bedraggled house, one of its shutters crooked, weeds standing as tall as mature corn. As I trudged toward the door, my head felt light and I thought for a moment I might faint. The pungent odor of rotting fruit wafted toward me. My stomach turned, and I took care not to step on the crab apples decaying beneath a tree. The door of the house swung open before I was even close enough to knock. The woman on the threshold looked to be about my age, but much larger in stature, her long dark curls tied with a simple ribbon at her shoulder.

"Miss Stone! I'm so glad you found us. Come in, come in. I thought your train was scheduled to arrive hours ago. You must be ravenous."

I'd forgotten all about finding the home where I'd been offered board and tentatively followed her inside. The interior of the house was in much the same condition as the outside, the hallway rug frayed at the edges, a wooden bucket tucked behind the door, the residue of the morning's milk not yet washed from it.

"We'll just come through this way," she said, leading me away from what looked like a sitting room, straight to the kitchen at the back of the house. She lowered her voice. "My husband broke his arm two months ago. He can't work at the mill until it's fully healed, so taking you on as a guest is a big help. You'll be sharing a room with my girls, but I'll make sure they make room for you." She took my bag from me and pulled out a chair at the kitchen table. "I'm Carrie, obviously," she said, smiling. "Sorry not to have introduced myself earlier."

"It's a pleasure."

She put a wooden plank on the table with a warm loaf of bread, slices of cheese, fig jam, and fresh strawberries. I hadn't realized how hungry I was until I dove into her offerings. The cheese rivaled my mother's, and I had never tasted better jam. I told her so.

"My mother always told me we're all born with unique gifts," she said. "Mine is putting up preserves, I guess. Anything tastes good with a little sweet on top."

I returned her smile and understood in that moment that the condition of the home had nothing to do with neglect. She was doing her best to hold her family together with what she had available to her.

"What do I owe you for the kindness of your lodging?"

She glanced down at the floor as a rush of red colored her cheeks.

"Would twenty-five cents do?" she asked quietly without looking at me.

"The meal alone is worth that." I placed the money on her table. She smiled and tucked the coins into her apron as if eager to swipe away any suggestion that there was more to her hospitality than pure kindness. But there was plenty of kindness in her, and I was grateful.

After I had my fill, Carrie brought me to the room I would be sharing with her daughters. I wasn't sure how many she had, but given the size of the bed, I hoped it was no more than two.

I thanked her for the kind hospitality and explained that I had to head out to knock on more doors, probably right up until the time of the lecture.

"I'll see you at the church," I said.

"My husband doesn't approve of a lady speaking in mixed company. But I'll be sure to wait up until you get back."

Fatigue threatened to swallow me again. My own host wouldn't even be coming.

"Thank you for supper." I made sure to keep my voice cheerful. There was no time to entertain self-pity. I had a job to accomplish.

There was one more street I had seen from the train stop that I hadn't yet walked down. Crossing in front of the general store and a tavern called the Black Kettle, I kept as close to the side of the road as I could to make room for carriages clanging past. I sidestepped a small puddle just as a carriage slowed behind me, the horse's hot snort grazing my neck.

"You must be the lady preacher we're hearing about," a deep voice said. His words had drink in them.

I looked up to see two men sitting on a lacquered seat, one face clean-shaven, one rough with a grisly beard.

"Not sure what you think you're doing here, little lady," Clean Face said, snickering. His bearded companion said nothing.

I tucked my trembling hands into my pockets.

"Well, you must come find out, then. Seven o'clock at the Unitarian church," I said, conjuring the sweetness of the fig jam in my voice.

The silent one raised his eyebrows, his jaw working some kind of lard.

"It would be wise to come early so you are assured a good seat," I added. "It's likely to be quite crowded."

Their carriage could have knocked me down with one sharp jerk toward the curb, but I stood my ground and waited for them to move on. I didn't realize I had been holding my breath until they turned out of sight.

As I pulled open the door of the Unitarian church that night, I was keenly aware that the success or failure of the evening would be up to me entirely. There would be no Ladies' Board standing in the wings threatening me with disciplinary action for daring to speak in public, no clergy admonishing me to keep my place—Pastor Green was nowhere to be found. It was both exhilarating and terrifying. And most surprisingly, the building was full.

All the town's wives, all those weary women who had barely conversed with me from the other side of their thresholds, must have dutifully told their husbands of their visitor. And nearly all of them, it seemed, had come to the church. Whether they were unable to resist the notion of seeing a woman speak to a mixed crowd—not that there were any women in the room—or they simply had no other entertainment to catch their interest was impossible to say.

The men barely noticed me over their banter at first, giving me ample opportunity to survey the crowd. They looked like a hardworking bunch, their broad farmers' shoulders fighting for space in the pews, each man used to having more room when their wives or children sat beside them on Sundays. The implicit equation behind that thought led me to understand that my audience stretched beyond Pastor Green's congregation, which could have explained the tussle erupting between two men in the second row, one trying to claim his usual seat, I presumed, a spot already occupied by an enormous gentleman who swayed as he rose to the challenge. The latecomer must have thought better of fighting brawn and liquor at the same time and retreated to a pew near the back.

A man in the fourth row noticed me at the pulpit, and his arm jab turned into a bench-long jostling. A wave of cleared throats rippled toward the back of the church. The echo of all the hushing bounced back to the front three rows, and the men closest to me looked up with startled expressions, as if they hadn't been expecting an intruder.

Someone said to his neighbor, "She's a little thing, now, ain't she?" which caused a fresh wave of murmurs and chuckles. I smiled and waited until the last voice quieted and there was no sound in the room save the shuffle of boots and backs on wood as everyone settled in. My thighs began to quake slightly as anxiety fluttered through me. I gripped the podium tightly and reminded myself that I was there to right a grave wrong. These men were there for one reason: to hear me speak. Whether it was for my message or for the spectacle was not my concern. Only what happened next was up to me. It was imperative to remain calm. I looked out one of the large windows to a grand and steady oak tree, its waxy leaves shimmering in the last of the evening's sunshine, and slowly counted to twenty before I spoke.

"Our great country," I began, "was born with a scourge on its soul. Our forefathers, my own grandfather, came here for religious freedom, for freedom from persecution, and then demanded separation from the motherland because our voices were not represented by the crown. We wanted better. We demanded more."

"Hear, hear!" someone yelled from the back.

A thrill ran through me unlike anything I had ever experienced. If standing in front of Professor Thome's classroom and putting words to my ideas for the first time had felt exhilarating, this was like running through fields of wildflowers, my hair streaming behind me, with no one within miles to catch me or slow me down. I was unstoppable.

"Our founding fathers nobly declared that all men are endowed by our Creator with the unalienable right to life and liberty and the pursuit of happiness. And yet, we have written into the law of our land the ability to do just the opposite—to imprison an entire race of men within the cruel bonds of slavery simply because of their ancestry and the color of their skin. Where does the Declaration say that one man can be owned by another, that men should toil for no pay, must suffer under the lash, and even meet their end at the whim of another? Can anyone tell me where in our great Declaration this idea is included?"

I waited, letting the moment flow over the crowd. I made eye contact with as many of the men as I could, daring them to answer the question. That was when I noticed a gentleman standing at the back of the room, leaning up against the last pew, his right arm tightly wrapped against his body. An unruly nest of brown curls perched on his head, and he looked uncomfortable, whether from the pain of his injury or from distaste at my remarks, I couldn't tell. If I could turn his expression into something more curious or thoughtful, I knew I would be on my way to winning at least some of the crowd. I watched him carefully as I continued.

"And if the gruesome physical abuse and stealing of one's freedom isn't enough," I said, "these men are further confined by being forced into a life of ignorance. The severest of punishments is meted out to any negro who dares try to learn to read. And do you know why? Because the white slave master knows that no sooner would a negro learn to read then he would understand the true evil behind his confinement, that white men lording over colored men is not preordained by God, as they are taught. No, the slave master knows that any negro who can read will quickly understand the truth of his situation as an unnatural one, and the truth cannot be stopped. As James Russell Lowell penned:

Get but a truth once uttered, and 'tis like
A star new born that drops into its place;
And which, once circling in its placid round,
Not all the tumult of the earth can shake.

"Those unjustly held down will rise up, must rise up to demand their rightful place in the world."

"Maybe you shouldn't have been taught to read either!" a fossil of a man yelled from the center of the crowd.

Laughter pulsed through the hall, and I willed myself not to falter. The man in the sling let a smile break into his pained expression. I hadn't won him yet, hadn't convinced any of them yet. But they were listening, and this was the moment to show them I would not be rattled by petty insults.

"Ah yes," I said, smiling. "But my ability to read doesn't hamper your own. And here is the crux of the issue. There is a fear gripping the slave master, gripping this nation, that if we allow the negro to experience the power of knowledge, the joys of freedom, then the white man will somehow be diminished. But does your neighbor's freedom reduce your own? Nowhere in the Bible does God or any of His teachings separate humans because of the color of their skin. Nowhere does it say that God blesses some of us, but not all of us. And do you doubt the word of God?"

The man with the sling worked his jaw as if chewing on this idea and nodded his head ever so slightly. I had planted a seed there. I could see it. And he was not alone. Like the hitch in a mare's cadence just before she begins to canter, I felt the energy in the room gather in, ready to run with me. The thrill of it was much like climbing to the very top of a tall tree and then stretching out to the last branch with a mixture of fear and exhilaration, with the sense that I just might be able to sprout wings.

"But we don't keep no slaves up here," a small man in the front row said, as if already pleading his innocence at the gates of Saint Peter.

"But will you welcome the colored man into your community once he is freed?" I asked.

Shouts of "Hell no!" and "Are you crazy?" and "Send 'em back where they belong!" erupted across the room.

"There is another truth I offer you." I waited again for the crowd to quiet. "You cannot condemn slavery without supporting freedom in all its forms for the negroes. Otherwise you are no better than the slave master himself."

"What do you know about it?" a man yelled, standing. I saw his hand fly through the air, and I ducked behind the dais just as a prayer book sailed past me. The slap of the leather against the floor temporarily silenced the crowd.

I looked at the faces before me. If they all turned on me, I would have no way to defend myself. My hand shook as I picked up the book and smoothed the crumpled pages, the banging of my heart drowning out all other noises in the room.

"I believe you will need this prayer book, sir." I worked hard to banish any fear from my voice. "For if we do not do everything to end slavery, we condone it. And if we do not embrace freedom for the negro, then we might as well be ripping children from their mothers ourselves, putting them up on an auction block to be sold to the highest bidder. If we are not willing to open our communities, our churches, our workplaces to the colored man, we might as well be holding the whip, fastening the noose around his neck, and hanging him from a tree."

"I don't need to hear a woman talk to me like this," the old man from the fifth row said, getting to his feet. He pushed past the others in his pew and stormed down the aisle, one or two from each row joining him like dandelion fuzz sticking to a skirt as he brushed by. I sensed a pull toward him and thought for a moment that the whole church might clear out, but after the first ten or twelve men left, the rest stayed in their seats, many with a look on their faces of a child caught stealing blackberries from a neighbor, not wanting to give up the sweet fruit clutched in their fists but not able to abide the look of disappointment on their mother's face either, knowing they'd done something wrong.

"Well then, I'm glad the rest of you are with me." I breathed out a deep sigh of relief. With the loudest dissenters gone, I sensed the opening of a space in the room that didn't exist before, a place where new ideas might be allowed to linger and be tested. Some men started to nod; others jabbed their seatmates and shared knowing looks. The man with the sling relaxed his stance, rolled his shoulder to work out a kink before rubbing it with his other hand.

"And so, gentlemen, as you go back to your homes tonight, as you tuck into your beds, think on the countless men who lay their backs on a dirt floor. As you kiss your children goodnight, think about the young boys who have been stolen from their families, never to see them again. And ask yourself if you can abide by anything other than helping to rid this country of slavery. Thank you for your attention, and God bless."

I looked out on the crowd, feeling sure I had done well. Any relief I felt, though, turned quickly to anxiety as I realized I hadn't planned what to do next. Should I be the first to leave the building, or would it be foolish to risk one of those men following me in the dark? But if I waited on the dais, would that invite conversation and precarious closeness to those strangers? And what if one of them lingered? Then I remembered the pastor's office just to the side of the pulpit. Pretending I knew exactly what I was doing—thanks be to God it was unlocked—I slipped inside, latched the door behind me, and waited for everyone to take their leave.

Sitting alone in the small office, my body shook with a combination of fatigue and triumph, pride and the residue of fear. So many thoughts and emotions raced through my mind. I wished Nette had been there to share in it all with me, to tell me which points had made their mark, where I might have done better. Would I have made Father proud, or would he consider me debauched, just like Abby Kelley? Would Douglass and Garrison have approved? I was sure I had shifted at least a few minds, pushed them in a new direction. Some walked away angry, resolved not to change their mind, and still others didn't know what to make of the proceedings and would wait to hear the opinions of friends and neighbors before forming their own. But I had drawn a crowd, and I had said what I had meant to say. The truth has a way of seeping in over time and finding level ground, like water after a rainstorm. I knew the ideas I had imparted would eventually sink in with someone. Maybe more than just one.

As soon as I was sure the church was empty, I walked into the night alone.

Over the next month I crisscrossed Massachusetts, from Pittsfield to Harwich, and traveled as far south as Connecticut and Rhode Island, nineteen towns in twenty-four days. My audiences varied in size and attitude, some more receptive than others, some downright hostile, forcing me to slip out a back door more than once for fear of being accosted after my talk. Many of my hosts were kind to me, generous with food and sleeping quarters, while some had no interest in speaking to me, leaving me to eat in silence and sleep on a cot tucked in a corner as far away from the rest of the family as possible. I didn't mind the separation, as those moments were my only opportunity to relax without strange eyes on me, without being watched as if I were a creature that might spontaneously grow a beak and claws. But I sometimes went for days without a friendly exchange, any hunger I had for company starved by silence.

Occasionally I was lucky enough to stay in a home with a lady of the house who treated me like a trusted friend. One such woman was Mindy Lowell. She was a year or two older than me and had six children. I offered to watch and distract them for her while she prepared supper, something I did whenever my help was accepted. Those were chances to give my hostesses a much needed reprieve from their broods, and there was no company I enjoyed as much. I loved to play hide-and-seek with little ones or read to them if they were lucky enough to have books in the house. I adored the ease of conversing with children. I found myself refreshed by their simple needs, their bias toward delight.

When I first met her, Mrs. Lowell wasn't far removed from birthing her last child, a perfectly round cherub with peach-colored cheeks and eyelashes as soft as the edge of a feather. Mindy put the babe in my arms one night, hoping I could coax her to sleep. I cooed and sang her a lullaby but found myself not wanting her lids to close. Her eyes were the color of pecans, full of trust and wonder, and she studied my face as if it were the map of the world. When she pawed at my breast, looking to suckle, I felt a stirring in my womb, something close to love, a swell of longing. I pushed my pinky into her little hand and reveled in the pressure of her grip, then felt a deep sadness wash over me.

The ache in my womb turned to something hard. You must understand that the idea of never being able to experience motherhood, the privilege of protecting a newborn with my life and being the center of her world in return, was difficult to entirely accept. I had chosen a different life, one without compromise, but in soft moments like this one, feeling the breath of a baby on my neck as she fell asleep, I allowed myself to imagine what I was missing. It was hard not to feel the loss of all I had sacrificed by choosing my path, and loneliness wrapped itself around me like a crusty blanket left out in the snow.

I do not tell you all this, Alice, to engender pity for me. I was living exactly the life I had intended, and it cannot be stressed enough how few women had that chance. Yes, it was difficult work. It took a toll on me physically, and of course it was not without moments of terrible self-doubt. But even as I drank in the smell of Mindy's baby, I also thought of Abigail and Willow. I was answering to no one but myself, and I was working for a cause that I believed in deeply. And it was not without reward, chiefly the fulfillment that comes with knowing I was making a difference in the world. It is always important to take stock of the impact we can make and evaluate if it is enough to fill our souls, don't you think? Would a life companion have added to the satisfaction of my purposeful life? I highly doubted it. Of course, my schedule didn't give me a moment's time to fraternize anyway, even if I had been interested in such a thing—meeting Harry happened in the least likely of places.

And regular letters from Nette kept me afloat. She sent them to every local Anti-Slavery office, her perfect penmanship greeting me at each stop. She worried about the danger I might be finding but never ceased to tell me how proud she was of my good work and the impact she was certain I was making. She sent news of her continued studies at Oberlin, how hard she had to push for the right to study theology. In my darkest moments, it was often her words that gave me the strength to face the next day, even as I missed her companionship dearly.

But it's not to say I didn't meet some extraordinary people along the way; in fact, one of the biggest benefits of my work was having the opportunity to become acquainted with some of the greatest thinkers of our time. It was on my initial trip to Boston when I was welcomed into such company for the first time.

Ah, now that's a night I will never forget.

5

By the time my train arrived in Boston for my first visit, I was starved and exhausted. I had spent the previous six weeks traveling through Vermont, New Hampshire, and Massachusetts. Just when I thought I might have some time to recuperate at Coy's Hill, a message came from Samuel May, the head of the New England Anti-Slavery Society, requesting my immediate presence. The note included a train ticket to Boston for the next morning. I had two simple hopes as I disembarked: that Mr. May's carriage wasn't going to drive me straight to an auditorium—surely I would have had more notice if I was to speak in the city for the first time—and that wherever I was to board would offer me my own bed. I needed sleep even more than food.

"You must be Miss Stone," a middle-aged fellow said to me as soon as my foot touched the platform. "Please let me help you with that." He relieved me of my traveling bag before I could respond.

"My carriage is this way." He seemed to be in a hurry. We walked through a large lobby with waiting benches and several ticket booths. A clock on the wall with arms longer than my own ticked near six thirty in the evening, and I began to suspect I was due in front of an audience after all. I hoped I might at least be able to wash my face before facing a crowd. I forced my legs, stiff from the long trip, to move faster so I could keep up with the brisk pace of my companion. Just outside the station, he threw my bag up into the back of a carriage and offered me his hand.

Unlike the open carriages of the countryside, where all passengers sit alongside the driver, or just one row behind, the area for passengers on this one was a wholly separate compartment, black and shiny with doors and windows, and I could see tufted cushions on the seats. I needed to ask one important question before being closed off inside.

"Can you tell me where we are going, sir?"

"To the Garrisons' house, ma'am." He offered me his hand again.

"William Lloyd Garrison's house?"

"Indeed."

He might as well have told me we were going to see President Polk. I froze just then, but his smile was unwavering. I finally found my feet and accepted his help into the luxurious coach.

I hadn't seen Mr. Garrison since the weekend of my graduation. Being asked into his home was something quite different from meeting him in a crowd, as thrilling as it had been. Perhaps he was writing an article on recent lectures for his *Liberator* and wanted to speak to me about my experiences? Being only a few months into the job I couldn't imagine I had anything to offer him that he didn't already know. And why bring me here so unexpectedly?

Despite all the questions racing through my mind, I couldn't help but notice the homes outside the window. Stunning brick mansions with windows fifteen feet tall, all flanked by enormous black shutters. Beyond one set of mullions I could see a party seated around a dining table with two silver candelabras in the middle. Up ahead, a white stone house with arches and turrets on top took up half a block, reminding me of illustrations I had seen once in a book about French royalty. The sky mesmerized with clouds as sheer as tufts of cotton pulled across a deep orange glow, all of it reflected in the huge windows of each home. Even the street was beautiful, wide enough for four carriages abreast but split down the middle by a long stretch of grass and trees. On our side, carriages went only in our direction, while the horses pulling in the other direction were on the other side of the divide. How civilized.

Less than ten minutes after leaving the station, we pulled up in front of a lovely brownstone, three stories high with a flight of steps leading up to a huge black door.

Having collected me and my bag, the driver lifted and lowered the large brass knocker and then stood to the side. Almost immediately, we were dutifully greeted by a woman in an apron and another woman I took to be the lady of the house, who rushed down the hall behind her. Sparkling jewels in her hair matched the deep maroon of her silk dress, an intricate brocade at the bodice. I pulled my coat a little tighter around me, thanking my mother silently for my one satisfactory garment.

"Lucy Stone, there you are!" She moved gracefully toward me, her arms outstretched. "I am so pleased to finally meet you. William just raves about you."

She took my hands in hers and kissed me on both cheeks before pulling me inside the vestibule. Everything whirled about me, like when my brother Frank used to spin me around on his shoulders and then plop me back on the ground to see if I could walk in a straight line. I never could.

"Dinner is about to be served. As you can see, we have an excellent group tonight." She gestured to a huge sitting room to her left, where several gentlemen stood in front of a hearth drinking aperitifs, even though it was too warm outside yet for the fire to be lit. "Evelyn will show you upstairs. I'll make sure nothing is served before you join us, but I'm afraid there won't be time for a proper bath. I hope you understand."

"Thank you," I said, a beat later than was polite. I looked back at the closed door and realized that I had failed to offer thanks to my driver. Everything was moving a bit too fast.

Evelyn was already halfway up the stairs with my bag—how odd to have a servant do such a thing for me—and I hurried to catch up. She led me up two flights and down a hall to a bedroom unlike any I had ever seen before. The dark mahogany bed was twice the size of my own at home, with a massive headboard and what looked like a carved pineapple adorning each corner. The sheets and coverlet looked fine enough to be stitched into a formal dress, and the pile of pillows beckoned me to lay my head down and fall into sleep. On the other side of the room, a triptych of tall windows pushed out toward the street, beneath them a sitting area with a couch and two chairs. Each curtain looked substantial enough to suffice as a winter coat for a giant.

"Would you like me to unpack for you?" Evelyn asked, placing my bag on a small bench beside a dresser.

"Will I be sleeping here?" I asked, feeling even more unmoored than when I heard that William Lloyd Garrison himself had spent time complimenting me to his wife.

"Yes, ma'am." If she found me foolish, she didn't let it show through her placid expression.

"Thank you so much," I said, wanting to express my gratitude for all of it somehow. Then, "I mean, no thank you. I'm happy to unpack for myself." I'm sure Evelyn suspected by the weight of my bag that there wasn't much inside. She must have been instructed to ask this of all the guests.

She nodded and stepped away, quietly closing the door behind her.

Looking about the room, I suddenly realized there was no washbasin, and I hadn't asked her for a sponge or towel. There was no looking glass either to check the mess that must be my hair. Noting a door on the far side of the bed, I opened it to hang up my coat and to my surprise found an entire room dedicated to one's toilet. Not only did it have a washbasin, but there was a full-size ceramic tub with claw feet. Between the two was what looked like a privy bowl covered with a porcelain seat. The water in the washbasin looked fresh, and three small towels were stacked on a chair beside it. Imagine, an entire room to oneself for washing up!

I set to wiping the grime of travel from my face and brushing my hair and pulling it back into a tidy bun as quickly as possible. I didn't want to keep Mrs. Garrison and her guests waiting. Back in the bedroom, I tried not to linger on the fact that I had no other dress to change into. But I did have a beautiful blue scarf Nette had gifted me. I fastened it with my mother's church pin and hoped it would suffice.

Back downstairs, I crossed the threshold of the sitting room to join the other guests. It reminded me of the grand gathering room of President

Mahan's house at Oberlin, but with much finer furniture. I quickly counted seven people other than the Garrisons, only two of whom I recognized.

"Welcome, Miss Stone," William Garrison said, crossing the room to take my hand. "We have been eagerly awaiting your arrival."

The idea that this man was eager to see me, Lucy Stone, was thrilling beyond measure. I tried to keep my face from bursting into a ridiculous grin.

He placed his hand at my elbow, steadying me as he ushered me toward the group. He was tall and lean, his nose, in profile, the same perfect triangle as the portrait of him I had hung in my dorm room. The angles of his face and limbs fit with his approach to abolition, direct and to the point. He often warned his readers that harsh language was required when circumstances were dire. But in his own home, he clearly enjoyed the role of magnanimous host.

"I am pleased to introduce my great friends, Ralph Emerson and Henry Thoreau. Gentlemen, this is Lucy Stone."

I began to wonder if in my weary state I had stumbled into some kind of dream. Could I really be meeting these men? I held out my hand in greeting. Mr. Thoreau was a bulky, stalwart man. He smiled kindly behind his fulsome beard. Mr. Emerson looked to be almost twenty years my senior and appeared more fragile.

"What a pleasure," Mr. Emerson said, taking my hand. I immediately regretted the nights Nette and I used to read his essays and make fun of his lofty language and overly dense prose.

"I believe you have previously met Frederick Douglass," Garrison said.

Douglass was much shorter than Garrison, but his presence took up far more space. His face was wide and wizened, and while he clearly took care with his elegant clothing, his enormous mane of hair indicated he would not allow himself to be entirely restricted by the customs of New England. I considered the audacity it would take for me to free my hair from the confines of a traditional bun and wear it naturally in mixed company. The mere thought of it made me blush.

"Of course," I said, shaking his hand. I hadn't seen him since Oberlin either, and had spoken to him then for the briefest of moments. The weight of the company I was to join for repast began to press on me. Was I really meant to be joining this group?

"It is wonderful to see you again, Mr. Douglass."

"And this is Mr. Wendell Phillips, and his wife, Ann." Garrison gestured toward a woman perched on a settee to my right. She made a poor attempt at a smile before looking away. I hoped she wouldn't prove to be a repeat of President Mahan's wife. I knew Phillips's name well as one of the great Boston abolitionists. My father had long admired him right alongside Garrison. Unlike his host, Phillips had been born to a wealthy family and was Harvard educated. He had given up his legal career to fight slavery. While known as a fiery orator in his own right, everything about him was rounded and substantial, suggesting a man who took his time to digest serious ideas and then put the full weight of his stature behind everything he did.

"You have been making quite a name for yourself, Miss Stone," he said while shaking my hand.

"Is that right?" I asked, wondering if he too had ties to Oberlin and had heard of my name in those circles. I hoped his wife, who was still silent, was nothing like the matrons of the Ladies' Board.

"Garrison's paper certainly has you front and center. Sounds like you have been stunning audiences from here to Stockbridge. I can't wait to hear you myself," he said, finally releasing my hand from his vigorous shake.

This both delighted and stunned me. I hadn't read one issue of *The Liberator* since setting out on tour. On the rare occasion I spotted a copy beside the hearth in a house that boarded me, I never had time to sit down and actually take it in. If I had been mentioned in Garrison's broadsheet, my father surely would have seen it, too. Had he read those passages aloud to Mama? I hoped it made him proud to see my name, his name, on those pages, that he hadn't tossed them into the fire.

The next shock arrived as I took in the elegance of the dining room. The white silk draped across the table was fine enough for a wedding dress, the brass candelabra an intricate tangle of branches and leaves holding fourteen perfect tapers. Above every plate sat two small silver bowls, each with a tiny spoon for personal portions of salt and pepper. I told myself that a fork was a fork and a spoon was a spoon and tried not to feel uncomfortable with the weight of them in my hands.

Once conversation got under way at dinner, any discomfort fell away. Not since college had I been around a group of people with such thoughtful opinions and well-constructed arguments. It was a thrill to listen to the ideas bandied about, each challenge or question designed to help tighten a point. Much of the early conversation revolved around Mr. Emerson's newest essay on wealth, and I assumed I would have nothing to contribute. I knew nothing about it.

"I agree entirely with Mr. Emerson," Mr. Phillips said. "All men should have the ability to avail themselves of the labor of another. Only then can we truly enjoy what life has to offer."

"But surely if we live a simpler life," Thoreau countered, "if we have fewer possessions, smaller homes, we have no need of such extensive labor to maintain it all."

"Perhaps a solitary life allows that," Phillips said, "but if you are supporting a family, there is need for a bigger house, for more to maintain."

Mr. Emerson hesitated to defend his own philosophy. I suspected he pined to have print in front of him from which he could read, rather than being expected to respond in the moment to questions and critiques. I soon found, with some surprise, that I had many more opinions on the topic than I had first assumed. Seeing an opening, I worked up the courage to speak.

"Fewer possessions doesn't mean one doesn't have to work hard simply to stay fed and keep warm," I said.

"True enough," Thoreau said, "but working the land can also be a pleasure, can help us remain close to what is important."

I loved the farm and missed it well. But the work was draining, especially when the necessity of providing for an entire family meant that no one person could make the choice to sit idle for a day and go hungry for a night. The needs of the whole put pressure on everyone.

"I compliment you, Mr. Emerson," said Frederick Douglass, "as long as your definition of wealth assumes that those who labor are paid a fair wage for their work. There is great pride to be taken in earning a decent living. But if a man of power feels he can avail himself of labor for less than a fair sum, then both men are poorer for it."

"Not to mention women, who are often left out of the equation altogether," I said, earning a disapproving look from Mrs. Phillips. "Women labor on a farm, too."

"Does Mr. May not see to it that you are fairly compensated for your work, Miss Stone?" Garrison asked, looking alarmed.

"As long as I am paid the same as any man, it is quite fair indeed, Mr. Garrison."

Everyone's spoons stopped in mid-motion, hovering above their soup terrines. I immediately worried I had spoken out of turn as every eye at the table focused directly on me. When no one spoke, I took the opportunity to clarify.

"I am extremely grateful for the opportunity to earn a wage while supporting the cause. There is no more important work at this time in our country's history."

All silverware went back in motion and a collective exhale freed the room of tension. Except Mrs. Phillips, who quietly put down her spoon and stared at her bowl, as if she had seen a field mouse floating among the vegetables.

"Indeed. Let us speak of this before the night gets away from us," Garrison said. "We plucked you out of the countryside, Lucy, because there are a series of lectures advertised for this weekend here that the Anti-Slavery Society would like you to join. While we have Mr. Douglass in town, he will be speaking three times. Stephen and Abby Foster will be there too, and we thought it would be wonderful to add you to the billing."

Now it was my turn to let my spoon fall motionless. I had imagined more times than I could count the impact of moving a single person in a crowd as deeply as Abby Kelley. She was now married to Stephen Foster, a man my father had long admired for his anti-slavery lectures, and—I hoped it hadn't been lost on my father—a man who obviously supported the idea of his own wife speaking in public. She was a unique force, but at least, I often told myself, I was doing my best to stand in where she could not be, fill rooms where she wasn't present. I had never dared to imagine sharing the same stage with her. Would I have anything to offer the audience beyond what she already provided? And how could I possibly add anything to the powerful presence of Frederick Douglass himself? There was no one more qualified to speak to the horrors of slavery and no one more eloquent. Douglass was not to be matched.

"I think you may have given our guest a shock, darling," Mrs. Garrison said.

"Is this acceptable to you, Mr. Douglass?" I avoided all the eyes staring at me. Except his. I needed to know if he approved of such a plan.

"I welcome the help, Miss Stone. I hear you are quite persuasive. We can never waste an opportunity to make sure the audience is so utterly convinced that they spread our ideas themselves. I think we will make a wonderful team." He raised his glass toward me.

"I would be honored," I said, and lifted my own glass in his direction.

After that first trip to Boston, a pattern emerged. Every few months, when the difficulties of unknown towns, hostile crowds, and shared beds began to weigh on my soul, my itinerary would bring me to Boston or New York for a two- or three-day lecture series.

While the schedule of talks, dinners, and meetings was intense whenever I was in a big city, those trips always felt like a reprieve, a chance to cleanse myself of hardship. I could remove, if only for a few days, the emotional armor protecting me when I was alone in unknown territory, the required layer I had to put up against strangers who wished me ill or disapproving eyes that might turn on me within a house where I slept.

And the luxuries provided to me in each home I visited were unparalleled. I stayed in bedrooms with their own fireplaces, had butlers offer to polish my boots while I slept, was given my pick of three different newspapers over the morning meal, and was sometimes offered a private driver for my day about town. These comforts were commonplace to the generous friends of the cause who boarded me, and they were more than happy to share them.

As lovely as the accommodations were, nothing pleased me more than the opportunity to work side by side with such like-minded and accomplished people striving for the same goal. Mr. May invited me into strategy meetings, where we plotted out the best towns and cities for lectures and how to advertise upcoming talks, limit travel expenditures, and excite newly won champions to donate.

I made countless new friends, some who quietly supported the cause from the side with their money, some who actively nudged their friends toward involvement. Others, like Mary Livermore, were more active, lending her talents and expertise directly to the movement.

I became fast friends with Thomas Higginson, a preacher who reminded me of my brother Bo. He was a staunch abolitionist determined not to let the robes of his profession quash his most important beliefs. He was a counselor to me in many ways, guiding me when I was in search of a new way to convey my thoughts to a crowd. And given that he spoke to the same congregation each week, he also advised me on how to encase the same themes and ideas within different structures and stories, arriving at the same place by way of a unique path. I frustrated him slightly because I never wrote down my speeches, so he wasn't able to review them unless he heard them firsthand. But his suggestions helped me put a new spark of energy or insight into my lectures, making each one more powerful than the last. The hard work toward a shared goal created a camaraderie among us that I cherished.

Until my fourth trip to Boston. That's when everything changed.

6

The warmth within me rose the closer the train got to Boston. The winter had been particularly cold and difficult thus far. Nette had written to me, worried after my health. Cholera had struck multiple classmates at Oberlin, several of whom had died because of it. I knew all too well the price my own sister had paid. Traveling as I did among strangers and sleeping in homes with less-than-ideal opportunities for hygiene made the risk of contracting such an illness much higher. Nette was constantly berating me for my hectic schedule, admonishing me to take care lest I end up infirm or worse. But I counted on her letters like bread and water. She always knew how to bolster me and make sure I knew I wasn't forgotten as I tramped around the countryside. I hoped my replies offered her some measure of support as she continued to do battle with the overseers at Oberlin who weren't at all convinced that advanced studies in theology were fit for a woman. I told her their policies were no match for her determination.

I was looking forward to this particular stop in Boston, in the middle of February, not just because I knew both my bones and my spirits would be warmed by my surroundings. There was much at stake in this visit.

The Anti-Slavery Society had decided to give me lone billing at my lecture on Friday night, and Samuel May told me they were expecting upwards of two thousand attendees. Apparently due to the coverage Garrison was giving my talks in *The Liberator*, including snippets quoting some local papers whose editors found my appearances in their small towns an abhorrence, more and more city folk were clamoring to hear a lecture from Lucy Stone. I still hadn't gotten used to seeing my name in print. One article stated, "With Lucy Stone set against slavery, the South should take notice," while another claimed, "The small woman with big ideas mesmerizes as soon as she speaks." Not all the coverage was flattering, however. An editor from Burlington, Vermont, wrote, "Lucy Stone takes a whiskey shot before every talk, and is known to order two or three more after, more than happy to let any gent who comes her way foot the bill." The lies some newspapermen were willing to tell to sell their papers were incredible. Fortunately, *The Liberator* was always at the ready to question outrageous claims, but it was hard not to imagine my parents reading these falsehoods without being there to defend them.

I had prepared a talk that I could only hope would live up to the expectations of those who knew me only as a name but had yet to hear my passionate plea for abolition. I also knew many of my friends and supporters would be in attendance, and it was equally important to me to perform well and validate the confidence they had placed in me.

I was also hoping on this trip to discuss with Mr. May an increase in my pay. Traveling the countryside was far more expensive than anticipated, and my wages barely covered the cost. I was lucky to have ten cents left over at the end of each week. My boots were already worn thin, I needed a second dress so the first could be properly laundered, and I worried for my ability to survive with no savings were I ever to have to take time off due to illness or a visit home. If I could prove a success to such a huge crowd in Boston, surely he would be able to convince the society to raise my wages.

Upon arriving at South Station, I saw three posters tacked up behind a peanut vendor announcing: "Lucy Stone on the Scourge of Slavery, Lyceum, 7 P.M." My name, front and center. Suddenly embarrassed, I turned to see if anyone had caught me gawking. Hats and shoes brushed past me, their owners eager to hop into a carriage or meet a loved one. No one gave me a second look.

❧

The day of my lecture, excitement and determination coursed through me and I decided to leave the Garrisons' home for the Lyceum an hour earlier than necessary to take a walk in the brisk air and clear my head. I took the opportunity to pass through the Boston Common so I could see Hiram Power's sculpture, *The Greek Slave.* It had caused significant controversy from the moment it was unveiled and was temporarily on display in Boston as part of its tour through the Americas. There had been much discussion about it at dinner the night before, all the women at the table scandalized by the appearance of a full-size female nude in a public place. "How are children to play in the grass with such a figure close by?" they wanted to know. The artist had defended his subject's nudity by pointing out that the slave had not disrobed by choice like some harlot preparing for a romantic tryst. She had been stripped of her clothing by Turkish slave brokers, making her worthy of our deepest empathy. He also argued that her piety, obvious by the small cross dangling from her discarded robes, kept her wrapped in a kind of protection more holy than any human garment. My dinner-mates found this explanation wanting.

There was a small group gathered in front of the statue when I approached, and I waited until they moved on, so I might have a moment to view it on my own. As soon as I stood at the feet of that woman, all commentary from the previous night fell away. She was uncommonly beautiful, her marble skin unblemished, her expression calm and loving. Nothing could shake the faith this woman had in her own humanity, in God's desire to keep her soul and spirit unharmed by the reality of her station. And yet she looked away, her face in profile, as if sparing us our own shame at her nudity. Her left hand pulled against her chains to cover the lower parts of her womanhood, her modesty intact even in the face of such injustice. An onlooker seeing only her face would not suspect her harrowing circumstance, but no one could miss the shackles at the center of it all. This beautiful, strong, pious, and proud woman was a slave. Chattel. Like so many of us. And yet so many of my sisters did not see the chains that bound them. Too many women eyed this statue with pity while having no idea they were looking at some version of themselves.

Emotions swarmed me in an unfamiliar way. *The Greek Slave* was the first outward representation I had ever seen of the naked truth of our sex, colored or white, Greek or American. Beautiful dresses and silver salt dishes couldn't hide the gross injustice in every home I had ever visited. The lot of us were all chattel, all chained.

A quiver started in my legs and worked its way up my body, until my fingernails vibrated with a certainty unlike anything I had ever felt—stronger than my determination to go to college, greater than my desire to study rhetoric, more potent than my resolve to endure whatever hardship might be slung at me in order to speak out for abolition. I knew I also had to speak out for the elevation of my sex.

There were only two women standing in the garden at that moment, this extraordinary slave, whose voice would be forever frozen in marble, and me, who had been given a voice that could soften stone.

I was lost in my thoughts of *The Greek Slave* when I arrived at the auditorium. I barely noticed the throngs of people waiting in line for entrance to the event, barely heard the instructions of the stage manager, who told me where to stand to best catch the light from the row of candles set up in the proscenium. I hardly said a word to Mr. May, who wished me luck before introducing me to the crowd. And once I was onstage, I could no longer pretend that the plight of my fellow sisters in my own country was an inconsequential issue.

Words flowed from me without hesitation. I implored the audience to weep for the enslaved on the plantation but to save some tears for the enslaved in their own homes.

"So many of us are raised to envision holy matrimony as the winning of a brass ring that will make the rest of our lives secure. But we are unknowingly putting ourselves inside a cage, in a place with no rights beyond what the husband chooses to allow. In marriage we become no better than chattel to our husbands."

Uncomfortable gasps rose from every row. I knew I had their undivided attention. I went on to describe the insights and opportunities my education had given me and asked them all to consider why society at large chose to fully educate only half of our own population. Why was it that the half of the family expected to raise the children was not given the highest level of education in pursuit of even that simple goal? And for those women who wanted to utilize this education to enter a profession of their own, why should it be assumed that she would be any less qualified than her husband for his same job?

The speech was like a cleansing of my soul, a chance to give the thoughts and ideas that had been bubbling up in me since my childhood a public hearing. A radiance shot through me, propelling me to greater eloquence than I had ever before achieved. The words came from deep inside, from a never-ending well of emotion and determination to change what needed to be changed. All the while I was careful not to let my voice hit a fever pitch. I felt such certainty in the rightness of my words that I had no need to yell them. Like a tributary that cannot be stopped in its path down to the sea, my voice flowed over the crowd, cleansing it, too. It felt triumphal.

When I finished, a smattering of the audience broke into applause. The rest sat in stunned silence.

Samuel May stomped out of the auditorium without looking back. He was furious.

❧

"This is not what we pay you for," Samuel said. We were at the Anti-Slavery Society offices the following afternoon. My previously arranged meeting to discuss an increase in my wages had been turned into something quite different. Samuel May was an older man, likely in his fifties, with a soft beard that encircled his chin. His normally kind eyes were stern, his anger from the night before clearly not greatly dissipated.

I hadn't slept that night after the speech. I could not stop a great rush of energy from pulsing through me. While I had known for some time that speaking on behalf of those wronged by our laws was my calling, I now recognized what I needed the focus of my work to be. I also knew that the Anti-Slavery Society had a very clear mission, and helping free women from the injustices of the Constitution was not central to it. But these men understood well the issue and had supported my work despite my sex. They never questioned my ability to lecture for them just because I was a woman. They paid me the same as my counterparts on the speaking circuit who were men. I knew they agreed with the principles of my argument. Many of their donors must have felt similarly. Perhaps a joining of forces was the answer. There was no reason to forgo one cause for the other. Why not speak about both of these great wrongs from the same stage, to the same audience, with one compelling message?

I woke determined to convince May and the others of this. I had no interest in parting with the Anti-Slavery Society. Not only did I need the job—the only other thing anyone would hire me for was teaching, an enormous step backward—I didn't want to stop fighting for abolition. And this group had become like family. For the first time in my life, I fit in, my skills were appreciated, and I was doing work of which I could be proud.

"I apologize that my remarks took you unaware," I said. "I didn't know what direction they would take until I took the stage. I simply could not ignore what was in my heart. But these topics are intertwined. Surely discussing one doesn't dim the light on the other."

"The people last night came to hear anti-slavery. You gave them women's rights. It's not right."

"How can I speak with conviction about one injustice and completely ignore the other? That's not right." He had to see reason eventually.

"You must understand how my hands are tied. The money we have raised is for anti-slavery activities. That is what my budget allows me to fund. Nothing else. We are about abolition. And so are you. Don't forget that."

He reached for my hand in friendship, but I drew it back. I was surely an abolitionist. But the fact that I had spent so many hours and miles, spoken to so many people, without including the plight of my fellow women now seemed absurd.

"Before I was an abolitionist, I was a woman. I must also speak for women."

"There is no ready stage for it, Lucy. No interested audience outside of sewing circles."

He wasn't wrong. I didn't know if any public venues would allow a speech on women's rights, let alone if anyone would attend.

"And yet, it's what I must do." I felt the truth of it all over again.

"I don't know what you want me to do." He leaned back in his chair.

I had been naive. As much as the Anti-Slavery Society had welcomed me, a woman, as a lecturer, they supported me only insofar as I furthered the cause of abolition. They had no inherent interest in elevating women. And just like I couldn't give Oberlin my words when they wouldn't allow me the stage, I could not take the stage solely for abolition anymore.

"You don't have to do anything. I shall resign. No longer will I lecture for the Anti-Slavery Society. I will never cease to advocate for abolition, but I need to work for women's rights, too."

I swallowed hard, my statement hanging between us. In so many ways it was the last thing I wanted to do, but it was the only way. He said nothing at first, perhaps waiting for me to retract my statement.

"How will you survive?" he finally asked.

"I have always found a way, Mr. May," I said, and left his office.

I had no idea how I would survive. Speaking was my life, my calling, and I had just walked away from the one paying job available to me. The image of what lay ahead almost brought me to my knees.

On my way back to the Garrisons, I thought about what I would tell my host. William Lloyd Garrison had been my idol, my first champion, and the one who had helped me make a living as a speaker. He had welcomed me into his home countless times and introduced me to his closest friends and allies. And I had no desire to abandon the abolitionist cause. I knew slavery to be a terrible instrument that was shredding the very soul of our republic. But neither could I ignore the injustice inside every house I visited. From the finest laid dining rooms to roughhewn kitchen tables, the status of women was no better than an indentured servant. It could no longer be ignored. Not by me, anyway.

I made my way back through the Common, comforted to see the *Slave* still there, her expression unchanged. The sun reflected off her skin, allowing me a measure of hope, even though I knew it would not warm her on that winter day. She exuded a peaceful calm that gave her an unbreakable strength. I would have to find the same within myself to carry on.

When I arrived back at the Garrisons' house that evening, Evelyn took my coat and ushered me directly to the small sitting room at the back of the first floor. It was used for intimate gatherings of family or close friends, and I had always felt lucky to be welcomed there. It was not where I had pictured delivering my news.

William stood when I entered. Helen remained on the couch, beside their guest, a young woman with deep brown eyes that reminded me of my sister Rhoda. I could tell even from her seated position that she was tall like my sister had been, but she was as thin as the stem of a dandelion.

"Lucy, I would like you to meet Juda May," William said. "She has just recently come to us from South Carolina. She escaped three weeks ago."

Juda nodded her head at me and smiled without showing her teeth. I reached out in greeting and felt the hard calluses inside her palm, the dryness of her hands. She looked to be no more than twenty-five, although something like fear or sorrow was engraved into the edges of her eyes and mouth.

"We are trying to help her get to Ohio," Helen said.

Juda nodded her head. "I think my son might be there."

"How old is he?" I asked, sitting next to her.

"He's got ten years on him by now." Her eyes said the rest, how badly a child needs his mother, how desperately she missed her son.

A glance and a smile passed between Helen and William.

"We knew you two would get along," Helen said. "You must both be tired."

"And we have a big day ahead, Lucy," William added.

I winced. He was expecting me to speak alongside him and Wendell Phillips the next night for the Anti-Slavery Society. He had no way of knowing I had just quit. This was no time to discuss it, but I felt like a traitor in his house.

"I've set Juda up in your room, Lucy, I hope you don't mind," Helen said.

"I'll take you there."

I couldn't help but laugh a little at Juda's expression when I showed her the bedroom.

"I feel the same way every time I walk in here. You won't believe the bathroom."

After washing up and changing into my nightdress—Juda stayed in her cotton shift—I sat on the side of the bed. She padded across the room to a cot I hadn't noticed had been nestled into a nook by the sitting area.

"No, this won't do," I said, standing again.

"I'm sorry, ma'am. I told Miss Helen it wasn't right." She pulled the quilt and pillow off the cot. "It's better if I sleep outside the door."

I met her halfway across the room and put my hands on her shoulders.

"Juda May, no friend of mine sleeps in the hall. I meant that the cot is not sufficient for a good night's sleep. And please call me Lucy."

She looked at me, puzzled. I took the quilt and pillow from her, placed them back on the cot, and led her over to the bed. I pulled back the coverlet for her before walking around and getting in on the other side. She didn't move, just stared down at me, her arms wrapped around her thin frame.

"I used to share a bed at home with my little sister. It was half this size," I said, patting her side of the bed.

Juda slowly let her arms drop to her sides. Carefully climbing onto the bed, she pushed at the mattress and ran her hands across the soft sheets, as amazed by the comfort of it as I had been on my first night, I was sure. She leaned back into the pillow gingerly, as if testing if it would hold her. She eventually tucked her legs under the quilt but remained in a sitting position. She grinned, showing her teeth for the first time. The flame of my oil lamp reflected off her dark eyes, reminding me of how the sunshine had glanced off the shoulder of the statue. And I saw in those eyes a deep yearning for her son.

Of all the time on the road I had spent trying to reconcile the fact that I would never have a child of my own, it was another thing altogether to imagine the devastation of losing a child. Could she still feel his touch, hear his laugh, remember his little-boy smell?

"Will you tell me about your son?"

"He was no more than seven when I saw to his escape. He got out, but without me."

"Will you tell me?"

She explained that the key to any escape was distracting the master of the plantation. He preferred to sleep during the day while his managers watched over the slaves in the fields, but he prowled the grounds at night, shotgun in hand. The property was too small for anyone to run off when he was making his rounds. The only thing enticing enough to keep him indoors after dark was his need to satiate a certain hunger, and his hunger was always for Juda May.

She knew well that violence triggered her master, and song transfixed him. Whenever she did something to offend—drop a spoon in the kitchen or forget to don her apron—he was quick to rage, and rage filled him with desire. He would first strike her across the jaw, then push her across the room and take her with her face pressed against the wall. At least she didn't have to look at him and it was over quickly. But sometimes he would ask her afterward to sing one of the songs he heard floating into his window from the fields during the day. He would hold the tip of his rifle against her quivering lip and make her lie down on the bed and sing. She had to look at him as she sang, watch him moving above her, his bloated face contorting as he slowly, slowly worked himself up again. If she looked away, he hit her and forced her to keep singing despite the blood dripping down her throat. Afterward, he would fall on top of her and sleep like a corpse, burying her under his sweat and filth. Sometimes she would lay trapped until dawn.

And so, she sang unbidden that night, and her son escaped.

"And now I have finally gotten myself away, and the only purpose left to me is to find my baby, to give him back his mother," she said, her voice calm and sure.

I had no idea what to say.

I wondered at her strength, at her willingness to trust me with her story, at the horrors she had endured. She had described it all without a quiver in her voice, no self-pity, only grace. She knew this story as well as the inside of her own palm, every detail a part of her now, and her steady recounting of it all stunned me. I had tried not to let my eyes grow wide at the misery she related, tried not to let my own emotions add to the weight of what she already carried.

She let out one long breath and then moved off the bed.

"Thank you, ma'am, but I think I'll be more comfortable over there." She pointed across the room.

Before I could form words of protest, she had tucked into the low-slung canvas and pulled the blanket over her thin body.

"I haven't had a bed to myself my whole life," she said sleepily. It wasn't long before her breathing became a low murmur.

No longer under her steady gaze, I couldn't tamp down the pressure pounding its way out of my chest. Something unwound from my heart, like the innermost strand of yarn coming free from its spool. My exhaustion from being on the road now seemed a petty complaint, my fear at having only a curtain to separate me from drunken men as I slept felt exaggerated, but hearing her story reminded me of those things. My childless life was nothing in comparison to the loss of her seven-year-old boy, and yet I felt the void of motherhood keenly just then, the belly that would never grow, the soft skin of my breast that would never be suckled. I knew my own struggles under the tyranny of inequality to be minor compared to what she had already experienced, let alone what was surely to come for her. And yet we were both forging our way in a society built to cage us, both forced to do the bidding of undeserving masters.

Tears were an indulgence I had managed to avoid most of my life, but my shoulders shook with each of these thoughts. I burrowed into the covers and pressed my face to the pillow to stifle my sobs. I wept for my sisters—lost to illness before they could fully experience life, for the lonely hours I had behind me, and the multitudes of miles ahead of me, for the horrible injustices built into our republic, for the resulting anger that I sometimes worried might harden my heart. I wept for *The Greek Slave*, in all her glory and shame. And I wept because I knew that the long climb against the injustice Juda and I would both face for the rest of our lives would mostly be a solitary one. Even in this most intimate of settings we were still alone, she and I.

I cried quietly until the raw places inside me grew numb, until my sharp thoughts dulled, until I could breathe without a rush of tears blocking the air in my lungs, until weariness overtook me and quieted me long enough to welcome sleep.

The next morning, I drifted awake, the images from Juda's story still darkening my mind, my pillow slightly damp. I had no idea how late into the night I had indulged my inner miseries before finally giving way to my own fatigue, but daylight had rushed in far too quickly.

Evelyn was opening drapes in the room and saying something about breakfast. Juda was gone. I felt the comfort of sleep dissipating like a dream I could no longer grasp in the morning light.

"They're waiting for you in the dining room," she said impatiently, and left the room.

I tidied up and dressed as quickly as my foggy brain and heavy limbs would allow. I couldn't in good conscience spend another day in the Garrisons' home without telling them about my resignation. But how could I do that now? Juda May's story rushed back in all its gruesome detail. I had spent my life in pursuit of abolition, and the country was far from accepting it as its future course. I honestly had no desire to abandon the cause. Resigning had simply been the best way I knew to express to Mr. May my deeply embedded need to begin the call for women's rights. I was in the perfect position to speak aloud on the topic, and it was up to me to start. And I still didn't understand why every speech couldn't address both injustices inherent in our society: slavery and the indentured servitude of married women. And was not Juda a woman, too? She was on her way to freedom from slavery, but another kind of servitude would still hold her back.

When I got to the dining room, I was surprised to find not a family breakfast in process but a meeting between William and Samuel May. William sat at the head of the table with Samuel to his right. Both men stood when they saw me, but rather than move toward me, they fidgeted in place, like schoolboys caught stealing chalk.

"I cannot accept your resignation," Samuel said as soon as I stepped through the door.

I waited for one of them to say more. I had given Samuel no reason to think I would change my mind, and I tried to read William's face to gauge if he was angry. He pulled a chair out for me.

"You have become an extremely valued member of the Anti-Slavery Society, Lucy," William said, "and it would be a shame to lose your oratorical abilities. We need you."

I waited.

"I understand you wish to lecture on behalf of women's rights?"

"I can no longer ignore the grave injustices faced by women." I tried to invoke a marble-like calm.

"Can I ask you one question?" Samuel said. "You have made great progress in your speeches advocating for others. The way you implore your northern audiences to think beyond their immediate needs and consider the plight of people on the plantation, the way you ask them to recognize the bleak future that awaits a country built on slavery. Don't you think some of that power comes from the fact that you have nothing to gain from your argument?"

"Are you suggesting a woman should not advocate for herself? Do you feel this way when Frederick Douglass speaks on behalf of his kind?"

"Well, he is a total anomaly. An escaped slave who educated himself under the most dire of circumstances and is now as well-spoken as any Harvard man," Samuel said.

I shook my head at the irony of the statement. But I had no desire to fight with those two, especially if they might agree with my proposal. Dual-topic lectures made perfect sense.

"I would welcome all the support you can offer. It would be wonderful to have a cadre of respected men advocating for the rights of women and to join these two great causes. It would make a powerful statement."

The two men glanced at each other. William continued.

"Of course we support you, Lucy. But unfortunately, Samuel was quite right in his assessment. The funds we have raised on behalf of the Anti-Slavery Society must be used only in service of promoting abolition, nothing more."

My eyes fell to my lap, disappointment flooding me. I had allowed myself to imagine them actually considering my proposal. I'd dared to hope they might see me in the same light as any of the other important thinkers who had been invited to dine in that room, men who were respected because they dared push boundaries, because they were authors of ideas that would change the world. I had wished for too much.

"I suppose I should go pack my things," I said, getting to my feet. I would miss that lovely house and the steady counsel of these men. They had treated me exceptionally well from the moment I had met them both.

"Please hear what we propose," Samuel said. William nodded at me, advising I sit back down. I stayed standing.

"We would like you to continue to lecture for us on the weekends. That's when the crowds are the biggest anyway. It will allow you to make the most impact. During the week, you can speak on women's rights on your own account. Of course, with the smaller schedule, I'm sure you will understand that we will have to reduce your pay from six dollars a week to three. But you will be free to focus on women's rights for five out of every seven days."

I was barely surviving on six dollars a week and couldn't possibly manage on three. And I would have no official backing while speaking on women's rights, a topic no woman or man had taken on in public. I had no idea how to organize venues for women's rights lectures on my own or how I would find enough money to pay for my travel and living expenses during the week. And if funds ran dry, could I even count on a pillow for my head at Coy's Hill? Father still hadn't given me his blessing for supporting the cause he treasured most, and now I would be taking on issues he abhorred. I might become a pariah in my own home.

I thought of Juda. I thought of *The Greek Slave*. I thought of my mother. Of Abigail. Of my sisters. I knew I had to do what I could for all of them.

"Four dollars a week," I said.

Both men jumped to their feet and shook my hand.

❧

That night I took the stage at Faneuil Hall after Garrison and Phillips had spoken, making me the headliner. They trusted I would stick to abolition, and I was good to my word. But I focused on a slightly different angle than I had in any of my previous lectures. There were a significant number of women in the crowd, and I decided to appeal to their motherly instincts.

"Imagine, good ladies here tonight, knowing that the best thing you could do to save your child would be to give him up, to send him away, knowing you might never see him again. I met a woman last night who did just that. You see, she made a plan of escape from the plantation where she was enslaved, not for her own freedom but so she could get her seven-year-old son away from the hard labor he would face as soon as he was old enough to work, to spare him the terror of being ripped from her without warning and sold to an unknown master. She made a plan to save his life. She teamed up with four friends who were young and fast and had devised a clever route of escape. It all rested on time, on their ability to be at least an hour into their journey before the master noticed them gone. There was only one thing that ever distracted him. His insatiable desire for the boy's mother. And so, she sacrificed herself so the others could get away, so they could get her son to safety."

Hands flew up to mouths with gasps and much head shaking. I gave them as many details as I dared, while sparing them the story of Juda's singing.

"The boy escaped, but she then had to wait three long, lonely, terrifying years for a chance to get away herself, and she has been trying to find her son ever since. And so, imagine coming across this brave soul in her attempt to escape. Could you send her back to that inferno? And what of her young son and those four friends who agreed to take him for her? Could you turn them away from your homes? Would you not offer them hot food and safe shelter? Or would you call the authorities? What a poorly chosen word. Authority. Has God given any of us authority to treat another human with so little dignity, with so little humanity? How could you do anything but help these good people if you could?"

I paused and looked at Juda. She was standing in the wings, out of sight of the audience, her thin shift replaced with a simple blue dress Helen had given her. Her hands fidgeted, but she stood tall, unashamed. I wondered if she had any idea how much her strength had buoyed my own. She had rescued something in me, for me, and I had laid down my small woes that night. She nodded at me. I held out my hand, and she joined me onstage.

"This is my brave friend, my sister." The audience inhaled collectively.

"She is the one who has survived the horrors I described to you. We have an opportunity to help her go forward, to find her son. Please give what you can."

Samuel May was the first on his feet, beaming and clapping. The rest of the audience soon followed suit. Samuel passed his own hat into the crowd. Juda's eyes grew wide as she saw it fill to the brim with bills and coins. We collected more money in one night than in the previous three weeks combined.

I couldn't help but wonder if I would be able to move an audience to contribute even one-tenth of that amount in support of women's rights. Without it, it would be difficult to survive and impossible to avoid complete disgrace back home. I had no choice but to try.

7

I'm sure you can well imagine the difficulties I faced then, Alice, scraping together enough money to speak on women's rights during the week while continuing to lecture on abolition every weekend. It was all compounded by the reaction I received to the notion of elevating our sex. While I had significant experience dealing with audience members who found the idea of equality between the races offensive, their misgivings were often theoretical. Most people I spoke to did not own slaves, nor did they personally know anyone who did. Yes, they were still a part of the system of slavery, but they did not see it in their everyday lives and homes. But the idea of women having the same rights as men rattled every household within the sound of my voice. Not only was the response to the concept harsh, but to my surprise, the loudest detractors were often other women. It didn't take long for me to understand just how threatened married women were by the suggestion that they deserved opportunity outside the domestic sphere, as if the idea of women having value beyond the home implied that they no longer had value within it.

And my railing against marriage laws made many assume I was against the idea of a male and female union altogether. It was an easier conclusion to reach than entertaining changes in the law to make the contract fair on both sides. As you can imagine, the more resistance I encountered on the topic, the surer I became that marriage in its current form could never be for me.

My one pleasant surprise since setting out on my own had been my ability to draw listeners to my women's rights lectures. Apparently, everyone had seen my name in one local paper or another. A shopkeeper who doubled as town councilor showed me a copy of his *Springfield Republican*, in which Wendell Phillips was quoted as saying I "spoke words with a rare eloquence, with a power that has never been surpassed and rarely equaled." And a member of the Northampton Anti-Slavery Society read me Frederick Douglass's pronouncement that I was "one of the most attractive and effective advocates for abolition anywhere." And so, even those who weren't inclined to hear a lecture on women's rights were drawn in by my name. When I passed the hat after my talks, however, only a smaller percentage of the audience was willing to show appreciation. I felt lucky to gather enough coins on any given night to pay for the expense of the hall and lodging. With only four dollars a week coming from the Anti-Slavery Society, paying the rest of my expenses, from travel to meals to printing flyers, was another story.

I was beginning to question the sustainability of it all when Laura Hutchinson invited me to join her family onstage one night rather than compete for the same audience across two venues. Laura was part of a troop called the Hutchinson Family Singers. She had one sister and two brothers in the act, and they often entertained at large anti-slavery rallies. Laura was the eldest and therefore the leader. I had always appreciated their talent and the level of professionalism they brought to their performances, but one thing gave me pause. I knew they charged admission.

It felt wrong somehow to charge people up front while hoping to gain their trust, while asking them to open their minds to a new way of thinking. Putting coins in a passed hat was a voluntary act, a sign of appreciation for a lecture well delivered. I worried my comments would be held to a higher level of expectation if those in attendance had to pay an outrageous sum just to enter the building—twenty-five cents apiece! But the Hutchinsons often drew a large crowd, and having access to their audience was appealing. I decided to take them up on the offer.

In between a lively repertoire of songs by the Hutchinsons that opened and closed the show, I did my best to educate the audience about the backward laws of our land and the multitudes of antiquated beliefs we had all too readily accepted. I spoke of women forced to stay with their abusive husbands rather than leave their children behind. I told them about how misled many of us have been by faulty interpretations of the Bible. The term "helpmeet," for example, when used to describe a wife's relation to her husband, has been misunderstood to mean something like an indentured servant, the one required to help the other. The true meaning of the word, I explained, was someone who kept another company as a full intellectual equal. I assured them that educating women didn't preclude anyone who so desired from becoming a housewife, but it would make her a better mother, a truer companion. I contended that the vast array of skills women had mastered to run their households could be utilized in a wide variety of professions outside the home, allowing them to contribute to the financial stability of the family. I spoke as passionately as I knew how and was rewarded with an extraordinary ovation, women and men alike on their feet, clapping and even shouting a few "bravos." I was relieved not to have spoiled the show.

After the hall had emptied, Laura brought me to the owner's office on the second floor to collect our pay. He held up his hand to silence us as we entered. He was counting a mound of coins on his desk, moving them from one pile to another under the close light of his lantern. We sat quietly and waited as he scratched some figures onto a piece of paper and then swept the coins into a tin bucket with a clatter.

"Quite a night, ladies! By my count, we brought in thirty-four dollars tonight. Half goes to the house. So that leaves eight fifty for each of you."

He opened the center drawer of his desk and carefully counted bills out into two piles, then reached into the bucket and added five dimes to both. Laura picked up the stack closest to her, but I didn't move.

"But you are four performers. I am only one. Surely that should be considered—"

The owner interrupted me.

"Take your business elsewhere, ladies. I've got to close up."

Laura smiled at me, put her money into a small velvet pouch, and walked out of the room. I scooped the rest of the bills and coins off the desk and hurriedly followed after her, not able to catch her until we were on the front steps of the hall. Her family was waiting for her there.

"Judson, John, Abby," she said, addressing each of them in turn. "How much of the proceeds from tonight did we agree should go to Lucy?"

"Half," they all said in unison.

The bulge of the bills in one fist and five coins in the other still seemed impossible. I couldn't pull the surprise off of my face.

"But if you think you should have more than half . . . ," Abby said, her words trailing off with something like a question mark at the end. She was the youngest, and I could hear the soprano in her speaking voice. Her flax-colored hair fell in long ringlets, and she rather reminded me of my little sister, Sarah.

"Shush, Abby," Laura said. She put her hands on my shoulders. The pouch tied to her wrist rested on my collarbone. "One thing our daddy taught us about this business: Never underestimate your own value. That's what the rest of the world is there for. And they will never think you are worth more than you tell them you're worth. We will happily perform with you any time, Lucy Stone. Just say the word."

I never spoke again without charging admission.

My change in circumstances was immediate, my income more than tripling overnight. I finally bought a second dress and new boots and was able to afford meat at least once a day. Those comforts buoyed me as I continued my solitary work, seven days of every week for the next three years, speaking to thousands of people over the course of any given month, never knowing if my next audience would be welcoming or hostile. But I knew my message was beginning to make inroads, that women were beginning to consider their own potential, or at the very least had begun to understand that they deserved to be treated as more than chattel. They were entitled to rights of their own.

The progress I sensed every time I spoke came to me in tangible form in a wonderful letter from Nette during the summer of 1853.

Dear Lucy,

I hope this letter finds you healthy and well. I'm so pleased that you have taken my suggestion to heart and are finally having a sojourn at Coy's Hill. I hope the old landscape is restoring to your soul. No one deserves a few weeks of rest more than you.

You will note a new return address on the envelope, which I am pleased to say will be my home for the foreseeable future. While I've enjoyed the many pulpits that have had me as a guest speaker over the last two years, and I've found the creation of compelling sermons for various audiences as spiritually and intellectually stimulating as ever, you know how much I've longed for a congregation of my own. Not to say that one sermon cannot have lasting impact—you know yourself how much you can shift a person's thinking in a single hour—but the ongoing conversation that happens within a congregation, the opportunity to guide the collective growth of a community, is where I've always set my sights.

As tempting as Horace Greeley's offer was to work for the new interdenominational chapel in New York City—it is only to you I can admit that he offered me $1,000 for the job! Can you imagine that much money for one year's work?—I felt accepting it would compromise my desire to minister to a traditional congregation, to be a pastor just like the many who have come before, despite the difference in our sex. Just when I began to fear I might be forever overlooked in this pursuit, I received word from the little hamlet from which I write you now, South Butler, New York, that they were in need of my services. The salary is less than one-third of the other, but the privilege feels enormous. On September 15 of this year, I am to be the first woman ordained in our country as a Protestant minister! Even as I put these words down on the page before me, I can hardly believe them.

Do write to tell me you can be there to cheer me on. There is no one I would rather have there to bear witness to the moment.

Until then, I hope you are enjoying every day at Coy's Hill. Give my best to your parents.

With much love to you, my dear friend,

Nette

She had done it! I hugged her letter to me and looked out across the orchard of my youth. It had been seven years since Nette and I had first met, since we had confessed our ambitions to each other under the cover of night. Since then, she had earned an advanced degree and visited countless congregations to spread her good word. I had spent more than five long years on the road lecturing for abolition and women's rights. We were living our whispered dreams and had finally come into our own.

❧

I couldn't remember the last time I was in one place for more than a few days, making the prospect of a full month at Coy's Hill—I had finally saved enough money to feel the time off could be justified—as gratifying as it was indulgent. Milking cows, cooking meals, and pressing cheese were all a welcome change, and waking to a familiar scene out my window each morning a great comfort. The more rooted I felt, the more freely my thoughts could roam, like a Hosta plant multiplying in fertile ground. I began to see daily chores as a wonderful way to accomplish two things at once, the hands handling the physical work while the mind puzzled on something else.

On one particular Sunday, with everyone else in the house gone off to afternoon services at church, I decided to tackle the job of whitewashing a swath of the kitchen ceiling that had gone gray with smoke from the stove. Standing atop a chair, first washing, and then painting, I found myself mulling over an idea that had long intrigued me: starting a paper focused solely on women's issues. I imagined having an office where I could work every day, staying in the same location while spreading new ideas and bold arguments far and wide, perhaps further than I was currently able to do in person. I was so caught up in my thoughts that I didn't see the man standing at the door.

"I'm sorry to interrupt. I come to you on recommendation of Mr. Wendell Phillips," he said. I placed my brush in the bucket but stayed on the chair.

"I am Henry Blackwell. My friends call me Harry."

"I didn't hear a horse or carriage."

"I walked from town. I find a good walk an important part of the day."

He wore a dark suit and sensible leather shoes. He was not a tall man but had a striking combination of black hair and eyes the color of a blue medicine bottle. Had he said Blackwell?

"Are you related to Elizabeth Blackwell, by chance?"

"She is my sister."

Elizabeth had become the first licensed female doctor in the country. Her solitary rise in medicine was nothing short of extraordinary and I had long wanted to meet her.

"We have met once before, but I doubt you will remember," he said.

I considered him more closely. He was quick to smile, and something about his expression was almost impish, mischievous, and earnest all at the same time. I had met hundreds of people in my time lecturing but doubted I would have forgotten that face.

"No need to worry. I think you were quite distracted at the time. It was three years ago. You stopped into the hardware store my brother and I own in Cincinnati. You asked ever so sweetly if we might cash your check right away as you had to immediately reboard your train."

A faint memory tugged at me, too hazy to retrieve, but it could have only been one occasion, when I was on my way home after Luther's ordeal. If I had looked as horrid as I felt that day, I wondered that he might remember me favorably.

"That was a difficult time," I said. And what did I look like now, my hair hastily thrown into a bun, my bloomers not properly pressed? I hadn't been expecting company.

"I carry a letter of introduction from Wendell Phillips." He patted the breast of his jacket.

"To what end?" The ceiling was nearly finished, and it was annoying to be interrupted this way, but the fact that he was Elizabeth Blackwell's brother did intrigue me.

"I told him I was very impressed by your speeches. I've heard you twice in the last year, once when you spoke at the Massachusetts State House, and then at the anti-slavery meeting in Worcester."

"And why did you not approach me then, Mr. Blackwell?"

"I wanted to be sure to be introduced properly, and with the referral of someone who might know us both. Please call me Harry."

Such an introduction usually came with entanglements. I dipped the brush back in the paint and lifted it to the ceiling.

"And if you inquired about me with Mr. Phillips, I'm sure he told you I am not interested in suitors, if that is your business." I kept my gaze squarely fixed on my task.

"Mr. Phillips told me many things about you, and that was primary on his list. May I help you with the ceiling?"

"No thank you. And what else did he tell you?"

"That you love this place more than any other, and that you don't easily accept help in your endeavors."

"Are you here to help with something?"

"Apparently you require no help with the ceiling."

"And what might one need to know about you?" I asked, still wondering why Wendell would have sent him my way. He understood more than most men why I was not interested in the folly of courtship. And by then, I was thirty-five. Well beyond marrying age.

"I intend to make my fortune producing beet sugar." He smiled when I glanced down at him. He had good teeth, and the smile looked at home on his face. He was younger than me, still not out of his twenties, I guessed.

"Beet sugar? I didn't know there was such a thing."

"It hasn't been perfected yet, but it has one ingredient that will make it the preferred sweetener across the republic. Can you guess what it might be?"

"Beets?" I liked beets just fine but couldn't quite imagine putting them in my tea.

"Well, lack of an ingredient, I should say. No slave labor. I hope to put sugar plantations out of business."

I stopped painting.

"I have a friend whose father makes clothes only out of cotton picked with paid workers. Is there no sugarcane farmed this way?" I asked.

"I'm sure your friend also told you that such cotton costs three times as much as the cotton from plantations. It's a difficult business proposition. But my sugar will cost the same as the other, or less."

"A bold vision," I said.

"Is there any other worth having?" The mischievousness I had seen in his eyes lilted through his words. We looked at each other for a moment, and I lost track of whose turn it was to speak.

"Can I help you down?" he asked, reaching up toward me.

When I took his hand, something rushed through me, as if touching him connected me to a root system different than my own. His hand was smooth and cool despite the heat, and after I stepped off the chair, he kept hold of me just a moment longer than necessary. I had almost never touched a man's hand without a glove between us, and it was usually in the transactional motion of a handshake. This felt different, more intimate even than a kiss on the cheek from a friend.

"Do you have a favorite spot?" he asked.

"Pardon?" I rescued my hand.

"Here on the property. Is there a place you prefer above all others?" His tone was earnest again. I had never been asked this before.

"The top of the hill. It's a rocky climb, but you can see for miles from there."

"I would very much like to see it if you would be willing."

The request felt intensely personal, like he was asking me to share secrets with him even though we had only just met. I should have put him out just then, but I felt a bit confused, unsure of the right thing to do.

"Mr. Blackwell, I have potatoes to peel. And I'm still unclear as to your purpose," I said, wiping my hands on a rag.

"I felt we should be acquainted. And I am very good at peeling potatoes."

He smiled again, and I could not help but smile in return. I suddenly had the urge to prove to him that he couldn't learn everything about me through a simple conversation with Wendell Phillips, as dear a friend as he was.

"All right, Mr. Blackwell. If we can get these potatoes peeled in the next twenty minutes, I will show you Coy's Hill."

"We will get them peeled faster than that. And please call me Harry."

I learned a great deal about him as we worked through the pile of potatoes. Not long after his family had come over from England his father had died, leaving him and his brothers to support the family. In addition to Elizabeth, he had a second sister who was also on her way to becoming a doctor.

"So, you see, I have grown up in a household entirely supportive of a woman's right to a profession and to her independence. I do not see how a woman would want anything less."

The potatoes took us longer to finish than he had predicted, but a walk up the hill sounded delightful to me, and I didn't want him to think I had put him to work with the intention of denying him the views. We set out from the house just as the sun was beginning its long descent from the hottest part of the sky toward the promise of a cooler evening. His legs were not much longer than mine, and our strides matched easily.

"The bloomers must make walks like this much more enjoyable for you," he said.

"Quite." I rather enjoyed how the breeze played with the billowy fabric without restricting my stride.

"Before we spend another moment, I must be frank. While Mr. Phillips did indeed impress upon me that you are not interested in suitors and have no intention of marrying, I am here to convince you otherwise."

I felt a heat rush through me and was grateful not to be wearing a tight corset that would have trapped it next to my skin.

"That's quite direct, Mr. Blackwell."

"I felt it important to get to the point. I realize I may not have much time."

"I'm not sure you realize how long this walk is." Perhaps offering Coy's Hill had been a mistake after all. Would I have to defend my stance the entire time?

"I have heard you speak, and I have read much about you in the papers. It is obvious that you value well-constructed arguments and consistency of thought. I hope you will hear me out." I could feel him looking at me. I allowed a quick glance at him but didn't turn my head. I already knew his eye contact to be persuasive, and I needed to maintain my composure.

"Then I am sure you must realize how much I have thought through this issue myself. I do work that I believe to be crucial to the future of this country, and while it carries a sacrifice to me personally, there is no sacrifice too big if I am able to help generations of other women. It would not be possible were I anything but my own person."

"Ah, but this is where I intend to change the assumptions. My vision of marriage involves two completely independent people who pursue their callings, even maintain pecuniary independence." His tone was not urgent, but rather philosophical, the way I had heard Emerson deliver his views on transcendental thought.

"The law does not see it that way," I said, but I was highly intrigued by his sincerity on the topic.

"No man is going to be summoned to court for allowing his wife to have access to her own earnings."

"But do you see your need to use the word 'allow'? It is the husband's choice alone whether he is lenient or holds strictly to the law. I have no need to put myself in that position." My heart rate quickened, not from the beginnings of our climb up the hill but because of conflicted emotions. This lovely man was speaking so frankly to me of marriage, possibly with me in mind. And yet my life's work had all started from the need to change marriage laws. I could not become party to a relationship governed by those arcane rules any more than Juda May might move back to South Carolina because she preferred the climate.

"But here is the crux of it. You exemplify a life of independence as an educated person who can earn her way and make her own choices. A very compelling model. But what of the multitudes of women who intend a husband and family? Would it not be more powerful to prove that a woman can pursue her professional dreams—speak, write, preach, practice medicine and law—and be a wife and mother also?"

I had never thought of it in quite that way before. I'd had "Spinster!" thrown at me like a machete many times, the slinger considering it a painful insult. It conjured the lonely woman too wretched to attract a man, or a daughter forced by responsibility to care for her parents past her marrying age, leaving her doomed to spend the rest of her life alone. That was not my life, but it was true that most young women were deathly afraid of such an outcome. For those with no aspirations beyond keeping a home for a husband and children, a husband was the critical ingredient.

In my silence, he continued, his breath and words coming in spurts now that we had reached the steepest part of the climb.

"If it be true that a woman who has a profession cannot be a wife and mother, it justifies to a great extent the argument of the antagonists who say that women who are wives and mothers should not exercise a profession. Can we not be true to our whole nature?"

"Whatever is currently unnatural about my choices is made necessary by the horrid wrongs of society, by circumstances I'm afraid may not change until the dirt covers all of us now living. I will admit it is a sad necessity"—a shiver ran through me at this admission—"and one that I hope to save multitudes in the future from needing to experience. But to accomplish that, I must stay the course. I trust you understand." I looked back at him as we crested the hill.

He gave a slight nod, working hard to steady his breath. Sweat beaded on his face, and I had the extraordinary desire to wipe it off his brow for him, to offer him something cool to drink and to sit with him in the shade to learn more about him. That wouldn't do.

"And now you can see why this is my favorite place." I walked to the western edge of the clearing at the top of the hill. "Can you see those huge crags of rock down to the left, partly covered in vines?" I asked, pointing. "My brother and I called it the rock house. We used to hide in there and pretend it was our castle."

"And were you the princess or the knight?" He stood beside me.

"Scullery maid to my brother's stable hand." Luther and I never imagined great wealth, only that we secretly ran the castle, making sure all servants had plenty to eat and the best rooms for sleeping without the king bothering to notice. I missed him.

"And that wide swath of treetops is our orchard. My second favorite spot. If I cannot be on a hilltop, I prefer to be surrounded by trees. I loved to climb them as a child, and I had hundreds to choose from down there." As I stepped to that side of the clearing, he followed.

"This is gorgeous indeed. We seem to be above the birds."

Several robins popped up from the top of an apple tree and sped off across the field. The sky had just begun to take on a deeper blue and purple, heralding that magic hour of colors splashed across the heavens. I had only ever enjoyed this view with my siblings, three of them lost to me now. Given the hectic pace of my life, I hadn't ever had the chance to experience it with someone who didn't grow up here. Not even Nette had come here with me. I found I greatly appreciated having a companion to share in this moment. Something like joy skipped across my heart.

"I must say one last thing," he said. His boots crunched on the dirt as he turned quite purposefully toward me. It seemed rude not to at least turn my head his way. "I knew from the moment you stepped into my store that we might be compatible—more than compatible, even. I'm sure I wasn't wrong. But I do believe the most important thing is for you to stay true to yourself, mind and soul. If your true self needs to be solitary, then so be it, but if something changes, if your true self ever wants something different, I hope you will not neglect that new truth and will allow your mind to change to meet the needs of your soul."

I found his words mesmerizing, dizzying, and had the urge to grasp his arm to steady myself, but that would have sent entirely the wrong message. I took a deep breath and looked back out over the horizon.

"I thank you for your gentle words, Mr. Blackwell. My views have changed on certain subjects, and I hope this trait will not be lost on me in the future, when warranted, but I'm afraid I see no possibility of change in this one." I then added, against my better judgment, "No matter how much I might desire it."

Did his countenance shift as I spoke these words? I chose not to look at him directly to find out lest I falter.

"And now I must get to boiling those potatoes. My parents are due back shortly."

As we walked down the hill, conversation flowed easily. If he was disheartened or disappointed, he did not let it show. He asked me about my recent work at the state house, and he told me more of his travels in the east. He described in detail his visit with Sarah and Angelina Grimké, the latter now known as Mrs. Weld. He was thoroughly impressed by both sisters and spoke highly of Angelina's husband. Had he chosen to speak to me about these particular sisters—two of my idols—to impress me, or was this simply the kind of conversation one could regularly expect from him?

"Would you like to join us for dinner, Mr. Blackwell?" I suddenly asked as we crossed the field toward the house, surprising myself.

"I must take my leave. But might it be acceptable to write to you, Miss Lucy, as a friend?"

"I would like that."

"Thank you for a most enjoyable afternoon." He tipped his hat in a half bow before turning in the direction of town.

I watched him go—his sprightly gait suggesting he might be whistling a tune, his soft shoulders open to the landscape—and, for a moment, found myself wishing he would stay.

8

Three weeks later, my train rattled out of West Brookfield just after sunrise, chugging slowly at first, and then picking up speed as a long line of oak trees stretched back toward home. The sun winked and blinked through the branches, giving the impression that the orange and yellow was being emblazoned on each leaf as I watched. I wished I was leaving Coy's Hill in a happier state of mind.

My visit home had ended badly. Father remained disgruntled about my work. While he had seemed resigned to my oratory, he was furious that I insisted on spending a substantial amount of my time on women's issues while progress toward abolition appeared to be slipping. I tried to impress upon him how linked the oppression of negroes and women were at their base, how even Garrison and Douglass wholeheartedly supported my dual efforts, but he had no ears for it.

"The Whigs are falling apart," he said one night, slapping the latest copy of *The Liberator* against the arm of his chair. Mama flinched. "There's talk of doing away with the Missouri Compromise, but unless we have enough foot soldiers on the right side of this thing, I'm not sure how we keep every new territory from adapting slavery."

The flicker of the fire threw shadows into the folds of Mama's face. Being away for months at a time made changes in my parents appear more dramatic, perhaps—like seeing a honeysuckle bush bursting with pollen one day and hibernating against the cold the next—but this visit was the first time my mother had looked old to me, bone weary, finally worn out by life. Her hands were less steady, her eyes not as bright, her hair a wispier and whiter version of itself.

"And your friend's book isn't helping," he said. I hadn't seen a copy of *Uncle Tom's Cabin* in the house anywhere and wondered if he had actually read it or was simply reacting to criticisms he had heard. I knew better than to ask.

"It has done a great deal to increase sympathy for negroes in this country," I said.

"But Stowe practically endorses colonization. How does that help?"

"Her book will do more good than harm."

"How can you say that? You know freedoms for negroes must be total, including living where they please." He paced in front of the fire, rubbing his head furiously as if trying to scour away ash that had scorched him from the hearth. "If you insist on continuing to embarrass us by speaking in public, how can you spend a moment of your time lecturing on anything but the great crisis of slavery?"

I embarrassed them? I looked at Mama. Her mouth curved down at the edges.

"Imagine if I could vote, Father. If all the women who support abolition could cast our votes accordingly."

"Wives will vote the way their husbands do. It would be counting twice as many ballots to arrive at the same result. A complete waste of time. You should spend yours more wisely." He reached for his mug of cider, his fourth of the evening.

I had endured criticism in conservative papers railing against me, had stories circulated about me tossing back whiskey in taverns with any man who was willing to entertain me or paying for lodging in unseemly ways, but that was all no more than a bee sting compared to the knife edge of my father's words. And my mother's inability or unwillingness to disagree with him openly only deepened the wound. I understood her fear, and her years of trained subservience, but it pained me still.

As I formulated a response in my mind, the old dark snake arrived. It slid up my spine and threatened to constrict around my neck, while an insistent thrum started between my eyes. It had been years since a debilitating headache had crept across my skull and dug in its fangs. I had to immerse myself in darkness immediately if I had any chance of staving off its worst effects.

"I'm not feeling well. I need to retire early," I said, turning toward the stairs without even kissing Mama goodnight.

"Is it that easy to scare off the famous Lucy Stone?" Father said, his voice growing louder.

"I think it's best we discuss this another time." My vision narrowed, and the light from the fire scorched the inside of my head.

"Some fighter for your blessed cause you turned out to be." He waved at the air like someone sweeping away a gnat.

I couldn't say more. Speaking created more noise in my head than I could tolerate. I took the stairs slowly, as any increase in my heart rate only increased the pounding in my head. I doused my lantern as soon as I had made my way to the bedside. Without even removing my clothes, I buried myself in the dark.

I stayed in bed the whole of the following day. Each time I woke, the argument with my father resurfaced, and I winced at the ugliness of it, of the pain it likely caused Mama. She crept in and sat on the edge of my bed now and again, caressing my forehead like she used to do when I was a child. I kept my eyes closed so we could both stay in a sweet space of tenderness. Her touch helped me fall back away from the anguish.

I thought I heard her whisper, "You always were my brave one," as I drifted off, but it could have been a dream.

The headache subsided by late the next afternoon, leaving my mind coated with a milky residue, my thoughts aimlessly disconnected. After sitting up for a while, managing the light in the room without pain, I decided to test the workings of my brain and reached for the book of Plato beside the bed. It had arrived not long after Mr. Blackwell's visit, with a long letter. It gave me comfort to know there was another man, a different man, who respected me and my work. I unfolded the carefully written pages I had tucked inside the volume and read them again.

Dear Miss Lucy,

Please accept the enclosed volume as a token of our friendship. I am told this translation of Plato is of highest quality, but as a true Greek scholar, you will have to tell me if that is so. I will picture you reading it with the breezes of Coy's Hill keeping you cool, I hope far cooler than the heavy air I have found back in Ohio.

I have reflected much on our conversation in that sacred place, and I thank you for sharing your thoughts with me so openly. A thought struck me afterward, and I would welcome your views on it. It seems to me that your view of marriage as a necessarily constricted institution depends very greatly on the individuals within the particular relationship. Most men, I agree with you, are not interested in granting their wives equality. And sadly, I think you are also correct in your estimation that most women don't actually desire men who are willing to give up their power so easily. While you complimented me greatly on my views of equality, I know for a fact that many women see this same course of thought as unmanly, and therefore not worthy of any husband. But what of two people who do believe in such equality? Then might not their union create something better for each of them than either can create on their own? Wouldn't any life of purpose be more successful if embarked on with another? I hope so, as I know it is what I most desire. And if two people cannot accomplish more than they could alone, I will remain unmarried and adopt a dog for company.

Of course, you do a world of good helping narrow-thinking men expand their views on the capabilities of women and do the same for women who continue to underestimate what their role might be. The world is lucky to have one as unselfish as you to put aside all your other needs to push for freedoms for women and for the continued work you do on behalf of negroes. I fear I am not so selfless. I feel the need to firmly establish myself before I can dedicate my time to these things alone.

But they are not unrelated efforts. I also believe that pecuniary independence has much to do with the marriage equation. Not just that the woman have her own funds, but that the man have enough means not to depend on his wife for the drudgery of keeping the house. Is this not what keeps many women from pursuing intellectual and professional pursuits as much as anything, their inability to get out from under the weight of household chores? Hence my continued quest for material wealth so that I might have my affairs settled enough one day to offer a marriage that allows for true independence on both sides.

I thank you for indulging this long letter. I am as ever,

Your friend,

Henry B. Blackwell

I enjoyed the company of his written words, much as I had enjoyed his presence on the day he visited me. His thoughts on what marriage could look like were truly progressive and his arguments well-constructed. I'd written back to him to thank him for the gift, careful to reply solely as one would offer a response to an interesting part of a conversation with a friend, determined not to give him the wrong impression.

Dear Mr. Blackwell,

I send my sincere thanks for the book as a token of our friendship. You will be happy to hear that it is a fine translation. I am pleased you continue to further your thoughts on the equality possible in marriage. When you find a woman worthy of these ideas, I'm sure you will both benefit greatly.

I do encourage you, however, not to put such high priority on financial success. What can begin as a reasonable goal can easily become an obsession with the material, a never-ending pursuit that then pushes good works to the side for the duration. While we all need enough to survive, I do believe it is through working to better the world that we thrive.

I have much travel in my future, heading to Cleveland by way of Ithaca and Seneca with an indulgent rest in Niagara right before the next convention, so I will not be reachable at this address for the foreseeable future.

I remain your friend,

Lucy Stone

The morning of my departure, Mama handed me a small satchel with bread, two apples, a chunk of her cheese, and a jar of preserves.

"So you don't get hungry on your trip," she said, kissing my cheek. "And a letter came for you yesterday afternoon. I put it in the bag for you also. Good to have reading on such a long journey."

Father drove me to the station without a word. The squeaks and groans of the carriage accentuated the silence he insisted on perpetuating. We had barely spoken since our argument, and I had decided not to address it further, keeping the peace for my last few days for Mama's sake. But I could see the tension between us etched in her face.

"Please take care of Mama" was all I said to him as he left me at the station.

Once West Brookfield was long gone in the distance and the train reached its full speed, I thought back to Mr. Blackwell's visit again and tried to recollect more clearly the day he suggested we had previously met in Cincinnati, three years earlier. It was difficult to pinpoint the moment, so jumbled as it was with fatigue and sorrow from that awful time.

I had eagerly accepted several lecture invitations in Chicago that summer, knowing it would give me an opportunity to visit my brother Luther in the small farm town outside the city where he had settled. I hadn't seen him in years and couldn't wait to walk his farmland with him and relive even a tiny bit of the childhood we had spent wandering Coy's Hill together. I had always felt more myself whenever I was with him.

It was an exciting time. I had been working with two friends that year, Paulina Wright and Mary Livermore, to organize the first-ever national women's rights convention, slated for September of 1850 in Worcester. We had put out a call, received signatures of support from more than forty prominent reformers, and were developing an impressive slate of speakers who would bring the issue of women's rights to the fore in the mind of the nation. It was sure to be my most significant achievement yet.

By the time I was ready to leave Chicago for Luther's, the newspapers were full of grim news. Cholera had pockmarked the countryside, with little rhyme or reason for which household it might attack next, and I was advised to turn back for home. Something told me to press on, and I paid a driver double his wage to take me to Hutsonville.

When Phebe opened the door to my brother's house, I could see in her eyes how gravely ill he already was. She held their young son on her hip awkwardly, his legs not able to wrap fully around her bulging belly. The little boy, Sam, looked just like Luther as a child to me, his curls stuck to his forehead with sweat, his dark eyes blinking at me over the fist jammed in his mouth. I put my hand on his back and forced my lips into a smile but didn't have the time to get acquainted with him. Luther needed me.

"Where is he?" I asked, already headed up the stairway behind her.

"First door on the left."

The lone candle in the room sputtered as I opened the door, its flame swaying with the shift of air in the room. The windows on either side of the bed were wide open, but the balmy night offered no breeze, only the sound of peepers from the bogs I had ridden past on the long lane in. The room had a sour stench, which I followed to the chamber pot across the room.

Luther didn't stir, his head half buried in the pillow. His sheets were awkwardly wrapped around one leg, suggesting a struggle that had left him entangled and helpless to fix it. A column of sweat darkened the center of his nightshirt.

I sat on the bed and took his hand in mine. It was limp and very warm. I noticed a damp cloth hanging off a bowl on his nightstand and gently wiped away the beads of sweat at the edge of his hairline. His neck was stretched out awkwardly, as if he had thrown his head to the opposite side of the pillow, and I could ever so slightly see his life beating there, erratically. He didn't stir until I laid my cloth on his chest, hoping to take some of the furious heat from his body. He turned his head toward me in what seemed a tremendous effort and opened his eyes just enough to take in the light of the candle.

"The baby," he murmured. Always the protector. Even in his dazed state, he knew it was too dangerous for Phebe to nurse him.

"It's Lucy. I've come to see you well."

He closed his eyes and tried to squeeze my hand, his fingers barely tapping my skin before falling open again.

I stayed with him through the night, leaving his side only to empty out the chamber pot and refill the basin of water by the bed. He hardly moved, but his breathing was even, and I allowed myself to hope it was the kind of deep sleep that might help him regain his strength, not the kind that is only one step from the beyond.

As the sun came up, he opened his eyes, wider this time, and he tried to lift his head. I braced his shoulders and bunched the pillow behind him. In the morning light, I could see how pale he was, the dark gray patches below each eye looking almost as if he had been in a schoolyard tiff.

"How do you feel?" I asked.

He shrugged and with great effort pulled his tongue away from the roof of his mouth. I tilted a small cup of water up to his lips. He took only enough to wet the inside of his mouth.

"Little Lucy," he said with some difficulty.

He had always called me that, his reminder that he was the older brother, the bigger brother, even when I beat him in a footrace. Underneath his teasing, I always heard pride in the fact that his little sister could run faster than a boy.

The only place I consistently outpaced him was in intellectual pursuits: memorizing Mama's Bible verses, solving mathematic problems, making sense of Homer. But none of that mattered to him. Luther was a true boy of the land. While I loved the farm for the jutting rocks, the view from the hill, the acres of trees that offered their shade in summer and their glistening glory in the winter, Luther loved the farm for the dirt, for the worms that fertilized the ground, for the patient work of coaxing a crop to fruition. He had come to Illinois, where huge tracts of land were easier to come by, where he could run a farm operation of his own.

Luther had never been much for writing letters, but we shared a bond that didn't rely on such details. I had been closer with him than any of my siblings, including my sisters. He and I had walked through our childhoods side by side. With only eleven months between us, we were practically twins. He had always known how to taunt me or praise me to get me to take on one of his chores, and I always knew what he was thinking before he had to say a word. In his eyes was deep sadness for how I might tell Mama she had lost another child without breaking her heart, without shattering mine, and extreme worry over what would become of Phebe and Sam and the new babe without him.

"Your boy looks just like you," I said. "Must be stubborn like you, too."

He smiled ever so slightly, but the skin around his cheeks didn't follow, as if there was too much to lift.

"Tell me," he said, unable to complete the sentence.

As kids, whenever we had a spare hour or two and the weather was amenable, we'd run out to the orchard, climb our favorite trees, and then lie down in the shade munching on our fill of apples. Luther would always say, "Tell me everything," and then listen to me ramble on about all the new things I'd discovered that I thought he should know, like how the Thompson boy had slipped Eliza a note or that the blacksmith was behind on paying Mama for cheese. He would listen to each tidbit and my theories about what I thought might happen next. When I ran out of family news, I would tell him about the novel cousin Abigail had given me to read—swearing him to secrecy, as novels were not allowed in our house—or share something I had learned from the judge. Luther rarely asked questions, no matter how far-fetched what I told him might seem, and would sometimes even fall asleep in the shade while I talked. It suddenly occurred to me, as I sat beside his bed, that perhaps he wasn't interested in any of it, but simply liked the sound of my voice.

"I saw the most beautiful vegetable garden while visiting a home in Pennsylvania recently." I talked, and he fell back into a deep sleep.

I stayed in his room through another night, holding his hand tightly when a muscle cramp caused his body to lurch and trying to keep him cool with my one rag, dipping it into the water, wringing it out, and patting down his tortured body. I came out twice to nibble on bread Phebe brought up to me and tried to answer her worry the only way I knew how, with a squeeze of her arm and a promise that I was keeping him as comfortable as possible.

Thirty-eight hours into my vigil, Luther's grip jarred me. I had been dozing, my hand in his, and I jerked my head up, half-expecting him to speak to me. His shoulders clenched, his eyes widened, and then I watched helplessly as a long, slow exhale left his body. My hand emptied out as his fingers opened in their final surrender. I tried to hold on, to coax him back to me. My body began to shake, and my grip on him made us both quiver, as if some last living part of him was passing back into me and some piece of my soul was being sent off with him. We were grown from the same earth, shared the same roots, and my world wouldn't be the same without him in it somewhere.

But he was gone.

It took me some time before I was able to summon the will to leave the room. I found Phebe sitting at her kitchen table, Sam playing in the dirt on the other side of the screen door. I didn't have to tell her what she already knew.

She slouched over a cup of tea, her hair pulled hastily back into a greasy bun, her face as lifeless as a dried-out prairie.

"I had three miscarriages before Sam. I thought I might never be able to give him a family, the son he wanted. Your brother didn't give up on me. He said we'd have our family when the time was right."

She paused and held her apron up to her eyes, wiped her nose with it.

"He barely had time to show Sam how to plant his first seedling." She pushed her teacup aside and laid her head in her arms on the table. I rubbed her back for a few moments as she heaved in silent grief before stepping out the screen door.

I bent down in front of Sam and put a handful of dirt into his bucket. He looked up at me with anxious eyes, the same eyes I had just closed for the last time. My own eyes began to swim. I took a deep breath and willed a smile onto my face.

"Should we go plant something with this soil?" I asked. He nodded tentatively.

I offered him my hand, picked up his bucket, and led him out toward the fields my brother had so lovingly tilled and harvested. I had no idea how large his farm had become.

"Your father always liked my stories. Would you like me to tell you a story?"

❧

We buried Luther two days later. Afterward, I walked among the daffodils and daisies in the graveyard, taking time to read the headstones. I wanted to understand who my brother's neighbors in the afterlife would be, given he was so far from his own kin. I hoped the stones would tell me something to suggest good people, honest and hardworking families that loved and took care of one another. It would be too lonely for him otherwise.

Some stones were too old to read, some newly etched for babes barely older than Sam. Two larger inscriptions caught my eye. One read, "Here lies Richard M. Morrison, beloved doctor of Hutsonville, keeper of healing secrets, 1782–1835." Under that read, "Hannah, wife of Richard, 1785–1837." Another stone read, "RIP William G. Forrester, first cowboy of Hutsonville, 1762–1829." Beneath his name was etched, "Marjory, wife of William."

All the family stones called out the same order of things, a man who was known for doing something, a woman who was simply a wife. And now Phebe wasn't even that.

With no way to farm the land on her own and cholera still spreading across the state, Phebe and I decided that she and Sam should come back to West Brookfield with me. At least my mother would have a grandson as some comfort for the loss of yet another child.

On the third day of our trip east, the heat hovering at the back of my neck and winding around to my cheeks could not be fully explained by the late August temperatures. I tried to tell myself it was a delayed reaction to the work of settling Luther's affairs while my grief bubbled around the edges of my heart, but I was used to work with little rest, and I began to fear the worst.

By the time we arrived in Utica, I could barely make it to the boarding house. I paid for separate rooms and asked Phebe to wake me two hours before our train was set to depart the next day, which was almost twenty hours away. And then the world went black.

I vaguely remember not being able to rise out of bed but somehow convincing Phebe that she and Sam had to stay away and had to catch the train or else their tickets would be voided—an untruth, but I had to ensure they would continue on. She had to get to a safe place before the baby came. The last thing I did before I lost all ability to function was give her a two-dollar note and ask her to have the boardinghouse owner send for a doctor.

I don't remember him coming and didn't wake for four days. I know this only because when I rose briefly, unsure of where I was, I found four bowls of soup lined up outside my room, the innkeeper apparently not wanting to be accused of failing to feed her guests. I also discovered a bottle of pills on the nightstand next to a glass of water. I took one and tossed and turned through several more soup deliveries, wracked with bouts of scorching fever and visions of walking barefoot through January snowdrifts, the cold making an icicle of my spine. In my delirium, I found myself chased by an angry mob, then skidding down Coy's Hill, the rocks digging into my back, then standing in a huge convention hall for hours, the empty seats never filling, my speech recited forty times over into a void, then chasing after Luther endlessly, my legs not responding properly, his limp hand always just out of my reach. Every time I crawled back to the present, I forced myself to take another pill, not having any idea of the stretch of time since the last dose but somehow aware they were my only salvation.

I have a faint memory of touching the soup spoon to my lips, the liquid long gone cold, the smell making me gag. But I also knew I needed nourishment. I might have had one bite a day, I cannot be sure. I held onto the edges of my bed like they were the sides of a raft that might tip me into a winter stream if I didn't lie very still. I drifted in and out of consciousness without any sense of night or day or how many of each passed through my room.

When I was finally able to eat half a bowl of soup without spilling the contents back out into a bucket and perceived I could walk the distance from my room to a carriage and from the carriage to the train platform, I made up my mind to head home. The woman sitting in a little study off the front hall barely looked up at me.

"You owe ten dollars," she said. A king's ransom.

I detached my tongue from the roof of my mouth to speak, a painful memory of Luther edging into my brain. How was I alive and he wasn't? I looked at the bottle still clutched in my hand. I squinted at the barely legible words: *Chlorophyll with Quinine, take 2 times every day for Typhoid Fever.* Not cholera. Its only slightly less deadly cousin. Relief and guilt coursed through me in equal amounts.

Her bosom heaved as she sighed. I had more than worn out my welcome.

"Seventy-five cents a night for the room and board. Plus, a dollar for the sheets. I'm going to have to burn those." There was no sympathy in her voice.

My mind tripped over the numbers, and I had to calculate it several times before I could be sure. Twelve nights I had been there? Twelve nights with barely a drop of food and only as much water as it took to swallow a handful of pills?

"Don't tell me you don't have it," she said. "I seen you in the papers."

It was shortly after that when I must have stumbled into Mr. Blackwell's hardware store, an uncashed check from the Anti-Slavery Society my only lifeline for getting all the way home. I still couldn't picture the store, or him standing behind the till. But all these years later, he had sought to find me nonetheless.

❧

I now opened the bag of provisions Mama had given me and laid out a small repast of cheese and fruit on the jilting train table. As I ate, I read Mr. Blackwell's letter.

> *My Dear Miss Lucy,*
>
> *Your kind note was the first thing that greeted me on my return from Wabash, and I am writing quickly in hopes that this reaches you before your departure north.*

I very much appreciated you questioning if my need to earn properly before marrying or before devoting myself to a life of principle, as you have, is mere love of money or blind ambition rather than a sound philosophy. Perhaps you are right, and money is not needed before doing either of those things—you have certainly proved this for yourself. But I fear I cannot be considered a man of value unless I have achieved success on some level of financial measures. I hope this does not make you see me as selfish or less passionate about equality, abolition, or women's rights. Please know I think of little else each day. But I continue to believe that moving our shared ideas beyond theory and putting them into actual practice is as strong a protest against the ills our founding fathers infected us with as anything.

I am quite glad my idea that a marriage might be less of a prisoner to its name than to the individuals that enter into it struck you as not altogether wrong. There is too much to say on this topic for the size of the sheet before me. Important thoughts of this kind should not be rushed, and you will understand that I have not the luxury of time at the present.

You say you are stopping in Niagara on your way to Cleveland for the next convention. If your schedule has not changed, might you be open to having me come meet you there? While I do not mistake your words for anything beyond the thoughts of one friend sharing ideas with another, there is still much to say that is better addressed in person. Please let me know if you are amendable to this. It would be a true pleasure to have another long walk and puzzle through these important ideas together.

I look forward to your earliest reply.

Yours ever,

Henry B. Blackwell

I laid down the letter beside my half-eaten apple and looked beyond the window to the fallow fields rushing by, my mind a torrent of conflict over what he had proposed. Seeing him again would be lovely, but it was not without risk. Despite being a grown adult, a woman who spent every waking moment fighting for the right of independence, the expectations of how such a woman should comport herself were difficult to unload. There was certainly nothing wrong with taking a walk in the public eye, as he suggested, to discuss important matters. I had done so many times with other gentlemen, Mr. Garrison and Mr. Phillips and others. But to prearrange a meeting in a place that was neither home for either of us nor a work location could easily be interpreted as something else. Of course, hundreds of visitors arrived in Niagara every day, those mesmerized by the great rush of the falls, the clouds of spray created by the never-ending crash of water, the noise that silenced everything else. I had been once before and found it to be remarkably soothing, perhaps the one place where I felt truly still. I had been looking forward to two days of utter peace and wasn't sure it would be the same were it to be interrupted.

Of course, I had already shared the magic of Coy's Hill with Mr. Blackwell, and his presence had not diminished the effect of that place. In fact, the conversation had almost heightened the experience. But perhaps that was because it was entirely unexpected, a spontaneous exchange of ideas that would be impossible to re-create.

And I could not deny the real danger of sending this gentleman a false impression of my intentions. Were we to meet in Niagara, I would have to be diligent in communicating that friendship was the only course for us. Were this possible, would not conversation with Mr. Blackwell be a welcome addition to my visit?

I didn't have long to decide. If I wanted to accept his invitation, I would need to post a reply to him within the week. And it would need to be crafted carefully. Of course, I could simply fail to respond in a timely manner, which would put an end to the matter.

I was still puzzling through these competing thoughts when it was time to change trains in Albany, and I still hadn't arrived at a conclusion several hours later, as I pulled into the station in Ithaca. As the train chugged to a halt, it was a delight to see Susan waiting for me on the platform, waving her hat, and all thoughts of Mr. Blackwell fell to the side in anticipation of what lay ahead.

9

I'm relieved to see you looking so well," Susan said, holding both my shoulders in her hands to look at me squarely. "How was your time at Coy's Hill?"

"It was a much welcome rest. You, however, have been on the go nonstop, it seems." If she was weary, none of it showed on her face. Determination sparked in her eyes.

I had first met Susan three years earlier, thanks to Elizabeth Cady Stanton. I know you dislike Mrs. Stanton, Alice, and it irks you to no end that the *History of Woman Suffrage* touts the gathering in Seneca Falls as the first national women's rights convention and treats the great convening in Worcester as an afterthought. But the meeting at Seneca Falls was an important moment in our movement. Yes, her gathering was much smaller than Worcester and without a widely distributed call for attendance could hardly be called national—her one small ad in the local paper didn't reach most of us or give adequate notice to attend. But it was groundbreaking nonetheless. And I must tell you that Elizabeth had always been gracious in her encouragement of me personally. She wrote me several letters before we ever met, congratulating me on a speech she had seen printed in a paper or cheering me on for my decision to charge admission to my talks, and she threw her full support behind Worcester, despite not attending herself. So when she invited me to her home to discuss the third planned convention, I eagerly accepted.

It was immediately apparent on my first visit what a split life Mrs. Stanton led. Her front lawn overflowed with the gleeful sounds of children set loose on a summer day. Two boys raced by my carriage as I pulled up to the house, one in pursuit of the other, while another tickled a toddler rolling in the grass. I was considering joining the game of tag when my hostess stepped through her front door to greet me, a fifth child perched on her hip. Her dark hair spun in ringlets around her face, her blue eyes a perfect match with the jumper of the cherub clinging to her side.

"Lucy Stone, it is grand to finally meet you in person. Come, come, you must be wilting. Let's have some lemonade and cookies," she said, waving me down from the carriage.

"Charles and James, why don't you take the little ones to pick some raspberries? Eat your fill, but bring some home for supper." She briefly watched the two older boys chase each other and held up her hand, as if considering interrupting their fun with another instruction, but then waved the thought away.

"Harley will bring in your bag," she said in my direction, and turned to go inside.

I was pleased to see Elizabeth wearing bloomers. Amelia Bloomer's invention of a tunic that hung down to the knee over loose pantaloons eliminated the constriction of corsets and long heavy skirts, providing freedom of movement previously unimaginable. And yet, wearing them stirred almost as much controversy as speaking to mixed audiences. Doing both at the same time put those of us in the public eye to the test.

Elizabeth's bloomers were made of a fine light cotton, the tunic flowing over her ample hips, the color a pale green with tiny flowers embroidered at the hem. I wondered at a wardrobe vast enough to include the perfect fabric for the heat of August while being formal enough to receive guests. I was lucky if my clothes were a good match for the season, let alone any particular occasion, which the heavier silk bloomers I wore decidedly were not. Was such an array of choices a comfort or a burden? I had never had the finances or the time, not to mention the space in my valise, to worry much about it.

Elizabeth had of course signed the call for all of our national conventions—which had by then become annual events—but I had long wondered why she hadn't attended in person. Now I understood why. All those children would keep any woman squarely focused on the home front. Lucretia Mott had told me Elizabeth became so restless after being forced to move from Boston by her husband that her writing on women's rights was the only thing keeping her from pulling every ringlet from her head. But I could see she was at ease with her children, happy even. She adored them and they her. Yet any envy I felt about her bustling family evaporated as I quickly calculated the years of education and work I would have lost producing such a brood. I couldn't imagine giving up one of those years, let alone five or six more.

I followed her into a house that was much larger than it appeared from the outside. The front hall stretched deep into the space, with several doors on each side. Elizabeth's study, which led out to a veranda, had a round table with four dainty chairs and a lace tablecloth, slightly damp in the center from the large pitcher of lemonade fighting off the heat.

"I hope you don't mind, but I invited another guest I thought you should meet."

A woman, a few years my junior, came around the table as we entered. She leaned toward me with a hopeful smile, much like the young women who approached me after one of my speeches, eager to talk and anxious to shake my hand.

"Miss Stone, it is such an honor. Susan Anthony." She thrust her arm toward me.

"Please call me Lucy." I noted her strong grip and willingness to look me directly in the eye, a welcome change from the demure greeting more common from other women. Standing at least a head taller than me, her open expression and angular body suggested a contemplative mind coupled with a certain eagerness to speed up the flow of incoming ideas. Where laugh lines graced Elizabeth's round face, Susan's was completely smooth, as if not yet imprinted by any moments that might last. The gray cloth of her dress indicated a simpler life than the one Mrs. Stanton obviously enjoyed.

"Susan lives not too terribly far from here and has recently shown interest in our crusade." Elizabeth shifted the baby onto her lap and poured the lemonade. "As soon as I knew when you would be coming, I invited her to join."

"It was your relic speech that caught my attention," Susan said. "It made me consider devoting some of my time toward women's rights."

I relished converting any talented individual to the cause, and if Elizabeth Cady Stanton saw potential in Miss Anthony, she would surely become a valuable asset. And I was gratified to hear that my relic speech had been appreciated. It was such a blur at the time. I wouldn't have remembered anything about it had the *New York Tribune* not printed it in full. It arose from my experience in Luther's graveyard, all those names on stones, listed as nothing but a wife. "A wife is nothing but a man's relic. A thing left behind," I think I said, with an impassioned plea to change the marriage laws. I had removed myself as the headline speaker in Worcester, at first unsure I would even be well enough to attend after my bout of typhoid, and certain I wouldn't have the strength to stand onstage if I did. But on the third day of the convention, as I pictured all those headstones surrounding my brother, I could sit quiet with the idea no longer.

"You said the law gives married women no more rights than the family cow," Susan said. "I was struck by that. I always thought that most of what holds women back is simply learned behavior, what men expect of us, and what we are taught to expect of ourselves, which is bad enough. But the law is a powerful barrier. It needs to be changed."

"It all needs to be changed," Elizabeth said. "It's a shame conventions don't do any real work."

I lowered my glass without so much as moistening my tongue.

"Oh, don't be insulted," she said, bouncing the child on her lap. "They must be had, I suppose, but the real work needs to be petitioning law-makers. The best speeches would do more good if they were spoken into the ears of legislators."

"If you don't mind me saying, I do think there is value in turning the views of the people first," Susan said. "Public opinion must be chiseled rock by rock until the lawmakers know the avalanche will bury them if they don't move."

"True. I suppose those with the power have no incentive to create change otherwise," Elizabeth said.

I couldn't help but marvel at the instant fluidity of our conversation. My mind turned over all the good we could do together with such like minds. I decided to share an idea I'd been contemplating.

"I do often think that we could make significant change through a paper devoted to our cause. Think how much good *The Liberator* has done, or Douglass's *North Star*."

"That's the best idea I've heard in a long time," Elizabeth said.

Her praise buoyed me. I smiled despite myself.

"The challenge is in funding it." A paper couldn't be run on encouragement alone. "We barely have enough funds to put up the next convention."

"Lucretia tells me some don't want Abby Foster back for Syracuse," Elizabeth said, putting two more cookies onto her plate.

Abby gave one of the most controversial speeches in Worcester, suggesting blood might need to be shed to achieve our goals. She often ruffled the collars of her audience.

"Many in the crowd were upset, I'm afraid," I said. "But women who have never faced violence have no right to judge her."

"And a little shock never hurt anyone," Elizabeth said. "Sometimes staking out the extreme is all it takes for the middle ground to look less dangerous."

"Perhaps she was asking a more fundamental question about what we are willing to give up for our liberties. Men were willing to die for the revolution," Susan said. "Are we?"

"Violence is a man's idea," Elizabeth said. "Like so many of the bad ideas we are fighting against."

I thought of Garrison, Phillips, Douglass. Some of my greatest supporters were men, and none of them espoused violence in our work.

"I think the women are harder to convince than the men," I said. "There is fear that we're trying to take away the role of mother or housewife, everything they know."

"Speaking of which, I need to get this little one into his crib for a nap," Elizabeth said. "I'm sure you two can find much to discuss."

Susan and I dove almost immediately into more personal conversation, all of which felt as vital as it was natural. We discovered quickly how much we had in common—neither of us married, both of us long-time supporters of abolition, both raised in simple households—and how much of our experiences had been different. Susan was brought up as a Quaker, and her people valued women equally to men. In meetings, women and girls spoke just as frequently as did men and boys. More than one woman in her family had achieved the revered position of High Elder, and women's opinions were welcome at the dinner table on everything from farming to politics. Her father expected as much of her as if she had been a son, giving her no need for outrage or revolt. It was almost impossible to imagine. I had no idea what it might feel like. I had claimed my freedom only by escaping from the confines of my childhood home, while Susan found society at large far more confining than her Quaker past. Our paths collided at just the right time.

We took long walks in the evenings while Elizabeth ushered her children to their beds. Cicadas filled the air with a constant hum as the sun and the moon traded places in the sky. Linked arm in arm, we shared our childhood dreams and our current frustrations. Susan talked a great deal about her father, a liberal thinker and Garrisonian—the word lifted my heart. He owned factories and stores and taught his daughters the rules of business, encouraging them to learn a life of independence. A strict Quaker, however, he never allowed song or dance or toys in the house, and he refused to sell spirits in his general store or employ anyone who suffered from the drink—both of which he was warned would make running his business impossible. But he persisted, even managing to host a barn raising without serving a drop of gin.

"He once bought a camel cloak with an enormous cape to keep him warm on his business travels," she said. "The elders found this to be against the rules of plainness and forbade it. My father asked if they would rather lose a valued member to death by illness or to a rule too rigid. They allowed him the coat."

I told her about my horrific discovery in the Bible as a child of God's curse that women's "desire shall be to thy husband, and he shall rule over thee," how I told my mother the translation had to be wrong and declared I would one day learn Latin and Greek so I could correct it.

She laughed. "The Bible can be quite harsh, I suppose."

By the third day, I realized I hadn't felt as comfortable with anyone since being side by side with Nette. It made me miss her terribly.

"You must meet my friend from Oberlin, Nette Brown. She and I swore a long time ago that we would never marry."

"I've known for some time that marriage wouldn't be for me either," she said.

"Then can I ask why the relic speech meant so much to you?"

"You said, 'A husband or father is never all a man is allowed to be.' I never felt unequal in any way until I started teaching and discovered how much lower my pay was than my male counterparts. It infuriated me. And when I tired of teaching, I understood how little else was open to me. My father would have encouraged me or my sisters to take over his factories when the time came. He had trained us for it. But he lost everything in '39. Suddenly there were no options available to me. I had been taught to be independent, but it is clear to me now that we are considered of no value if not a wife or mother, but anyone who is a wife, by law, has no independent value. It is a trap of dangerous proportion."

I had said as much onstage countless times, and yet seeing Elizabeth with her baby, the way she inhaled his sweet scent and absentmindedly stroked his cheek, made me wonder if there weren't precious parts of life that defied logic.

"Do you ever think about what we might be missing? Despite her claims otherwise, Elizabeth is so happy being surrounded by her children. Do you ever long for a family?" I asked.

"Independence outweighs all that. Just think how much *she* is missing. She has a brilliant mind, but she's stuck inside her house. You and I can get out there and make a difference."

Surely there was value in the act of raising boys who might treat women far differently than our fathers did. But Susan was unlikely to be persuaded. And anyhow, I would be grateful to have another woman at the ready for work on the road.

"You must come speak at the next convention," I said.

"No, no. I'm good for organizing. I can travel, put up notices, get people to sign petitions, write letters, anything you need, but not speaking. That's clearly your specialty," she said.

"But you've spoken for temperance before. And surely you spoke at your meetinghouse."

"Temperance is an idea I grew up with, so it comes naturally to me. And speaking in meetings is different. There is never an expectation of a well-conceived speech, just an invitation to share a thought or a feeling if so moved. That's easy for me. The other is quite terrifying."

Not to mention having books and rotten fruit thrown at you, I thought.

"You'll find your way," I said, squeezing her arm.

On our last morning of that first visit, Elizabeth seemed distracted by her husband's impending arrival. She interrupted our conversation to speak to the cook each time he came to see to our meal.

"You'll have the pheasant on hand for tonight?" she asked him when he arrived with our morning tea. When the fellow came back with the eggs and biscuits, she asked, "We did discuss apricot sauce, did we not? Or should we have the sherry sauce?"

When he attempted to clear the table, she pulled her plate back and turned it in her hands.

"I don't think this pattern will do for tonight. Please fetch the stoneware with the hunting scene, if you would. Oh, and some fine cheeses for dessert would be lovely, I think."

The cook finally sent off, we were settling into a discussion about the merits of petitioning various states for municipal school voting—who could disagree that decisions about a children's schooling fit squarely into a woman's domain?—when she interrupted herself with details of our departure.

"Have I mentioned that Harley will take you ladies to the train after our midday meal? That will give me just enough time to prepare for Henry's arrival," she said.

She kept smoothing her hair, appearing nervous, and had adopted a more businesslike tone than usual, perhaps trying not to let her anxiety show. Did her husband frighten her at some level? I had met Henry Stanton at an anti-slavery meeting once before. He'd seemed gentlemanly enough and was an avid supporter of abolition, but he had famously stormed out and threatened to resign when Abby Kelley was elected to a leadership role in the organization. What must Elizabeth have thought of that? Did they discuss such things at home, the reformer and her perhaps less-than-supportive husband? I couldn't help but wonder if all the children pattering about had the same cause to thank as we Stones: too much whiskey, and force.

After breakfast, she announced there would be no more disruptions during our final morning together, ironic considering she'd done all the interrupting. She asked her maid to watch the baby and set her eldest son in charge of a treasure hunt for the other children. Once we clearly had the room to ourselves, she was all business.

"There are two important items I would like to discuss having added to the official agenda for the convention, Lucy," Elizabeth said, pushing a curl off her face before placing both hands on the table. "Divorce and birth control."

Had my thoughts about her marriage and childbearing crept onto my face? The subject of divorce had long been debated by reformers, a complex topic indeed. But birth control? I had no idea what to say.

"It's quite simple," she said. "Women will not be in full control of their lives unless we can divorce men whenever necessary and without losing custody of our children, and we will never truly be free unless we own our own bodies. Birth control is required."

"As you know, there is a motion under way to support legalizing divorce where there is drunkenness—"

She interrupted me. "Not just on the grounds of drunkenness. For any reason. Failure to requite love, inability to provide, et cetera. Women should not be stuck in a marriage they don't want to be in, period. Without this right, men can be as crude and loveless and careless as they like with no threat of consequences," she said, her passion coming through.

"And you believe men should be able to initiate divorce for all the same reasons, I presume," I said.

"Of course."

"I couldn't agree more, but it's really a human rights issue, not a women's issue. If we take it on as purely a women's issue, we run the risk of alienating too many men. If men and women take it up together it would have more chance of success."

"Poppycock! What man will be interested in that?"

"The same ones who are supporting changing the property laws for married women," I said.

"And aren't those the men who will be at your convention?"

We debated this for some time, until Susan raised her hand to silence us both. "Lucy, will you take it to the executive committee for discussion as an item to be included?"

We had discussed it as a group many times, and I knew where my colleagues would come out on the issue, but I demurred.

"Good. Now, on to the second topic," she said.

It struck me how much more assertive Susan was than a few short days before. I wasn't the only one drawing confidence from this formidable trio. Our roundtable suddenly felt like she was at the head.

"Is this part of the same issue: if a man is forcing himself on his wife, should this not be grounds for divorce?" Susan asked.

"Certainly. But I'm not speaking of rape. I'm talking about a woman's desire to be intimate without necessarily producing a child," Elizabeth said. She refilled all our teacups with a steady hand, as if we were discussing the preferred way to trim roses.

Susan and I both sat back in our chairs, quiet.

"Oh, good lord. Why does everyone always think it's only for the man's pleasure and women should have no interest without wanting a baby? You unmarried ladies have missed out on a lot!"

"Elizabeth!" Susan said.

Heat rushed up the back of my neck, and I felt foolish for being embarrassed, yet I was embarrassed just the same. My sisters had spoken to me about the thrill of kissing a boy, but pleasure in procreation? What was it even called if you weren't creating anything?

"Honestly, men just visit a brothel whenever they get the itch. We have to go and get ourselves married," Elizabeth said. "And even then, there's no stopping the endless flow of children. Don't get me wrong. I adore every one of my children, but can't a woman look forward to seeing her husband without worrying about having another mouth to feed?"

I stopped my hands from flying up to my face in shock. I had never heard anyone speak that way. Was the nervousness I saw in her earlier actually excitement? Did "preparing" for his arrival mean taking time to beautify herself to catch her husband's attention. *For her own pleasure?* I had long believed that women needed the right to refuse their husbands without censure, but she meant something else entirely.

Elizabeth went on.

"And you two. Why shouldn't you be able to enjoy yourselves even though you aren't married? Because the Bible says you shouldn't? Hogwash. That's just another rule men made to keep their women 'unblemished.'" She poured herself more tea and topped off our cups, though neither Susan nor I had touched ours. When neither of us replied, she sat back in her chair and shook her head. "Must I explain everything? Surely you both know there are countless methods—pessaries to block the way, tonics, prevention powders?"

I wasn't the least bit familiar with these methods, as she called them, and given the size of her family, I wondered how common they really were.

"Anyway, birth control should be on the agenda. In the end, a woman's right to her own body might be the most important right of all. Without it, we don't have much."

I had heard all the arguments against women's rights shouted at me from audiences over the last few years: If women walked all the same halls as men, then children's faces would stop getting washed!, dinners wouldn't be cooked!, whole households would become dustbins of chaos! All of it was patently ridiculous, of course, but did we need to set them to worrying that babies wouldn't get made at all?

"There are more basic concerns that need to be addressed first," I said.

"Are there?"

It struck me then that Elizabeth, the only one among us to be married and have children, was the one arguing for divorce and birth control.

Would Abigail have divorced Jeb had that option been readily available to her, saving her from a loveless life? Perhaps Susan and I underappreciated these two issues because we weren't living through them. Or maybe Elizabeth simply relished occupying the position of being the most radical person in the room.

I looked around Elizabeth's personal study then, with its fine pewter candlesticks, stacks of books, and lace curtains. Beyond the window I could see the cook pushing a wheelbarrow brimming with radishes, corn, and apples, all purchased from the farm next door. No one inside this house had dug in the dirt, pressed the cheese, snapped the necks of the fowl that would be presented at dinner. Mr. Stanton clearly wasn't stingy with his income, or if he kept more than his fair share, there was still plenty to go around.

I considered, not for the first time, whether it was easier to be a revolutionary when you had all the comforts anyone could ever require. A needy person has less to lose, but Elizabeth would never have to worry about her children starving because of her ideas.

❦

Susan and I stayed in constant touch after that first meeting, seeing each other whenever possible, relying on written correspondence in between to stay abreast of the other's activities. She put her organizational skills to work on behalf of the cause immediately, helping to circulate pamphlets and petitions and encouraging influencers she knew to consider the grave injustices women faced. After more than two years of cajoling, and thanks to a long series of letters with Elizabeth at their fulcrum, I finally managed to convince her to speak alongside me. I was in Ithaca now for that purpose, and Elizabeth had written her a speech for the occasion. I assured Susan that she would find a welcome audience. I hoped I was right. I didn't know how she might react if we had an angry mob on our hands.

We linked arms as we left the station. There was so much catching up to do beyond what we'd been able to share in our letters, and conversation flowed freely as we walked to the lovely inn on Green Street where I had reserved a room. The innkeeper, a burly man who looked more suited to chopping down trees than minding an inn, wrote down our names and interrogated us before handing us the key.

"There can be no men brought here," he said. "I keep watch."

"We can assure you that won't be the case," I said. "We are here to give a talk at the meeting hall tonight. Perhaps you would like to come listen?"

He clutched the key more tightly. "You're not those two ladies who've been pushing an end to liquor, are you?"

I shot Susan a warning glance. She and Nette had become fast friends, just as I'd hoped, and had spent the last three months campaigning for temperance together.

"No, sir, we'll be speaking about women's rights," I said.

He studied each of us for a moment before dropping the key on the blotter.

"I lock the main door at nine o'clock. No visitors."

We thanked him and trudged up the stairs to our room.

"Did you hear that Elizabeth is expecting again?" Susan asked, leaning into a pillow on the window seat.

I nodded. "She wrote to me last month."

"Really, that woman needs to get hold of herself."

I laughed, but Susan wasn't smiling. As much as I knew her to have a wry sense of humor, she was genuinely disappointed that Elizabeth would have another infant to mind. I remembered watching Elizabeth with the baby on her lap, absentmindedly brushing his forehead with her lips, his tiny fist clutching her dress near her breast.

"I'm sure we'll all have times when we'll be more active and times when we will need to rest. It's part of why we need each other," I said.

"Objects in motion tend to stay in motion, my friend. You and I will always be in motion. It's up to us to get the objects at rest back in motion."

"How do you feel about the speech?" I asked. I was to speak on the importance of education for women, and she on the disabilities of women in the professional world, her first lecture on women's rights. I had no doubt Elizabeth had constructed a compelling argument, but I still wondered at Susan's willingness to recite the words of another. But the most important thing was for tonight to go well for her so that she might join me permanently in this fight.

"I wish now that I had asked her to write a speech on the vote," she said. "Nette and I secured 2,800 women's signatures for our temperance law. Do you know what the legislature did? They laughed. They said we might as well have had children sign their names for all the power those signatures held."

The determination I had seen in her eyes earlier lit up, like the hottest part of an ember at the bottom of a fire.

"Nette told me," I said. Nette had been equally energized by the work and disheartened by the outcome, but she would not be dissuaded from making temperance the focus of her energies, as much as I tried to pull her out on the lecture trail with me, too. She had joined me at every convention, but otherwise her main priorities were her congregation and temperance.

"Do you think you'll win suffrage in Massachusetts?" Susan asked.

"They have promised us a hearing date, but I'm not full of hope," I said. Wendell Phillips and I were petitioning to have the word "male" stricken from the state constitution in order to give women all the same rights as men, including the right to vote. We had garnered tacit support, but the majority of legislators saw our request as a loss of something more than a word.

"We must press for the vote everywhere," she said.

"Why don't you speak on suffrage tonight, then?" I asked.

"I don't have that speech," she said, looking alarmed. "I can't just stand up and speak on something without preparation."

I shrugged. "Maybe next time."

"I will talk to Elizabeth about it, ask her to prepare something."

I nodded. All I wanted was for her to have a successful evening. If she were willing to turn her attentions from temperance to speaking for women's rights on a regular basis, I would have the fiercest ally of them all. I was sure of it.

10

As soon as we entered the meeting hall that night in Ithaca, I could tell the space was used for everything from dances to cattle auctions. We arrived early and walked past two men playing billiards at one end, the crack of the balls echoing off the pine walls of the structure. Two others were setting up the speaking area. One swept hay and piles of dirt from the floor while the other dragged long benches and chairs from the edges of the room onto the newly clean spots. Neither of them paid us any mind.

The faint smell of dung permeated my nostrils, and I walked toward one of the large windows for relief from the odor. They were all cracked open just enough to let in the crisp fall air without removing all the warmth from the day's strong sunshine. A lantern hung between each window. I wasn't sure how bright the light would be from those once the sun went down but hoped it would be enough. The seats faced a small wooden platform, no more than one foot high and six feet long, the spot from which the town clerk likely called meetings to order. I estimated the space could hold eighty to one hundred people, if we were able to fill it.

I found an annex at the far end of the room and suggested to Susan we wait there for the audience to arrive. I had been told a storekeeper would be taking payments at the entrance—fifteen cents per person—and we could start whenever we liked. I knew to wait long enough for the majority of the attendees to greet their neighbors and settle into a seat, but not so long that those assembled would grow restless.

The room had only one small window, and Susan looked hot and fidgety in her black silk bloomers, a relatively new outfit for her. There were no refreshments anywhere to be seen—something I had begun to expect—and I worried about the friendliness of the location after all.

Susan's lips moved as she silently read from the paper Elizabeth had sent. I listened to the sound of boots shuffling into the building and the growing hum of conversation, jokes shared, benches clunking when repositioned for comfort.

"Where are your notes?" she asked once she finally looked up from her lap.

"I don't write down my speeches."

"You must be joking," she said, clutching her sheet of paper.

Reading from prepared remarks had always felt confining to me. While I scribbled down ideas and concepts constantly, I found it much easier to compose while walking outside or riding a train, the recitation in my head enough to etch a picture of what I wanted to say in my mind. Our secret debating club at Oberlin had prepared me well in this regard.

"Would you like to go first? What would make you comfortable?" I asked.

"I would be most grateful if you went first. This way I can get a feel for the crowd."

We walked into the noisy hall. Not only was every seat filled, but a row of men stood behind the last group of benches. I was pleased to see at least twenty women in the audience. They gave Susan and me their full attention when we stepped onto the platform, while their husbands continued to talk across them or were turned fully around, in conversation with someone behind. There were two chairs on the wood slab. I removed one to make enough space to stand comfortably. Susan sat.

"Good evening," I said. "Thank you for coming." And then I waited. As the crowd sounds slowed and silenced, I continued to hear the intermittent clack of billiard balls from the far end of the room, obscured from view by the row of standing men. The audience didn't seem to be bothered by the noise, so I began.

"Tonight, I would like to share with you the idea that women and girls, poor and wealthy alike, should be given access to the same educational opportunities as men."

A few boos went up from the crowd, but I pressed on. It was important that Susan learn not to be dissuaded by naysayers.

"We expect our mothers to be in charge of the education of our children, to teach them to read, to guide them through their studies, and yet we do not see fit to educate these future mothers to the greatest extent possible."

"Worked out okay for me!" a man standing in the back shouted.

"Did it now?" I asked. A few snorts of laughter punctuated the air.

As I continued on with my arguments for not only high school-level schooling but the kind of advanced education I had received, a small commotion outside the window nearest me caught my attention. It sounded like a wagon or large barrel was being dragged toward that side of the building. Two heads bobbed at the bottom of the sill, and a nozzle appeared. Before I could move out of the way, frigid water doused the side of my face and dress. A snort of laughter punctuated the eruption of water, and the women in the audience all screamed with surprise. The spray was so strong that as fast as it soaked my tunic and bloomer trousers, the hose turned on itself and fell out of the window. Several men hurried over to look for the culprits, while conversation broke out in every row.

Susan jumped to my side. She was somehow still dry.

"I'm fine," I whispered to her. I wiped the water from my face but otherwise stood completely still. What had been a refreshing breeze now felt like an icy wind, but I willed myself not to shiver lest I look intimidated. I knew I simply had to erase any shock or discomfort from my face and wait. I forced a smile.

As the roar of laughter and conversation died down and the audience found me still standing there, silence again began to settle in the room. Even the billiard balls stopped clinking.

"As I was saying," I continued, "educating women should not only be considered important for teaching our children. Education can also open the doors of every profession to our sex."

The shock on the faces in front of me was plain to see, and not just because of the content of my remarks. There was no shortage of amazement that I had chosen to continue speaking. Stunned silence was followed by nodding and applause as I finished. I worked hard to keep a satisfied smile from blooming across my face.

"For the second part of our evening," I said, "which will feature a lecture on the limitations on women in the professional arts, I am delighted to introduce Miss Susan B. Anthony."

When I turned around to change places with Susan, she looked terrified. The paper she held tightly shook in her hand. I took hold of both of her arms and squeezed, holding on for a moment to steady her.

"Courage," I said.

I sat in the chair as she began her remarks, feeling lucky that the water hadn't touched my backside, so I didn't have to sit in the cold of it. I gently held the bodice of my tunic away from my skin and wrung bits of water from it as surreptitiously as possible.

"Ladies and gentlemen, I thank you for your audience," Susan began. "As you all know, women do great and noble work inside the home, raising children and keeping house, but for those who need or seek employment outside the home, there are few professions available beyond factory work. We are welcomed as teachers in schoolhouses, again a worthy profession, and one that should be better compensated, but there is no ability today for a woman to take on the mantle of lawyer, doctor, or pharmacist."

As soon as she started to speak, her nervousness seemed to fall away, or she buried it so deep inside it was undetectable. Elizabeth's words matched well with her voice, clear and strong. Nonetheless, the billiards began to crack again, and a few more men at the back joined the game, perhaps weary of so much talk. Before long, all three tables were in use. Susan's jaw grated at each pause in her remarks. I stood.

"I'm sorry, gentlemen, if you may, could you please cease the playing until we have finished? These people have paid good money to hear this lecture."

"Don't see why," one of the men said.

"Ah, perhaps you haven't been able to hear us all the way back there."

I looked at Susan, and as if reading my thoughts, she nodded.

"Let us come closer to you," I said. "Then you'll be able to hear."

We both stepped off the platform and walked down the small aisle between the benches. The audience swiveled in their seats as we headed toward the back.

Susan grabbed one of the abandoned chairs and placed it beside the center billiard table, put one hand on its back, and reached out her other to me. Smiling, I gave her my support as she climbed onto the chair and then up on the table.

"What the heck!" one of the men exclaimed. "You'll scuff up the table."

"No need to swear," Susan said, leaning over the man, before straightening up and standing strong and tall atop the table. "Now can you hear me?"

With that she finished her remarks. It took everything I had not to laugh out loud at her audacity. The room broke into applause, and one man insisted on swooping her off the table to help her to the ground.

"That's the best entertainment we've had in this town in years," he said, clapping her on the back as if she were a showman.

She gave him a perfunctory smile, linked her arm in mine, and out we went into the night.

Not until we had safely locked the door to our room did we allow ourselves to break out in laughter.

"That hose! You were dripping like a girl gone swimming in a lake. How on earth did you keep your composure?" she asked.

"They will never play billiards again without thinking of you," I said. "Where did you find the nerve?"

I peeled off my wet clothes and wrapped myself in a quilt while Susan went to fetch a pot of tea. Sitting atop our shared bed, a candle burning down on the table beside us, we talked late into the night. We discussed the triumphs and setbacks of the past year, admitting the deep failure we both felt when the result we envisioned didn't materialize, and agreed we could bring each other great strength working side by side. And then we started to laugh again.

"Wait until Elizabeth hears this story," she said.

"I wish she could have been here tonight."

"The more babies that come, the longer it will be before she'll ever leave that house. At least I don't have to worry about you going down that path."

Thoughts of Harry resurfaced. I said nothing in reply.

But I had been right about Susan. Now that she'd gotten a taste of the pulpit, she would take every opportunity possible to speak out for our cause. She would prove to be unstoppable for the rest of her life.

❧

After three more speeches in and around Ithaca, we traveled to Elizabeth's house for another weekend together. The property had changed since my first visit, having taken off its light summer frocks to wrap itself in earthy hues. The soft pink and cream roses that had dominated her side yard were pruned back in anticipation of coming frost, and lines of birch trees had transformed from verdant screens to bright yellow sentinels of fall. The biggest change of all, of course, was the promise of another squawking newborn, soon to be the sixth child of the house. Little Joseph had switched from Elizabeth's lap to Susan's while his mother rested her hands on her growing belly. Susan barely missed a beat in conversation as she fed him pieces of biscuit from her plate and held a small glass of water for him to sip.

"I hear Theodore Parker is your latest convert in Boston," she said, bouncing Joseph on her knee.

"I have to give Wendell the credit for that. But the good preacher has delivered four powerful sermons in our defense. Did you see the pamphlet?" I had funded the publication of Parker's last lecture—one of the more useful aspects of making money was the ability to invest in such things. Those who were unwilling or unable to attend lectures often garnered as much from reading strong arguments in print as they did by being at the event in person.

"He won't be much use on the topic of divorce," Elizabeth said, rubbing her belly absentmindedly. I pressed my hand on the flat of my own stomach, wondering what it must feel like to grow an entire human being there.

"Elizabeth has written quite a declaration in support of divorce," Susan said. "I think it should be read at the convention."

One thing I had learned about this pair was that Elizabeth rarely gave up on her ideas, no matter how premature they were, and Susan stood at the ready to do her bidding regardless.

"I don't see us winning many friends among men if we are seen as trying to convince a room full of married women to demand the right for divorce," I said. I had been called many things in my time. "Home wrecker" was not an epitaph I wanted added to the list. If a husband was a drunkard or violent, so be it, he had ruined the home first. But I didn't think the populace at large would stand for the larger debate.

"And since when do we care what the men think?" Elizabeth said. "And this is for unmarried young women as much as anything. Marriage is a contract, and women of today should be wary about entering into it unless there is a way out, for any reason, on both sides."

"And what of control within the union?" I said. "Is it not almost more fundamental for a woman to have a say over her own body, even when she is married?"

Susan set Joseph on his feet, steadied him, and then patted his rump. She told him to go find his brother Marcus and then leaned forward on the table. "Say more."

Mr. Blackwell's theories on marriage had set me to thinking about what might be possible, what assumptions about marriage were so deeply ingrained into society that even I hadn't been able to see beyond them. These assumptions needed to be articulated, challenged, and discussed if anything were really going to change.

"The contract you speak of assumes that in exchange for shelter and financial stability, the wife will fulfill all her wifely duties, chief among them performing the act of relations whenever the husband demands, with no thought given to the desires of the wife," I said.

"Why again would anyone sign up for that?" Susan said, looking at Elizabeth.

"I didn't know any better, dear," she said with a smirk. "This was my point earlier."

"Even worse than having to give up property and possessions to a husband," I continued, "the wife is duty bound to give up her own body whenever asked. This is simply not right."

"Did we not discuss this the last time we all sat in this room?" Susan asked, looking a bit impatient.

"I believe I was speaking of relations without the desire for children, but you are talking about marriage without relations? And you're the one worried about getting the men on our side?" Elizabeth asked.

"Not entirely without relations, but it should always be a mutual choice, not something expected at will."

"Find the man who will sign up for that and you have found a demigod," Elizabeth said, laughing.

The sky behind her was quickly turning a deep peach color. I hadn't had a moment in Ithaca to reply to Mr. Blackwell's invitation and was now running out of time.

"When is your post collected?" I asked Elizabeth, suddenly distracted. "I have something I must send off first thing tomorrow."

"Four in the afternoon, but Harley can take it to the postmaster for you in the morning if it's urgent."

I excused myself and went up to my room to compose my note to Mr. Blackwell. I didn't think it was right to leave him with no answer to his entreaty. I tried several versions before settling on something short and to the point.

> *Dear Mr. Blackwell,*
>
> *I would be pleased to receive you in Niagara for a conversation between friends. I will be there from October 6 through 8 inclusive. Please leave a note at the Grand Falls Hotel as to where I might find you.*
>
> *Sincerely,*
>
> *Lucy Stone*

I held the letter in my hands and considered what I might be setting in motion. Was it unreasonable to think I could have a deep friendship with an unmarried man without it going any further? Or was I testing my own desire to hold that line? I didn't have the answers, but memories of our time together invaded my thoughts regularly, and I wanted to see him again.

The next morning, I took my letter to the stables and gave it to Mr. Harley with coins for postage. I was still unsure if I was making the right decision, but it was now out of my hands.

I found Susan and Elizabeth taking breakfast on the back porch. A gentle breeze played at the edges of the tablecloth, and I welcomed the idea of spending as much of the day as possible outside. As diligent as we were in our work planning last-minute details for the convention, we spent far too much time inside Elizabeth's house for my taste. I pulled one of the rocking chairs nearer to the small table, laden with berries and egg soufflé, a teapot and cups, and jumped into the conversation midstream. Elizabeth was predicting the passage of the Kansas-Nebraska Act and the likely end of the Free Soilers. We debated the future of the Whig Party in some detail and had begun to discuss what might become of Martin Van Buren and John Hale when one of Elizabeth's young sons came running to tell his mother that Joseph had cut his knee on a rock. While he was barely bleeding, he could not be consoled. He needed her.

"Take me to him, darling." She hopped up and followed her son off the porch.

As I watched her go, I considered for a moment how fortunate I was to be contemplating matters of the world with these women, but how little time we spent discussing everyday life—gardening, art, the shape of the clouds, how to corral a fussy six-year-old.

"Is everything all right, Lucy?" Susan asked me, leaning back in her rocker with her teacup in hand. "You seemed rather distracted last night. Is it your parents? How do they fair?"

"My visit ended poorly." We had been so absorbed by our work in Ithaca that I hadn't yet described for her the quarrel with my father. "Perhaps I shouldn't expect him to change. But what is as disturbing is the effect on Mama. I know she must agree with much of what we are fighting for, but she's not allowed to admit to it. She has no practiced way of refuting him. Not that she hasn't stood up to him in her own way, behind the scenes. Do you know she used to sell an extra wheel of cheese now and again without telling him, just so she would have enough money to buy fabric for our clothes? That's how stingy he is."

It felt disloyal saying this out loud, but putting words to my frustrations always eased the pressure, like loosening the hooks of a corset.

"Ironically, Father is resigned to me speaking on abolition, maybe even a little bit proud. But I'm not sure my mother is yet comfortable with the idea of me lecturing at all. She'd much rather me write like Elizabeth does, in the background."

"While being married and nursing a brood, I suppose?"

"It hasn't hampered her thinking. Maybe it's made her all the more revolutionary."

"Like a prisoner gone mad, scribbling on the walls of her cell," Susan said sardonically. "I can't imagine our dear Mrs. Stanton would have chosen this if she'd been awakened to women's rights earlier. She didn't know any better."

"But she loves her family." I'd never seen her complain, no matter how many times she was pulled away to bandage a scratch or to put one of her children to sleep.

"Of course she does. It's precisely why she's stuck in between. Imagine if you were caged up at home, unable to go out on tour, hampered from stepping onstage. Let's just be grateful you and I never have to worry about that."

What kind of world were we sculpting if family was to be the enemy of work? Was there no way to have both?

Out past the pond, I saw a horse and wagon trotting down the long country road toward town—Harley with my letter. I did my best to mask the unfamiliar flutter of anticipation that was making it rather hard to breathe.

11

The moving wall of water that was Niagara made me feel the divine Presence, something larger than myself, bigger than us all. It moved as fast as a spark toward a never-ending stash of dynamite, loud and continuous. I tried many times to follow a section of the river with my eyes, marking the place it arced over the edge of the cliff and hung in the air—that moment between being pushed by the current above and pulled by gravity below—and then tracing the progress of a specific mass of water as it plunged. But it was as futile as trying to fix one's eyes on a patch of dirt beneath a horse's galloping hooves. Whatever portion of water I tried to track was inevitably swept under, lost to me, the dizzying exercise a useful reminder of the benefit of contemplating the entire system at once, in all its beauty and danger, not just its smallest parts.

Harry and I sat together on a bench downstream from the main viewing platform, listening to the rush and tumble and watching couples and families stroll by. We had already walked for almost two hours that morning and decided to rest our legs for a spell before continuing on. I found silence to be just as easy with him as conversation.

We had quickly slipped back into a theoretical debate about the merits of marriage, discussing in detail the notion of whether two people could remain truly independent in marriage. The church espoused the "oneness" created by the sacred bond. If one did not subsume themselves to the other, was it a true union? Had he not said as much in his letter declaring that two people together could become more than their separate parts?

He draped his left arm over the back of the bench and spoke to me directly.

"I do believe there is something sacred in an intimate relationship. A feeling that heightens everything to a different level."

His searching eyes coupled with those words sent a shudder through me. I hoped the slight chill in the air would stop the heat within from crawling up my neck and across my face.

Just then a woman appeared in front of us, standing so close I couldn't imagine how I didn't notice her approach. She wore a fine blue woolen coat and matching hat. Her purse slid to her wrist as she bent over us.

"I'm so sorry to interrupt, but I had to ask. Aren't you Lucy Stone?" She was breathless and looked only at me, as if the other side of the bench were unoccupied. I nodded my head, feeling a mix of annoyance and surprise. I was used to being recognized in public but had never been interrupted in the middle of such a personal conversation. She might as well have arrived unannounced at my kitchen table.

"I knew it. I told my mother it was you. I saw you speak in Fitchburg not too long ago. I wanted to tell you how inspiring you were. You are."

"Thank you for saying so." She made no move to walk on. "Can I be of service in some way?"

"Not at all. I apologize again." She glanced at Mr. Blackwell and then back at me. "I didn't mean to interrupt. I just had to meet you. Goodbye now."

I raised my hand in a small wave and turned back to Mr. Blackwell.

"Does that happen often?" he asked quietly as our visitor moved away. He seemed more impressed by her recognition of me than annoyed by the intrusion.

"More than I'd like."

The young woman and her mother were feeding ducks absentmindedly and continued to look our way.

"Let's keep walking if you don't mind." I was careful to keep a healthy distance between us as we set back out on the path.

"Is everything all right?"

I pulled the collar of my coat up against the misty air, which had grown cold.

"Perhaps a cup of tea."

We walked back into town. My hotel served high tea, but it was now out of the question to be seen there together. Being recognized in this far-off place reminded me how much the papers loved a good scandal.

"Part of it is these bloomers, I'm afraid," I said once we were safely tucked into a booth in the back of Moorings Restaurant, famous for their afternoon scones, which were served with local maple syrup. "They make me stand out too much. I can't tell you how many times on a train women insist on sitting next to me and talking to me for the entire trip when all I want to do is close my eyes and have some quiet."

"I thought you enjoyed this fashion."

"I do enjoy the practicality of it. You have no idea how horribly restrictive the normal dress is to the simple act of breathing. But needing to constantly defend it is exasperating. Did you see the article in *Harper's*?"

No thanks to a host of sneering articles that compared our "Turkish Dress" to some kind of circus attraction, even friends had become wary of the outfit. I had recently visited the Livermores in Delaware, and their daughters implored me not to wear the bloomers in public. They were afraid of being mobbed in the streets by those who liked to jeer and felt uncomfortable bringing me calling to houses of families who might not approve.

"Susan has begun to wonder if our lectures would be taken more seriously if we took the question of dress out of it."

"You're not thinking of giving it up, are you?"

"I told her it was hogwash to think that anyone hears our words any differently based on what we are wearing." But it was all beginning to take its toll.

Our conversation continued through three pots of chamomile and the lighting of the sconces on the walls. Between eating a late breakfast, walking the length of the river more than once, stopping at several benches along the way, and then taking tea, we had spent almost four hours together, much longer than I had ever intended. Our conversation flowed with ease, and it felt as though we could keep talking well into the night. Nonetheless, we had perhaps reached capacity for one day.

I watched him as a companionable silence fell over us. As thoughtful as he was, he still carried something boyish about him that made me want to giggle, my mood taking flight every time he looked at me. He was in constant battle with one lock of his dark hair that insisted on falling into his eyes, and when his hand wasn't busy swiping it away, his fingers were usually drumming on something: his leg, the table, the back of a bench. At first, I thought it was nervousness, but after some time I decided it was an outward sign of the constant workings of his mind. He seemed to always be puzzling over something.

"I have a proposition I hope you will consider," he said. "My family home is no more than half a day's train ride from Cleveland. I have told my family so much about you, and given how close you will be, it would be such a shame if they didn't have the chance to meet you after the convention."

"Mr. Blackwell, I thought we understood each other." I was unable to keep the exasperation in my voice.

"Certainly you can call me Harry by now." He was undeterred. "I know there are many people in and around Cincinnati who would love to hear you speak. I have taken the liberty of inquiring at several venues and am confident I could set up six different lectures for you on women's rights and at least four large talks on abolition if you were willing to spend some additional time in that part of the country. Transportation is easy enough to arrange, and the local paper would be happy to write a few articles to publicize your visits. And Mother would be delighted to have you stay at our house for the duration."

This all came out in a rush, presumably so I would hear all the details before formulating any kind of protest. The opportunity to lecture in a new city was always of great interest. And having someone who knew the territory organize it all for me was an extraordinary offer, not to mention having a welcoming place to board. And I couldn't help but feel a bit pleased. While he had claimed in a letter not long ago to be hesitant to devote himself to furthering important causes before he found strong financial footing of his own, perhaps he was reconsidering that stance. Or was this all designed as a means to another kind of end? Was it horrible to think that might be true?

"I'm due in Kentucky next month for two weeks of lectures."

"Then the timing is perfect. I'll accompany you to the convention in Cleveland. Directly afterward, you can spend two weeks with us, and then you will be closer to Kentucky than if you'd gone back east."

"That is quite a lovely offer." It really was too compelling not to seriously consider. "I don't know what to say."

"Say yes." He grinned in a way that made his blue eyes spark, just as the unruly black curl fell across his forehead.

Harry kept good to his word and organized a dozen talks for me in and around Cincinnati and well beyond, the visit stretching to three weeks. He saw to my every need, and his mother could not have been more welcoming or lovely. She expressed sincere interest in my views on women's rights and my predictions for when and how we might see progress, such a difference from my own mother that it made my heart hurt.

Harry's older brother Sam came to the house often for dinner, and I found him to be no less handsome or thoughtful than Harry, perhaps just not as mischievous. Harry would tell childhood stories of their escapades stealing sugar candy from the local pharmacist or putting worms in the desks of particularly prim girls in school, while Sam would steer the conversation to the job they shared in the mills as boys to keep food on the table. Their mother beamed at all of it. His sisters Elizabeth and Emily were in New York City focusing on their medical careers, and I was sorry not to have the chance to meet them. If they were anything like the rest of the Blackwell clan, I was sure I would enjoy them immensely.

I had organized countless speaking tours in unknown cities and towns on my own by then and realized quickly how much easier it was with Harry by my side. His devotion to my work went beyond the beautiful words of his letters to earnest action. I found myself looking forward to perusing the morning papers with him at the breakfast table every morning, discussing the attendees he expected at each venue, who I should be sure to meet, who I should avoid at all costs. His concern over every detail, over me, was quite endearing. We also discussed the relative merits of his mother's plum cake versus my mother's sticky pudding, and our joint preference for piano concertos over the opera. We were never at a loss for companionable conversation.

On our last night in Cincinnati, Sam and his mother left us alone in the parlor. The more I tried to thank Harry for his help and guidance during my time there, the more he brushed it off as nothing remarkable, assuring me that I was the one doing the real work. I moved to the couch where he sat. Without thinking, I put my hand on his.

"It is important to me that you know just how deeply grateful I am." I don't know why I touched him in that way. In all our time together, even as we leaned close to review a guest list or read a newspaper article, we had rarely actually touched.

He took my hand in both of his. A sensation ran through my body, like the combination of hot and cold that comes when warming near-frozen hands in front of a blazing fire, soothing and uncomfortable at the same time.

"I would do anything for you, Lucy. And right now, I would very much like to kiss you."

To my utter amazement, I very much wanted to be kissed, to feel the touch of his cheek against mine, to fall into the curve of his arms. I found it difficult not to lean in his direction and we were suddenly close enough for me to deposit words from my mouth directly into his. Our lips briefly brushed.

I jerked back.

"This can't be, Harry." I hated saying it but knew it was true.

"You know it can." He gazed at my lips as he spoke.

My good senses were on the verge of escaping altogether. I knew I could not allow a kiss, but why did my stomach feel as though an army of ants were running for cover? I pictured a craggy rock scraping the bottom of my foot in order to gather myself. I removed my hand from his and pushed back to a comfortable distance.

"Until marriage laws change, I cannot—" I searched about for the right words. "I cannot abandon my beliefs for the convenience of my heart."

"But is it right for heart and head to be in constant battle?" He looked at me with a combination of tenderness and regret. I wanted to offer comfort in some way, but this was no longer an intellectual argument.

"Please let's not do this. We've had such a lovely time."

He studied me for the longest of moments, and I feared what he might say. After all he'd done for me these last weeks, he had every right to rebuke me, to send me on my way in the morning and tell me he never wanted to see me again. He stood to stoke the fire.

"Who will board you in Kentucky?" He kept his back to me, but his tone signaled a return to harmless topics. His willingness to indulge the fickle movements of my heart sent a wave of affection through me, and I wanted to reach for him all over again. Instead, we discussed my itinerary and compared notes on the little we each knew about Kentucky. The next morning, we parted as if nothing more than business had passed between us. But we both knew something had.

12

Three months later I arrived in Philadelphia to give a lecture at the Musical Fund Hall. The day dawned cold and cloudy, the sky covered in a layer of gray that looked ready to crack and drop shards of ice on the ground. I had arranged to arrive a day early to get some rest before the speech, which would be the most important for the cause of women's rights thus far. In the north, I had begun to draw crowds as large for women's rights as they were for abolition. I had less experience in Philadelphia. The home of Benjamin Franklin and Betsy Ross, the city brought revolution and free-thinkers to mind. It was still a city of influencers, and I would be speaking at its largest venue.

I splurged for the Independence Hotel, a comfortable place where I could find quiet and privacy. At three dollars a night, I was spending more on board than on travel, and using up almost half of what I carried in my pocket, but I told myself I had earned the right. Other than a short visit to the Garrisons for the holidays, I'd lectured with not so much as a day's rest since my time with Harry in Cincinnati.

He and I had kept up our correspondence since then, and he continued to address issues of male and female relationships from a philosophical perspective. I appreciated the exchange of ideas and reasoned it could do no harm from such a distance. I could not take back the emotion I had allowed to spill out that night but trusted he understood my conflict and would not push me beyond my limits. I could not deny that leaning up against that limit had been thrilling. A slight tinge of it came back to me every time I saw my name written in his hand on the front of an envelope.

And so it was when I checked into the Independence. Atop a small bundle of letters waiting for me was one from Harry. The pile also included some official notices from the Anti-Slavery Society office, several calling cards from local residents, and notes from Susan and Lucretia Mott's husband, James. It would be a luxury to sit beside the fire in my room, read my mail, and pen any needed replies when the spirit moved. No need to dash off hurried notes before jumping on the next train.

After unpacking my small valise and asking for tea to be delivered to my room, I sat down to open my mail. Practicing some modicum of discipline, I started with Susan's letter.

Dear Lucy,

I am beyond myself with confusion over what to do about these interminable bloomers. It has become an unending burden to constantly defend my dress and fend off hooligans who desire to taunt me on the street. But no fight is ever easy, and so I had determined to stay the course. But then I received your letter on Tuesday last suggesting that you are not sure yourself if the bloomers are worth their trouble.

If you, who can change anyone's mind about anything with your voice like a harpsichord and your message as direct as a steel blade, cannot turn the tide on this change of fashion, I'd like to know who can? And if you are to turn away from it, how can I possibly continue?

Please write as soon as you are able to let me know if you are truly ready to go back to the old. It would help me to know better what I should do.

Your dear friend,

Susan

There was an addendum on the same page, written in a different hand.

P.S. I've given them up and told Susan not to put so much worry into the thing. I've had shorter dresses fashioned without the trousers for casual wear that I think are a delight and I will have my pick of long or short for more formal occasions. Please tell her not to fret so.

P.S.S. If any rumors make their way to your ears, pay them no mind. Clearly they are patently ridiculous.

Yours,

Mrs. Stanton

I had to laugh. Susan made such a good fighter because she was earnest down to the last lace of her shoes, but she did worry a great deal what people thought of her. Elizabeth was good for her in that way. People's impressions of her were the last thing she ever concerned herself with, which drove her detractors mad. I wondered what rumor she was referring to that might be circulating about her now. She did know how to cause a stir.

I decided I would write Susan back after my lecture, so I could share news of its reception with her, and let her know that I had chosen, for better or worse, to wear only long dresses in Philadelphia. I needed to conserve my energy for bigger battles.

I opened the letter from James Mott next. He had been instrumental in securing the Musical Fund Hall for my talk, and I was eager for any further introductions he might suggest while I was in town.

Dear Miss Stone,

I hope this finds you well and shored up with much confidence for your lecture in Philadelphia. Lucretia and I are both eager to hear how you are received there and will be watching the papers for an account. If you have time, do drop us a note with your own assessment.

I am sorry to have to deliver upsetting news to you in advance of such an important event, but I wanted to be sure to get word to you sooner than later. It seems there has been a bit of rumor circulating involving you and Mr. Henry Blackwell. Apparently, his appearance at the convention, or rather, the fact that you arrived in Cleveland on the same train, caused quite a stir. A young lady inferred that she had seen you riding together from as far away as upstate New York, stirring the pot, as you can imagine. The fact that you spent time at his mother's home afterward has thrown some talkers into a frenzy.

So has begun the rumor that Lucy Stone is getting married. Those who know you well of course know this to be absurd, but I do offer some caution. Putting too fine a point on your refusal to ever marry while spending time with an unmarried man might force the rumor-mill to spin out a different tale, worse than the first.

This is such sordid chitter chat. I hope I am doing the right thing by even bringing it to your attention. You know that Lucretia and I have nothing but the utmost respect for you, and we simply wanted you to be aware of all this so that you might be careful. I know you don't want a scandal standing in the way of any of your good work, and good work it is indeed!

Please let us know if there is anything we can do beyond, as always, defending your good name and steadfast honor at every opportunity.

Your friend,
James Mott

I strutted circles in my room at a furious pace and almost tore up the letter. A thundercloud of anger overtook me, and I roiled in it. How had my actions possibly given anyone fodder for gossip? I knew the papers were always on the hunt for scandal, but this cut to my core. I hadn't indulged in so much as a kiss, and now people who knew me personally were suggesting something untoward? The unfairness of that was hard to swallow.

The truth of my feelings came to me with a rush of clarity I could not deny. I did long for Harry to touch my cheek, brush his lips against mine, tell me he would love me above all others. I wanted to fall into his embrace, wrap my arms around him, and return his affection. Was that wrong?

I slumped back into the chair, holding Harry's letter for a few minutes before opening it. The thin parcel felt blemished now, as if our private correspondence had been invaded, burdened with something impossible to throw off. I reluctantly unfolded the page.

My dear Lucy,

Just the quickest of notes to wish you all the luck the angels can rain down on you for your talk in Philadelphia. I know how important it is to you, and I know exactly how wonderful you will be.

Thank you for your kind and wholehearted letter. Despite your good-natured suggestions to the contrary, you and I both know we created a connection between us that cannot be ignored. I do fear that the longer we are apart, the more the memory will fade, so I want to remind you of what you know is true, even if it is not convenient for your heart, as you said. Job waited fourteen years for his Rachel. I trust you will agree he was a reliable fellow. He is no match for me.

Sending this off in the hope it will arrive in time. I will be cheering for you from afar. Write when you can to tell me every detail of your success.

As ever yours,
Harry

My hand fell to my lap and misery overcame me, a deep sorrow filled with the inescapable fact that the place in the world I had carved out for myself came with an impossible trap. My reproaches against marriage law—never marriage!—had somehow barred me from taking the one step toward partnership that would be considered natural for any other woman but me, the supposed model of female independence.

What was I doing? Who was I trying to fool? This man had laid out his heart to me and I had allowed myself to pretend, even for a short moment, that I might be able to reciprocate without severe consequence. But I would never be able to reconcile what I wanted for my life with what was needed in the world. My emotional desires had to come second to the urgent work at hand, and I could not do that work within the current structure of marriage. James Mott's letter said it all. I would never be a wife because Lucy Stone couldn't possibly be a wife. And any suggestion that I was an advocate for free love, that I was entertaining relations outside of marriage, would be a disaster. Such a claim would invalidate me entirely and erase any inroads I had made in convincing society that women's rights was no threat to the sanctity of the true marriage bond.

A new wave of sadness and shame broke over me. How had I led Harry so far down this path? I had been playing at a cruel game. It could not continue.

I penned my response swiftly, doing my best to make it as unambiguous as possible.

Dear Harry,

I have always been alone in this world. I have made plans, taken action, and made decisions without the need of advice or permission from any other person. I have kept my own counsel and shared my deepest thoughts and emotions only with myself. I have created a life with the intention of doing good and important work in this world, and it brings me more satisfaction than is likely to be experienced by most men in our society. I cannot change my course. Even when I ask myself, "Might there be good reason to change?" the answer comes back as a constant refrain: "No." Your Rachel I am not meant to be.

You are a dear man. I hope you find the woman you deserve. Perhaps someday we might even be friends.

Lucy Stone

I sealed the envelope and found myself in the lobby, standing at the foot of the stairs without any memory of having walked down them. The gentleman at the front desk eyed me with concern as he took the letter from me, promising to see it posted, and then quickly looked away. Climbing what seemed a never-ending stairway back up to my room, I caught sight of myself in the mirror on the landing. A sheet of water covered my cheeks, tears streaming from my eyes, my own small Niagara. I didn't realize I'd been crying.

I walked to the Musical Fund Hall the following morning. I hadn't had much stomach for breakfast and decided a walk was in order. It was a bright and clear day, the chill in the air encouraging everyone to move at a good clip. I matched the pace of those around me and banished all dark thoughts, refusing to allow them to tarnish the day. It was an important one.

I hoped I could gain entrance to the hall, meet with the manager, and survey the space. I liked to stand up on a stage before talks when possible to get a feel for the size of the place, the position and arrangement of the audience. And this theater was different than any other where I had spoken before. It was known for having nearly perfect acoustics, which meant I could speak as if I was having a conversation with someone only a few feet from me and be heard equally well in every row. It was hard to imagine given its size, a truly proper venue for an opera or symphony.

The hall was large, close to eight hundred seats, with a mezzanine and boxes on each side. It was difficult not to feel quite small on that stage. I had spoken to far larger crowds about abolition, but this would be the largest gathered purely for women's rights.

The manager was a small man who rather reminded me of a squirrel on the hunt for acorns. He stood perfectly still whenever I spoke, as if he had to sniff the air to hear me, but then scurried about as he talked, picking up stray handbills or straightening chairs. I followed him about as best I could.

"Half the seats gone already, ma'am," he said, grabbing a broom and walking up the aisle away from the stage. "Usually it's just a rush right before show time, but people have been buying them up all week."

This was excellent news. The papers had been giving notice of my visit for the past two weeks, but I knew new cities could be tough to crack.

"Do you have a room where I might wait this evening before the lecture begins?" I preferred to arrive at the venue well ahead of the crowds if at all possible. In Burlington, Vermont, so many people had wanted to speak to me and ask me questions as I made my way down the aisle, I had to rudely break away just to get the talk started.

"One costume room on either side of the stage. Take your pick." He pointed with his broom and continued in the opposite direction toward the entry hall.

Following him into the vestibule, I admired the carved arches of the doorways and the civilized ticket windows, each with a strip of glass separating the customer and the seller, an elegant attempt to curb transmission of cholera and the like. A handbill announcing my lecture was tacked next to every window: "Lucy Stone, 'The Legal, Civil, and Professional Rights of Women,' 7 P.M., 25¢." It seemed an almost outrageous sum, but apparently it hadn't deterred ticket purchases so far. I quickly did the math in my head. I could clear nearly ninety dollars on this trip after expenses. That was an astonishing figure. It would go a long way toward organizational funds for our next convention and printing important articles in pamphlet form for distribution.

And then I saw it. Another small sign tacked below the handbill, no more than twelve inches from my name: *NO NEGROES*.

"Sir?"

He turned and lifted his pointy nose into the air, waiting for my next words.

"Why does this say no negroes?"

"'Cause that's what it means. That's the rule."

"No one told me of this."

"Always been this way," he said, his broom moving sand and dirt to the sides of the entryway. "Everyone knows it."

"Some of my audience may never have been here before. This must be changed."

"Not my hall. I just run the place."

How could I have been so stupid not to have known this? The farther south my travels took me, the larger the negro population, which also meant there were more explicit rules.

"All those people who bought their tickets in advance? Haven't had to turn anyone away yet, if you know what I mean. This is an expensive ticket. I wouldn't get too worried about it."

"But what of people who live outside the city, who might travel here for this occasion and not know the rule?" I asked, more to myself than to him. And the principle of the thing was unacceptable. There was only one solution.

"I can't speak if you are planning to turn people away."

He let out a long sigh, the point of his nose almost drooping.

"Look, lady, I turned down two different vaudeville shows 'cause you had the place booked. All I know is you owe me half the ticket draw, sixty dollars minimum. A cancellation means refunds, and I won't be refunding anyone until you show me you can pay in full."

I blinked at him, stunned. Sixty dollars? To turn away hundreds of people who had probably never heard an argument in favor of women's rights before? That would be foolish. But neither could I condone the deplorable circumstances. It went against everything I stood for.

My lecture was set to begin in less than eight hours. I leaned against the wall, feeling an enormous weight press on me. There was no one to turn to for counsel. There was no solution that didn't bankrupt me of money or character. I couldn't afford either one.

I left the hall and spent the next several hours pacing in my room, turning over in my mind the various outcomes of different courses of action, weighing good against bad, and bad against worse. By the time I left for the talk, I knew there was only one choice available to me. In fact, I thought it to be a rather clever idea.

As I waited in the wings for the curtain to go up, I considered who had gone before me in this famous hall. Had Charles Dickens thought about the readers who would be barred from the place before speaking here, or Jenny Lind before performing, or had it not even crossed their minds? Were the people in this audience so used to walking past signs like the one at the ticket window that they didn't see them anymore? I wanted to stomp onto the stage and rail at them, tell them they should be ashamed, tell them to get up out of their seats and walk out. But I too had been blind to not expect it. I had learned a similar lesson once, the night May reprimanded me for delivering a women's rights speech to a crowd that had come to hear about abolition. This night, a full house had paid good money to hear about women's rights. I owed it to them to at least give them that.

I walked onstage and stood quietly, waiting for conversations to die down, for feet to stop shuffling, for programs to be laid on laps. And then I talked about marriage laws, property laws, the opportunities lost when women were not properly educated, the opportunities gained by opening professions to the fairer sex.

It was hard not to be distracted. A balloon of emotion rose at the back of my throat every time I thought about the enormous doors at the front of this stunning marble building, slammed shut on a whole race. But I pushed on.

I shared stories of my own schooling and implored that audience not to be frightened by the prospect of women sharing the rights of men, but to welcome the benefit of having a wife as able to converse about complicated topics as they, of having children reared by mothers who understood more about the world than simple household accounts. I made sure to give them their money's worth in argument, ideas, and good counsel.

And then I changed the subject.

"But I made a mistake in coming here, and you made the same by buying a ticket," I said. A murmur filtered across the crowd. "You see, the owner of this venue has seen fit to exclude negroes from this hall, individuals who can pay the price of admission, just like you, but they are barred from attending simply because of their race. This is an abhorrent policy, and I would never"—I paused—"*ever* have chosen this venue had I known of the horrid rule in advance. And neither should have you. I won't be back until this policy is changed, and I implore you not to buy another ticket here until the same is true."

This raised a full titter of gasps and conversation among seatmates. *Does she actually mean to say we should miss the symphony? Avoid the theater? All because of a silly rule?*

"Let me tell you what it is like to be a supposedly free negro in this state," I continued.

A few gentlemen rose from their aisle seats, smashing their hats back on their heads as they walked out of the auditorium. I hoped it was in indignation about the policy, but their body language suggested it was disgust with me.

I told them the story of Junior Ryley, who had come to Philadelphia from Barbados to build ships, how slave hunters had captured him and sent him to Alabama. How he spent three years suffering the lash and hard labor with no pay before his family found him and organized the paperwork to prove his freedom. How he was beaten to death before he could board his train home.

"Maybe you are sitting in your seats wondering what this has to do with you. You do not run a plantation that enslaves other humans. You have given no personal help to slave owners and their henchmen. But don't we help them when we do nothing? The same holds true for our politicians. How can the Whigs or Free Soilers condemn slavery while at the same time they hold meetings with judges and legislators who are known slaveholders? Isn't that like cutting deals with pirates while outlawing piracy? It is the same thing we do by being in this hall, by buying a ticket from a venue like this, and I deeply regret taking part."

The crowd fidgeted, unsure what to make of me now.

"Easy for you to say. We already paid!" a man shouted from the balcony. Many in the audience murmured their agreement.

"I would give you all your money back if I could. But fully half of it belongs to the owners of this sinful place. But please know that I will not be accepting so much as one dollar from tonight's lecture."

With that, I walked off the stage.

Any triumph I felt from what I had considered to be a bold act was quickly replaced by regret. The reaction from the world at large was swift and brutal. The Philadelphia papers were harsh, but I had expected that much. That I had "insulted their venerable hall," and tried to "overlay my Yankee ideals on a city not my own" was to be expected. They had even managed to compliment me in a backward kind of way, saying it was a shame I had allowed my "insistence on insulting my esteemed audience to ruin what had been an otherwise intellectually stimulating experience."

What took me entirely by surprise was the vehement reaction I received from my own dear friend, Frederick Douglass. Without contacting me first to air his complaints and allow me a chance to respond, he unleashed his fury to the public, writing a scathing article in *The North Star* opining that I should have refused to speak the moment I knew the hall would not admit negroes. My failure to do so suggested I must have known it was segregated all along and had chosen to schedule a lecture there anyway.

As if this rebuke wasn't enough, I was devastated to learn he'd kept a promise he'd made to me years before and had encouraged several friends who lived outside the city to make the trip to hear the venerable Lucy Stone, assuring them it would be worth the two-hour journey. They'd arrived well before the event sold out but had been summarily turned away, those big oak doors closed in their faces. The very thought of it horrified me, and a deep layer of guilt and shame took hold.

James Mott, who'd been instrumental in scheduling the lecture, came immediately to my defense. He wrote to Douglass, confirming that we knew nothing of the policy in advance. Given the last-minute discovery, he contended that I had done the right thing by taking the opportunity to educate the audience and went so far as to point out that there were many abolitionists in Philadelphia who did not shun the city's omnibuses even though those very buses refused colored riders. Should they not be equally reprimanded? My talk, Mott insisted, had done more good than harm.

Douglass did not relent. I grew increasingly certain I'd made a terrible mistake and began to question my own motives. Had my desire to stand on that grand stage and impress the influencers of Philadelphia clouded my view? Had the cost of cancelling played a larger role in my decision than I was willing to admit? Was I no better than the plantation owner who claimed to loathe the "peculiar institution," as they insisted on calling it, but was reluctant to give up the profits provided by free labor?

I ran away to Nette's house to stay out of the public eye while the tempest roiled, and the next few weeks passed like I imagined a long and difficult labor might—crescendos of pain separated by periods of waiting, dreading the next wave of regret and shame that would inevitably tighten its excruciating grip. She was a great comfort to me, but I found my stomach lurching each time the post arrived, a daily opportunity for my detractors to send sharp missives my way, and I quickly regretted forwarding my mail there.

One of the worst letters came from Lydia Mott, who sided firmly with Douglass despite being a distant cousin to James. She described what I had done as inflicting devastating and unsurmountable harm to the women's movement and articulated her disappointment that a person she had previously considered to be of strong character would debase themselves by putting aside their values to curry favor with the high society of Philadelphia. Each letter and article questioned my intentions, slashed away at my self-worth, and left me flayed and raw.

Even a letter from Susan did little to boost my spirits.

Dear Lucy,

Elizabeth and I both agree you are not to be blamed. You did the right thing not squandering the opportunity to further our cause. Sometimes a choice must be made. We have long known our actions will not please all, and we must simply press on.

With you in sisterhood,

Susan

Even they misunderstood. I hadn't meant to choose between causes but had tried to advance both at once. I shuddered when I dared to imagine what Father must have thought of me. Had his own daughter so lost her sense of right and wrong that she had sacrificed her morals in the name of some mangled notion of progress? Had she perpetrated an act as abhorrent as purchasing a slave off an auction block? Had I?

I found myself slipping into a deep melancholy that threatened to drown me, body and soul. Getting out of bed felt impossible, as if the quilts were stitched full of lead, a great weight pinning me to the mattress.

I lost track of the sun rising and the moon changing shape. I often woke in the dead of night and slept when lines of light appeared around the edges of the curtains. I worried I would no longer be able access a vital source of energy, that whatever had fueled me for so long in the face of adversity was now lost to me, never to be recovered.

Nette was patient with me, never questioning the hours I spent in bed, the blank stares I offered when she checked on me. But after a week of leaving me to my dreary existence, she began to coax me out of bed for meals and insist I come outside with her for a few minutes to take in fresh air, if even just to stand on the front porch. I would wrap a blanket around my shoulders and follow her out into the icy air. The longer we spent outside, the longer it was necessary to sit by the hearth to regain warmth in our fingers and toes. She would then ask me if I didn't mind chopping carrots for the soup she was making, or if I might knead the dough for a loaf of bread.

Eventually, she asked me to help her with a sermon she was working on by writing down the words as she said them aloud, allowing her to compose on her feet while I captured her thoughts in ink. We did this for an hour or so each day, Nette pacing in front of the hearth or gazing out the window as she spoke, me dutifully taking down every word. At first, the simple act of putting pen to paper was meditative, the curling of a's and s's and linking them with l's and h's a soothing exercise. Then the letters combined into words like "righteous" and "courage" and "sacrifice" and wedged their way into a part of my brain that had gone dormant. Full phrases then pushed themselves through the opening: "striving for kindness" or "reaching for the better parts of one's heart."

"How about if you change 'heart' to 'soul'?" I asked on the fourth day transcribing for her. "I think that might better capture what you are trying to articulate."

"But don't you think they might miss the point if I take out the word 'heart,' since we are talking about how we treat others?" she asked, her gaze steadily fixed on the snow falling outside the window.

"No, no," I said, certain the other would make it stronger. "You must use the word 'soul.' The soul is the greater of the two, the definition of who we are."

Nette turned toward me, grinning broadly, and only then did I realize that the help she had requested hadn't been for her at all. I steadily improved after that, remnants of myself coming back to me daily, reattached inside with stitches I hoped would hold.

Just when I felt almost whole, the postman arrived again, this time with a letter from Harry. I hadn't heard from him since I'd sent off my cutting reply to him from Philadelphia. I asked Nette to read it to me, trusting she would stop if it was too brutal. I wasn't sure I was ready to handle the ricochet of anger and hurt my last note to him must have caused. At the time, I told myself I was doing him a favor, lessening future pain by making my message as clear as possible, the way Father had taught us to quietly sneak up on a chicken and twist its neck before it could register fear. Swift and definitive. But now I wondered how I ever thought I had the right to consider his fate to be in my hands, to assume I could wield that kind of power. Another hasty and horrible mistake. I couldn't blame him for being severely disappointed in me, but I wasn't sure I could handle it.

Nette sat beside me and read the letter out loud.

23 February, 1854

My dear Lucy,

I have lost track of your whereabouts and dispatched this letter to the Anti-Slavery offices, hoping it will find you without too much delay. I have been following the papers closely and sincerely hope this entirely unjust lashing has not been overly injurious to you. Knowing you as I do, I worry otherwise, but I implore you not to let this storm douse the noble light that you hold up for the rest of the world. It is in desperate need of that light.

We all have moments of regret, things we wish we had not done, or said, or perhaps even privately put to paper. But who are we as humans if we cannot forgive each other these small drops in an otherwise endless ocean? I prefer to let the salt buoy me and will continue to float unabated, just knowing that you are somewhere in the same sea.

Please send word that you are well as soon as is convenient for you. I have included an address in Wisconsin. I am headed off to purchase land for a group of investors. There is tremendous potential in real estate, and I think it might be the path for me.

I am as ever yours,

Harry

Oh, dear Harry! He hadn't turned away from me, as hard as I had been on him. I had forgotten what tears of joy felt like until just that moment.

"How extraordinary," Nette said. "Who is this man?"

I told her everything then, the content of our discussions, the proposals embedded into every letter, about our time in Niagara and at his home. I described his wonderful family and how he organized lectures in Walnut Hills and Cincinnati and Louisville and Youngsville for me, and how we discussed each success and nuance of my talks in the carriage afterward, sometimes allowing for a circuitous route to elongate our time together. How we had touched hands and almost kissed. And then the awful letter I wrote to him after receiving James Mott's warning.

"Your complexion has changed completely while you've been speaking of him," she said. "You and I may have pledged long ago never to marry, but if a marriage could exist that was entirely different than those that have come before, would that not be a wonderful thing?"

I had watched James and Lucretia Mott together many times. Theirs did seem a marriage almost of equals. He promoted her in every way and even helped nurse the children. But Quakers lived by a different set of rules. She could be a wife without compromise, be married and still a High Elder in her community.

"I just don't know," I said. "This has all been awful enough. Can you imagine the next fury to erupt were a headline to announce that Lucy Stone has broken down and married? It's impossible."

"Nothing matters but the truth in your heart, and God knows the truth of it all."

I wished that brought me comfort. The laws were the laws and would still make me nothing but chattel were I to succumb to my heart. I laid my head on her lap.

"Do you love him?" She stroked my hair.

Was that what it was, this deep longing to be near him?

"Please don't tell me love conquers all, because I have no proof." I was glad she could no longer examine my face for answers.

"Nothing has ever been easy for us. Do you think we will discover, in the end, that it's worth it?"

"Yes, I do," I said, daring to answer two questions at once.

"When will you see him again?"

"Why continue something that is just going to be torture for both of us?"

"It's not like you to give up. What about when your father refused to buy you books? Or you were not allowed to debate? Or lecture on women's rights?"

I loved Nette for remembering the story I had told her so long ago about the day my father handed Luther five cents for a schoolbook and stated very clearly that he would not pay the same for any book for a *girl*. How I went to the woods and foraged for chestnuts until my apron was bursting with them and traded them for shiny coins so I could buy the book myself. It was my first taste of victory, and I had been chasing small triumphs ever since, collecting them like precious nuts that might have the power to unlock my future.

Could that future actually include a husband, or was that like trying to grow a tree out of an acorn that had never been nurtured in fertile ground?

13

Spring burst once again from nature's frozen cocoon. Each tree reached out to its neighbor with festooned branches that had been desolate and deformed just weeks before, a kind of poetry blossoming in the sky. The air danced with jasmine and lilac, and the humidity encased my skin in warmth. I wondered anew at my doubts that spring would prevail, at my regular willingness to allow a cold layer of doubt to drive me inward.

I had replied to Harry's letter, tentatively reopening our communication, testing the strength of the old territory of one friend writing to another. He wrote of the wide and startling beauty of Wisconsin. He described never-ending tracts of open land, pine groves that opened without warning onto acres of wildflowers, the trout jumping from streams as if showing off their glistening silver hides. I found myself wishing I was there with him, enjoying the raw beauty of new territory.

By April, a long six weeks since the Musical Fund Hall scandal, I had pulled myself away from the comfort of Nette's home and joined several speaking panels in Boston. The heaviness in my stomach slowly dissipated as I discovered that the passing frosts of winter had taken with them the Musical Fund Hall controversy. As far as I could tell, everyone with an opinion had said their piece and miraculously moved on to other more urgent issues, shoring up support for the underground railroad being at the top of the list among many of my colleagues.

The Fugitive Slave Law had produced much of its desired effect on the North, the fear of fines and imprisonment making even some staunch abolitionists suddenly less willing to actively help escaped slaves. Each time a ship arrived from Virginia or the Carolinas with an escapee hiding amongst its cargo, information had to be passed more carefully, plans laid more quietly, even in Boston.

When Anthony Burns snuck off the *Sweetwater* in March, Garrison and Phillips moved into high gear. Burns had found a way to educate himself thoroughly prior to his escape, much like Douglass, and they saw in him the makings of another great abolitionist leader. But Burns's slave master was known to be one of the savviest of the South, and not likely to tolerate his escape. The Anti-Slavery Society had pressed all its agents into extra work during these times. I was more than happy to help and found that my colleagues had moved beyond my transgression, appreciating my abilities and diligent efforts above all else, which was an enormous relief.

After a month in Boston, another request for assistance arrived via the post, this one from Susan, who was launching her own insurrection in New York. It felt good to be useful, to once again fill each day to the brim before the clock ticked past sundown, unlike the days at Nette's, which had stretched like taffy. I would be ever grateful for her support and equally amazed by having needed to indulge in it quite so completely.

Walking down Albany's main thoroughfare, I hurried to keep up with Susan's long stride. The dogwoods lining the streets were a riot of pink and white against a bright blue sky. She treaded on the carpet of waxy petals like a general headed to war, her long gray dress growing thick with pollen at the hem.

"First we must be sure to see Bainbridge. We won't be able to gain access to Sullivan until we have a signature from Bainbridge. Albany County is tougher on this sort of thing than Tompkins, so we have to be mindful of taking wins as quickly as we can, losses only when we must."

I had learned to let her run down her complete set of instructions before interrupting and listened for the next three blocks as she reminded me of every player we might encounter and their particular view of things. This was Susan's territory. She had become a student of New York State politics and was convinced the time had come to fight for a change in property laws. Elizabeth had written numerous editorials at her bequest perfectly timed with official statehouse visits or dinners with a key influencer. How she managed to produce an invitation to just the right table at just the right time was a wonder to behold.

"Now, I know Bainbridge is very impressed by your lectures on professional freedoms for women—he has three sisters and two daughters—so our angle on the property law is that it's the next logical step in this sequence. This is less about marriage rights and more about property in his eyes. And avoid the topic of divorce at all costs."

We turned onto State Street and took five steps in silence.

"And do we mention that we are seeing Mr. Callahan tonight?" I asked.

"I wasn't finished. Bainbridge's secretary is named Florence, and small talk annoys her considerably. A simple greeting will do. Only mention Callahan if he does first. If he knows about it, that gives us a good idea that the old gang is taking notice. Ready?" She stopped at the entrance of an austere edifice still buttoned up against winter despite the rising temperatures.

I followed her down a hall to a room on the far side of the building, bright with light from two large windows. The long bench situated between them had the straight back of a church pew, which I suspected had been specifically chosen for its lack of comfort. The only other piece of furniture in the room was a desk, behind which sat a young woman working on a ledger. As soon as she saw us, she popped up and held out her hand in greeting.

"Miss Stone, I can't tell you what an honor it is to meet you. I'm Florence Hedicker. Your lecture here last year inspired me to take this job. Spending money of my own."

"And you like the work?"

"My father is against it, but I try to keep my own counsel."

"And your mother?"

"I tell her there is no harm in earning a little money until the right boy comes knocking."

Even this young girl saw work and marriage as incompatible. The idea was as ingrained in our culture as roasted chestnuts at Christmastime, and I wondered what it might take to change that.

"Perhaps you could knock on his door, Miss Hedicker, to let Mr. Bainbridge know that Miss Anthony is here for our appointment?" Susan said, peering at Florence over her glasses. She had begun to wear them recently, thin wiry rims that sat high atop the bridge of her nose. They made her look older and more severe, both of which I assumed were on purpose. "We don't want Mr. Bainbridge to think we have come here just to chitchat." She shot a look of admonishment my way.

"Yes, of course. I apologize. Please have a seat."

"Lovely to meet you," I said.

The poor girl didn't say another word to us while we waited.

The meeting with Mr. Bainbridge did not go well, and after a four-day stint in Albany, we retreated to Susan's house in Rochester to regroup and wait for word of whether our petition would be taken up at the statehouse. Mr. Callahan had agreed to write directly, and we still hadn't heard anything. Susan became increasingly agitated and had already begun to compose letters of protest in case the motion was not furthered. I hoped we would have our answer before I had to leave. I had promised my sister Sarah a long-overdue visit on my way back to Boston.

Susan sat at her desk, scribbling away, a row of small portraits gazing at her from the top of the secretary. In various frames made of wood and silver, she had lined up photographs of twelve different women she said gave her inspiration, a choir of friendship and encouragement. It was a little disconcerting to see my own likeness looking out at me from over her shoulder.

I contemplated what advice the group might give Susan in support of her efforts.

"You might consider a softer approach," I started. "It never hurts to ask after one's family, their cattle or crops, before diving into business. They are starting to call you Little Napoleon, you know."

The *New York Tribune* had coined the term but was not the only paper to take it up. Susan sat up straighter, if that were possible.

"A redundant phrase, by the way. And what idiots. Do they not know how much taller I am than he?"

I laughed.

"Here he is," she said, catching sight of the postman walking up the brick walk to her door. "Perhaps we will have an answer now."

She swooped down the front steps, her hand outstretched for a small stack of envelopes. She looked through the pile as she made her way back inside, disappointment evident on her face.

"Well, at least we have heard from dear Mrs. Stanton, and there is also a letter for you."

If she'd bothered to read the return address on the envelope, she made no comment. My correspondence with Harry had continued unabated, and I could not ignore the quickening of my pulse every time I held one of his missives in my hands.

Susan broke the seal of Elizabeth's letter as she sat back down at her desk. When it was clear she did not intend to read it aloud, I stood.

"I think I will take in some fresh air." I stepped away to the privacy of a small porch at the back of the house.

4 May, 1854

Dearest Lucy,

I hope you and Miss Anthony are finding success in New York and not working yourself to the bone. Two more driven women God never put on this earth.

I was ever so glad to receive your invitation to visit with you at your sister's house in Gardner next week, which I accept with pleasure. It will give us much needed time together, "under the trees and away from curious gazes," as you say, to explore everything that cannot be fully expressed with pen on paper.

I find I cannot wait, however, to offer an idea for your consideration in advance. Given that you say it is the backward laws of this land that keep you from following your heart, why not protest them outright? Why not marry while simultaneously protesting the laws as they are? Why couldn't we create our own contract to serve as the governing law of our own marriage? I propose signing a document stating that all of your financial holdings would belong only to you, that your professional and personal decisions are yours alone, and that you will not be subservient to me in any way. Our marriage, our way. We would not be the first to lodge such a PROTEST, but with your name attached to such a document, it would immediately be printed in papers across the land. What better way to educate the world on the abominable state of current marriage laws? And no one would question if Lucy Stone has given up reform. Instead, you would show the world that you do not intend the will of lawmakers to hold you back from your true course. Think of what good it would do!

And I of course would profit most of all, as there would be no greater joy than for you to call me husband, and me to call you wife.

Do not reply via the post on this. Your letter is not likely to arrive before I strike out for the east. But think on it, dear Lucy! I look forward to hearing your thoughts in person. I count each minute as a day, each day as a week until I see you next.

Until then, I am, as always your,

Harry

I read the letter a second time and could not help but smile and shake my head in admiration of such a bold idea.

"I trust he isn't trying to organize another speaking tour for you?" Susan said, standing at the open door to the porch. "We don't have time for any more petty rumors."

She sat down next to me. I reflexively turned the letter over in my lap.

"He has been remarkably helpful to me, to the cause. We always need supporters on our side"

"A rather rudderless fellow, though, wouldn't you say? The only part of the rumor about you two that struck me as having merit was the idea that he might wish for you to be his mast and sail." She fanned herself with Elizabeth's letter.

"I beg your pardon?"

"You may still think of yourself as a farm girl, but you are a farm girl who has earned more than most men ever will. What does Mr. Blackwell have to call his own beyond his family name, a name made rich by the women of the family, by the way?"

"He hasn't quite found his way yet, is all. He has just begun to explore real estate in the West. Speculators are going to have a lot to say about how this country expands." I didn't know if real estate would prove to be any more profitable than his hardware store or beet sugar, but I felt the need to defend him.

"Helping the cause out West, then, would be a good use of his efforts, I would think. No need to pester Lucy Stone." She handed me her makeshift fan. "Mrs. Stanton sends her regards and has enclosed her latest treatise. She would like you to review it and add any comments or edits. She intends to circulate it to all the eastern papers." She handed me three pages of vellum covered in tiny text.

As my eyes scanned Elizabeth's article, my mind drifted to Harry's proposal. Was it true what he said? Would creating our own contract be enough to separate one marriage from the morass, symbolically if not legally? Could that be enough for me?

I pictured us strolling the land by Sarah's house together. Her property wasn't nearly as rocky or steep as Coy's Hill, but it was lovely nonetheless. I envisioned a long discussion about the concept of a marriage protest as we walked, the sun setting over the holly trees, his earnest arguments enveloping me in a soft embrace. And then I dared to imagine taking his hands in mine, our fingers intertwined, and finally saying the words that had been winding their way up from my heart for so long. *Yes, Harry, yes.*

14

I arrived in Gardner just when news of Anthony Burns's capture reached us. His owner, Charles Suttle, had hunted him down, and federal marshals had arrested him, setting the trial for the following week. The call rang out far and wide to launch a massive protest of the proceedings. A stroll beneath the trees with Harry would have to wait. I met him at the station in Gardner, and we caught the first possible train to Boston.

The city roiled. Swaths of black crepe covered storefronts. American flags hung upside down from blackened windows. The streets teamed with people chanting "Stop the kidnappers!" and "End this vile proceeding!" We merged into a stream of protesters, and I tried to discern where the current might take us. A man in a long dark coat stood atop a wall by the Granary Burying Ground on Tremont Street, waving people toward the water. I yelled up to him.

"I've only just arrived. Where is help needed?"

"Nearly five thousand are gathered at Faneuil Hall, awaiting instructions."

I assumed Garrison and others from the Anti-Slavery Society were there. They would be formulating the plan.

Harry's grip tightened on my arm as we moved with the crowd. Farther down the street I noticed that the doors of Tremont Baptist Church stood open, a stream of men and women pouring down the steps. The mostly negro procession diverged from the masses ahead. I veered to the left to join them and asked one of the women where they were headed. Red lines webbed the whites of her eyes.

"There's no reasoning to be done. We're going to rescue him, make sure they don't ever find him again." She said this more as a proclamation than anything, a brick clutched in her hand.

"We must join them." I was certain of it.

"Better to hear the plan." Harry pulled me in the other direction.

"These people already have a plan, Harry. There is a life at stake." I pushed farther into the rescue party. Whether he let go of my arm or the crowd separated us, I wasn't sure, but there was no time to waste.

Nearing the federal courthouse, a swarm of people rushed the steps and launched bricks and stones at the building. I saw Thomas Higginson and six or seven other men carrying a huge beam, bashing in one side of the double doors to create a way in. Another group of men hacked at a side door with axes. A brick flew over my head and crashed into one of the stately windows, shards of glass toppling from their mullions like falling daggers. A militiaman rushed past me, followed by an endless number of officers, all of them holding muskets or swords. I yelled out to Higginson just as the deafening crack of a rifle split my words in two. One of the men next to him fell back, his grip slowly loosening on the beam as he slunk to the step, blood already staining the white stone.

Cries of anger rose from the crowd, a desperate and primal call. I tried to get to Higginson but could not keep pace with the swath of militia. A wave of uniforms enveloped me and spit me backward like used ammunition. Clubs swung in the air; men fell to their knees.

"Lucy!" I heard my name somewhere in the fog of my raging stupor. "Lucy!"

Harry's hands were around my waist, and he dragged me from the fray.

"No!" I struggled against him. "We have to help."

He flinched as a rock smashed through another window. "This is not the way, Lucy. It's too dangerous."

I could not fight him off, and he pulled me to the doorway of the building across the street, his breathing ragged as he took my face in his hands.

"I thought something was going to happen to you." Relief cascaded over his face.

I stared at him in disbelief. My safety was hardly the point.

"Let's go to Faneuil Hall," he said. "There has to be a better plan than this."

I continued to look back toward the courthouse and the mayhem as I reluctantly followed him in the opposite direction. Harry tugged on me each time he sensed my hesitation, his desire to get as far away from the tumult as possible growing more evident with every step, his back turned to the entire proceeding. Perhaps I should have been grateful for his attempt to keep me away from danger, but instead I resented him for it.

As we crossed the brick courtyard in front of Faneuil Hall, I could see through the large arched windows that the great meeting hall teemed with people. Most everyone I had ever worked with in Boston was likely there, trying to devise a strategy that would alter the course of things. I hesitated. There were men of action inside that I respected, and I was no longer sure it was a place Harry belonged.

"We shouldn't be seen together. I'm sure you understand." I hurried into the building without looking back lest I find him standing motionless, with no idea what to do next.

❧

Over the next week, I took up my old room at the Garrisons'. I did my best to push all thoughts of Harry and the plans we might have made in Gardner to the side. Whenever I found myself wondering if he had secured lodging somewhere else in the city, or if he had simply left, I admonished myself for allowing thoughts of him to interfere with the important work at hand. I'd been foolish to let it occupy so much energy. But I don't deny that I wondered where he was, my heart jolting every time a knock came on the Garrisons' door, hoping it might be him.

City officials and abolitionists alike came and went at the Garrisons' through each long day, the news increasingly grim. The court ruled that Burns was indeed Suttle's property and therefore guilty of escape. President Pierce designated a navy vessel to take him back to Virginia and ordered federal troops, 1,500 militiamen, and the entire Boston police force to keep the peace while Burns was delivered from the courthouse to Long Wharf.

If slavery's claws could stretch all the way to Boston, I knew that nothing was safe. No person could expect freedom.

We all dressed in black the day of Burns's departure, women wearing veils of mourning, men in black gloves and hats. The street could not be seen below the thousands of feet that marched down Commonwealth Avenue, the wide strip of grass that ran down the middle swarming with people. A group of men at the head of the procession balanced a coffin above their heads with the word "Liberty" painted on its side. Liberty in all its forms was dead. I thought my heart might break.

Standing atop the Garrisons' steps, preparing to join the throng, I saw Harry across the street, leaning on a tree. My breath caught in my throat. He looked dapper in his mourning clothes, but his posture suggested a man already defeated. He straightened when he saw me, and I told William and Helen to go on ahead. I suspected William might have seen Harry also, but he didn't question me.

After the Garrisons had disappeared into the crowd, I nodded at Harry, and he joined me on the steps.

"How are you? I've been worried about you," he said.

"This is a terrible day."

We walked wordlessly the rest of the way to the wharfs. When we reached Atlantic Avenue, I pulled on Harry's sleeve and headed left. I couldn't tolerate the crush of the crowd any longer, fifty thousand strong they would tell us later, and none of us able to change the course of that day.

We wound our way through the crowds until we were at the mouth of Commercial Wharf. From there we could see the massive navy ship in port, a sea of black streaming from the water's edge all the way back to the statehouse. Harry turned a crate on its side to make a bench. The familiar comfort of sitting beside him came back to me, mixed with a good deal of confusion. I wanted to take off my glove and touch his hand, but I kept my hands firmly clasped together in my lap.

"This has been a long week," he finally said.

It was one of the longest of my life. I had wrestled with two impossible conundrums. How had this country, formed on such noble ideas, come to this? If the government could be so brazen in its defense of unjust laws, what hope was there for any of us? These thoughts mingled with the memory of Harry flinching as panes of glass rained down from the courthouse, of his desire to seek safety over action. Was Susan right about him? Was he a man without direction, a man simply willing to do my bidding? As flattering as that may be, was that what I wanted?

Susan and I spoke the same language in our life's work. She might have rough edges, but she would never be held back from an opportunity to get something done unless she was shackled to a moving train going in the opposite direction, and even then, she would find a way to convince the conductor to set her loose. That was the only way I knew how to live. As lonely as that life could be, I had no right to turn away from the work. Anthony Burns needed it. Juda needed it. Our country needed it.

"I'm not sure this Union can survive as it is," I said, that sad truth catching in my throat.

"But might not the protest mean something?" His voice sounded as weary as my own.

"It was a valiant effort. But it failed. And here we are." I gestured vaguely toward the crowds in the distance, waiting for Burns's ship to set sail.

"Failed? We haven't even had a moment to discuss it."

I realized then that we were talking about two different unions, two different protests. Sorrow and something close to defeat wound their way around my vocal cords and I wasn't entirely sure I would be able to speak.

"I meant the country, Harry."

He nodded slowly and looked back out over the water. The cannon announcing the ship's departure fired. I closed my eyes and pictured the musket striking down the colored man by the courthouse. I hadn't ever learned his name. And I couldn't help but wonder, would the shot have found Higginson instead if he'd not been white?

"I have a lot of work to do before the Anti-Slavery Convention next week." I would rework my speech and call for the dissolution of the Union. I was no longer willing to consider these slave states cousins while waiting for them to right their wrongs. "Are you attending?"

"I have plans to go back to Wisconsin with my brother for a month or two. The opportunity is ripe there. I leave tomorrow."

That jolted me. Perhaps it was just another sign that we weren't suited for each other after all. We had both let the last week slip by, me without considering that I might be running short on time to see him, and he without taking the initiative to find me, even though he knew the Garrisons' house to be a likely spot.

As I watched Burns's boat sail toward the horizon, I felt like I was watching everything good drift away. We had been unable to keep this man safe, even in the cradle of the revolution. And now I was letting my one chance for love, for motherhood, for having a family of my own, slip out of sight. This was a good man sitting beside me, but we couldn't seem to navigate our way toward each other. I had always sworn I would fight my fights on my own, but I couldn't ignore the bottomless pit of sadness that idea had cracked open in my heart.

I put my hand to my clavicle and cleared my throat.

"Good luck," I said, wondering if what I really meant was good-bye.

15

I spoke nonstop after Burns's capture, certain the country was on the brink of extinction and finding the divide of opinion on slavery and its solutions stretched to a breaking point. I added the topic to most of my women's rights speeches and often scheduled additional lectures during the week on abolition alone. It had become increasingly clear that the ideas of freedom and equality for all could no longer be entertained as some interesting theoretical argument. The stakes for each state in the union were high, and emotions ran hotter than ever.

Thoughts of Harry would tug on me during lonely hours on a train, when I took meals by myself or on the rare occasions when I made time for a long walk. Whenever my heart swelled with a thought of him, the feeling would quickly be overshadowed by the image of him rushing out of harm's way in Boston, reluctant to risk himself for the greater good. He was not a man of action, and the country needed action desperately. I had been right to put reform first. I still faced headwinds at every turn.

One day that fall, in Jamestown, Rhode Island, my lecture was almost thwarted by a group of teens that followed me about and ripped down my flyers as fast as I could tack them up. They didn't try particularly hard to go unnoticed, keeping five or six horse-lengths behind me, daring one another to come even closer and steal the remaining stack of papers directly from my hands. I knew I should head down a busy street, somewhere another adult or business owner might recognize one of them and scold them for their insolent behavior, but the teacher in me couldn't resist an opportunity to mold their minds. I turned down an alley toward the wharf where I had seen a line of men unloading crates of goods from a large boat the day before. The docks were quiet on this still morning, unusually warm for October, and I could feel the boys closing in on me, emboldened by their surroundings. Fear licked at the back of my legs, but I maintained a steady gait so as not to unleash more of their energy by running after me. As soon as I reached the first stack of crates, I turned on my heel to face them.

"Good morning, boys."

Sand kicked up where they stopped. I appraised them, realizing they were younger than I had originally thought. The tallest of the group looked unsteady on legs too long for his knickers, his knees protruding like knots on a birch tree. The other two appeared to be brothers, their faces still soft with baby fat.

"I see you've taken an interest in my flyers."

They glanced at one another with expressions I had seen in my classroom hundreds of times before, their brows knit in a bunch while calculating whether to respond to my friendly tone and risk admitting their crime or flee and demonstrate cowardice in the face of a defenseless woman. I knew what I had to do.

"I trust you can read the title of my lecture?"

"Yes, ma'am," the tallest one said quickly, looking down at the flyer in his hand. "The true costs of slavery and the case for . . ." He trailed off.

"Abolition," I said. "Do you know what that means?"

He shook his head. The other two did the same.

I patted the stack of crates behind me. "One of you hop up here."

None of them moved.

"Don't tell me none of you are strong enough to pull yourself up there."

The older of the two brothers, whose feet were as unwieldy as duck flippers, bounded past me and pulled himself onto the crate as easily as he might mount a horse.

"I need you to stand up."

He shrugged and followed my order.

I backed up and stood beside the two other boys.

"Now, how much do you think he's worth?" I asked, crossing my arms over my chest.

"Ma'am?" the tall one asked.

"He looks to be of good stock, healthy, and ready to have a growth spurt, I'd say. I bet he is very strong. He could probably load a whole carriage of wood in half a day." The boy on the crate tentatively pushed his shoulders back, proud of my assessment. "I think someone would pay at least one hundred dollars for him."

"One hundred dollars? For him to stack wood? Who pays that kind of money, and where can we sign up?" the younger brother said, laughing.

"Not to pay him. To own him. To take him away from home forever and to work for the rest of his life for no pay whatsoever."

The boy on the crate hunched into himself.

"No one would sign up for that," the smallest one said.

"But what if he had no choice? If not even his parents could stop bad men from stealing him away?"

All three looked confused and grew decidedly quiet.

"Come down off that crate."

I stood close enough to the boys to touch them and looked into each of their eyes in turn.

"Boys your age are auctioned off down South every day. These boys are forced to stand up on a platform in front of a crowd, sometimes naked, while slave owners bid for them. And they know, standing there, that whoever buys them will take them away, and they will never see their mother or father or siblings or friends ever again. They will work in the fields for no pay until the day they die."

The eyes of the boy who'd been on the crate opened wider, and the other two examined the sand at their feet.

"White men buy and sell people on their plantations the way your fathers might buy a hog, but I bet your fathers treat livestock far better than these people are treated, young boys exactly like you. The only difference between you and them is that they are negros."

I squinted at the sun beating down on us, suddenly aware of the dust in my throat, of how hot the day had become.

"So, I am here to talk to the good people of this town about this problem, make sure they understand it, and figure out how we can rid this country of slavery. But no one will come to hear my lecture if they don't see my flyers."

The mouth of the youngest of the group began to twitch, and I thought he might cry.

"Ma'am?" the tall one said. "There is a park on the other side of town where families go for picnics on fine days. You could hand out flyers there."

I smiled. These young boys needed only to be asked to rise to the occasion, be given the chance to do something useful.

"I'd be grateful if you took me there. And can one of you put my flyers back up?"

"Yes ma'am," the two brothers said in unison, and ran off back toward town.

Several days later, I set out once again for Pennsylvania to give as many lectures on abolition as I could before the convening of our fourth annual Women's Convention, which would be held in Philadelphia for the first time.

The courtroom I had secured for my talk in Chambersburg was filled with a respectable-looking group, the men taking off their hats upon entrance, the women sitting primly with their hands in their laps. They each politely paid their ten cents at the door, took theirs seats in an orderly fashion, and I was allowed to speak without interruption. But while no one directly called out their opposition to my ideas of negro and white equality, I could feel the resistance to the idea rumble through the crowd.

I wondered if the simple fact of being in a courtroom had saved me from flying insults or debris, but I also found it difficult to refute sentiments that weren't spoken aloud, left to fester rather than offered up for a reaction. It almost made me wish for a raging fire I could work to extinguish rather than the slow gathering of smoke at my feet, the source of which I couldn't easily identify. I finished my remarks to muted applause and much shuffling of feet.

I donned my coat and hat and waited for the last of the crowd to depart before setting off myself. I wanted to thank the man who had unlocked the space for me and lit all the lanterns.

"Miss Stone." He dipped his head deferentially at me. "I'm sorry to say that I will not be able to open the courthouse for you again tomorrow night."

"But I have advertised two nights of lectures, Mr. James. We had already agreed."

"Tomorrow is the Sabbath, and upon further reflection, I find myself unable to condone any act of commerce such as yours on the Lord's day, as it is not condoned by God. People paying for a lecture, that is. Nor can I sustain being paid to light the room and work the door on the Sabbath. It is against my faith."

I appraised his face, trying to determine if the content of my lecture had brought him to this decision or if he was giving me a true account of his feelings. He held a crumpled hat in his hands, his eyes skipping off mine.

"I would not want you to do that which you feel is wrong. Perhaps there is another who could be engaged?"

"There is no one else authorized to use these keys."

"I see. And I don't suppose there is another location in town you could suggest that would be open to my lecture on a Sunday?"

I was fairly sure I had seen all of Chambersburg during my stroll from the train station to the Victorian house where I was boarding. Despite the large number of residents, the town had but two churches, a feedstore, a firehouse, one tavern, and a bank.

"I'm afraid not," he said.

"Then I trust you will be on hand, good sir, to tell anyone who arrives tomorrow evening that the courthouse is closed? Without pay, of course." I left him standing with his hat in his hands.

I walked the short distance to the inn under a bright starry sky and found myself wishing Harry were with me. I longed for his good counsel on what he thought of the crowd, if I'd managed to get beneath the veil of good manners they all wore, or if their opinions had indeed gone unchanged. He'd been an excellent judge of such things during my western tour, often offering insightful suggestions for driving a particular point home.

I pulled up the collar of my coat, the chill of the night wisping around my neck. I imagined the comfort of a warm arm around my shoulders, how much more enjoyable the night would be in the company of another, in the company of Harry. I knew these thoughts were foolish, but the impending cold and the accompanying reflex to turtle inward this time of year exaggerated the unnatural state of loneliness I insisted on maintaining. I hadn't seen or heard from Harry for five months, and it felt like an eternity.

There was no train coming through Chambersburg until Monday, and so I found myself with an entire day and evening free on the Sabbath. As I settled into the parlor, I was pleased to find multiple newspapers left out on side tables and stacked on shelves. Either the owner had an insatiable appetite for printed news from various parts of the country or he considered it an important amenity for his guests. I wondered if God had indeed intervened on my behalf, giving me not only a day of rest but unfettered access to news from near and far.

I was already ensconced in the *New York Tribune* when the innkeeper appeared with hot tea and biscuits.

"That is grim business," he said, eyeing the front page before me.

"Just awful." The story of the SS *Arctic* had dominated the news over the previous week. It was bad enough that more than three hundred passengers had perished off the coast of Newfoundland, but as more details emerged about the horrific behavior aboard, it was hard not to feel ashamed for humanity. After a brief celebration that eighty-five lives had been saved, it began to dawn on rescuers that the lucky group of survivors were all men, sixty-one of them members of the crew, despite the presence of hundreds of women and children aboard.

I immediately wanted to know more about these survivors. Were they traveling alone? Had they no sympathy for the women and children? Of course, no mother would abandon her child, but had husbands abandoned their families? Had strong young men leapt over women clinging to their babes to gain their places in a lifeboat without so much as a look back?

The idea disgusted me, and at the same time I found myself confused by my own outrage. Had I been aboard, should I have expected "protection"? Was that in the purview of an independent woman, married or not?

"Captain survived," the innkeeper said, pouring my tea. "Went down with the ship, but they found him floating on a broken paddle wheel two days later."

I felt some measure of relief that at least the captain had not abandoned his passengers. A chill ran through me as I imagined him during those hours adrift at sea, knowing his crew had failed him and so many had perished, clinging to the detritus of his ship, one last remnant of humanity, yet utterly alone.

The innkeeper fidgeted at my side. "I hope you don't mind me saying, but I'm hearing some people didn't take too kindly to your speech last night. I'd be careful going out alone if I were you. Once church lets out, there's no telling what trouble people start to look for."

I stiffened in my chair. "Thank you," I managed.

As I watched him leave the room, I caught sight through the kitchen door of his wife and daughter sitting at their own table, the little girl lapping up oatmeal from her mother's spoon like a bird. He kissed each of them lightly on their foreheads, a gesture as natural as pouring a cup of tea. The wife squeezed her husband's hand just before he backed up a step and closed the door.

That afternoon, I turned my attention to several letters I was overdue in composing.

12 October, 1854

Dear Susan,

I'm delighted to hear you were well received in Illinois. I regret that we have not been able to visit together this fall to do some planning for Philadelphia, but I have had a full slate of speaking engagements in Pennsylvania leading up to the convention. Hopefully we will fill the halls with more supporters from this state if I can turn hearts and minds in our direction. I wonder if you feel the weight of this broken country bearing down as I do. I've begun to envision the book that will be written entitled "The Rise and Fall of the Republic." I do not know if the great work done against slavery will be mentioned even as a footnote, but after the country is dissolved, when a more just world looks back, I'm quite sure they will understand our anti-slavery activities to have been the noble course, the right course. I hope the same can be said for our women's rights activities, although I have begun to see that our work will likely blossom like the aloe plant, only after one hundred years. If it takes that long for us, my dear friend, the effort will still be worth it even though we will be no more than ash in the soil, nourishing the plant.

Since I cannot be with you, I wonder if you could discuss with Elizabeth the idea of knitting together the ideas behind these two grand causes. It seems to me, given the dire situation of the country, that we should begin a demand for universal rights. Why speak to one need from one platform and to the other when standing in the building next door? The foot soldiers for change are largely the same in both movements. Why not link them? The country has done an equal disservice to us all, and a call for a universal solution might be our best course. I will be considering this as I prepare my remarks. Discuss this with Elizabeth if you will. Perhaps a well-placed editorial from her and some words for you to bring to the convention would be possible.

I will be sorry to miss walking the pond with you and discussing all of this and more. Please do give my regards to Elizabeth.

I am as ever, your faithful friend,

Lucy

I wrote several other letters—one to Nette and one to Thomas Higginson, with whom I had kept up a regular correspondence since Burns's capture—before turning back to the litany of newspapers strewn about the room, the privilege of having so much printed information at my fingertips a rare luxury. Looking for a more hopeful story than the last, I scanned the headlines of multiple papers, until I caught site of one that read: "SLAVE RESCUE IN OHIO HAILED."

Salem, Ohio, 10 October, 1854

In a test of the Ohio Supreme Court's recent ruling that any slave voluntarily brought into the state can be considered free, a young slave girl of eight years was pulled from a train as it stopped at the junction in Salem on the 8th of October. Word had been dispatched in advance to the attendees of the Western Anti-Slavery Convention being held at Slater's Hall that a couple with a baby were on a northbound train from Tennessee with the slave girl. More than 500 individuals were waiting when the train arrived.

Eyewitnesses state that the girl was asked, "Would you like to be free?" When she answered in the positive, she was pulled from the train. A tussle broke out between several passengers and those who had come to get the girl, but she was reported to be unharmed. The leader of the rescue team, a Henry B. Blackwell of Cincinnati, was arrested for kidnapping and will stand trial.

The slave girl was immediately renamed Abby Kelley Salem, in honor of one of the original female abolitionists and the town of her rescue.

I read the article three times before it fully sank in. The words "Henry B. Blackwell" and "leader of the rescue team" were indeed side by side, brothers in arms, one defining the other. My Harry had led the effort to rescue the girl! He had clearly put himself at some risk, physically and legally, and they had successfully taken the girl from her master, changed the trajectory of her life! But then I realized that he wasn't *my* Harry, and my stomach churned while my heart raced.

I jumped from my chair and paced the room, not knowing what to do with my sudden energy. I wanted to throw my arms around Harry, and congratulate him on his noble act. Yes, that was the critical word, he had acted on behalf of the cause, for the benefit of the girl, without thought of the consequences. Better yet, he'd likely had plenty of time to consider the consequences in advance and he still chose the right course of action. I felt a sense of pride well up in me, a pride I knew was not mine to claim. But he was clearly his own man, and he had done what he knew to be right. I knew him to be a decent man, and this was proof that he was capable of more goodness—more action—than I ever imagined.

Everything around me took on a new life. I noticed for the first time the sun blinking through the fine lace curtains on the windows, speckling the walls with leaf-like patterns. The grandfather clock clanged with sweet notes, and a scarlet ember in the fireplace popped like a firecracker, as if all in celebration of Harry's courageous deed. My heart swelled again, and I knew it to be something larger than pride.

I took out my pens and my stationery and poured out my feelings to him. While the laws of marriage still caused me great consternation, I longed for a way to escape the unnatural loneliness I had chosen again and again. I wanted to believe that because we knew each other so much better than foolish young lovers who wed blindly, and because we had been so frank about our true hopes and desires, there was a chance for us to create a union unlike any other. I told him all this and more, writing furiously into the afternoon, the previously sun-dappled walls fully in shadow, the words on the page no longer easy to see.

I closed by asking Harry if he would consider meeting me in Pittsburgh in two weeks' time, my last stop before the Women's Convention. We needed to see each other in person, have one more frank conversation away from prying eyes, address one more lingering issue. Could he meet me there? Would his trial interfere? Was I too late?

It had been five months since I'd seen Harry last. I could only hope he hadn't erased me from his heart. I sealed the envelope and held the letter to my breast before bringing it to the innkeeper for the next day's post.

16

I received no response from Harry as I traveled through Pennsylvania, despite having given him my full itinerary in my letter. Each post office I visited to no avail reminded me of my days at Oberlin and the endless waiting for a message from home. After claiming nothing but blank stares from the postmasters in Pittsfield and Lancaster and finally at the front desk of the Allegheny Hotel in Pittsburgh, worrying thoughts consumed me.

Was he still detained in jail for the supposed kidnapping? Surely they could not find him guilty when he'd simply escorted off the train a girl the law deemed to be free? I had not considered, however, her young age. Could they call it kidnapping because she was a minor?

Or perhaps Harry simply had no wish to see me again after my treatment of him in Boston. I feared I had tried his patience for the last time. And it was entirely possible I had given him too much time to be swayed by his sisters, Elizabeth and Emily. While his mother and his brother Sam had taken to me during my time in Cincinnati, I knew Elizabeth and Emily did not consider me to be worthy of their brother. Despite their status as single professional women, they did not approve of my lecturing and running of conferences. They were both surprisingly conservative and believed that the unladylike act of speaking out cast our sex in a less-than-favorable light. They were certainly not alone in their opinion.

But deep down, I knew there was another reason they didn't consider me suitable for their brother, and it was even harder to swallow. I didn't have the pedigree or the birthright of their class. They were wary of "Yankee women," and I was decidedly one of those. They hailed from a proper British family, while I came from a farm. They had been highly educated, and I had barely scratched together enough schooling to attend college. None of this had made a difference when I was convinced Harry and I weren't a suited pair, but now it mattered to me greatly.

In between my lectures in Pittsburgh, I spent my time in a small library off the lobby of the Allegheny. I told the front desk that anyone looking for me could find me there, which began to look like a ridiculous announcement after two days passed without a visitor of any kind.

On the evening of the third day, I was about to head up to my rooms for a quiet night when I heard my name coming from the corner of the lobby. My heart wobbled, hoping that Harry had come for me at last.

"Ah, if it isn't the famous Lucy Stone," a man dressed in a proper waistcoat and trousers said as he entered the room, his coattails flying behind him. I did not recognize him.

"Gentlemen, she is in here," he said over his shoulder. "Allow me to introduce myself. I am George Talbot of Pittsburgh. We were just at our club when Joseph Phelps here told us of your speech from last night. We would have gone if we could, but when I learned you were staying just next door, we thought we should take the opportunity to meet you and continue our debate in person."

I shook several hands as nine or ten men filed into the room and each found a chair or brought one with them. A gentleman near the back of the room entered with a bellman at his side, offering a tray of whiskey. I declined.

"You don't preach on temperance on top of it all, do you?" one of them asked.

"I find I am able to counter the effects of alcohol only if I keep it out of my own system." This brought a laugh.

"Mr. Phelps here says you believe women should have equal opportunity to men in all things," Mr. Talbot said.

"Yes, I see no reason why that shouldn't be the case." The soft couch attempted to swallow me. I pushed myself to the edge, where I could straighten my spine.

"I don't know how much you know about steel manufacture. It is at the heart of this city. Do you expect women to go to work in the steel mills? Take up forging irons?"

"Indeed." The men snickered. "But I expect better than that. I believe that one day they will occupy the offices high above the mills, and they will be the lawyers seeing after employment disputes, and even play a role in running the railroads."

"Ha, she's after your job, George!" a man in a tweed coat said, tipping his glass in Mr. Talbot's direction. His coat wasn't as finely hewn as the others and I could tell his hands had seen their fair share of proper labor.

"I think your cause would be better served, Miss Stone, had you not brought up the negroes last night. You might convince some that a woman has similar mental capacity as a man, but then you dare to say there is no difference between a white man and a man of color?"

"Are you a Christian, Mr. Phelps? Only an infidel doesn't believe God's word that all humans are born of one blood. God does not differentiate."

"But the niggers are a different creature. Another species," a man across the room said.

"I am a Christian," Mr. Phelps said, "but that doesn't mean I believe every section of the Bible."

"An infidel indeed," I said. "I have been called the same, Mr. Phelps. But surely God does not speak of two kinds of humans in creation. We are all the same."

A new arrival at the door of the library caught my eye. I looked up to see Harry standing there, his hat in his hands. His dark curls played at his temples, his eyes the blue of the Niagara sky. It took all of my will to keep myself from leaping from my seat. I smiled with my eyes, hoping he would see my delight at his arrival.

"I will say you know how to spin a tale, Miss Stone," Mr. Talbot said. "But if what you envision comes to pass, if women are doing man's work, what will become of the children? Will we end up without any babies at all, with no heirs to carry on our families?"

The men harrumphed in agreement and clinked their glasses.

"Let me ask you." I leaned toward the man in the tweed coat. "Did your mother work hard when you were a child?"

"Yes, ma'am, she did," he said with some pride. "She was always scrubbing or weaving or cooking. She even took in mending from our neighbors for a little extra."

"And did you go hungry because your mother was so busy? Did you lack for what you needed?"

"No, ma'am." The rest of the men said nothing.

"Gentlemen, only when you recognize what women have to offer the world and support your wives and daughters in following their dreams and vocations will we ever realize the American dream as promised to us in the Declaration."

They turned to one another at once, erupting into their own individual protests: "I'll be damned if my wife . . ."; "But they don't have the skills to . . ."; "I'll be dead and gone before . . ."

I smiled at Harry across the fray.

"Thank you for coming, gentlemen," Harry said, raising his voice as he walked into the room. "I'm afraid Miss Stone has a prior engagement and will need to leave it at that."

After hasty good-byes were exchanged and I had shaken every hand, Harry ushered the group out of the room. Before turning to me, he closed the huge double doors leading to the lobby, sealing us in privacy. I knew it wasn't proper but decided not to care.

"Oh, Harry, you came." I rushed toward him.

A serious expression hardened his face.

"Did my letter not reach you in Pittsfield? I took too long to write it. There was too much of importance to say to rush it."

Did I misunderstand his purpose in being there? What had his letter said?

"Tell me everything." I sat on the couch. He had every right to spurn me.

"It has been the most trying of months. They finally dropped the case, of course, but it took some doing by Carlysle, a family friend who is a lawyer, to put a stop to it. Some wanted the whole thing to be played out in court, but there were no grounds for a real indictment."

"I am so proud of you. You were heroic."

"Not everyone sees it that way. Half our hardware customers have decided to buy their goods elsewhere. And a group of men in Memphis have put a ten-thousand-dollar prize on my head. But none of that mattered the moment I got your letter, Lucy. Tell me in person what you wrote on the page. Is it true how you feel about me? The future we can have?"

I scanned his eyes. They were soft again. The swelling in my heart that I had tamped down over the many months of our separation pushed on my chest. I forced myself to stay composed.

"I do hope so, Harry." I reached for his hand. "But I told you we needed to have one more conversation. There is one more thing I need."

"Anything. What is it?"

I hesitated. These last weeks spent waiting to hear from him had made me almost desperate. I had imagined the relief of finally expressing my true feelings and showing him what was in my heart without qualification or shame. I wanted to plan the future with him, one we would share. I couldn't bear to lose it all now. But I reminded myself this was no trifle I was asking for. It was critical to making our future work.

I took a deep breath.

"I need to keep my own name, to continue to be known by the name Lucy Stone only."

It was the only way I could think of to ensure I wouldn't be subsumed by marriage. If Harry was prepared to protest the law, willing to agree that I was not his property nor did he own anything of mine, it only stood to reason that I should not carry his name. But I knew it was asking a lot, perhaps more than anything else we had previously discussed. As far as I knew, no married woman had ever failed to take her husband's name. The fact that people like Elizabeth Cady Stanton insisted on announcing with the signing of every guest register that she was a Cady before becoming a Stanton still offended women and men alike. What I was asking was another order of magnitude more radical. I couldn't help but wonder if my father would be horrified or pleased.

"I thought you would be proud of the Blackwell name." Disappointment tugged at the edges of his mouth.

"I would be proud to say I am the wife of Henry Blackwell. But I must remain Lucy Stone."

He let go of me and stood. He placed one hand on the small hearth in the corner of the room, his back to me. My heart bunched up and pounded in my ears at the expense of any other sound in the room. I allowed myself to imagine, just for an instant, the two of us at a kitchen table, a baby on my lap, Harry's soft kiss landing on both our foreheads. I almost cried out for want of it, how it would hurt to lose that image forever. How I would miss him if he left me now. Yet I could not give way, not at this final juncture.

"Lucy," he finally said. "We have agreed, have we not, that you will keep all your possessions, you will keep your own counsel and can make any professional decisions you deem the best for you? You will always maintain the right of custody of any children, and we will live together to the extent made possible by both of our careers, is that not right?" There was no malice or injury in his words, but it did sound like a long list.

"Yes, you have agreed to all of that, but—"

"Then what is left in a name?" He came back to the couch and laced a hand in mine.

"My name is who I am." The mass at the back of my throat threatened to produce tears.

"No, that's not what I mean. We have decided you should keep everything that is yours, and I mine. It only stands to reason that you should keep your name."

"Oh, Harry." I allowed myself to wrap my arms around him then, my tears spilling onto his jacket.

We didn't open the door to the library for the next thirty minutes.

❧

I arrived in Philadelphia for the annual convention two days later. The new Pennsylvania Railroad got me there in record time, and I was able to meet up with Nette and Susan for a late supper the night before it began. It had been bittersweet leaving Harry. It was harder to say good-bye than ever before, but it was also a parting layered with promise, knowing we would be embarking on a future together.

"Lucy?" Susan asked. "Do you agree?"

We were taking dinner in my rooms at the Girard House and had opened the balcony doors to an unusually mild October evening. I took my eyes off the trees lining Chestnut Street and forced myself back into the room.

"I'm sorry, what did you ask?"

"We haven't seen each other for months, and I feel as though I can hardly capture your attention. Are you quite all right?"

"I'm perfectly fine. In fact, better than I've felt in years. Could you pass the salt? I'm ravenous."

"I'm relieved by how well you look given the schedule you've been keeping," Nette said.

"I will tell Mrs. Rose that fifteen dollars is more than enough to reimburse her travel expenses," Susan said. "People have gotten lofty ideas in their heads. She can't honestly think this room or this meal is paid for by the convention. Everyone needs to economize."

"Thank you for handling that." I was accustomed to covering all costs associated with long-distance travel and accommodations out of my own earnings and was often surprised by the amounts some of our speakers claimed were necessary for reimbursement. I greatly appreciated Susan's support.

"Fortunately, this is her only trip this year," Susan continued. "Recently, when a switch broke between Washington and Arlington, I found myself passing the time with the foolish game of adding up how many hours I have spent on trains and in hired carriages this year. Would either of you like to guess the number I came to?"

"Four hundred," Nette said.

"Eight hundred and seventy-two," I offered. I had played this game myself.

"Just shy of that number, yes."

"That's impossible," Nette said.

"If there is no wind for the flag," I said.

"Keep moving and it will fly," Susan finished.

"Honestly, you two must take better care not to tire yourselves out. Where will the rest of us be if you two expire?"

"Closer to having some rights." I raised my water glass as a toast.

"Marriage rights, at least," Nette said. "It sounds like you have been taking this state by storm, Lucy. The *Tribune* said there were no shortage of men in Pittsburgh lined up in the lobby of your hotel, ready to genuflect and propose. That's a direct quote."

"They said what?" I choked on my sip of water. I hadn't bothered to read the papers during my last day with Harry, nor since arriving in Philadelphia. Had we been noticed in the library?

"Ha!" Susan said. "I must compliment that reporter. How I do enjoy the image of those steel barons kneeling at the feet of the one woman least likely to ever accept a man's entreaty."

I wished the breeze off the balcony were cooler just then, certain my face was the color of a radish.

"Lucy?"

I had written to Nette of the awful day of Burns's removal from Boston and how I had essentially sent Harry away. I had also admitted to her that I wasn't at all sure I had done the right thing. She smiled and raised her eyebrows at me.

"What on earth is going on here?" Susan asked.

I had hoped to wait to tell Susan by letter if possible, the better to temper any explosion she might aim my way. But if I couldn't gain comfort in my decision with these two friends, when would I ever?

"I haven't even told my family yet, but Harry and I are to be married."

Susan blanched. "Good lord. That Blackwell man?"

Nette grabbed my hand in both of hers. "I knew your heart would win in the end. He's a good man."

"A good man? I heard he toppled a baby off the lap of its mother when he was trying to rescue that slave girl," Susan said.

"You know that's untrue," I said. "Harry wrote a wonderful editorial detailing the whole episode."

"But marriage, Lucy?" Susan said. "We don't have time for such things. No wife can log thousands of miles of reform work. We agreed not to be distracted by personal folly."

"It will not slow me down in the least. Not one bit." I had no idea how to be a wife and a reformer at the same time, but I certainly hadn't promised Harry a typical domestic life. He knew this would be a marriage like no other.

"Until the first baby arrives," Susan said. "Then I will be abandoned again."

"I don't even know if God will grant me children at my age." I had waited so long that at thirty-six, I wasn't sure if I could even conceive. Conceive! The thought of being intimate with Harry made me blush.

"Oh, babies will come," Susan said. "And then you will be no better to me than any other married woman. How could you do this?"

"Susan!" Nette said. "Surely you don't mean that."

"You should know something. We have agreed to protest the laws of marriage when we wed. We are writing our own marriage contract. I cede no legal rights, to my possessions, property, or, yes, even theoretical children. And I will be keeping my own name."

"Interesting." Susan sat back and smiled for the first time since my news.

"You won't go by Blackwell?" Nette asked.

"I shall remain Lucy Stone only." I was proud of Harry all over again for supporting me in that decision.

"Are you sure? How will anyone know you're married?"

"Salmon Chase has assured me there is no law that stipulates the taking of one name over another. Our marriage will be perfectly legal, and I will be the wife of Henry Blackwell while still being exactly who I am, Lucy Stone."

"Well, if you must, I wish you nothing but happiness, you know I do. I just pray you won't abandon me in the midst of your wedded bliss," Susan said flatly, although she looked directly at me when she said it.

"You know I would rather die than abandon this cause. Or my friends."

"I'll count on you for that," she said somberly, and excused herself from the room.

We were married on a beautiful spring day in 1855, looking out toward Coy's Hill. It had taken us seven months to find an agreeable day in both our schedules for the ceremony, and while the wait seemed interminable, I was pleased that we would join hands after the milkweed had already popped up from its winter slumber and while the bees shimmered in the sun.

Harry met my parents for the first time the night before the wedding. Mama and I roasted chickens and corn while Father sat with Harry on the front porch. When she and I were quiet, it was easy enough to overhear bits of their conversation.

"Lucy tells me you're going to let her keep working?" Father asked.

"It's not up to me, sir. She is her own person."

"I see. And what do you do for work, exactly?" Father asked, pulling on his pipe.

"I am a land agent for some investors in the Midwest and am currently thinking about buying into a publishing company in New York. Agricultural books."

"Can't put experience in a book. Takes a lot of hard work is all."

"You do have a beautiful place here, sir."

I smiled and went back to peeling potatoes, reminding me of my first afternoon with Harry. So much had changed for me in just two years.

"Are you sure you want to settle in New Jersey? So far away," Mama said, kneading dough next to me.

"New York City is full of opportunities for Harry right now, and it is a central enough place for my travels." Despite my dreams of making my own home somewhere in Massachusetts, I understood Harry's need to find a profession that suited him. I had given him $1,500 of my earnings for land investments in Wisconsin, and he had encouraged me to settle the remaining $4,500 of my savings in my own name in bank bonds before we married. He was determined to use as little of my money as possible and make his own fortune.

"How can you keep traveling like you do and care for a family, dear?"

My choices had always confused my mother, made her worry I misunderstood the way things worked and would be forever disappointed.

"Harry and I have agreed to support each other in all ways, Mama. We will manage."

"Young men often make promises they can't keep." She covered the dough with a dishrag to let it rise.

"Harry's not like most men." I wished I could explain to her how different I intended my life to be. I didn't know how to tell her that the awful circumstances she endured had provided much of the inspiration to sculpt my life from different clay. It felt like a cruel compliment. I hoped she had found more happiness than had been obvious to me.

"Leave this for a minute," she said, wiping the flour from her hands on her apron before taking it off and draping it over the chair.

She brought me up to her bedroom and held up a silk-and-lace dress, the color of pale roses. I had never worn so beautiful a garment. It must have taken her months to make, and I could tell with one glance that it would fit me perfectly.

"It's stunning," I said, afraid to touch it lest I mark it with dirt from the potatoes.

"I'm so happy you have at last found your way." Droplets appeared on her lashes like dew on blade of grass.

The next morning, Reverend Higginson arrived from Boston with his wife, Mary, to perform the ceremony for us. I was grateful for the effort. The West Brookfield church had seen fit to expel me years earlier for daring to speak in public, and I could no more be wed by a minister from that church than ask a known slave owner to dinner.

My brother Bo arrived soon after with his three children and Phebe and her two in tow, Sam looking handsome in a pressed shirt tucked into his knickers. Bo and Phebe had been married for three years now, a turn of events I was certain would have pleased Luther. They had made a lovely home together just down the street. Despite Phebe's life having taken this happier turn, I had a new appreciation for the heartache she must have endured. The prospect of losing Harry that way seemed unthinkable to me.

I was sorry for Harry that none of his family were there, but we would board the noon train to New York for a separate celebration with

Elizabeth and Emily. Despite their doubts about me, once our engagement was made official, Elizabeth wrote a lovely note to welcome me into the Blackwell fold. I was quite sure I still didn't live up to the societal standards either of the Blackwell girls had held for their brother, but I was not beyond trusting I could prove them wrong with time.

I was also sorry not to have my sister Sarah there, but the trip was too much to ask with her young children still underfoot and a ceremony that would take no more than thirty minutes.

Throughout all my years speaking to crowds, walking streets by myself, calling conventions to order, I never felt a twinge of nervousness the way I did on that day. As I stood beside Harry and looked into the periwinkle blue of his eyes, I prayed we were making the right decision. There was no man I could imagine feeling closer to or trusting more than he, but could we make a marriage work? Could I be a good wife? Would I become a mother? Would I truly be able to finish my quest once I was married? I was now bound with a vow to try.

Harry read the Protest aloud, standing proud in a proper waistcoat. He had taken great pains with every word, detailing each of the laws we stood against and the equality within our marriage we intended to observe. Father scowled throughout, the words and the glare of the sun likely causing him equal discomfort. Mama's smile never left her lips. Clearly, she was relieved to finally marry off the last of her children, no matter in how unconventional a manner.

Almost as soon as the ceremony began, we promised to love and care for each other in sickness and in health and were pronounced husband and wife. I was now a wife.

Harry was patient with me on our wedding night, gentle and loving. I was shy at first, reluctant to remove my clothes or let down my hair. But his touch on the inside of my elbow, the edge of my shoulder, then the top of my knee felt like the heat of sunshine, and it didn't take long before I wanted to be covered in it. For the first time in my life, I lost myself completely, allowing a freedom of emotion and a surrender of thought I had never before experienced. Both gratitude and regret rippled through me for all I had missed in refusing to welcome a love like this into my life long before. How bottled up I had been, how unwilling to access my deepest desires. This was union, only possible by giving myself over wholly to another, only possible because I trusted Harry so completely. I knew he would never hurt me.

The pleasure of our intimacy was overwhelming, and I didn't want to waste a moment of it with sleep. But a kind of drowsy contentment eventually overtook us. I lay my head against the silk of his nightshirt, his arms wrapped around me, and fell asleep to the rhythm of his breathing.

We woke the next day in New York City, the bliss of the previous night lingering about me like a gentle fog, to find that our wedding was front-page news. We would come to discover over time that our Protest appeared in full in countless papers, including *The Liberator*, the *Philadelphia Inquirer*, the *Charleston Courier*, and even the *Jackson Citizen* in Minnesota. But on that morning, I had only a copy of the *New York Times*. Over soft-boiled eggs I read, "Miss Lucy Stone has succumbed at last. In spite of all her diatribes against the tyranny of marriage, and her assertion of woman's rights, she has come under the yoke, and is now the lawfully wedded wife of Mr. Henry B. Blackwell."

Under a yoke? They had missed the whole point! The happy fog of the night before gave way to a familiar dread. I thought the decision to marry had been the hard part. How wrong I was.

PART II

17

I hope you have some sense now, my dear Alice, of why I held myself at bay from the threshold of marriage for so long and how I finally allowed myself to be picked up and carried across. It was such a difficult decision in some ways, and an obvious choice in other ways. All I wish for you is a future that matches what's in your heart and what you want out of your life. Of course, getting to the altar is only half the story, and the wisdom of any decision can't really be judged by what came before as much as by what came after. So, I think it important to give you a sense of the changes in my life that naturally unfolded after making such a choice. I don't intend to sway you one way or the other, but please forgive me if any of this is difficult to hear.

It's hard not to blush a little thinking back on those early days. During our first few years of our marriage, my work continued uninterrupted. Good to his word as always, Harry did not place any restrictions on my hectic schedule, nor did I on his. We both traveled constantly, he still in pursuit of financial success, me for the cause. What did change was that we had a shared home to come back to. While we didn't have nearly as much time together as either of us hoped for, it was truly magical when we were able to spend the evening reading by our own hearth before retiring to our very own bed. There I was, sitting at the fire with my husband, just like my mother had on so many nights with my own father, except Harry and I came to our seats as equals, discussing the news of the day with respect in each other's opinions, and we could retire upstairs with no unreasonable expectations between us. I found a sense of calm whenever Harry was near and was ever grateful that he'd waited for me to find my way to him. My Job indeed. I could only hope the suffering I had caused him in the process was duly replaced by the joy we shared as a married couple, as intermittent as it was.

An unexpected outcome was the need to frequently convince others of the verity of my name, even though it was the same name I had carried my entire life. Not having any idea what to make of a married woman who did not use the moniker "Mrs.," I was often forced to at least identify myself as a wife. When signing the contract for our house in New Jersey, even though I purchased it with my own funds, I had been required to sign as "Lucy Stone, wife of Henry Blackwell." I employed the same bulky signature whenever we checked into a hotel together, simply to appease the worries of the clerk.

The biggest change of all, of course, came three years after our wedding. Just when I'd begun to believe I was destined to be childless after all, I gave birth to you, Alice, my beautiful baby girl. What a miracle you were. I adored watching you sleep, your lips mouthing at little bubbles, your face perfectly round with almost no hair to disrupt the smooth orb of your head, your tiny hand laying half open like a tulip unfurling from its bud. You rolled it into a fist when you wailed, often with a good portion of my hair locked in your grip. But when you were quiet, I loved nothing more than nuzzling you and feeling your soft skin against my nose. I remember it all perfectly even now.

Harry missed too much of it. Although we had relocated to New Jersey directly after our wedding so he could pursue an important job opportunity in New York City, his job put him on the road more than he was home, sometimes for months at a stretch. He deplored missing so much of that miraculous time, your triumph at holding your head up on your own, the way your eyes studied my face as if to memorize every expression, your shock at pulling a tassel from the edge of a lace doily.

Motherhood is truly a wondrous thing. It changed me. It softened my edges and sharpened my defenses all at once. The smallest coo could make me swoon, and the reminder that my girl would be considered less than a full citizen in this country rankled me, giving me ever more determination to work for change. But Harry's long absences meant I had to temporarily stop lecturing. While he encouraged me to leave our little cub, as he called you, in the care of others from time to time, he didn't understand that I could not abide having any other woman calm you when you yowled or smile back at you when your giggle revealed one small tooth sticking out from your gums. The one night I went to speak in New York was full of endless faces that were not yours. Every squeak of a door came to me as a baby's helpless whimper. I yearned for your breath against my neck, and the tightness in my breast served as a potent reminder of where I was supposed to be.

It was exactly as I had feared: I couldn't tolerate being away from my child long enough to dig into work in earnest, but I still missed it desperately. I participated in every way I could from our kitchen table, planning conventions, circulating pamphlets, supporting my friends from afar, but it wasn't the same as facing detractors directly, of changing minds with a well-chosen phrase or a powerful retort. Had Harry been home more, perhaps I would have laid you in his arms, satisfied that you were at least with your father, and been more active, but I didn't have that option.

I had imagined more than once accepting one of the many speaking invitations I regularly received and taking you on the road with me. I pictured standing up onstage with you swaddled in my arms, demonstrating for all to see the possibility of providing for a child while doing important work. But then a rock or book would fly across the image, shattering the reverie.

Please know that this isn't about you, Alice. I would give up everything all over again for the delight of being your mother, for the wonder of watching you grow. But I want you to understand that marriage and motherhood can create what feels like an impossible choice. I struggled mightily to find my way.

The distance from Harry made it much harder. He wrote frequently, but the news was often the same.

8 July, 1859
Dear Lucykins,

I hope you and the little cub are doing well together. I'm sorry to say that my time in Illinois, it seems, will stretch into its fourth month. I wish I could afford to pack up and turn away from this job, but I fear that's not possible. I just learned that the Saxton Company had debts previously unrevealed to me, and so I now own my part of those debts from its closure. How I wish I hadn't used any of your hard-earned money to buy into this business, as the investment is now tied to my waist like an anchor in a deep sea. I have been trying to sell off some of the land I purchased in your name for you, but the recession has made sales very slow and prices less than fair. But don't lose faith, dear wife. I still believe that investment will prove profitable in time. And once I can pay down the loans I took for my own parcels, I should clear a tidy bundle that will finally show I am worthy of the faith you have put in me.

In the meantime, I am happy to report that I'm having success selling my various books and encyclopedias in the West and feel confident I will eventually be granted a healthy share of the profits. We can use it to pay down our near-term debts. I enclose this quarter's salary for what little it will cover.

You will also be proud to hear that I have begun to speak on occasion for the Western Anti-Slavery Association. Of course, I can only devote as much time to this as my professional responsibilities will allow, but given my actions in Salem, they see me as a leader of sorts. I am told my lectures are received well. I did learn at the feet of the best speaker of our time, of either sex, so I have you to thank for any success I find in that area.

I love you with my whole heart, wife, and find this separation from you to be endless. I count the days until I can be back in our little kitchen, hearing your lovely voice and the coos of our sweet daughter.

I am faithfully yours,

Harry

I looked up from the letter and gazed at you, napping in the same cradle my mother had used to rock all of us to sleep. She had given it to me as a wedding present, hoping I would be able to fill it with many children of my own. It was the only object in the house I didn't buy myself, and it was my most cherished possession. It fit perfectly in a small nook between the kitchen and our sitting area, and next to a bookcase neatly stacked with volumes I couldn't wait to read to you. I had promised you on the day you were born that the one thing you would never lack was books.

The rest of the kitchen was in some disarray. The cucumbers and carrots I had pulled earlier in the day mocked me from the counter, the bucket full of as much dirt as vegetable. Before I could start peeling, I needed to wring out your diaper cloths and dressing gowns and get them on the line while the sun was high in the sky. And the whole house needed sweeping, a task I had neglected for the last week as I nursed you through a cold.

Not that it was a large house, but it was our house, a sweet cottage with an apple tree out front and a garden patch behind. It was the first place I'd called home since leaving West Brookfield twenty years earlier. The ability to lay my head down night after night on the same pillow was not something I had experienced since Oberlin. I only wished Harry could enjoy it with me. The short time we'd shared here, sitting by the fire at night reading to each other before slumbering peacefully in our wedding bed, felt like a dream. I might have doubted its verity without you as proof of our wedded bliss, and the next baby I was sure was growing inside me.

But Harry's letter left me unsettled. Our finances were becoming increasingly dire. The mortgage on the house cost us dearly. I had made the five-hundred-dollar down payment, but the interest payments were barely covered by his salary. I had lectured as late into my pregnancy as I thought safe, but those earnings were eaten up quickly by loans on Harry's western land holding and the money he invested in the publishing company. Despite our best intentions of leaving my savings untouched, the amount was down to a thousand dollars. While I would have happily turned it over to Harry if it meant he could come home, he insisted that he could not call himself husband if he relied solely on my earnings, not to mention that depleting those savings entirely would make our situation even more precarious. Getting back on the lecture circuit or selling off land holdings were our only opportunities for some kind of financial security and it didn't appear either of those were likely to happen anytime soon.

Trapped in the little kitchen so far from home, I thought often of Coy's Hill, of the wide spaces and craggy rocks I loved so well. I wondered if the bald eagle I had seen soaring there as a child, or her offspring, might still be there. On one of the many days I visited the judge back then, he had let me use his illustrated Audubon guide to identify the hawkish bird I had seen one morning. I remember being fascinated to read that the bald eagle had a dainty call, no more intimidating than a sparrow. It was news to me at the time that a fierce animal didn't need an angry voice. Father didn't think it possible that a bald eagle would nest on our property, but I liked the idea of her and decided to believe she lived there anyway. The judge's book taught me that eagles mate for life, each built as the perfect complement to the other. The female's larger size is ideal for warming the eggs and nestlings when they are young. The male is smaller, sleeker, better suited to hunting for the family. But the female was known to catch fish or scavenge for food when necessary. Could the father just as easily warm the nest? Did he feel diminished if the mother did the hunting?

I turned my back to the vegetables and laundry and took up my pen to write Harry an encouraging letter. I cupped my growing belly, delighted at the idea of giving you a sibling. But I was glad I hadn't yet written to Harry of my pregnancy. He certainly didn't need any more pressure. Instead, he needed my congratulations on his current successes and my assurance that all would be well in our happy home whether greater fortunes came along or not. My pregnancy would be a wonderful surprise when he finally did come home.

I'd scribbled no more than the date at the top of the page when a loud knock startled me. While I knew the names of most of the families who lived nearby, I had yet to find a friend among any of the ladies, and so didn't expect a visit. Many of them, I surmised, were not quite sure what to make of me, or perhaps of the me they read about in the papers. The Franklins were the lone family I thought might have some sympathy for my work, might even support it, but with a house to run and a baby to care for, there was little opportunity for tea and conversation.

You started to cry. I barely had time to wrap a blanket around you and take you in my arms before an even more insistent knock rattled our door.

I opened it to find a gentleman in a dark suit and silver spectacles holding a folder.

"Mrs. Blackwell?" he asked.

"Lucy Stone, if you please."

"I have here a letter dated the eighth of March stating that you refuse to pay your taxes." He looked at the papers in his hand.

"Then you would know my name is Lucy Stone, as that is how I signed the letter." I rubbed your back, hoping the whimpers you were gulping back wouldn't erupt again into a full-blown howl.

"I have come to collect the $32.50 owed to the town of Orange for this property."

"Mr. . . . ?" I inquired.

"My apologies. Mr. Haverford." He momentarily lifted the hat from his head and tipped it at me.

"Mr. Haverford, as stated in my letter, I am refusing to pay taxes because I am refused the right to vote, and I do not intend to pay any taxes until I am given that right."

"Mrs. Blackwell—I'm sorry, Mrs. Stone, there is no statute that makes it legal to object to taxes on those grounds, well, on any grounds, really." He adjusted his glasses as if to see me better.

"I believe a small revolution was started in the North based on this very same idea. Do you know of it?"

"I don't see what that has to do with this," he said, impatience starting to register in his voice.

"I suggest you think it over, Mr. Haverford. Taxation without representation? I think you will find it to be the very same thing. Now, I need to tend to my baby. Good day to you, sir." I closed the door and secured the latch with a click.

They could send me as many notices, through the post or in person, as they liked. I was not going to give them a dime.

❧

Several weeks later, I sat again at the kitchen table, trying to get through as much paperwork as possible before you woke and squawked for your midday feeding, when a rattling at the door again interrupted me. The first knock didn't wake you this time, so I decided to finish the letter I was reading before accepting the disruption.

Dearest Lucy,

It is impossible to describe to you how tired I am as of late. The schedule of speaking engagements and the miles of travel continue to be relentless. Somehow knowing you aren't on a parallel set of train tracks, or standing on a wooden box turning over the minds of an unruly crowd somewhere makes this work all the more lonely. I cannot do it without you.

You said in your last letter I should try to hone my own words, to own my own speeches, because I know it all in my heart. Do you truly believe I can? It may become a necessity. Have you heard that Elizabeth is expecting her seventh child? How can six not be enough? Please tell me you have gotten the need for children out of your system and will rejoin me as soon as possible. We need your voice, Lucy. Without it I fear my lonesome chorus will be drowned out by a million anti-womaners.

The minute Nette began to have babies I knew she would be lost to the cause for years, but Lucy Stone? Please write to me of your intended schedule for coming back out to the public. We need you desperately. I need you.

With love,

Susan

I brushed an unruly clump of hair off my forehead, trying to remember the last time I'd washed it. Susan had no idea how depleting caring for a baby and a household could be. I cupped my belly again, knowing the work was soon to increase, as would my hiatus from agitating for the cause. But if she saw it as a holiday, she was badly mistaken. The thought of riding a train by myself, sleeping without the cries of a child piercing my dreams, and standing in front of an audience all sounded as lovely as a long walk up Coy's Hill with nothing to bother me but the wind in my hair.

At least Nette understood this now. To my great surprise, Nette had fallen in love with Harry's brother Sam during a visit to us all in Cincinnati the summer after we married. My dear friend was now also my sister-in-law. She had already delivered two children into the world, and I suspected many more were in her future. She gave up the pulpit for her family, and I could not blame her for that choice, knowing as I did how strongly the call of a mother's bosom is to her children. Exchanging letters with her on the topic brought great comfort.

But I did miss the road. I did miss speaking. I missed the intellectual conversation at dining tables in Boston, the camaraderie of debating issues of reform and honing my own point of view. But motherhood came first for now. You needed me. And the new baby would need me. My purpose for the near term was to protect you both, to provide for you, to keep you both safe. I was nothing if I couldn't do that.

The knock on the door came again, and I reluctantly answered it. This time Mr. Haverford had a constable with him.

"Mrs. Stone, I trust you saw the notice in the *Courier*?"

"What notice?" I hadn't read a newspaper in weeks.

He sighed and opened his brown leather folder to read from a document. "It is ordered by the County of Essex and town of Orange, New Jersey, that property from 8 Cone Street in Orange be seized and sold in order to pay the $32.50 and $1.25 interest owed in back taxes. The sale will begin promptly at noon on the third day of August on the lawn of 8 Cone Street. All buyers welcome." He slapped his folder shut.

"But that's today." The clock in the parlor had just recently struck eleven. They were intending to run some sort of sale on my own yard within the hour? "I don't understand."

"Everything in this house is your property, Mrs. Stone?" Mr. Haverford walked past me uninvited and into the front hall.

"Yes, but—" I started.

"Johnson, choose whatever items you think might add up to the needed sum and bring them outside. I will catalog the inventory," Mr. Haverford said, and then turned to me. "As I said when I first visited, you are required to pay your taxes. We will see to it that the city gets its money before the end of the day."

His gruff voice and stiff heels scraping the wood floor finally woke you. Your whimpers included a hungry cry.

"Gentlemen, I need to feed my child. You will have to come back at another time."

"Court order, ma'am. Whatever room you need for privacy, we won't disturb you, but we must have the sale ready by noon."

Your whimper rose to a wail. I had no choice but to retreat to my bedroom. There was no latch on the door to keep the men out, so I dragged a trunk from the foot of our bed across the room and sat on it with my back to the door. Perhaps sensing my impatience, you writhed and protested before eventually latching on. For the next quarter hour, I was hopeless to stop the two strangers as they banged around the house, apparently taking anything of value light enough to move outside.

When I finally buttoned up and made it back downstairs, I could not believe the items they had chosen, a full mockery of justice on display. They'd seized my portrait of William Lloyd Garrison, and one I had more recently purchased of Salmon Chase, the lawyer, now a Supreme Court Justice, who had assured me that keeping my own name was perfectly legal. At least I could take comfort in the fact that Garrison's likeness would not appeal to a wide audience. But there was more set up for sale. As if calculating that taking purely decorative items would not create enough of a hardship, they had dared to remove my kitchen table and put it on the lawn, placing upon it our brass clock, which had been a wedding gift from Wendell Phillips. None of this compared to the final item out on display: your cradle.

I gripped the cotton of my skirt and tapped my fist against my thigh. The memory of Abigail losing Willow came rushing back to me. I had been powerless to help my cousin then, and had I had the money, I would have settled her husband's debts myself. Anything to save her from the heartache of that loss. But I now understood his cruel act to be much more than a monetary transaction. It was an expression of power. He had taken from her the one object of her affection, her source of joy, her place of safety, and he had done it on purpose, leaving her no choice but to rely on her new husband entirely. I had worked ever since then to ensure I would never be in such a position.

I did have the money to end the current folly. Hidden in the lining of a coat upstairs for emergencies was enough to settle the matter right then. This man would never expect that a mere wife, with her husband away, would be able to pay such a debt. But just as in Abigail's case, there was far more at stake here than money, and I would be damned if I was going to give into the real issue so easily.

"Ah, there you are, Mrs. Stone," Mr. Haverford said, turning to me, a slight smile creeping onto his face. Was he actually enjoying this? "Would you care to reconsider? If you will agree to pay the tax, we would be happy to put everything back."

"And will you see to it that I can vote in the next school board election, or for the upcoming mayoral race?"

"Certainly not."

"Then carry on," I said, and shut the door.

I sat in my chair beside the hearth, staring at the spot on the wall where Garrison was supposed to be, while you made happy popping sounds in my ear. Managing without a kitchen table or cradle would be a particular challenge. The nearest woodworker lived an hour's carriage ride away, and orders often took a month to be completed. And the cradle could never be replaced. As foolish as it was to be wrapped up in material things, it was the one thing I owned that had touched my mother's hands, my only physical connection to my past. How, after all these years, could I still be rendered so powerless? How could these men do such a thing and then go home and look their children in the eye?

Rage simmering in my gut, I left via the back door of the house, careful to cut a wide path back toward the woods so as not to be seen. I made happy murmurs for you as we walked, hoping to keep you from sounding a cry that would give us away. Rounding the edge of our small plot of land, I stepped onto the road and headed toward town. Within ten minutes I stood on the Franklins' threshold, letting my own knock rattle their door.

The sun had been gone from the sky for at least three hours when the first cramp seized my belly. I didn't know the exact time because the brass clock was gone, sold before Mr. Franklin managed to join the throng gathered in front of our house that afternoon. With my money in hand, he yelled out a figure for everything remaining on the lawn—not realizing the most valuable item had already been taken—and brought the entire auction to a halt. Happy to have their work done for the day, Mr. Haverford and the constable left with their profits, taking Mr. Franklin at his word that he would come back for the goods as soon as his son returned from town with his carriage. Under the cover of darkness, he helped me move everything back inside the house.

The shock of the pain in my abdomen forced me to drop the knitting needles on my lap and grab the arms of my chair. It was too early for anything close to labor. I knew I was no less than four months along, but certainly no more than six. I cradled the bump at my waist, the size of a cantaloupe, and tried to take long and slow breaths. I needed to stay calm. Perhaps it was just a reaction to the meal I had eaten too fast after the trying day, or maybe it was a muscle cramp from lifting the Chase portrait back onto the wall. But on my second, deep breath, I knew something was terribly wrong. Everything clenched inside me again, like a rope tightening around the neck of an unruly calf.

I forced myself out of the chair, trying to measure if I had strength enough in my legs to make it to the Franklins' again. It seemed unlikely I could walk the distance while clutching you in one arm and my cramping belly with the other. The next wave of pain sent me to my knees. Liquid seeped through my undergarments and down my thighs. I stuffed a wad of yarn into my jaw to clench against the agony and to stop myself from screaming out. I didn't want to scare you, asleep in your cradle. Against every desire to keep the baby inside me, my body insisted on pushing. Searing heat attacked my lower back like a branding iron, the yarn dissolving in the vise grip of my teeth, my moans almost impossible to contain. I pushed into an endless stream of pain until suddenly, like so many sheep I had seen release their lambs by squatting in the mud, I delivered a tiny boy onto the rug in front of our hearth.

I gathered him into me, frantically wiping the mucus and blood from his face, willing him to whimper, begging him to breathe. I pulled a throw blanket off the couch and swaddled him, even while the chord still stretched from between my legs to his tiny belly. I sat on the floor and held him, trying to warm him, cradling him in the way that always soothed you. His eyelids were impossibly tiny, no bigger than a clover leaf, his entire body smaller than a half loaf of bread.

I begged him to stay in this world and began to weep. In between sobs, I told him about his big sister, about his father. I promised him he would always be loved, murmuring over and over that he was my beautiful, beautiful boy. I don't know how long I rocked him, only that when the room was finally void of my own noises, I had to face the fact that he hadn't made even the tiniest sound, had never taken one breath. My baby was dead.

18

I have no idea how much time passed between the night I lost the baby and when Harry finally came home. I did notice the grass turn inward at some point, allowing its bright green to fade to the color of the sandy soil beneath. The strawberries shrank and withered, the roses rotted on the vine. The days blurred into one long wait for another sleepless night, the nights stretching toward another day in which I could not scrub the sadness from the house. I fed you whenever you cried out for it. I fed myself when dizziness signaled it had been too long since my last meal. I was grateful you had no words to ask me about my silence. I couldn't find anything else to be grateful for.

I didn't have the heart to write to Harry of our loss. I had told him nothing of the expected addition to our family, and sharing both pieces of news at the same time seemed cruel. I considered asking him to come home to me, but I felt in no condition for adult interaction, even with Harry. I held on to the hope that I would eventually find my way through the fog of grief and confusion and be able to accept his comfort.

Letters began to pile up, unanswered. I remember a congratulatory missive from Elizabeth. She had read about my tax refusal and lauded it as "perhaps the most effective protest one could wage from the kitchen." What would she say if she knew the cost? After some stretch of weeks, the letters took on a more anxious tone, Harry worried I was angry with him for staying on in the West, Susan suspecting motherhood had finally so consumed me that I had given up all thoughts of reform. Maybe I had.

The longer Harry's absence dragged on, the more withdrawn I became, ready to blame anything and anyone outside the walls of our tiny cottage for my loss.

One morning I noticed frost clinging to the bedroom window like cobwebs, winter once again attaching itself to our lives. That afternoon, Harry came home. Despite the mixture of damp and dirt caked on him from the long trip, he appeared vibrant and strong. The look on his face told me what he saw: an apron that hadn't been laundered in weeks, a tangle of hair barely caught into a bun, a thick layer of dust on every sill. I could find no way to tell him what I had endured. It had become part of me, as hardened and immovable as bone. Taking it out would break me.

Harry's gaze turned from me as soon as you toddled into the room. He scooped you in his arms and twirled you in the air, the glee on both of your faces almost pushing a smile across my own.

"I didn't expect you today. I don't have anything in for supper," I said.

"Things have been hard on you." He attempted to smooth the hair from my face.

I bent to pick up a wooden pail.

"I'll just pull up some potatoes, and I think I may still have some rice in the larder," I said, heading out to the barren vegetable patch before he could say more.

That night, after pulling off his travel clothes and sponging off, Harry tenderly gazed at you, curled up in bed beside me.

"Shall I bring her to her crib?" he whispered.

"This is where she sleeps," I said, and closed my eyes.

Several weeks after Harry's homecoming, he rocked you to sleep while I cooked apples for a pie. I knew it had the makings of a happy scene, but I couldn't seem to ignore the weight of my own eyelids or the wad of sorrow stuck in my throat like an uncooked ball of dough.

Leaving your cradle, Harry removed the wooden spoon from my hand and guided me to the seats in front of our hearth.

"We promised many things to each other, Lucy, and one was to always speak frankly. What have I done to upset you? You were so encouraging of my endeavors out West. But now you hardly talk to me."

I couldn't form the words to tell him how completely I had failed in everything. I was no longer the brave lecturer he had followed about the country. And now I was failing in my wifely duties also, barely putting meals together for our table or keeping the house in order, turning him away at night even though he had coaxed you to start sleeping in your own room. The act felt dangerous to me now. But mostly, I couldn't find a way to tell him how completely I had failed as a mother. I was unable to save my baby, had rendered the words "brother" and "sister" meaningless in our family. I stared at the rug, at the place where our son had entered and departed this world, all in the same moment.

"I'm sorry I left you alone for so long."

"I told you a long time ago that being alone is my natural state," I said, and went back to the pie before I let anything more hurtful come out of my mouth.

The days continued on in a blur, with nothing to lift my spirits. Harry restarted the newspapers, which only made things worse. Anti-abolition violence was surging in border states, and retaliation was becoming common. When we read about Charles Sumner, a Massachusetts senator we knew well, being beaten with a cane on the Senate floor by a colleague from South Carolina because of an anti-slavery speech, we knew those chosen to govern were unlikely to agree on an acceptable solution to the scourge. And then John Brown was captured at Harper's Ferry. Father wrote me that if Brown was sentenced to death, he felt the country wouldn't recover.

A previous version of myself would have rushed out to speak on these things in public, to help the people of our country see the rights and wrongs of it all, but I could not call up that other person. She was latched away behind some hidden door I could not locate, and even if I could find it, where was the key? And I felt sure I would not find it while living so far away from my fellow reformers, from those whose dedication to change had long sparked fire in me and given me free access to a well of confidence and inspiration.

And so, I continued on in a half-numb state. What happiness there was came from simple daily interactions with you—reading to you, watching you wobble and then steady yourself on your feet—and quiet time in the evenings when I could lose myself in a book of poetry and for a moment pretend all was well. I even made it through one whole evening without staring at the faded spot on the rug I had scrubbed until my hands were raw with bleach.

And then I received a startling letter from Nette.

21 November, 1859
My dear Lucy,

I do not know how to put this on paper other than to write the horrible truth of it—we lost our sweet Mabel. Barely six months old and swept away from us so fast it felt like she had been pulled from my arms by a rogue wave on a summer's day. It has taken me weeks to be able to write these words, to fully accept that she is gone. I wish you could have met her, seen her rose-colored cheeks, the perfect pucker of her lips, the great joy she brought with her tiny presence.

I have been wrestling to understand for what crime God chose to punish me. Was it my insistence on preaching as a woman? Or had I left the window by her crib open on too chilly a night? Had I not loved her completely enough? What failure of mine had caused this tragedy? What failure could be equal to such punishment?

I have Samuel to thank for helping to lift the burden of these questions from my soul. I thought he would not understand the depth of my motherly grief, but then I found I could not carry it alone anymore. Only in recognizing my own deep sorrow in his could I start to release the darkness from my heart.

I know now that God had other plans for my sweet angel. She was called back into His safekeeping because she was too good for this world, too bright for our daily chores. It was not my failures, but her grace that called her back to Him.

Thank you for shouldering the burden of telling Harry he has lost a niece and assure him his brother is as well as he can be.

I wish you could be with me to offer your own loving comforts.

I am, as always, your sister,

Nette

Oh, my dear, sweet Nette. Her words broke me wide open. I understood the magnitude of her loss all too well, as I knew she would understand mine. And I was so grateful for those simple words. *It was not my failures, but her grace that called her back to Him.* Could I allow myself to believe that? Had my son died not because of my failures, not because I was dreaming of returning to reform while growing him in my belly, but because he was too good for this world? Because God wanted him back to bring greater light to the beyond?

I walked out of the back door and fell to my knees next to the garden, forgetting that it was too cold to be outside without a coat, not noticing the ice on the ground. My sobs came out in steamy puffs, my chest heaving with the urgency of it. Clutching the letter to my breast, I let the tears fall freely. They were the first I had allowed since that horrible night.

I felt the weight of the blanket on my back before I felt the warmth of it. Harry crouched beside me, his arms wrapped tightly around me, his voice shaken by worry.

"What is it? Is it your mother?" he asked.

I knew no gentler way to tell him the news than with Nette's heartfelt words. I handed him the letter and saw his face droop as he digested the news. His brother, his closest friend, had lost a child. I saw the bruise land on his heart as clearly as if I had pounded it into him myself. But when he looked at me, his eyes held a question. He understood how upsetting their loss would be to me, but he had never seen such emotion pour from me. He knew there had to be something else.

I stood and walked to the back edge of the property, to a pair of young maple trees that gave our yard shade in the summer. I pushed aside frozen leaves to reveal a mound of dirt and the miniature cross I had made to mark the place where I had wrapped our little boy in a white blanket, tucked him inside a tiny pine box, and delivered him back to the earth.

"We were to have a son. He came too early. Stillborn." I could say no more.

Harry pulled me into him and held me close. I wanted to melt into his embrace, to let him warm the frozen shards in my heart that made it hard to breathe. What I felt instead was the ground beneath my stockinged feet turning my body to ice.

"Why didn't you tell me?"

Men never lose what we lose, never endure what we have to endure. How could he ever understand?

"You weren't here." As cruel as I knew those words to be, as much as I recognized the moment as one that could have brought us together, I was trapped inside an impenetrable shell. I pulled away.

"I need to answer Nette's letter," I said, and left him standing in the cold.

Harry watched me carefully after that, wanting to console me but having no idea what might help. He left for New York City most mornings for work at A. O. Moore and came home each evening hoping for a true reconciliation. Knowing some female issues aren't ever questioned by men, I explained that trying to conceive a child within a year of a miscarriage was ill-advised. After that year passed, I told him that at forty-two, I was likely too old to have another healthy baby, but not too old to get with child. I could not risk it, nor did I want to. It was this last part he did not understand.

"There are ways to avoid unwanted outcomes," he said to me one night as I lay down on my side of the bed.

Another winter had come, and his breath puffed white against his pillow. The hot-water bottle at the end of the bed was doing no good.

"It's too cold for Alice to be sleeping alone. I'll get her, so we can warm her up," I said.

"I'll get her," he said, sighing.

But I knew he never minded anything involving you. And Harry could do no wrong in your eyes, then. Your first word was "Papa," and you loved nothing more than story time atop his lap. Unlike the books I had at the ready to read to you, Harry invented stories of his own. Some of them went on for weeks, each night starting at a new "chapter" of his wild tale.

One of your favorites involved a character called the Raspberry Girl; do you remember it? This girl discovered bushes in her garden that sometimes grew raspberries laced with sugar, as if confections fell from the sky like snow. When she ate one of these special fruits, she turned into a tiny fairy and had access to a whole kingdom in the forest too small for human eyes, unless of course you knew where to look. Harry described miniature doors hidden in the knots of trees and secret passageways through the stems of flowers. Every chapter was a new adventure. I marveled at his ability to weave such a tale, and the utter delight it brought you. I wished more than once that I could find a tiny door with a passage into my own heart.

"More, Papa," you would say, now almost four and able to voice what you wanted. "Tell the one about the house inside the acorn."

Seeing you two so happy and comfortable with each other, I announced a decision I had been mulling over for weeks.

"I have been invited to speak with Henry Ward Beecher next month, and I plan to accept. It is only in New York, so I won't be gone more than a night."

"Do you hear that, Alice? Mama is going to lecture again!" he said without a moment's hesitation. An empty well inside me filled with tenderness for him. He always supported me without question. How had I forgotten?

"I think I will title the lecture, 'Women's Rights and Women's Wrongs.'" Yes, it had a wonderful ring to it. "I trust you will be able to stay home with Alice for me?"

I knew he would be disappointed not to come with me, to listen to all the lectures and confer with the attendees afterward, but this part of our marriage we knew how to do.

"Of course. And guess what?" He turned you toward him on his lap. "We get the whole day to play in the gardens and look for ladybugs, and a whole evening to catch fireflies. No chores!"

You clapped your hands with delight, and I did my best to ignore the twinge of envy that threatened to contort my smile into something else. I had no right to feel anything but grateful.

The thought of lecturing again sparked an old urge that spread through me as fast as a match to dry kindling. If this first lecture went well, if I felt my old confidence come back, perhaps I could arrange a string of lectures in New York and Pennsylvania. Maybe we could all travel together and Harry could mind you when I was in meetings or up onstage. I began a mental list of all my favorite venues, all the places I knew would have me back.

"Is there a date for the lecture yet?"

"I believe it will be in mid-March. Sometime after Lincoln's inauguration. Beecher intends to use his speech to apply pressure on him to finally support abolition and not fall prey to the desires of gradualists."

"Any time in March should be fine. I hear they're expecting an extremely healthy harvest of beets in Maine this coming season. I plan to travel north soon to inspect the situation."

It had been years since Harry had contemplated beet sugar production. I had no idea he still thought it a viable business.

"You're leaving again?"

"Obviously I won't go until after your lecture."

As it turned out, we didn't have time to worry about trips to Maine or how I would lecture with Harry away. Anderson surrendered Fort Sumter to Confederate soldiers on April 13. The Civil War had begun.

19

You and I spent much of the war at my sister Sarah's house in Ware, Massachusetts, do you remember? She moved closer to West Brookfield when my mother fell ill, and we took turns nursing her in her final days. Our first visit there was meant to be temporary, but Harry's constant travel and our financial situation left me in no rush to return to New Jersey. We had sold the cottage in Orange for one in Roseville. While it made good sense to dramatically reduce the size of our mortgage, and for Harry to be closer to the city, there was little space there for raising a child. I eventually used what remained of my savings to rent a house in Ware right next to my sister's and enrolled you in school. Sarah's daughters became like sisters to you, especially Emma, and being near my own sister was a comfort I hadn't indulged in years.

My mother left this earth peacefully, like a glorious sunset fading too quickly from the horizon. My father's decline was much less graceful and more difficult to watch. He lost his eyesight, which for an incessant reader is paramount to taking the reins from a horseman. Either Sarah or I needed to be with him at all times in those final months, the other with Sarah's children and you.

One night, after I read to Father several excerpts from the latest issue of *The Liberator*, he fell into a deep and lengthy silence. I thought he'd fallen asleep in his chair, until he suddenly sat up and said, "I was wrong, and you were right."

I was stunned. After taking a moment to digest such uncharacteristic words coming from my father, I wanted to ask him about what exactly he was willing to admit he'd been wrong. But I said nothing. It occurred to me that he might have forgotten who was in the room with him. Or he could have been having some kind of reverie, imagining a conversation on some inconsequential topic. Might he have been articulating some long-overdue apology to my mother? I so badly wanted to believe it had been his intention to speak these words to me, though, that I didn't say anything for fear of ruining the possibility.

It was difficult to think of my parents as gone. My mother, as little as she understood the choices I had made, had always been my emotional and moral center, the warm glow in my life, the one place I could look to be soothed of whatever ailed me. She made motherhood look pleasureful—not the hard work I knew it to be—all while raising seven children to my one. And as much as the responsibilities of the house occupied every moment of her day, she never failed to notice when something irked or upset me, her soft fingers inquiring at my brow, her warm eyes enfolding me with understanding. A daughter is never quite the same without her mother, and I felt the loss deeply, as if the hearth of my life would forever sit empty and cold, no more bright flames to take the chill from the world.

Father was the font head of revolution to my running waters. As much as he didn't agree with my particular cause, it was his insistence on standing up for what is right, even if it meant the defection of friends and criticism of neighbors, that had set my course in life. The loss of both of them left me untethered, as if the hands steadying my kite had suddenly let go, leaving me wobbly.

Just as disorienting, bayonets took the place of intellectual debate and reform work. Most agitating ceased while the sons of the nation fought for its future. I was ready to go back to work, but there was no organizing to be done, not via the post as I had done while trapped in my kitchen in New Jersey, nor was there anywhere to speak. I was rendered as useless as a wrangler with no steed.

I was, however, able to focus my attention fully on you, Alice. Your curiosity and dependable disposition made you a wonderful companion, and our bucolic days and cuddlesome nights filled empty spaces in me. And the distance from Harry suited me. Each day that had passed since I stepped away from speaking had pushed some essential part of me further into the shadows. I found it easier to portray steady moods and a pleasant demeanor in letters.

And then, four long years after the war began, it ended, and I hoped I could find my way back to the person I had once been. I was desperate for it.

"Do they see the folly of this amendment, or are they merely simple in the brain?" Elizabeth asked from her seat at the kitchen table in Ware. Flowers covered every inch of her dress, the yards of fabric hiding the chair beneath her and giving off the impression of a wide rose bush potted in the middle of the room.

Susan set the kettle for tea and sliced the loaves of bread while I poached eggs and mixed bits of ham hock with rosemary and dill from the garden. She and I had become facile cooking partners at her home in Rochester, where you and I had visited her as often as possible during the war, snatching stretches of time to plan for the future. The South winning had been unthinkable, but the prospect of such an outcome dominated every waking moment. And as much as we prayed for a Union victory, it was unclear how we would ever weave the country back into the same cloth, let alone make progress mending its many other deficiencies.

"They must do something to override the Black Codes. The Thirteenth Amendment is meaningless if those laws are allowed to stand." I moved the skillet away from the heat.

"But as soon as negroes are considered citizens, the official population of southern states will increase, giving them the right to more representation," Elizabeth said. "That's just foolish by any standard. That will just mean more southern congressmen who won't give us our due."

"Surely you can't expect freed slaves to continue to be counted as three-fourths of a person," I said.

"Do they have even three quarters of my education?" She slathered marmalade onto a slice of bread.

I had learned not to respond to every shocking comment of Elizabeth's. She tossed them out like a card thrower, only expecting a few to land their mark. It was often easier to ignore them and hope they floated out of sight.

"The real problem," I said, placing the eggs and ham on the table, "is the wording. We have to get the word 'male' out of the amendment. Sweet pea, come to breakfast," I called.

You had been squirreled away with one of Harry's stories all morning, as you often were. As much as we were apart from Harry, he kept you close by sending the beginnings of all those stories that you could add to before mailing them back his way to do the same. We shuttled them back and forth in our letters, some tales stretching to several pages before you or your father would finally pen "the end," with the end of one always leading to the start of another. Back and forth your writing would go.

"Haven't all 'men' always been created equal?" Elizabeth asked with a snort.

"More than equal," Susan said. "But 'men' has always been understood to mean people. 'Male' is a specific designator of sex that has never been in the Constitution before. It means all persons who aren't women. It would set us way back."

"It's used three times in the Fourteenth Amendment. There is no mistaking the purpose," I said.

"Aunt Susan, do you want to read my story?" you asked, handing over a piece of paper with your large loopy writing covering it entirely. We'd been working hard on your penmanship, and I could see that your letters were even and straight.

"Will you read it to me after breakfast? I don't want to get the page dirty at the table."

You nodded and dutifully placed your story on the windowsill, counting the minutes, I was sure, until you could share it.

"You know Sumner best, Lucy. You must convince him to find a different way to draft the amendment."

"He owes us. He said himself that the spark for emancipation began with our petition," Elizabeth said. "History will give Lincoln all the credit now that he's been canonized, but Sumner knows our part in it."

Our biggest achievement during the war was amassing four hundred thousand signatures in support of emancipation, the largest number ever gathered on any issue. Susan worked tirelessly to orchestrate that feat, and it had surely helped to sway Lincoln—he hadn't been fully committed to emancipation until it became a political necessity. His assassination had vaulted him into the pantheon, securing him a leading role in a slightly different legend, but regardless, the right outcome had prevailed.

"I'll get to Sumner." I stood to clear the table. As I turned toward the counter, a rush of heat overtook me as swiftly as if the kitchen stove had spewed its burning embers onto the floor at my feet. I put the plates down and leaned over the sink as sweat pricked every inch of my body. As soon as I could be sure I wouldn't swoon, I turned back to the table.

"Are you having your changes?" Elizabeth asked.

"I think it must be starting. Alice, dear, you may be excused," I said, not wanting you to hear such adult conversation.

"I'll find you later," Susan whispered, and patted you on the back as you hopped down from your chair. "Sit, Lucy, I'll do this." She rose with Elizabeth's dishes in her hands.

"Has everything gone dry?" Elizabeth asked as I dropped back down into my seat.

"Dry? I'm living in a constant pool of humidity even though it's October." I wiped my brow with my napkin.

"Not that. The other. Where my rivers ran deep, I'm now all dried up. The husband plows on as if there's no change, but I might as well be a bucket full of sand."

"Good lord!" Susan said from the sink. "Is this the kind of thing you married ladies spend your time talking about?"

I knew no other lady, married or not, who had such conversation. Not even my sister and I spoke of these things. Besides, Harry and I hadn't been together in that way in a long time. He never forced himself when I wasn't willing, and after the miscarriage I forgot how to open myself to him. I missed the closeness, the intimacy, and sometimes wondered how to go about rediscovering it, but Elizabeth's description of what it might feel like now sounded awful. Did she give herself over to it now merely to please her husband? That seemed out of character. Maybe it was her way of trying to find something she had lost.

"Can we get on with the business at hand?" Susan wiped her hands on a dishrag and rejoined us at the table. "There's much to be done to get our petition for suffrage properly circulated."

"I don't think it should call for universal suffrage," Elizabeth said. "It might be misunderstood that we are primarily calling for suffrage regardless of *race*. But if colored men win the vote before we do, there will be that many more men able to stop us from getting the vote. This petition needs to call for suffrage regardless of *sex*. We must make ourselves clear."

"The Constitution should be repaired once and for all, not in bits," I said. "It only makes sense to join forces and demand the vote for all citizens, regardless of race or sex, black and white, women and men, all of us."

"But surely you see the progression of things, Lucy," Susan said. "If the Fourteenth Amendment does pass with the word 'male' in it, giving rights of citizenship to black men, it designates women as less than full citizens more clearly than ever before. The next logical step could be the suggestion of giving black men the vote before it is given to us. I agree with Elizabeth. We need to use this petition to get ahead of that possibility and specify that we demand the vote for women, alongside all other citizens."

"But the time for sweeping change is now." I was sure of it.

"Let's be sensible about this. If the currents are strong toward universal suffrage, then by all means we position ourselves to catch the momentum," Elizabeth said, leaning on the table such that it tipped slightly in her direction. "But if the current goes the other way, let us not forget that we sit in different boats."

I wondered if that was how she saw the waterway of progress, black boats and white boats floating toward the same future, but separately. Were there male boats and female boats, rich boats and poor boats? Did one set of boats have the privilege of taking the lead with an unencumbered view, while the rest of the rowers saw only the backs of their countrymen? How far was she willing to take that idea?

Mrs. Stanton and I often disagreed on such things, likely due to our different backgrounds, she of a privileged home with easy access to books and schooling. The thing we shared in common was having fathers who could see us as nothing but inferior beings. Elizabeth would have made an exceptional barrister, or even a judge had such an avenue been available to her. Her articles and essays were all written with the supporting evidence and airtight logic of Supreme Court opinions. Those willing to concede that genius was possible in a woman lauded her as one of the best minds of our generation. And those who would never entertain such outlandish ideas did sometimes find themselves complimenting an impressive article, having no idea that the E. C. Stanton who had authored it was indeed a woman. Despite all of this, her father took exception to everything she published. Even though he was a barrister himself and must have appreciated the logic of her arguments, he could not bring himself to see her as anything but a woman stepping far outside her appropriate sphere. He told her once that he was ashamed to call her daughter. They hadn't spoken since. Being cut loose from her father's mooring gave her a certain freedom of thought, but I also understood the heartbreak that comes along with that.

"We are in agreement, then. This petition will speak to women's suffrage," Susan said, before I was at all sure we had agreed on anything.

It was critical to get this right. Our call to action would be signed by the three of us and circulated to thousands of reformers, asking for their support before being presented to Congress.

"Let me talk to Charles Sumner," I countered. "Let me try to convince him to remove the word 'male' from his amendment. I think showing him that we are prepared to circulate a petition calling for universal suffrage gives us a stronger case and may give him some leverage with his colleagues."

Susan and Elizabeth looked at each other across the table. Coming to a decision with them was always a bit like talking to a creature with two bodies and one head. They were of different stock, had different hearts, and would wrestle a topic with their separate arms, but they always spoke from one mouth, with one voice in the end.

"All right. See what you can do. But either way, we must begin our campaign before the year is out," Susan said.

I traveled all the way to Washington, D.C., to have Charles Sumner tell me, in the politest of ways, that he could not find a way to clearly construct the Fourteenth Amendment without the word "male."

His barrister's desk divided the room in half, the brass lantern atop it more finely wrought than anything in my own home, the rug at my feet obviously imported from the Orient. I thought I knew this man. I couldn't believe he was willing to allow the consequences of what he was proposing. The intent of the Fourteenth Amendment was to expand the title of "citizen," with all the rights conferred by that term, beyond white men. If it passed as currently written, only black men and no women would be considered full citizens.

"I have rewritten it at least twelve times. There is no way to keep the meaning clear without it."

"There are many other ways to write it, unless your main purpose is to specifically exclude women. It's not what I would have expected from you."

"My purpose is to author it so that it will be ratified, Lucy. I'm sorry."

"Not nearly as sorry as I am, Charles," I said, and left his office.

As I rode down Constitution Avenue on the way back to my hotel, the crane that sat atop the Capitol building cast a long, thin shadow over the road. The old dome had been removed to make way for what was promised to be a grander one, more fitting for the importance of such a public structure. I wondered who would be protected under the impressive new dome. Would the building represent all, or was the reconstruction of our nation just for show?

Even without winning the fight on the Fourteenth Amendment, I was not willing to give up on the idea of universal suffrage. I had learned reform at the feet of my abolitionist friends, and our causes were entwined. Fighting together was still our best course.

I arrived back in Ware to find you so engrossed in a game of skipping rope with your cousins that you didn't notice me until I tickled you from behind and lifted you off your feet. I'd only been gone two weeks, but you seemed to have grown an inch in my absence. I wondered what other, less visible changes I had missed.

Walking through the woods from Sarah's house back to ours, you told me about your adventures—building a fort made of leaves with Susie, drawing farm animals with Emma, and learning to make a bracelet from pebbles and string. Any worrying I had done about you while I was away was clearly for naught.

The butternut squash and the last of the red apples hadn't faired quite as well in my absence and were pushing past their prime. We would have to harvest what we could as quickly as possible and spend the better part of the next week peeling, chopping, cooking, and canning.

The postbox was full, with a letter from Harry on top. I was anxious for positive news. He had sounded confident in his last letter that he would soon be able to sell some of the western land he had bought in my name. I intended to use the profits to finally buy a proper home near Boston. I had no desire or reason to return to New Jersey and the idea of being close to my colleagues and participating in daily reform activities again boosted my spirits like nothing else.

"Is there a story for me?" you asked as soon as you saw the envelope in my hands.

As soon as I found the page addressed to "My Alicekins," you snapped it up like a baby bird squawking for food.

I sat at the table to read the letter intended for me.

7 October, 1865
Dear Lucykins,

Good news! I have finally sold several tracts of land at a healthy profit. There were enough proceeds to settle the debt on the remaining holdings, cover the losses on the lands with title troubles, and to pay back your original investment. I am pleased, though, to tell you that having been one of the first in this area, I was given first rights on several new plots, which I'm certain will increase in value even more than the last. As there was no time to consult with you by post, I'm sure you will agree with my decision to invest your proceeds back into this new area. Without your signature on hand the land had to be bought in my name. But do not worry. When these parcels sell at some future date, I will put all profits in bonds in the name of Lucy Stone, to whom they rightfully belong.

I plan to leave within the week and should be at the house in Ware by the week of November third to collect you and our little cub so that we may return together to New Jersey.

As ever, your loving husband,
Harry

I balled both my hands into fists, the letter in one of them, and closed my eyes. I tried to keep my breath steady but knew that tapping on my thighs, on the side of the chair, even banging on the table, would not satisfy the level of rage I felt pulsing through me. He had taken my assets, which represented a huge portion of my earnings, and put them in his name? With that one decision I suddenly had no claim to those investments at all. He had taken away the very thing I had been working for my whole life with one stroke of his pen, without even asking me. Harry knew this as well as I did, and yet he had chosen to do it anyway.

The furor crashed through my head like a raging waterfall, the noise of it so loud you had to call my name three times before I heard your small voice and opened my eyes.

"Mama, can you teach me to ride Sally?" you asked.

"We don't ride cows, Alice. We milk them."

"But Papa's new story is about a cowgirl who rides with brass stirrups and a snakeskin whip. She 'lassoes clouds to find secret messages hidden in the puffy parts,'" you said, reading that line from the page. "He said I could be a cowgirl too, if I wanted. What's a lasso?"

"Cowgirls ride horses."

"Not in Papa's story. She rides a cow named Spots."

"Papa isn't always right," I snapped, and regretted my tone when I saw you flinch. "I'm sorry, sweet pea. We'll talk about your story later. Now please go and fetch all the good apples off the ground before they spoil. Mama has work to do."

"Yes, Mama." You curled in on yourself as you shuffled outside.

I took a sheet of paper from the credenza by the hearth, intending to write back a scathing note, when I realized that Harry must already be on his way. The third of November had he said? I looked at my datebook. It was the fifth of November. He was due home any day now. I reflexively looked around the house. Every surface was covered in dust. I had no fresh food on hand save what little I could pull from the garden and had yet to pick up a new block of ice, so there was no meat. Eggs needed to be gathered and cream and bread made. You and I could live on oatmeal, syrup, and apples for a few days, but even Harry would expect better than that. The thought brought a new wave of anger. I had spent a lifetime ensuring I would never be judged by such things. And yet, in my rage, I wanted to prove I was capable of doing it all.

By the time Harry did finally arrive, you and I had managed to make apple crumble, put up preserves and compote, and stew a batch of potato and squash soup. My travel clothes snapped on the line in the brisk November breeze, and I had scrubbed and refilled the icebox with ham hocks and bacon. Somehow none of this improved my outlook.

After he twirled you in the air and smothered you with kisses, he put you back on your feet and held his arms open to me. I offered my cheek for a kiss and went back to the counter to peel and cut a pile of sweet potatoes. I watched from the corner of my eye as he presented you with a tiny telescope he'd found Chicago, which he said would help you look for deer and birds and magic clouds. With a squeal of delight, you ran outside to test your new prize. I couldn't help but wonder whose money he had used for such an extravagant item.

He sat at the kitchen table and watched me peel potatoes for a minute. I had hoped we might start fresh when he returned, but now I could not make myself look up and smile. The anger still pulsing through me made my hands shake.

"Did things not go well in Washington?" he asked tentatively.

"No, they did not. Are you hungry? Would you like tea and a biscuit?" I asked, already putting the kettle on the flame.

"Sumner should know better. What did he say?"

"It doesn't matter now. It's done."

As I dug into a sweet potato, trying to remove a dark eye from the surface, my hand slipped, and the blade sliced my palm. I dropped the knife and sucked in my breath.

"Are you hurt?" He jumped up and came to my side with a dishrag, ready to press it against the wound. I turned to the sink and tilted a bucket of water over my hand, a small stream of blood running through my fingers. The water stung, but I could see the cut was only superficial. I took the cloth from him, wrapped it around my hand tightly, and held it in place.

"Come sit down, Lucy."

My hand throbbed, bringing my anger closer to the surface.

"How could you, Harry? That was my property, and you put it in your own name."

"It's only temporary. As soon as it sells, I will transfer the money back to you." He said this as if it was a simple matter of fact, as inconsequential as borrowing someone's trowel for an afternoon of digging in the garden. "It's a fantastic opportunity. You'll be pleased with the results, I'm sure."

"Transfer back to me. Because it is now yours. This is not how we agreed to handle our affairs. And you speak like it's a predetermined success. What if you can't sell the land? You had no right."

"Do you not trust my judgment in such things? Have I not proven my abilities in this area?" he asked in a cajoling manner, as if I was questioning his ability to drive a horse and buggy.

I stopped myself from responding to that, from pointing out that he had only sold perhaps one-tenth of the lands he had purchased. Another 10 percent had gotten held up in title disputes or reclaimed altogether. The recent sale was promising, but we were by no means financially free of the shackles of real estate he had fastened around us. And I had plans for that money.

"You don't trust me to put the funds back in your name?" His voice was laced with something that sounded close to an accusation. I had touched a nerve.

"You know this is not about the money," I said.

"Isn't it?"

You burst through the door.

"Papa, I think I saw a woodpecker. Come see!"

He held my gaze for a moment, his brow hunched over his eyes, and then followed you outside.

❧

We had little choice but to move back to Roseville, my rent money having run dry. While leaving Sarah pained me, at least in New Jersey Harry's mother and his sisters were in close proximity. They had all offered to care for you whenever needed so I could get back to work.

When Harry announced he wanted to investigate beet crops again—in Ohio this time—I barely noticed. Susan, Elizabeth, and I had launched a tour of the entire Eastern Seaboard to promote the newly formed American Equal Rights Association, or AERA. I had convinced them that our best course was to officially join forces with the abolitionists. Our sole mission was universal suffrage, our singular message that it was time for the reconstructed republic to grant the vote to all its citizens regardless of race or sex. The three of us finalized and circulated our petition demanding universal suffrage and set off on a campaign to see it through.

Every mile, every speech, increased my confidence and energy, the old words coming back faster to me than I had even hoped. It was a thrill to be back in motion and fighting for the future. While it was difficult to be apart from you for so long—I missed your little giggle, combing your soft hair, hearing your stories at the end of each school day—I felt certain this was the moment when change would come, and I could not miss the opportunity to capture every mind, turn every opinion our way. And we used every means at our disposal.

One night, our southbound train from Albany got caught in a blizzard, stranded mid-stride. With no choice but to wait it out until the tracks were cleared, Susan, Elizabeth, and I decided to take advantage of our captive audience and convert every person to our cause.

"You take the front compartment, Lucy. Elizabeth, you go to the caboose, and I'll take the center. This way anyone who wants to escape one of us will find themselves walking into another one!"

We talked until our breath was frozen, the passengers practically waving white flags of concession.

❦

The longest separation from you came when I decided to aid the campaign in Kansas to promote state voting rights for negroes and women. As one of the newest territories, Kansas was wrestling with all the most important laws that would govern the land. We hoped such a new state might be more open to progressive ideas than states where a different set of rules was already ingrained.

I was tentatively optimistic when Harry decided to accompany me. We had not worked a speaking circuit together since I had visited his hometown, and not since he had done some lecturing of his own. His endless pursuit of financial gain was the villain that continually separated us, and I hoped this might be a sign. Perhaps he would finally prioritize reform over business success. I even dared to hope working together would bring us close again, like old times.

Harry's mother, Hannah, graciously offered to care for you while we were gone. Saying good-bye to you for what would likely be a three-month trip felt like cutting out part of my own flesh with a dull knife.

"We'll be back before you even notice we're gone," I said, trying hard to hold back the tears pushing behind my eyes.

"Write some stories for me," Harry said.

"I will, Papa," you said, with something close to excitement in your eyes before hugging us both and running off to play with the rabbits Grandma Hannah kept in her barn.

I wrote you as often as time and materials allowed.

4 June, 1868
Wichita, Kansas
Dear Alice,

I know you are only ten years old, my sweet pea, but I think it important for you to know the work that has taken us away from you these months. I was not much older than you when the greater world began to come into focus for me, and Papa and I know you are old enough to understand the concepts and ideas we are working for. Please read this aloud to Grandma Hannah if you like so you can ask her about anything puzzling to you.

First of all, Kansas is an incredible land. While travel here is difficult—there are often no proper roads and our horses need to pick their way through fields full of grass and plants taller than Papa—every stream we cross, every mountain we climb, every prairie we gaze upon is more beautiful than the last. We stay mostly in the log cabins of gracious citizens or in tents that we have gotten very good at assembling and disassembling as we go. It would be quite a rough trip for you, but I hope one day to bring you here to experience what it is like to be in newly discovered territory, with people trying to create their society almost from a set of raw ingredients.

We have met many people who are grateful we have come and who believe this new state is ready to do what the rest of our country has not yet had the courage to do. Because they have never had slaves, we hope they might be more open to giving negroes the vote, and there is a contingent who feels equally strongly about enfranchising women. Colonel Wood, a war hero and senator here, greeted us by saying, "With God and Lucy Stone on our side, we shall carry Kansas!" Of course, now that he has met your father, he is delighted to have him here fighting beside us. Others are not as interested in granting the vote to freed slaves or women. We never know which kind of people we will find.

Papa and I spoke today on the steps of a church and next to a field ripe with corn, and yesterday in a courthouse that hasn't yet had its roof secured in place. Just like when I lectured on abolition and women's rights before the war, we are sometimes greeted with more than a little bit of fear and anger. I do not tell you this to worry you, but so you will understand that this work is not easy, and it is when the conditions are difficult that the work is all the more urgent. Never fail to stand up for what you believe, Alice, even if you are afraid there may be dire consequences. It is only the consequences of our silence that are impossible to live with.

Grandma tells me you are a great help with the washing and cooking, and that you are working on a sampler with diligence. I am proud of you and look forward to seeing it when we return. Make sure you always ask how you can help before you do anything for yourself, no matter how nice the weather or how much you are enjoying your current book. I expect a lot of you, sweet pea, but I know you are equal to the challenge.

We miss you with more love than I have ink in my pen to express.

Enclosed is a poem from Papa. He asks for one in return.

With all our love,

Mama and Papa

One thing I chose not to tell you about in my letters home were the accusations regularly hurled at Harry and me that we were proponents of "free love." It had long been an exaggerated stance that women who wanted rights for themselves, and any men who supported them, were somehow advocating intimate relations outside of marriage, as if it was the logical next step. The whole idea was preposterous, and almost too shocking to dignify with a response.

"I don't believe you're even married!" I remember a man shouting from a crowd on Main Street in Wichita. Finding that the town hall we had secured for a lecture was otherwise occupied with a cattle auction, Harry borrowed the local fire wagon to use as our platform, pulled it up in front of the building, and lifted me aboard. The crowds gathered, if only to see who was bold enough to put a fire truck into service when there were no flames to be found.

"Your flyer says Lucy Stone and Henry Blackwell, and yet you call her your wife? Sounds to me like you don't know how to keep your own woman in line," one man called. He was small but wiry like a wild dog, hungry and angry in equal parts. I had a feeling he won most fights he started because he was quick enough to avoid real trouble.

"Maybe they just say they're married so they can love each other up!" another man shouted from the back of the crowd. He leaned against a hitching post, a bottle of brown liquid in his hand, his fingernails dark with dirt. "Is this how you want all your daughters to end up? Lovin' any man who comes through town? Next they'll be lovin' niggers."

"I assure you we are lawfully wed, by a man of the—" Harry's words were run over by several men in succession.

"Tell me, missy," a man said from the front row, looking up at me, "do you ride him like a mustang, or is it the other way around?"

"Gentlemen," Harry started, moving to my side.

"Or maybe we have it all wrong," the wiry one said. "A sissy like you following her around and speaking up for women? Maybe she don't use your name 'cause you don't bed her at all!"

Heat rushed up my chest. Having our intimate relations, or lack thereof, scrutinized in public was too embarrassing to take. Sleeping in tents and in the backs of wagons throughout Kansas hadn't been conducive to the marriage act, but even I couldn't put it all down to that. The searing glare of these men made it feel like an indictment of Harry's masculinity. It forced into stark relief that a close examination of our marriage might find it to be wanting. How much of that was my failure to live up to the expectations of a proper wife?

"Sir, if you please." Harry raised his voice over the chatter rippling through the crowd and addressed the wiry one. "Would you mind telling me precisely what actions occupied your wife this morning between ten and ten thirty?"

"I work for a living, mister. I don't know about you, but I don't have time to follow my wife around all day," he said, and nodded in response to a ripple of chuckles in the crowd.

"I see. And how did she know what to do if you weren't there to instruct her?"

"What are you saying, man? My wife knows how to run the house." His muscles flexed as if itching to be put to use.

"Indeed," Harry said. "Our wives are entirely capable without us. They do not need their husbands to tell them what to do or how to think. They should be fully represented."

"We represent them!" came a call from the center of the group.

"I highly doubt that," I said, keeping my voice as calm as possible. "And for the gentlemen in the crowd—I'm sure there must be at least some of you here. Who would you rather send to the voting booth: these unruly men, or your good wives?"

In the moment of silence that followed my question, we knew it was time to cut our losses.

"We thought so," Harry said. "Thank you for your time."

By August, twelve weeks of constant travel with as many as three lectures a day left our bodies and our bank account depleted. The money designated for the campaign was spent on printing thousands of tracts we distributed to anyone interested in learning more about the case for suffrage. Harry and I paid all travel expenses out of our own meager savings, $132 in all. What little money the AERA had raised we knew would be needed by Susan and Elizabeth when they came to Kansas to continue the campaign. Susan had no money to speak of, and Mr. Stanton had no interest in giving his wife any of his fortune for such an adventure. But we were ready to hand the campaign over to their trusted hands and diligently conserved funds to that end.

Watching the valleys of Kansas disappear as our train headed east, exhaustion filled me like dough rising in a bowl too small to contain its changing shape. I was looking forward to the normalcy of being home again. I had no idea how difficult home was about to become.

20

Despite my hopes to the contrary, Harry viewed his time in Kansas as a short hiatus from commercial endeavors rather than the start of a new set of priorities, and our time sleeping in wagons and pop-up tents had done nothing to increase the intimacy between us. You had faired incredibly well while we were away, as if my prophecy that you would barely notice our absence had come true, which left me feeling both relieved and less and less sure where I fit in. Harry's schedule and my continued responsibilities keeping the house running made committing to my previous levels of reform work difficult, while your increased independence meant you didn't always need me when I was home. My feet were planted on opposite sides of a riverbed, and I was stuck in between, with little to do but watch life rush past.

"Please come," Harry said one afternoon as he watched me scrub a petticoat on the washboard. "Everyone wants to see you and hear about Kansas. It's half a story without you."

We'd been home for almost a month, and I had yet to accompany him to one of his business dinners, which suddenly seemed to occupy almost every night of the week. I had no interest in uninteresting conversation.

"By 'everyone,' you mean a host of people I have never met. And you won't miss a step without me." I hoped he might leave before you came home from school that day so I would have some time to myself to catch up on correspondence. "Besides, I promised Alice sweet bread in the morning."

"Emily can watch Alice while we're at dinner, and we can all stay there. You know she loves my mother's sweet bread."

I felt the sting of that, even though I knew he was trying to be helpful.

"I don't want to stay at your sister's. And I'm sure Alice has had enough of it too." I slapped the dough into a smattering of flour. I could only count on so much goodwill from his sister and mother, who now lived together, and would prefer to take advantage of their kind offers to watch you for something worthy of the favor.

"Alice loved her time there, and my mother was incredibly generous to mind her as much as she did." His words prickled with annoyance. "And you have met Abby Patton once before. You would really enjoy her, and she is looking forward to seeing you again."

"I'm sure there will be ample opportunity. This is already the fifth time this month you have dined with them."

Ludlow Patton was a financier who had invested in some of Harry's original land deals and happened to have married Abby Hutchinson, the youngest of the singers I had shared the stage with more than fifteen years earlier. Just the thought of how young I was back then made my arms feel heavy.

"Working with him will be worth it. He's going to have another client there tonight who might be looking for land out West. If we can sell our holdings, it would solve everything."

"What exactly are you trying to solve?" I asked, almost daring him to put voice to the gulf between us. Or perhaps I was testing him. Did he even perceive a growing divide?

In Kansas I had dared to hope he was done with all his lofty plans for riches and business success. As much as I wanted the real estate to sell so I could regain my rightful earnings, I was increasingly concerned that he was stuck in one of his own stories and would never grow up.

"Next time, then," Harry said.

Only after he left did I realize he hadn't answered my question.

❧

I sent you off to read in your room right after dinner. I had neglected my mail for days and had a stack of unread newspapers sitting by the hearth. I turned up the oil lamp and opened a letter from Susan.

2 October, 1868
Topeka, Kansas
Dear Lucy,

Things here are worse than you described, or perhaps they have simply moved in the wrong direction since your departure. Any early groundswell in favor of the women's vote has nearly disappeared. It was apparent from the moment we arrived that the ballot item for the black vote has significantly more support. The state Republican Party is squarely behind it while being silent on women's suffrage. Your visit seems to have catalyzed an anti-women's movement which has gotten stronger by the day. Accordingly, Elizabeth and I have turned our attention solely to the question of women's suffrage.

Unfortunately, the funds you advanced to cover initial expenses have been depleted. I enclose an accounting of our expenditures since then, totaling $185. Please forward when you can. Luckily, we have found a new friend of our cause and are not abandoning the campaign while we await further funds.

Please write to all champions of women's suffrage you encountered while traveling this summer. We will need every vote!

Your friend,
Susan

I let the letter fall to my lap, dumbfounded. The original $250 I had advanced them was meant to cover the entirety of their campaign. And they had spent an additional $185? It was an outrageous amount under any circumstances, but the fact that they were neglecting the issue of negro suffrage made it all the more untenable. The AERA funds had been donated to further universal suffrage and nothing short of that mission. In my role on the executive committee of the AERA, I handled the finances and now felt complicit in a miscarriage of responsibility.

After an initial flare of rage reduced to a manageable simmer, I wondered if I was overreacting. Harry and I had written the instructions for their campaign together. Were they unclear? Where was he when I needed him? Having no choice but to wait until the next morning to speak with him, I opened the next letter, this one from Wendell Phillips.

4 October, 1868
Dear Lucy,

I am quite disturbed by what I am hearing from Kansas, to say the least. It seems that Miss Anthony and Mrs. Stanton have begun to share the lecture platform with a certain George Francis Train, I'm sure you know the one. If Garrison's editorial in The Liberator isn't enough to horrify, a Topeka paper lately reported that these three are drawing huge crowds, in no small part because they love to see what the dandy will wear next and they loudly cheer him on. Mrs. Stanton is seen to laugh right alongside him.

This is entirely unfitting for the AERA, or any friend of either cause.

Please talk some sense into your friends. They must cease association with this horrible creature at once.

Yours in spirit and friendship,
W. Phillips

I sorted through several issues of *The Liberator* until I found the editorial Phillips had referenced. Garrison called Train a "ranting egoist, crack-brained, and a semi-lunatic." My heart went cold when I read the next paragraph. According to Garrison, Train was widely known as an open and raving racist who had been against abolition from the start. He regularly "joked" that all coloreds were as dumb as a village idiot and how many of those did we want at the ballot? There was also a snippet from a speech Train had given to introduce Susan, describing her, to much laughter from the audience, as previously "four-fifths negro and one-fifth woman, but now is four-fifths woman and only one-fifth negro," a reference to her recent deprioritization of negro suffrage. He went on to praise her for this change because "if you spend too long with a nigger, you won't be able to smell anything else." Susan apparently said nothing in protest and thanked him for his introduction.

I could not fathom how this account could be true and almost hoped I was having an episode of delusion. But I knew in my core something dreadful had happened, and it momentarily robbed me of my ability to breathe, of my confidence in the future. How could Susan be party to this?

I don't know how long into the night I sat there. I could find no excuse or explanation capable of reversing the bitter poison of words I had been served, and I knew that once I swallowed, it would destroy something in my heart.

My despair only deepened come January. Susan and Elizabeth continued their tour with Train and brought their spectacle to the East Coast. Harry came home one evening with a newspaper and such a disgusted expression on his face that I almost turned away from the paper he held out to me. My first thought was that Garrison or Phillips had taken ill. Or maybe President Johnson had spoken firmly against universal suffrage.

When I glanced down, though, I saw a masthead I didn't recognize. *The Revolution*, it was called. And then I understood. Its editors were Susan B. Anthony and Elizabeth Cady Stanton, and its publisher was George Francis Train. An editorial by Stanton sat beside an offensive political ad for Train. The paper tagged itself "The National Organ for a New America," and supported "Educated Suffrage." This was the argument Elizabeth had started to form in Ware, a direct attack on allowing negroes to vote, as very few coloreds were allowed an education of any sort. They would not consider the negro vote unless women could vote first. White women.

I could no longer hope Susan and Train's relationship would peter out before the next audience gathered. It was now in print, for all to see, written in ink for all time. I had to do something.

"Starting a women's paper was your idea," Harry said.

"That's the least of the problem."

"Don't worry. It can't last. They'll be crucified."

"Do you honestly think that's what I want? Susan is the most powerful reformer I know. She is a force all her own. I don't want her crucified. I want her fighting on the right side of things. I want her back!"

Harry leaned away from me, as if avoiding a blow. I didn't realize I'd been yelling until the silence that followed rang in my ears.

21

The downward spiral of my moods after Susan and Elizabeth launched *The Revolution* defied explanation, or perhaps I am simply not the one to offer adequate description. The entire winter was a blizzard of emotion, and even crisp, clear days didn't cheer me. I lived in a kind of foggy state, battling a weather system that seemed to affect only me.

I cannot say with certainty who else could see the haze engulfing me. Fortunately for you, Alice, the font of fun in our house had not dried up, as your father was a continual source of mischief and imagination. You looked to me for the rules and for guidance on how to be a lady without being a supplicant, how to be a diligent student while maintaining a mind of your own. You didn't question my suggestions, I'm sure intuitively understanding it would be unwise to do so. Your confidence in my consistency helped me provide it, like a trellis that helps an unruly vine maintain proper form.

I'll never forget the day you came home from school distraught because a boy in your class said there was no reason for you to learn math, that girls didn't need arithmetic to make babies—do you remember?

I asked you how you'd replied.

"I told him he wouldn't be so bad at math if his mother had learned trigonometry like mine," you said, your eyes wide.

I remember suppressing a laugh and speaking to you sternly, telling you that what you had said was unkind.

"I know," you said, your pout starting to tremble. "But I didn't know what else to say."

I told you, "You will find that you are going to be better than boys at a lot of things in your life, and some of them won't like you because of it. But remember, while you have every right to excel in any subject or interest of your choosing, it will get you nowhere if you make others feel inferior."

You really did need to learn to watch yourself, but I indulged you then by suggesting you do some extra math while I prepared dinner.

❧

Relying again on Harry's sister and mother when I needed them, and despite the lethargy dogging me, I managed during this time to lobby for constitutional change at several state legislatures and deliver speeches I was told afterward had been compelling, even though I could barely recall them the next day. I accomplished this the way I imagine someone gone blind must navigate familiar rooms by trusting that the furniture has not been moved. Julia Ward Howe, the author of "The Battle Hymn of the Republic," found me after one particular lecture in Boston and simply said, "I am with you." I did not know to what I might ascribe having convinced such a bright literary light to join our cause but accepted her support with the silent gratitude of having made it across another great expanse without knocking something over.

Despite the extent to which I was able to overcome my dark moods in service of motherhood and the cause, however, I was utterly unable to do so for the benefit of my marriage. Like a child who struggles to be good in school all day and comes home only to throw a tantrum over nothing, I was dreadfully short with Harry. After speaking engagements were satisfied and organizational meetings complete, after your schoolwork was put away and you went off to read by lamp light, I could find no kind or cheerful word to say, no matter how hard I tried. And sometimes I didn't try at all.

"What is it?" he asked one night, kneeling in front of me with his hands on mine. "You are not the wife I know."

"Then perhaps you need a different wife."

By the time the sting of what I'd said pulled a small drop from my heart in the form of a tear, he'd already stood and walked away.

Looking back, I can see now the slow unraveling of the thread that had bound us together. Harry at first attempted to reason with me, then tried to cheer me, and finally found ways to be out of the house when I was in it. When I traveled to Boston or gave lectures in New York, he could always arrange to be home. But when I was home, he suddenly had unavoidable business dinners or other matters to attend to that kept him from coming home until late, or sometimes not at all. Over the course of the next year, we drifted past each other, sharing the responsibilities of parenthood, but little else.

One night was particularly dreadful. We were both at home for dinner for once, an unexpected and sullen affair that required me to carefully split two portions of pork and squash onto three plates.

After I washed up the dishes and you were sent off to finish your schoolwork, Harry and I settled beside the hearth as we used to, but he held no book in his hands, a sure sign he intended a discussion. I busied myself with reinforcing several buttons on a winter coat and waited.

"My association with Ludlow Patton will soon yield positive results, I am sure of it," Harry said. "His contacts are true prospects for the land out West."

I had heard this so many times I didn't respond.

"I will not lose focus on that. But I have some other ideas. There is talk of bringing the Dominican Republic into the fold as a territory, eventually a state. He thinks my skills would be well suited to diplomatic endeavors there."

"While being his real estate lackey there too, no doubt?"

"A lackey? How do you say such a thing?"

"Oh, Harry, you have been at his heels like a puppy for years."

"In an effort to support this family."

"Has it ever occurred to you that your efforts of support do more harm than good? I made more money every year on the lecture circuit than you have made in the last three, while managing to squander most of my earnings in the process."

I had never allowed myself to speak such things out loud but found it difficult to stop.

"And now you want to go away again? Far away?" I said, my voice rising. "The support you promised was to me, to your wife, to the cause of elevating women. Where has that gone?"

I tugged hard on the needle in my hands, choking the button with thread.

"I told you I would need to secure my own business success before I could devote myself to that life entirely." He spoke quietly, but there was a tinge of anger in his voice I had rarely heard.

"And when will that be, Harry? After I am too old to step onto a stage?"

He sat back in his chair, his jaw flexing, the hurt evident on his face even in the dim light of the fire.

"Must you always assume that your needs, your work, is more important than mine?" he asked, and left the room before I knew how to respond.

We didn't speak another word to each other for days.

❧

When spring finally came, it brought with it an opportunity for me to banish the cold from the house. The first sign of coming warmth was the tender leaves poking through bare branches of the dogwood trees. Then, almost all at once, thousands of pink and white flowers popped through waxen green, their soft petals flung open to sunshine and bees.

My foul moods dissolved as the dogwoods bloomed, and I began to wake with a renewed sense of excitement about the day ahead. I doubted the staying power of this enthusiasm at first, worried it might shrivel like the morning glory that shuts tight at the end of every day. But to my intense relief, it seemed to be lasting. By the time the wildflowers stood tall across our lawn and the first tomato plants began to offer fruit, my interest in all things had safely returned to me, and I felt confident my blues were finally gone.

I put a great deal of my reclaimed energy toward organizing the upcoming AERA convention, a critical convening to debate the Fifteenth Amendment, which proposed giving the vote to colored men. While the AERA had been founded with the mission of universal suffrage, the Fifteenth Amendment as currently written left women out. A united stance on the amendment was important, and I was deeply conflicted. I worried that casting aside women's suffrage now might leave us dangerously far behind, like so much dust flung behind the wheel of a wagon. But if the dual causes proved too heavy to carry across the victory line together, should both be stymied?

I also tried to be more attentive to Harry and began to see how much you relied on your father, how much you counted on him beyond his fun and imagination, as precious as both of those were to you. Your ongoing creation of joint stories and poems had evolved into a way to discuss anything troubling your adolescent mind. I remember one example in particular.

"How are 'The Three Cats' coming along?" Harry asked you one evening as we all sat by the fire, he and I reading, you writing in your journal.

You shrugged. "Tiger is in a bind. Boots and Betsy don't want to do anything anymore except prance and preen to get the attention of the local tomcats, and Tiger has to decide if she pretends to care about that just to be with her friends, or if she spends her afternoons alone."

I pretended to keep reading but listened carefully, my heart aching for you.

"That is a difficult bind. What will Tiger do?"

"She wants to scratch their eyes out."

Harry smiled. "Tiger's the best bird catcher in town, right? I bet if she sticks to that, it won't be long before Boots and Betsy get bored of their preening and ask her to take them on a hunt again."

"And if they don't?"

"Come here," he said. As gangly as you were, you still managed to curl yourself onto his lap when invited.

"There's no need for you to ever do anything you don't want to do. Sometimes interests change, and that can feel lonely, but anyone would be lucky to count you as a friend. Rose and Kitty will come around, you'll see."

"Do you really think so?" You laid your head on his shoulder.

Affection for Harry spread through me like warm honey. He was a good and steady man, such a wonderful father. Why had I allowed bitterness to creep into our marriage? Why had I turned so far inward instead of reaching out to him for support? My ill temper had created a gulf between us that sometimes felt impossible to cross. I missed our previous intimacy, our shared bed, our loving moments. I wanted nothing more than to build the bridge back between us. I needed to offer him some kind of olive branch, show him I still wanted to be his wife, in every sense of the word. I just hoped it wasn't too late.

"You mentioned dinner with the Pattons on Friday night?" I asked Harry the next morning. He'd taken to reading the newspaper at the breakfast table, a substitute for conversation I had appreciated through the long winter.

"Yes. I plan to stay with Mother. Perhaps through the weekend."

"I thought I would come with you. Your mother hasn't seen Alice since the New Year."

"She would like that. I can bring her."

"I meant that I could join you for dinner."

"No need. They're not expecting you." He talked into the printed pages he held up between us.

I had declined so many invitations to accompany Harry anywhere, he'd stopped asking.

"The Pattons have been good friends to you. I'd like for them to know it is appreciated." It didn't quite sound like the apology I had intended, but it was a start.

He put down his paper and looked across the table at me, as if confirming who was speaking to him.

"Very well," he said. "I will let them know."

❧

As our horse car clopped up to the Astor House in New York, a multitude of gas lamps threw their golden light onto the stone wall of the hotel, changing the color of the sky above. Men and women in top hats and gowns alighted from their carriages with the help of gloved valets and ascended the stairs to the grand entrance as naturally as I imagined them crossing their own thresholds.

I glanced at Harry and noted how comfortable he looked in his tails. I was wearing the same black silk dress and white collar I had donned for countless meals at the Garrisons' house in Boston, but now I worried if my simple outfit would stand out as peculiar in this gilded world of New York. I pinched my cheeks to bring some color to my face. The important thing was to appear cheerful and friendly.

While I understood that all tensions between Harry and me were unlikely to be erased in one night, I had high hopes this might mark a renewal of our partnership. I was here to support his business dealings, as he always had mine. I knew he would be a great help to me before and during the upcoming AERA convention, and the least I could do was ingratiate myself to his colleagues and potential clients.

"Good evening, Mr. Blackwell," the doorman said as he opened the door of the carriage.

I took Harry's arm as he led me up the stairs and into the lobby, an oval room festooned with huge flower arrangements and a running fountain surrounded by mirrored glass. We turned almost immediately to our right and entered the restaurant. The octagonal room, bustling with staff in waistcoats and the sounds of clinking crystal, glistened with candlelight. A vaulted ceiling sprang up from what looked like enormous tulips flung open atop gilded stems, each petal covered in a tiled mosaic. The floor mirrored the design above.

Across the room an orchestra played at a volume that wouldn't overwhelm conversation but was still loud enough to encourage dancing, and I surmised that the unusual ceiling wasn't just visually appealing but also offered the acoustics of a well-designed lecture hall.

Harry maneuvered us toward a large party seated on the outer wall of the room. I hadn't thought to inquire how many people we were to dine with and was surprised to count a table of twelve.

"Ludlow, my good man," Harry said, shaking the hand of the man at the head of the table before kissing the hand of the woman sitting to Ludlow's left.

"There you are, Harry," she said. "I was beginning to worry you had gotten lost."

I immediately recognized Abby Patton's blond ringlets and the lingering soprano in her voice, the youngest of the Hutchinson Family Singers. The last time I'd heard her voice, she'd been the one to suggest they would be happy to share more than half of the joint ticket sales with me. It was a sweet gesture that hadn't been lost on me. Her eyes matched the color of the large emerald at her throat.

"Mr. Patton, allow me to introduce my wife. Lucy, you of course remember Mrs. Patton."

"It's lovely to see you again," I said.

There were two empty chairs next to Abby. Harry held out the farthest one for me before depositing himself beside her.

Before I had the chance to properly settle in my chair, she addressed the table at large.

"Everyone, I am so pleased to introduce you all to Lucy Stone. Lucy and I performed together eons ago, didn't we? One of the most thrilling nights of my childhood."

If the age difference between us wasn't obvious to the naked eye, her description of me as an adult onstage while she had still been a child certainly did the trick. I smiled and nodded my greetings to the four or five people who had paused their conversations at her announcement. The rest of the table hadn't noticed our arrival. I was about to ask after Abby's siblings when the gentleman seated immediately to my left introduced himself and his wife as Mr. and Mrs. Rothschild.

Mr. Rothschild cut an elegant figure in a matching paisley vest and tie rather than the standard white fare. He had no gray yet in his hair, but he struck me as being several years older than me, nonetheless. His wife's hair was swept into a glamorous chignon with small flowers tucked in the curls, accentuating her high cheekbones and smooth skin. I guessed her to be barely twenty-five.

"Did you have a long ride in?" Mrs. Rothschild asked. "Mr. Patton always orders for the table, so there is plenty of time to go freshen up before dinner arrives, if you'd like."

I wondered if something was askew in my appearance and reflexively lifted my hand to my face.

"Don't let her start in on you," Mr. Rothschild said. "We've just moved to Central Park West, and Lolly now thinks that anyone who has come in from beyond the city limits must have traversed half the country."

"I assure you, coming from New Jersey is much easier than getting here from Kansas." I returned his small chuckle.

Mr. Rothschild raised his eyebrows and reached for his wineglass. I sipped from the goblet of water beside my place instead, the deep etches of the crystal refracting the candlelight. I had never held a drinking cup so heavy not made of pewter.

"Now tell me," she said. "Where did you perform with the Hutchinson family? What a thrill."

"I don't really consider it a performance."

"Oh, you're just like Abby. Always so modest. I bet you were a talent."

"Forgive my wife. She's too young to remember. Lucy Stone was quite a famous lecturer back in the day. Pressing the cause for women's rights."

"That's right." I was grateful for his acknowledgment, but had my day completely passed?

"And then you found your husband?"

Before I could respond, Ludlow clinked a spoon against his wineglass.

"Before the pheasant arrives, I'll just say to those of you heading to Palm Beach, including my lovely wife, I wish you a wonderful social season. Those of us left to toil away will try not to drink all the scotch while you are gone."

Ludlow smiled broadly as polite laughter rippled down the table. Harry wasn't smiling. I hoped I hadn't already misstepped somehow.

When the orchestra began to play a waltz, Mr. and Mrs. Rothschild rose to dance, and I took my opportunity to turn my attention to the Pattons.

"How long will you be spending in Florida?" I asked.

"Two months at least, I hope, unless it gets too dreadfully hot," Abby said. "But it's usually lovely through May."

"I've told Harry he shouldn't leave until he's sold every bit of land," Ludlow said.

"Land? In Florida?" I tried to keep my tone light.

"His holdings in Wisconsin." *My holdings*, I was tempted to say, but kept my expression steady as he continued. "The fat cats are all sunning themselves in Palm Beach already. Time to strike while the iron is hot. Now is a very good time."

I examined Harry's face for some sign that Ludlow was mistaken about his plans.

"And I will be able to accompany Mother and Elizabeth, which will be a great help to them," Harry said. "You know how much Mother is counting on the warmth and humid air to clear her lungs."

I knew Emily and Elizabeth were worried for their mother's health, but Harry had told me nothing further.

"It's such fun," Abby said. "You should come, Lucy. The water is divine for swimming, and the food at the club puts even the Astor House to shame."

"I've never seen you turn away an entree here, my dear," Ludlow said with a tinge of irritation in his voice.

"Lucy has an important convention she needs to attend," Harry said.

"A very important convention." I looked more directly at him. "And our daughter can't be taken out of school."

Was the distance between us even greater than I feared?

"You won't be missing much, Mrs. Blackwell. One party blurs into the next. And there's far too much dancing," Ludlow said.

"Speaking of which." Abby held her hand to her ear in an exaggerated way and tilted her head toward Harry. "Do I hear a polka?" She leaned across him and put a hand on mine. "I'm sure you won't mind if I steal your husband for a dance? Ludlow's such a bore about it, and your husband is always willing to oblige."

"Of course." I pulled my hand out from under hers.

Harry pushed back from the table and stood to help Abby out of her chair. He looked at me with an expression that was both defiant and resigned, like a dog that had been given a prime cut by one master after being starved by another.

"Mrs. Stone," I said after Harry and Abby were gone.

"Excuse me?" Ludlow asked.

"I am not called Mrs. Blackwell. It's Lucy Stone."

22

Harry left for Florida not long after the night at the Astor House. I tried to keep the mood in the house light before he left, to make it a place he would want to return to sooner rather than later. We had gone for so long without proper conversation, without kind or gentle words passing between us, that I couldn't tell if my efforts seemed forced or had gone altogether unnoticed. I longed for him to speak fondly to me. I had even hoped he might beg me to join him in Florida for a spell, but that was not to be.

As soon as he departed, I turned my attention back to my work and traveled to Boston to address the Massachusetts Joint Special Committee with Wendell Phillips on the topic of women's suffrage. He spoke elegantly on the need to eliminate the word "male" from the state constitution and urged the great commonwealth, first in so many things in the country, to be the first to enfranchise women. I followed his speech with an impassioned plea of my own. It was wonderful to be speaking beside my old friend again. The joyous stomping of feet in response to our remarks, and the decision of the committee to forward an amendment to the House for consideration that would give women the right to vote and hold office in the state, led me to momentarily forget my marital worries.

And being back in Boston, surrounded by my best reform colleagues, always lifted my heart. I visited regularly with the Garrisons, where there was much lively debate about the Fifteenth Amendment and the need to present a unified view on the issue as it went out to each state for ratification, and enjoyed uninterrupted time with Julia Ward Howe, Mary Livermore, and Miriam Phelps.

I had taken to staying at a small boardinghouse in the North End of Boston. Its proprietor was a wizened older woman who had turned her own home into a place women traveling alone or with their children could safely stay. She greeted me with a hearty hug whenever I arrived and offered hot tea and scones at the end of my longer days.

"A letter came for you today, Mrs. Stone," she said on an unusually warm afternoon for April. "I left it on your bed. And I took the liberty of opening your windows to take in the breeze."

"Thank you, Mrs. Balboa. I'll go have a look, I think, before I take tea." I skipped up the stairs. I hadn't heard from Harry since his departure and was eager for news from him.

When I saw the postmark, disappointment flooded my chest. The letter was from Susan. Harry had always been a loyal correspondent whenever we were apart, but the glitter of the social circle in Florida was apparently proving too much of a distraction for him. He had yet to send the simplest word to show that he hadn't altogether forgotten his wife. It had been over a month.

But the letter did hold interest for me. I hadn't heard from Susan since the Kansas and Train debacles.

25 April, 1869
Dear Lucy,

I am writing to ask after your itinerary prior to the AERA convention. Elizabeth and I would like to meet with you. Despite our previous quarrels over expenditures, this is an important moment to show our solidarity. None of us expected this fight to be brief or easy but continue to fight for what's right we must.

We should be in New York by the 10th of May. Will you be staying in the city? Send word and Mrs. Stanton and I will meet you.

Meanwhile, I'm hoping to hear good news out of Massachusetts soon. By the sounds of it, your speech at the statehouse was met with rousing approval.

Your friend,

Susan

I sat on my bed and considered the invitation. Their actions in Kansas and continued partnership with Train were no mere trifle, my disagreement with them on all of it not some small "quarrel," as Susan suggested in her letter. But Train was known to be unreliable and impetuous. A new project would catch his attention eventually, an opportunity for me to refocus theirs. Or better yet, perhaps they had already stepped back from him enough to take his full measure and were ready to break ties with him. I could only hope so.

If they desired a unified stance at the convention, that meant there was a very real opportunity for thorough and open discussion of the Fifteenth Amendment. It was a difficult situation. Our decades of work had finally brought us to the threshold of gaining universal suffrage: women, negroes, all of us leaning hard against the gates closed against us. But Congress was headed for a change in leadership, and time was dwindling to get something passed. Many thought negro enfranchisement stood a better chance, and so the proposed Fifteenth Amendment had been written to give the vote only to colored men. Supporting it meant willingly stepping aside as only half our battalion flooded through the palace gates with no guarantee of being able to push them open again. Eschewing the Fifteenth Amerndment would mean we could continue to apply our collective pressure, a force that certainly couldn't be ignored forever, but there was no telling how long we might all be left out in the cold. There was no easy answer, and I looked forward to discussing it with Susan and Elizabeth.

I dearly missed our fiery debates on topics such as this. We didn't always agree, particularly Elizabeth and I, but we did listen to one another, and more than once, we had let one change the mind of the other. While Phillips and Garrison were rigorous thinkers who challenged me and listened well to my own arguments, there was something different about having the female point of view, of debating an issue with someone for whom the debate wasn't just a theoretical exercise, but for whom the topic at hand held personal consequence.

I sat at the desk in my room, which was nothing more than a small table I had repositioned in front of the window and covered with a blotter and penned a response. I told Susan I would see them but could be in New York no sooner than the eleventh and suggested we meet the afternoon before the convention.

❧

The next morning, I gave my letter to Mrs. Balboa to post for me and walked to the Garrisons' house. I found William in his office. His normally friendly face was set with a grim expression, his gaze frozen in the middle distance. I was certain he hadn't heard me enter, or if he had, my presence was not enough to tear him away from whatever hovered in his mind.

"William, are you quite all right?"

His eyes moved toward me slowly, as if trying to focus, and then he tapped his knuckles on the paper on his desk. When I approached, he handed it to me.

It was the latest issue of *The Revolution*, and it didn't take long for me to surmise the cause of his dismay. The entire front page and almost all of the second was devoted to a scathing rebuke against him.

I lowered myself into one of the chairs on the opposite side of his desk and could hardly believe the words before me. Written by Elizabeth, the article claimed it was time to "unmask" Garrison's true character as a man who stood for nothing of merit except supporting those who agreed with him. She described the early abolitionists Garrison had gathered as a "motley crew," not worthy of an afternoon's attention, and mocked him for using a person's stance on the negro question as the sole measuring stick of their worth. Elizabeth argued that because emancipation was complete, and the "woes of the slave no longer needed to command the nation's attention," Garrison had become as "superfluous" to any discussion of the country's current affairs as a dancer standing in the wings of the stage long after the curtain closed. She called him "as dead as the Royal Dane," and suggested he should remain "in his sepulcher" rather than try to agitate for anything.

It was too much to take in all at once.

"I wrote that letter to Susan as a friend," he said.

I scanned back up to the top of the article and saw that they had printed in full a letter from Garrison addressed not to *The Revolution* but to Susan. It spoke of his admiration for her and all the good she had done for the cause of women and begged her to cut ties with Train. He used his own scathing language to describe the man and suggested that she and Stanton were doing severe damage to the women's cause by looking to Train and the Democrats for any help.

"People are starting to refer to this paper as the new organ of female suffrage, Lucy. And they devote six full columns of text to defending Train and his party. They have taken leave of their senses."

His normally bright eyes were filled not with anger but with sorrow. I knew he truly cared about the damage all this might do to the women's cause, but the awful way he'd been treated in print by two women he had once counted as friends cut deeply.

One letter from Susan and I had stupidly hoped she might be ready to abandon Train for more reasonable ground. How could I hope for any reconciliation of our views now? But my reply had already been sent. I would be meeting with them in less than a week.

❧

I brought the latest issue of *The Revolution* with me to New York. Before Susan and Elizabeth had even sat down, I dropped it on the coffee table between us.

"This is horrifying. Garrison has been a true friend to our cause, and you betrayed him."

"Betrayed him?" Elizabeth said, settling deeply into her chair and already brushing off my statement. "Did you read the words he used to describe our business associate? Garrison said he was headed for a lunatic asylum and called him a gorilla!"

"That was a private letter, and yes, Train should be put in an asylum. I just can't think what you two are doing associating with him at all." I struggled to keep anger out of my voice.

We were seated in a side room of the Grand Central Hotel lobby, my home for the duration of the convention. Susan suggested meeting in the office of *The Revolution*, but I opted for neutral ground. She didn't protest, which I took as a promising sign.

The room was paneled in dark oak, with a couch and several chairs placed around a mahogany coffee table. The plush carpet and bright fire in the hearth made it feel like a private den and reminded me of the room in the Allegheny Hotel in Pittsburgh where Harry and I had finally decided to wed. The thought stung my eyes. I had a ticket to the convention for him in my bag, still foolishly hoping he might suddenly appear. I pushed thoughts of him aside in favor of the conversation at hand.

"Surely you know Garrison is hardly unique in his views on that man," I said.

"You're so high-minded, Lucy. You too often forget to be practical," Elizabeth said. "Train has money, and he draws a crowd. Those are the two things our cause needs the most."

My mouth fell open at the brashness of that statement and how easily she could say it. Train was an abhorrent man. He could deliver the whole state of Kansas and a wagon full of gold and I still wouldn't consider sharing a platform with him. Was it really that easy for them to give up their principles for political expediency? Susan's expression remained unchanged. She sat up straight with her hands folded on her lap, content to let Elizabeth do the work of explaining. When I said nothing, Elizabeth continued.

"We spoke to thousands in Kansas we would never have attracted without him. And the paper? It has gotten nationwide attention in great part because people want to see what outlandish thing he might propose next. Meanwhile, we devote eighty percent of the space to the woman question. It makes it the perfect platform to further the most important issues."

Elizabeth spoke entirely without embarrassment or remorse.

"But educated suffrage? You know how discriminatory that is, do you not? It was strictly forbidden on plantations for slaves to learn to read and write."

"But it would allow us to get into the Constitution the idea that voting cannot be limited by race or sex. That's the wedge we need to stick into the door if we are ever to be allowed in. And it will assure that a bunch of uneducated idiots aren't able to vote before you or me," Elizabeth said.

"Idiots? If education is the measure, then it will be a full generation before negroes are actually enfranchised."

"And how long have we been waiting? I don't understand how you can want the vote given to more men, who can then turn around and block women from the same?"

I had previously considered Elizabeth a clear and consistent thinker. I was disheartened by her lack of integrity, her choice of whatever idea served her in the moment.

"They abandoned us," Susan said quietly. "We agreed to join forces and work together for universal suffrage, all citizens, colored, white, men, women. Do I have to remind you that's what the AERA was founded for? We worked tirelessly for it, all of us. But now they tell us we must wait in line behind the negroes? If we get at the end of that line, we won't see the vote for decades. Mark my words. They betrayed us, Lucy, and you should be furious."

"Of course I'm disappointed, but there were never guarantees. We knew all of it would be hard, and that hasn't stopped us yet. There just doesn't seem to be enough support in Congress for women's suffrage right now, while there is a growing urgency for negro enfranchisement."

"That's exactly the point," Susan said. "If Garrison and Phillips and Douglass were our true friends, they would keep the two causes attached and use support for the one to increase backing for the other, even if it takes more time."

I leaned back into the couch, my head spinning. She did have a point. If we allowed them to unhitch our cause from theirs, we might very well get completely stuck, a train car with no engine to pull it down the tracks. And we had played a major role in stoking the fires propelling them now. It was unfair to be left behind.

"We still have influence," Susan said. "But we must be united. We must stand together tomorrow and tell the convention that the women's caucus cannot support the Fifteenth Amendment. That our rights are no less important than any other. And then we work together until it is done. We are a formidable team, Lucy."

I badly wanted to be a team again. Locking arms with her when we first met in Seneca Falls had boosted my spirits in ways that I didn't even know I needed. She was the strongest ally I'd ever worked with, and I missed that level of camaraderie. I needed her friendship and counsel, and together our energies did feel like an unstoppable engine.

"We could also stand united and support the Fifteenth Amendment on the condition that our friends continue to work with us on behalf of women's suffrage," I said.

Susan and Elizabeth glanced at each other.

"That's not how politics works," Elizabeth said. "Once there is no heat, there is no fire. We must hold our ground."

"Thank you for asking to see me," I said. "I need to think this all through. And I also think it important to hear from our colleagues tomorrow."

"As they are going to want to hear from you," Susan said. "I trust you won't let us down."

❧

Steinway Hall was teeming with people by the time I arrived the next day. The city was abuzz with news of the last spike being driven into the rail line that would stretch from one coast all the way to the other. Many had come to New York to see off the first train to head west, and apparently word had spread that the AERA convention was likely to be highly contentious—excellent entertainment. Tickets to the proceedings were completely sold out.

Weaving my way through the crowd outside, I noticed a woman standing alone, looking a bit dazed. I remembered the spare ticket I had purchased for Harry, lonely in my purse.

"Ma'am, are you looking for a ticket to the convention?"

It took her a moment to register me before her.

"To this?" She gestured vaguely at the stone edifice behind her. "Certainly not."

"My apologies." I stepped past her.

"Be careful. The women in there want to wreck our homes," she said.

"Excuse me?" I turned back around to face her again.

"I'm interested in the negro question, but I hear there will be women speaking on the topic. Any woman crass enough to stand onstage is not worth hearing. Trust me. They're hideous."

"Perhaps you should hear what they have to say."

"Lucy," I heard from behind me. "There you are. We are about to get started."

I turned to see Stephen Foster, Abby Kelley's husband, beckoning me. I opened my purse and handed the spare ticket to the woman.

"You really should come listen," I said, and followed Stephen inside.

While the shade of the hall was a relief from the May sunshine, the marble walls and smooth floors had already lost their cooling effect, long overpowered by the hundreds of bodies in dark coats and wide skirts. It was steamy inside.

Stephen led me to the front left section of chairs, where he had thankfully saved a seat for me. The balcony surrounding the room was beyond full. There were even people sitting on steps or leaning against the walls. Heated debates were taking place in small groups huddled in the aisles and to the side of the stage.

Paulina Wright Davis, the secretary of the AERA, banged a gavel and asked for order. After several administrative issues were handled speedily, she announced the discussion of the Fifteenth Amendment and called upon Frederick Douglass for opening remarks.

Douglass took the stage, his wiry white mane as unruly as ever and his beard now almost as white. He was not a large man, but his stony expression coupled with a deep and resonant voice always commanded attention. He spoke eloquently of the good work women had done to help release the shackles from slaves and reminded the audience of his own long history of supporting women's rights.

"But this is the negro's hour. The Fifteenth Amendment is a matter of life and death. A freed slave who cannot vote is a man marked for slaughter. If we cannot make laws to ensure fair wages, no freeman will find work. If we cannot vote in laws that allow us to live in cities and towns of our choosing, the freeman will not be able to leave the plantation. Until we are considered full citizens, with the same rights as our white brothers, our lives will not be recognized as having the same value as a white man's life, and snuffing out that life will hardly be considered a crime. We must support the Fifteenth Amendment with the full backing of this organization and see it through to ratification."

Over the stomping of feet and calls of "hear, hear!" Susan's voice rang out. She was on her feet on the other side of the hall. Elizabeth occupied the seat next to her. She did not rise, but she wore the expression of a soldier ready to draw blood.

"This cannot be considered equal rights if women are not part of the equation," Susan shouted. "It is unequal and unacceptable!"

Voices rose in protest, and shouting began to pour down from the balcony as Paulina banged her gavel and urged the hall to maintain some level of decorum.

"Miss Anthony, you are invited to take the podium if you have something to say."

Susan pushed her way to the aisle and stepped onto the stage.

"You say, my good friend," she began, looking down at Douglass, who was now seated in the front row, "that this is a matter of life and death for the negro, that the freeman will be beaten in the street if he doesn't have the vote. But women are beaten in their own homes every day. And what of the colored woman? If women have no voice, you are only enfranchising half of your race. How do you explain that to your negro sisters? And what of the rest of us, educated, clear-thinking women who have been toiling on behalf of the negroes for all these years? We should not have to stand in line behind the uneducated and ignorant."

A rumbling of protests threatened to drown her out, but Susan raised her voice and pressed on.

"I hearby put forth two resolutions. The first is for this body to oppose ratification of the Fifteenth Amendment. The second is to put forth an amendment in favor of educated suffrage."

Paulina's gavel could not overpower the shouts and heated debate that erupted. Every third person in the hall, it seemed, was yelling his own insult or admonition.

"Educated suffrage is a sham!" yelled some, with others shouting, "Train is a racist!"

When Paulina was finally able to muster some amount of attention, she stood and took the podium herself. To my surprise, she defended Susan's position, stating that any use of race or sex as a qualification of suffrage was unfair, and that the organization had no claim to calling itself the American Equal Rights Association if it was ready to push women aside. Educated suffrage, she said, made common sense. Someone who could not read should not be allowed to vote.

Stephen Foster took the stage next and repudiated Susan's and Paulina's arguments. He argued that educated suffrage made a mockery of suffrage and threw his full support behind the Fifteenth Amendment.

As speaker after speaker took the floor and the temperature in the room rose to an ungodly level, the turmoil in my heart swelled to the point of suffocating me. I needed to speak my piece. Finally, I stood and walked up the steps of the stage.

I waited at the podium for the hall to quiet. Susan and Elizabeth eyed me with stern expressions. Several strands of hair had come unloosed from Susan's bun, and her face was uncharacteristically flushed. I considered the precarious nature of my position. If I supported them publicly now, we might lose today's battle, but we would be, as she had said, a formidable team and work relentlessly together. If I failed to show that support, Susan would be furious. Unlike Elizabeth, who could befriend an enemy without a second thought if it meant giving her some advantage and moved seamlessly from a public battlefield to tea with a foe, Susan waged war in a far more personal way. She would take any lack of support on my part as a personal slight. If I made it known publicly, she might never forgive me.

I took measure of the audience, so many friends and colleagues I had long admired. From Mary Livermore, who helped me organize the first convention in Worcester, to Wendell Phillips, these were people I had battled beside for years to bring our country to a better place. What a shame that we had landed here, divided, in turmoil, most in the crowd feeling we had no choice but to accept a half loaf of justice. I considered the hundreds of speeches I had made in my life on these two issues and wanted no part in choosing between them. I looked at Frederick Douglass and thought back on the night at the Musical Fund Hall and his severe reaction to the choice I had made. And then I thought about Juda May, and the girl Harry rescued from the train all those years ago. What had happened to her? Would the Fifteenth Amendment help either of them?

In the end, I knew there was only one thing to say.

"If one has the right to say that you cannot read and therefore cannot vote," I began, "we are reducing our freedoms, not increasing them. It is the same as saying that you are a woman and therefore cannot vote. We are lost when we break down our society into measurable increments and do anything not to give freedom to all. Women have an ocean of sorrows too deep for any plummet, and the negro too has an ocean of wrongs that cannot be fathomed. There are two great oceans, in the one is the black man, and in the other is the woman."

I paused and looked out over the crowd before continuing. The hall was completely silent. I knew my next words would have a broad and lasting impact, to me personally, and for the nation.

"I must speak out strongly in favor of the Fifteenth Amendment. I hope it will be readily adopted in every state. I will be thankful deep in my soul if any human can get out of this terrible pit."

Cheers and stomping of feet accompanied me as I returned to my seat.

The vote was immediately called to defeat Susan's two resolutions. As hands were counted, Susan and Elizabeth rose from their seats and marched down the aisle toward the exit. Susan glared at me as she walked past, something close to hatred seared onto her face. My heart felt too heavy for my chest, as if it had been turned to granite by her anger.

When Paulina lowered her gavel to close the matter, the bang of it was echoed by the door of the hall slamming shut.

That sound left my insides splintered like one side of a wishbone after the other has been forcibly snapped off. I yearned for Harry just then. He would have understood the choice I made, even applauded me for it. But I still hadn't heard from him. He knew well the significance of the convention and yet had left me to navigate on my own. Perhaps that was what he thought I wanted. Never had I felt quite so alone.

23

Back home in New Jersey, the untended gardens, unswept floors, and a large stack of unopened letters threatened to overwhelm me, but I let those all go in favor of spending the afternoon with you. Between my trip to Boston and the AERA convention, I had been gone for a month, and in my absence, it seemed as though you had grown from little girl to young lady.

While you were still only twelve, your mind was far more sophisticated than most girls your age. Spending as much time as you did with your aunt Emily had honed your love of both literature and science. Harry's sisters were incredibly well-read—my own mother's insistence that novels were scandalous had left me woefully behind—and I knew Emily offered you an endless supply of interesting books. Additionally, I imagined your dinner table discussions to include talk of Emily's patients, the latest medical cures available, and the vast quantities of scientific research she devoured on a regular basis. It was a full education on top of your regular schooling, and it had made you, my daughter, worldly and precise, at the ready to take on any conversation with maturity and discipline.

"Do you think we might purchase the next installment of *Little Women* when it comes out next month?" I remember you asking, as we ate our dinner of chicken and biscuits. "Aunt Emily and I have been reading them together, and I must find out what happens to Beth."

"I met Louisa May Alcott recently. She's lovely," I said, biting into a roll.

Your mouth fell open. "Could you ask her if Beth will be okay?"

"That would ruin it for you, don't you think?"

"Tell me what she's like. Could I meet her sometime?"

I couldn't help but wonder at your inner world. I was acutely aware that you were the same age I had been when the theft of Abigail's horse had set my life on its current trajectory. You had experienced far less hardship in your young life than I had, and I wondered if that had opened you up to a broader catalog of interests. Those interests were bound to be less urgent, but were they any less valuable?

I glanced at the stack of mail beckoning me from my chair by the hearth.

"I'll tell you all about her another time. But I'm sure you have plenty of homework to finish, and I suppose I should see to my correspondence."

The memory of what I found in that pile of mail jolts me back to the present, my grown daughter sitting before me, gulping down my stories as quickly as I offer them. I have worked hard to forget the pain of that time and try even now to tamp down the recollection. But my mind will not cease to churn, and the memory surfaces, unbidden.

After cleaning up the dishes, I sat by the hearth. Flipping through the envelopes I immediately noticed two letters with postmarks from Florida.

My heart leapt with hope. Harry hadn't forgotten me after all. I tore open the first letter.

1 May, 1869
Palm Beach
Dear Lucy,

I write with excellent news. Ludlow was exactly right in his estimation of the types of fellows that frequent this town and their appreciation of the value of real estate, particularly in the western direction of expansion. I have finally done it! I sold off all the land! My investors will be thrilled at the profits I can now deliver to them, and my portion of those gains is even quite a tidy sum. This of course means that I have sold your holdings entirely, and at a profit that exceeded even my lofty expectations. The income will be placed immediately into bonds in your name, so you need worry no longer about the intermingling of your money with mine.

I have suffered under the burden of these responsibilities for so long that the release of them makes me feel like a new man. I have finally proved my worth in the business realm and delivered to those who put faith in me enough of a return to fully justify that faith. I cannot tell you what good it does me.

Although my business here is technically complete, I have decided to stay another four or six weeks to rest and recuperate. You regularly advise us all to take better care of ourselves and there is no better place to restore one's soul than here.

Mother is much improved but worried about the coming heat, so she and Elizabeth will be headed home ahead of me. They will be well cared for by the droves of companions migrating north, so we need not be concerned about their safe passage. The extra quiet will do me good. I'm sure you will understand.

When you are next in New York, do go to the New York Trust Bank to sign for your holdings. The paperwork will be ready for you.

With my affection, I am as ever,
HBB

His letter stirred in me intensely conflicting emotions, and I had to read it two or three more times before I knew what to think. This was surely good news. Harry didn't have to include figures for me to understand that our financial troubles were now largely behind us. The sums he had promised were lofty indeed—such that I didn't think I'd ever see them—and if he'd actually exceeded those, we could live comfortably for the foreseeable future.

I also understood that Harry finally felt validated as a man. As much as he had vowed to support my causes and be one half of a marriage of equals, he didn't believe he would be taken seriously without proof of his own worth in monetary terms. While no one judges the wife on her ability to bring earnings home, the husband is judged on little else. He had been hobbled by that pressure and determined, since the day I met him and he told me of his beet sugar dreams, to prove he could provide. Now that he had made a little money of his own, he would be free of that pressure.

But rather than rush home to celebrate this good fortune with me, he was choosing to stay in Florida. That fact threatened to unleash an avalanche of sadness that had been pressing on me for weeks.

I remembered there was another postmark from Palm Beach. Maybe he had changed his mind and was coming home after all. When I pulled the second letter out of the stack, however, I realized it wasn't from Harry at all. It was from his sister, sent three days before his.

28 April, 1869
Palm Beach
Dear Sister-in-law,

I write under the assumption that certain rumors have made their way up the coast about your husband's carrying on with Mrs. P, and to let you know that both Mother and I are furious. The social scene here in Palm Beach has been on high tilt all spring, and their appearances together and lengthy tête-à-têtes while Mr. P is nowhere to be found have become all too frequent and increasingly embarrassing. As you can imagine, the situation is doing nothing to improve Mother's health.

But please do not overly fret. I wanted you to know that I confronted Harry just last night. I told him quite clearly that I found his behavior entirely unacceptable and implored him to cut off all ties and go home. As a husband and father, this is no way for him to behave, and with a married woman to boot.

I felt it important for you to know we are doing our best to corral my wayward brother and turn him back on the right course.

With affection,
Elizabeth

A sob escaped my throat, and I put my hand over my mouth to stop any more emotions from erupting. My Harry? This couldn't be happening.

But the dates on the two letters were inescapable. Whatever Elizabeth thought was occurring between Harry and Abby Patton, she had spoken to him about it before the end of April, and he had written to me on the first of May with a decision to stay. He chose to ignore his sister's admonition. I didn't need to guess who else was staying south beyond the social season.

I closed my eyes and rocked in my chair, unable to keep the tears from flowing down my face. I knew my moody spells had been hard on Harry, but had I really pushed him this far away? I used to be the earth to his moon. While he wasn't always physically here, his orbit back into my realm had always been certain, reliable. Had his affections wandered so far that he was now pulled in by an entirely different sphere, by a more womanly woman, one content to mingle and dance and spend her time coiffing her hair and polishing her shoes? Was that what he really wanted? Was that what all men wanted?

As twilight faded to darkness, I didn't bother to light a lamp or move from my chair. I just rocked and replayed the scenes from our life together, the tender moments we had shared, the bitter seasons I wished I could undo.

At some point my sorrow turned to anger, anger at his betrayal, anger that I had suffered through all his crazy business ideas—many attempted with my hard-earned savings—without an ounce of complaint, anger for every minute of my time I had spent cooking and keeping house for him rather than in service of the cause, outrage that he was proving himself no better than any typical husband, bored with one wife and drawn to a younger, more beautiful substitute. Hadn't he promised our marriage would be different than all others?

I almost left my seat to pen a scathing letter in response, to make sure he knew what I knew and exactly how much he had devastated me, forever cleaving us in two, that there was no coming back from this place.

But I hesitated. I had sent off a hasty missive to him once before, back in Philadelphia, when I had decided to fully cut ties and had then regretted it. I had a daughter to think about now. There were almost fifteen years of marriage history to consider. I knew him to be a good and loyal man, and the contradiction of all these truths left me numb.

Well past midnight, I trudged up the stairs, my head heavy with the weight of it all. As I stood beside our bed, I couldn't face lying there by myself, wondering where he might be at that very moment and with whom. Instead, I dragged the quilt and pillow off the bed and laid down on the floor, just like the many nights I had spent sleeping in the homes of strangers. Every thought of Harry, every memory, brought a new sob from my throat, and I forced myself to push them back down into my stomach so that I might survive the night. I clutched my pillow tightly and willed sleep to bring me solace for at least a few hours before the sun came up, possibly the only orb that could be counted on anymore.

❧

I took several weeks to think things over and make some plans. And then I wrote Harry the most important letter of my life.

30 May, 1869
Husband,

Please accept this letter as a missive from my heart. I have lately been hearing news from your sister of your "carrying on" in Florida, the details of which I do not feel are necessary to include here, except to say that your sister's disappointment in your behavior is no match for the sorrow this news has caused me.

This is in part because I know you to be a good and loyal man who would not willingly injure his wife without first feeling injured himself, or at the very least, in need of some affection he felt he was not receiving at home. I am filled with regret at the idea that I was less than what you needed or held you at a distance. It was never my intent.

I have fought all my life to prove that being a reformer doesn't make a woman "unwomanly," that rights for women don't threaten the home—yet you choose to carry on with another woman. A married woman? How can that not threaten everything I, we, have ever worked for? Please don't give our critics more fodder for their ridiculous notions.

I do not mean to let anger fill the page, and I do not write to ask you to confirm or reject the existence of a relationship with a certain Mrs. P, or even to apologize for it if Elizabeth's claim is true. In many ways, that is not important. I know it has never been the same between us since the loss of our son. I can offer no apology other than to acknowledge the change that loss rendered in me. But we cannot forget that you and I entered into a marriage bond like no other. We actively protested the laws of the land so that we might form a more perfect union. A consequence is that we put our marriage up on a stage like a P. T. Barnum creature for others to examine. And just like Frederick Douglass is so often held up as the one man who can stand in the stead of all escaped slaves, as wrong as that might be, our marriage is invoked as the singular opportunity to determine if a marriage of equals can be a marriage of substance, and if such a marriage can endure. Please let us not forgo that responsibility.

In your absence, I had no choice but to make some important decisions. You know that ever since heading off to Oberlin I have longed for a home to truly call my own, and that the commonwealth is where I long to be. Now is the time to plant the roots that will grow stronger with each passing year, not to be ripped up and relocated at every whim. With my proceeds from the sale of western land, I intend to purchase a proper home in Boston.

Additionally, I have finally succeeded in raising most of the funds needed for my woman's paper and will look for an office near Boston Common. I have spent many hours contemplating my future place in the cause and believe I can do just as much good, perhaps even more, by collecting and circulating news of the ordinary and extraordinary steps women are taking to improve their place in society. I have concluded that life on the road is no place for a mother to be. I have done it long enough. Alice deserves a home she can return to after the school day to find her mother there. I hope she will find her father there, too.

When we first met, you declared that we could do more good for the women's cause together than I could do on my own, and if we were married you would devote yourself to it. I hope you will maintain that pledge, and all the other promises we made on that day. There is so much work to do. The paper will be at the hub for me now, with the home and hearth at the center of it all.

I need you now more than ever. I'm sure you heard the news that Susan and Elizabeth secretly convened after the AERA convention to form a new National Women's Suffrage Association, without any invitation or notice to me. They of course are lauding it in The Revolution as the official organization of the women's movement. Such a claim alongside their encouragement of anti–Fifteenth Amendment sentiments is horrifying to me. Accordingly, on top of starting the paper, I have decided to organize a counter-organization and already have the support of most of our AERA friends. We will call it the American Woman's Suffrage Association, headquartered in New England, and hope our good work will carry the day. We will continue to include men among our ranks, which the NWSA has decided not to do, and we will continue to organize at the state level. You and I both know that amendments without support from each state do us no good in the end. With any luck, my new paper will have a much wider reach than The Revolution and will serve to properly bolster the AWSA and the cause.

But none of this will be satisfying if you do not return home to us.

Please write to tell us you will be coming to Boston and when we might expect you. You will never see two people more eager to see you than your cub and me.

I am, as ever,

Your loving wife

After posting my letter, we packed up the few belongings needed for our trip north and left New Jersey behind.

PART III

24
DORCHESTER, MASSACHUSETTS
1893

The morning light slides up the slope of land before me, waking each tree as it makes its long climb toward our house. The veranda looks out over Dorchester Harbor and the small cluster of Boston's buildings in the distance. My favorite settee was brought outside here almost as soon as Alice and I arrived home from the World's Fair, enabling me to watch the sun dance on the water and filter through the trees, and it is where I have been passing much of my time. As I had feared in Chicago, my old energy has not returned. The doctors haven't given a name to what ails me, but I have been under strict orders to rest as much as possible. I haven't been going into *The Women's Journal* offices, the focus of my days for more than two decades now. Equally disorienting, I've been unable to attend salons, speak at New England Women's Association gatherings, or accept dinner invitations where issues of the day are discussed and debated. Of course, so many old friends are gone now, both of the Garrisons, Wendell Phillips, Abby and Stephen Foster.

Even with so much time on my hands, I am of little use. I miss the satisfaction of milking at least one of our cows in the morning, checking on the goats, and harvesting the summer's bounty of tomatoes and cucumbers from the garden before heading off to the office. At least I can see the sweep of goings on from here and am on hand to remind Marguerite to feed the chickens and pick the strawberries before they overripen.

The house is too still, the size of it almost absurd without its usual thrum of activity. From the time we moved here, it bustled with Alice's cousins, many of whom boarded with us for a spell, the comings and goings of reformers in town for meetings, young people studying at MIT or Boston University who needed a place to stay, family visiting for the summer or a holiday. Now our rooms sit almost empty, fulfilling another of the doctor's prescriptions: quiet. I dislike my doctor and have sneaked out notes to friends inviting them for a visit.

The stillness gives me too much time to worry about Alice and what she might decide. I did learn a lot about Johannes during our long journey home from Chicago, in between the various stories of my life. She told me how they had met on the first day of the Hollowell Camp last summer—a retreat designed for artists and intellectuals; how they were both drawn there by the number of poets who regularly attended; how he was as amazed to find an American who enjoyed translating Armenian poetry as she was to meet someone from Armenia; how he was a great help with some of her more complex translations, patient in his explanations of phrases and concepts that are difficult to marry with English words; how he took to calling her "sireli," which means "dear one"; how they learned to play croquet together, surprising themselves by how much they enjoyed the activity, the peals of laughter every time they missed a wicket; how they found a special spot on the lake to watch the sun go down every evening. Her voice rang with affection when speaking of him. But my stories gave her pause, nonetheless.

She has grown quiet on the topic of Johannes since then, but I know she is still weighing his proposal. She quickly determined once we arrived home that she couldn't possibly leave until I fully recover, and so he will be returning to Canada next summer in hopes that Alice will meet him there, steamer trunk in tow, ready to embark with him to Armenia and on a life together. I have remained silent about the role of editor in chief—even though she has effectively been acting in that capacity since our return. I don't want my illness to complicate things for her. It is imperative that I show signs of improvement so she can make the right decision on her own terms, not out of obligation to me.

I am still rather amazed by the countless hours Alice spent listening to my stories in Chicago, choosing them over the attractions of the World's Fair during our final days there, asking me to continue throughout our journey home, her seemingly endless appetite for more. I am equally surprised by how easily old memories poured out of me, every facet appearing before me as if captured on a glass negative. Of course, I didn't share all the difficult details with her, although I spoke the essence of my truth in full. Instead, I would claim the need for an hour or two of rest and gaze out the window of the train, willing the most painful memories to rush past me as quickly as the landscape speeding by. As much as I wanted her to understand the challenges I faced in my life, I stopped short of anything that would shake her faith in her father.

"Your morning medicine," Harry says, stepping out onto the veranda and handing me a cup of hot water with my daily tincture of dandelion and pepsin.

I smile up at his slightly stooped frame, his white hair and beard offsetting the blue of his eyes. I raise the cup toward the sea. "Here's to a new day."

I have been truly grateful for every day since Harry made his way back to me.

He traveled north from Florida not long after receiving my letter and found me sitting on the front porch of this house. He said simply, "I've come home." His use of that word meant everything to me. Before going inside, I showed him why I had chosen this property. In addition to its proximity to the city—a mere three trolley stops away from *The Women's Journal* office and Boston Common—its expanse of land would allow us to keep a few milking cows, several goats, and a multitude of vegetable and herb gardens. But it was the trees that commanded my attention.

While there are many fewer than the orchards at Coy's Hill, there were enough for Alice to run between as a child, climb or settle against with a book, and the collective shade from their branches washes the yard in cool breezes in the hotter months. One in particular is my favorite, its wide canopy an entryway of sorts to our tiny forest.

It was there Harry brought me one summer afternoon, a day that would mark the start of the second half of our lives.

We had been living in this house for only a month and were still adjusting to our new surroundings and to being back together. The few items I had chosen to bring north from our temporary life in New Jersey were quickly swallowed by the multitude of rooms, allowing us time to consider how we would fill these new empty spaces, how we would adorn our future. The house was bigger than we needed, but just the right size once we began to share it with Alice's visiting cousins, reformers in need of boarding when they visited New England, and friends from near and far. It brought me endless pleasure to open our home to wise thinkers and to the young people who would be the wave of the future.

And it gave me great comfort that the title to the house was in my name. If the fact that I had enough money to buy such a grand house myself hadn't shocked the lawyers and bankers enough, they had been incredulous, as had so many before them, when I insisted on signing the papers as Lucy Stone *only*, reiterating to them that there is nothing illegal about maintaining the right to one's own name.

"You said you wanted a real and permanent home," Harry said on that summer afternoon. "One where we can all be together as a proper family."

I sensed he was trying to apologize for something, but we had already agreed not to discuss what had happened in Florida, so I was unsure as to his aim.

"I thought it important that we all be reunited."

I followed his gaze to the base of the tree. A cross had been newly etched into the bark, a small mound tucked into the earth below. I looked into his eyes, my throat not able to form the question.

"I went back to our old house in Orange, so I could bring him home."

I fell to my knees. I traced the carefully carved marking with my finger and then put my cheek to the dirt. Our boy was with us again. Something released inside me, a breath I could finally exhale. My sorrow had been understood by Harry and, in the same moment, gently laid to rest.

"Thank you" was all I managed once I got to my feet. I buried my face in his chest and let him hold me, no ice beneath my feet this time, only the warmth of his embrace. And I wrapped my arms around him for the first time in what felt like an eternity.

It has been twenty-four years since that day, its own lifetime.

"You're looking well this morning. I daresay on the mend," he says to me now.

I sip my tincture without responding. The doctor buoys his hopes, saying that with just the right amount of rest and quiet I will recover from this ailment, much as I have from bouts of pneumonia or bronchitis in the past. As much as I want to believe it, it is difficult to keep my own worries at bay. I subsist mostly on broth and warm cups of milk. Some days even that is too much for my delicate stomach. The tinctures are from the Blackwell sisters, the only remedies that provide some moments of relief. But I don't say any of this to Harry. He requires a steady diet of hope and possibility, and I see no reason to eliminate it from the house just yet.

"I'm headed into the office early, if you'll be all right. I'm expecting a long piece on the impact of the stock market crash on women's financial status."

As soon as we arrived home from the World's Fair, Alice and Harry began taking turns staying home with me while only one of them goes into the *Women's Journal* offices, fielding letters from subscribers and putting up articles. Having just one person in the office at a time puts a terrible burden on them both. At least they bring me pieces to review and edit, and we now hold editorial meetings as needed right here on the veranda, so we can agree on the most interesting stories to include, choose which letters to publish, or decide which column should be sent out for syndication. It is the part of the work I have always enjoyed most—filling our pages with examples of progress made by women in professional and political realms. The constant struggle to find funders and advertisers I could have done without. Fortunately for me, on top of adding plenty of editorial help, Harry willingly took on the role of publisher of the *Journal* when we moved here, and he has been managing that side of the business entirely for years now. He always was a salesman at heart.

"And will you be running the profile on Mary Ann Shadd Cary this week?" I ask. She was the first African American woman to publish a paper, *The Provincal Freeman*. I feel a kinship with her even though we never met. She died too young, of stomach cancer. The thought makes me wince.

"Yes. You should ask Alice to show you what she's got so far. And I'm going to add an editorial on the importance of publications run by those who sit the closest to injustice."

"From which seat?" I ask lightly.

"Good point. Perhaps I'll ask her to write that one also." He's always been sensitive to understanding when it is helpful for a man take up a particular issue and when it is best left to the directly aggrieved.

"Is there anything I can get you before I go?" he asks.

"Can you please ask Marguerite to soft boil two eggs for Alice? I think she'd like that this morning. And the roses need to be deadheaded. Perhaps Phillip could fit that in today?"

"Of course." He kisses me on the top of my head.

As I watch him go, I am amazed once more by how easily the particulars of our life together came back to me as I described them to Alice. While telling her nothing of his indiscretion in Florida or how I came to find out about it, I had shared more openly with her than I had thought possible the various challenges marriage had presented, even some of the difficulties of motherhood. Viewing it all from a distance has allowed me to consider it anew, like finally seeing a painting not as individual brushstrokes, but as a complete composition. Whether the portrait of my life is to be lauded for its originality or criticized for its many imperfections, I'm still unsure. I can only hope it gives Alice a clearer sense of the sacrifices that come with certain choices, of the responsibility she has to be honest with herself.

❧

The next morning dawns bright and clear, with a lovely breeze coming off the water. A perfect summer day. Best of all, it is a Sunday, so no one must go to the office. Harry declared we should have a picnic to celebrate my improving health, and I do not protest. Never has illness stymied me for so long, and it is high time for my full recovery. Besides, he knows how tired I am of being a prisoner in my own home. The daily walks I announced I would take have been infrequent at best, and often take me no farther than the goat pen before I think better of it and turn back. I'm sure he is equally bored of sitting with me constantly, watching for signs of improvement or decline, which is no way to waste a summer, or even a day. Being outside together will do us all good.

I catch myself in the mirror and notice there is a sag in my dress where the fabric once pulled tight around my middle. My wilting frame mocks my depleted energy, and I wonder if I'm watching an old lady slowly turn into a ghost. I pinch my cheeks to bring out color in them. I want Alice and Harry to see a strong woman today, to ease their worry about me. I want to soak up their certainty in my recovery and make it so.

Marguerite has fixed us a lovely assortment of bread and cheeses, blackberries and pears, lemonade and individual sweet cakes. Alice carries the basket, and Harry steadies me as we pick our way across the lawn toward the shady grove. As we walk by the chicken coop, we are greeted by squawks and the flapping of wings with each jump toward the fence to eye us more closely.

I hadn't considered how I would manage sitting on the grass for a picnic, but as we near the row of tall oaks that look out onto the harbor, I see that this has already been solved. A wide pile of pillows has been arranged at the base of one of the trees, so I can sit without having to lower myself too far and can lean comfortably against the tree. I laugh thinking about the number of chairs and benches inside that must be missing their cushions. Harry unfurls a large blanket beside the makeshift settee to complete the merry scene.

Alice sets out the food and leans against the one stray pillow not conscripted to hold me up. Harry pulls out a book of poetry from the bottom of the basket.

He is halfway through a Wordsworth poem when a sudden wave of nausea crashes over me. I concentrate on Harry's words and try to steady myself. I cannot allow anything to ruin this beautiful occasion, meant to mark the beginning of our return to normalcy.

"'They flash upon that inward eye which is the bliss of solitude,'" Alice repeats. "That makes me think of *a dream within a dream*. A lovely turn of phrase."

Perspiration pricks at my scalp, and I pray for the queasiness to pass.

"That calls for a little Poe, then, wouldn't you say?" Harry flips through the book to find the right page.

"Or how about 'To a Waterfowl,' Papa? Mama loves that one."

He searches for the poem in question, and as I watch the pages flip back and forth, I feel as though I am aboard a boat tossing on waves. My stomach lurches again, and to my horror, I gag and vomit onto the grass. I had little but warm milk this morning, and I can taste the curdled stench of it in my mouth. Alice jumps up and pushes a napkin into my hands. Harry is somehow already holding my shoulders, ensuring I don't tip over with the force of my heaves.

I want to tell them it is nothing, running through possible excuses in my mind, but none hold up to reality. I cannot lay this down to walking too quickly across our property—they were careful to maintain a snail's pace. Nor can I blame it on the heat of a summer day—it is dry and breezy. None of it would be believed anyway. We can all see that the milky puddle on the grass is stained with blood.

I look up at Harry and see the truth of it in his eyes.

25

Dr. Greer's face is grave. I know he wants to scurry off and speak quietly to Harry, but I insist he deliver his news to us both at the same time. Standing beside my bed, he takes off his glasses and explains that my symptoms are consistent with a tumor in my stomach, one that has likely grown considerably over the last few months.

"Stomach cancer," I say, thinking of Mary Ann Shadd Cary, who we so recently lost. How odd that she and I should suffer from the same thing. Even with all our work speaking out, did we still swallow enough to make us sick?

"There must be something you can do," Harry says. He is sitting on the edge of the bed, clutching my hand.

Dr. Greer's downcast eyes and lack of response say it all. I'm strangely comforted to know that my inability to regain my health since Chicago isn't a failure of effort, but part of a larger design, a process of its own volition. And my body knew the truth of it months ago. Much like an expectant mother cannot help but prepare the hearth and cradle to welcome a new life, a dying soul urges the release of all extraneous matter, encouraging the dispatch of all things that are no longer hers to hold. I see now how I've been shedding stories from my past like layers of my own skin, as if molting, readying for the next stage.

"Well, at least we have a name for it," I say in attempt to end the strained silence in the room.

I feel oddly relieved, knowing we can stop spending our time chasing remedies, waiting for improvement, and bracing for worse. Now we can face facts and get on with it. Embrace what remains. But Harry is struggling with the news. He really did believe I would recover from this latest ailment and carry on.

"I'll leave you two," the doctor says, and gratefully pulls himself out of the room.

Harry's eyes are the color of the ocean before a storm, dark and turbulent.

"Darling." I pat his hand. "Nette and Sam will be here soon. I must dress. Let's make this a happy visit."

"You should conserve your energy." He looks alarmed.

"I am no different today than yesterday. I will participate in every moment of this visit that I can."

He still hasn't moved, making it impossible for me to swing my legs off the bed.

"What will we tell Alice?"

This will be a great burden for her. If she was reluctant to go to Johannes before, she'll never go now. She won't abandon her father.

"Tell her nature has decided to claim me, take me back. And that I am not afraid."

And I realize that I'm not afraid. The deep sadness I feel, the sorrow threatening to gush from every pore of my body, is only for the thought of leaving Harry and Alice. How I will miss them.

"It gives me great comfort to know you will have each other. And I'm not going anywhere just yet."

Harry's face crumbles. He puts his head down in my lap, and his shoulders shake. I stroke the top of his head, his hair as dry as straw. I gaze out the window and force myself to stay composed. I can see Phillip snipping roses for the front table, taking care not to remove more than one bud from each vine.

"I do hope Marguerite has slaughtered the chicken by now. It will be more tender with a bit of time to rest," I say.

He raises his head and scans my face.

"She had it done before breakfast."

"See how well you all get on while I lay here doing nothing?" It is imperative that they harbor no doubts about how well equipped they are to continue on even after I am gone.

Harry wipes his eyes and stands, still holding my hand.

"If you wouldn't mind getting her for me, dearest. I'll need some help getting dressed."

After he is gone, I sit at my desk to pen a note I can no longer avoid.

14 August, 1893
Dear Susan,

Harry and Alice will likely put notice of my illness in the WJ, so you will learn this news soon enough, but I wanted you to hear it first from me. I am facing an illness that will be my last. It won't be long. The doctors agree there is nothing more to be done. I am not afraid. I only hope that where I am going will offer an equal opportunity to be useful.

I know you have lately been speaking in Kansas and so I hope this letter finds you soon, as I would be most grateful to have a visit with you while there is still time. Too much of the last twenty years have been spent in opposition to each other, but not a day goes by where I do not also remember our friendship. What we shared. I have much I'd like to say to you if you can manage it.

Do come if you can.
As ever,
Lucy Stone

I seal the letter as Marguerite comes in to help me dress.

"What would you like to wear today, ma'am?" Her eyes are pink at the edges. Harry has shared the news.

"Something cheerful, Marguerite. It's going to be a beautiful day."

❧

Nette sips her lemonade as she gently rocks her chair beside mine. She has weathered time well. At eight years my junior, she appears decades younger. She is still svelte, her bun painted with only a few streaks of gray, where my hair gave up its brown long ago. Our chairs face the lawn that slopes toward the apple orchard, and we watch Sam and Harry disappear around the corner on their way to inspect a beehive. Having Sam here has been wonderful for Harry. And four days with Nette an extraordinary gift.

"I am finding great comfort in the Bible lately," I say.

"Lucy Stone? Turning to the Bible?" Her voice is teasing.

"You know my qualm was always with the church, not the Bible. At least when it's translated correctly."

"The Book has much to offer in times of uncertainty."

"I must say, though, I don't see the afterlife as a place to lounge among the clouds. That sounds dreadful to me. I've decided that wherever I'm going next will have plenty of work to do, and I'll be just as busy there as I ever was here."

Nette laughs. "And I'm sure you'll stir up just as much trouble."

"Do you ever think about what life might have been like if we'd never married?"

"Do you?"

"I sometimes wonder how much further I might have been able to push things had I never had any other responsibilities," I admit.

"But aren't you glad of it? Where would we be without our children? You know Edith will want to come see you."

"I would like that very much."

Nette's daughter spent half her adolescence at our house after she started to give her mother trouble. I enjoyed overseeing the education of several of Alice's cousins in that way. It made us feel like a larger family, gave Alice companions.

"And Alice is doing a wonderful job with the paper, don't you think?" Nette asks.

"I do. It has been her life's work as much as mine. She and Harry are well suited as a team."

"She plans to write a book about you, you know," she says.

I think I have misunderstood her at first. Alice has told me nothing of the kind. Perhaps it is something she intends to take on if she leaves the paper. But still, the idea surprises me.

"She found my letters to you and had a slew of questions for me. I had great fun telling her my version of the Oberlin stories, and our early speaking days."

"Old letters?" I ask.

"She says there are boxes of them upstairs. Quite a project."

My body goes cold. I have kept every letter I have ever received. So has Harry.

"I should never have started all this," I say, almost to myself. "I should have left the past in the past."

"She is exceedingly proud of you, as she should be. You shouldn't be so reluctant to be properly recognized for all your accomplishments. I think a book is a wonderful idea."

"But there are letters she must never read, Nette." I look at her directly to make sure she understands my meaning.

She pauses for a moment before what I'm saying finally registers.

"Let me help. You should rest anyway." She is already standing. "Point me in the right direction, and by the time you arise, maybe I'll have it solved."

"Everything must be in her office on the third floor." The stairs are so narrow and steep, I haven't been able to climb them for years.

"It's settled, then."

Nette, as always, coming to my rescue. And it's a relief not to have to ask Harry to complete this task. I don't want him to think that memories of our dark time might be taking up residence again in my heart, marring any of the time we have left.

I lean on Nette as we walk through the foyer and up to my bedroom. I take my time, putting two feet on every step as I ascend. The grandfather clock on the landing tells me it's already almost two o'clock. By this time tomorrow, she will be gone.

Time is such a fickle friend. Sometimes it moves too fast, like a firefly that can't be caught. Other periods of time move like a mule with too heavy a load, the very weight of each moment almost too much to bear.

"Alice will be back by tea, so there isn't much time," I say.

When I wake, dusk is receding into night and my room is completely dark save for strips of pale light slicing through gaps in the curtains. I listen for the sounds of dinner preparations or the usual predinner conversations from below, but the house is silent. As my eyes adjust to the slivers of light in the room, which are growing brighter, I realize it is not dusk, but the earliest moments of dawn. I must have slept through teatime and straight on through the night. As much as I regret the time lost, I almost feel refreshed. I pull a shawl over the dress I'm still wearing from the previous day and find my shoes at the side of the bed. I move gingerly past Harry's door and hope I can make it down the stairs without waking the others. The quiet of the early hours reminds me of Coy's Hill, that suspended moment when anything seems possible.

By the time Marguerite finds me in the kitchen, I have reorganized the canned fruits in the pantry and have managed to lay out a traveling picnic for Nette and Sam, generous slices of Gouda, four scones, a jar of preserves, fresh blackberries, and three apples.

"Mrs. Stone, what are you doing? Please sit and let me finish."

"I can't seem to find a proper travel basket. I thought we had at least two in the pantry?" I continue wrapping the cheese in muslin.

"I could have come earlier if I had known you needed me."

"You spend enough of your day here as it is." I do my best to reassure her with a smile. Marguerite has been with us for almost six years now, my favorite of all the maids we've had over the years. I realized early on that I couldn't run the house without help, at first because my work left me without enough time to properly tend the vegetable gardens, or cook and clean for our boarders and other guests, and more lately because I'm too weak to do any of it. Marguerite is on the verge of running a household of her own. Replacing her won't be easy.

"What did you decide to serve after the ceremony, Marguerite? I've lost track of things. Half the fun of having your wedding here is knowing all the details."

She looks stricken by the question. I do worry about the stresses planning for her own reception might create around what should be a joyous day for her. Harry and I didn't fret about such things given our tiny ceremony and immediate departure.

"We are delaying, Mrs. Stone."

"But September is the perfect time."

I had been looking forward to cutting the hydrangeas just before they lose the last of their August blues and drying them for the occasion. As she lays out small handkerchiefs for the scones, I scrutinize her face.

"Is it Terrance? Is he giving you trouble?" I met her beau on several occasions, and he seemed to me to be a perfect gentleman.

"No, it's not Terrance, ma'am." She turns away from me toward the pantry. "I told him I'm not quite ready."

This from the girl who confided in me, almost apologetically, that her life's dream is a household brimming with at least five children. This from the girl who couldn't stop blushing for a week after her first dance with Terrance. This from the girl who began sewing her wedding dress the day after he proposed.

"This is because of me." I lower myself onto one of the kitchen chairs.

"No, ma'am. It's just not a good time," she says meekly.

How many of the people around me are delaying their living on account of my dying?

"It's the perfect time, and I would love nothing more than to have a wedding on this lawn to attend."

"But it's not right to leave you now. And Mr. Blackwell." She averts her eyes from mine again.

"So keep working after you marry."

"Terrance won't allow it. He says he's no husband if I still need to work."

"What if you want to work? It's not always about money."

"I shouldn't keep you, Mrs. Stone. Your guests and Mr. Blackwell are in the sunroom with Alice."

This surprises me. I didn't hear anyone come down after me. The day has gotten started and I didn't even notice. Time ticks on without needing any permission from me.

"I told them I would bring warm bread and tea," she says. "And then I can take care of the basket, all right?"

"Thank you, Marguerite," I say, without moving.

She nods and smiles and busies herself with the oven. I push myself up, walk to the door, and then turn back.

"Perhaps some creamed wheat?" I ask. "I'm sure they would like that before their journey."

As soon as I appear around the corner of the sunroom, Harry jumps to my side.

"How do you feel, love?"

Alice retrieves a blanket from the chest beside her chair, at the ready to place it on my lap. I still have Marguerite on the mind and wonder when exactly everyone started planning around my movements, in a constant state of worry. Did it start directly upon my return from Chicago? Or was it only after the doctor's declaration of certain doom? Or perhaps it was a steady progression, starting when my arthritis robbed me of my agility and a great deal of my strength. After fighting my whole life to prove I am not of the weaker sex, my body has betrayed me. And my family is the one to suffer the consequences.

"I missed your last day, and now leaving day has come too soon," I say, lowering myself onto the brocade love seat. "Can we convince you to stay one more day?"

Harry sits beside me. The upholstery is already warm from the sun beaming through the windows. I often think of this room as a birdcage encased in glass, with cushioned chairs and oriental rugs replacing perches and wood chips.

"I wish we could, but we are expected at Point of Pines," Nette says.

"Temperance again?" As much as I detest the effects of alcohol, I have long held that men are not likely to hand the vote to women if they think we'll take their drink from them.

"The platform will actually be broader than temperance. It will put forth that all men of intellect should rethink much about their day-to-day lives," Sam says. "You should write an editorial about that idea."

Two years younger than Harry, Sam has aged similarly, his hair the color of clouds, his cheeks sunken by age. But just like his brother, his eyes haven't lost their mischievous sparkle, and his memory is nearly perfect.

"Already in the works," Harry says. "I thought I'd take a go at that one."

Marguerite brings in a tray of tea and bread. Alice helps her deliver small bowls of oatmeal. I take one so as not to turn attention my way.

"And what do you hear of the recent Board of Lady Managers meetings?" Sam asks.

"We continue to get an astounding number of letters decrying the 'shameful disagreements' among the women there," Alice says. "It seems men can argue and shout, and as long as they don't break out in fisticuffs, no one takes notice. But one public disagreement between women and it becomes national news."

I sit back and listen to this group discuss the issues of the day, wishing I could suspend this moment, make it last a little longer. I glance at Nette and can see by the downturn of her mouth, even when she tries to smile, that she is thinking the same thing I am. Today is the last day we will likely ever see each other.

I have been more than blessed to have her in my life. There is symmetry to the fact that Nette and I married brothers, that we unexpectedly opened our hearts, and in doing so, solidified our sisterhood in an entirely new way. I think back on the many moments in my life that were defined by her presence, our hours of practicing rhetoric together, the urgent conversations that stretched long into each night, our shared understanding of motherhood and its losses, her unwavering support of me after the Philadelphia scandal, after everything. The list is endless.

"Not to rush, but your carriage is prepared whenever you are ready," Phillip says from the doorway.

Nette and I lock eyes then, and she can no longer mask her deep sadness. I find I must momentarily look away.

"Your visit has done us a world of good," I say. "Thank you for making the journey."

As we walk toward the front door, Harry and Sam make promises to see each other soon, even though they know the distance will likely keep them apart for months, if not an entire year. Alice hugs Nette and then hurries ahead to say good-bye to her uncle.

Nette's arm is linked in mine, her head on my shoulder as we amble through the foyer. It reminds me of so many sunset strolls we took in college, and I appreciate that she has momentarily forgotten who is the one now that most often needs holding up.

"I put the letters in your desk," she says.

"Thank goodness." Relief floods me, and my legs almost give way.

"Alice has organized everything by year up there, which made it considerably easier. I hope I found the ones you were looking for."

"Thank you. For so many things, my friend. For so many things."

The threshold looms above us.

"I will miss you, sister, more than you know," Nette says.

"Don't worry. We will meet again, of that I'm sure," I tell her.

We embrace for a long moment. I do believe we will be reunited in the great beyond, no matter what form it might take, but it is difficult to let go of her now, this sister of mine. She is the one person who has understood every hardship I have ever experienced, every mood that threatened to drown me, and was always at the ready with a steady hand to pull me up. I will miss her so.

I reluctantly release her and watch as she and Sam climb aboard the horse car. I stay in the doorway, my hand in the air, until I can see them no more.

❧

As soon as Harry leaves for the *Journal* later that morning, I ask Alice if she wouldn't mind making a fire in my room.

"Maybe you'd like to sit in the sun?" she asks. "It's quite warm outside."

"No thank you. I was awake very early, and I think I will have a small rest."

After she opens the flue and prepares the fire, she turns and appraises the room. Stacks of old *Women's Journal*s sit atop a trunk in one corner, and a pile of books next to my desk threatens to topple over from her scrutiny. She picks up the afghan from the floor near the hearth, refolds it, and drapes it neatly across the back of the chair. She looks again at my desk and I know she would like nothing more than to tidy it up.

"Thank you for the fire, sweet pea. I'll be down in time for tea today."

She demurs and closes the door behind her. Once I hear her footsteps descend all the way down the stairs, I open the center drawer of my desk and find the small stack of letters, all postmarked 1869. Two from Florida, one addressed in my own hand.

I quickly reread the two from Florida—the one from Harry announcing his land sales and his intention to stay past the season, the other from his sister, the words just as harsh now as they were then. The superstition of the church maintains that bad things come in threes. For me, it has always been twos: my tax protest and losing the baby; the Musical Fund Hall debacle and rumors of untoward behavior between Harry and me; Kansas and *The Revolution*. And then these two things: Harry's betrayal and the final break in my partnership with Susan. This last pair is full of almost as much loss as the first, the feeling of being utterly alone still visceral. I still can't understand how she lost track of her senses so completely. Her sense of fairness and justice. She, who I had thought the most morally resolute of women! And Harry. That cut too deep to probe. It seemed best to just close up the wound before there was any threat of infection.

I open the last letter in the stack, the one I wrote to him, and try to remember if I felt as clear as the words sound now, if I was as confident in the future as I portrayed on the page.

> *When we first met, you declared that we could do more good for the women's cause together than I could do on my own, and if we were married you would devote yourself to it. I hope you will maintain that pledge . . . With my proceeds from the sale of western land, I intend to purchase a proper home in Boston . . . With any luck, my new paper will have a much wider reach than The Revolution and will serve to properly bolster the AWSA and the cause . . . You will never see two people more eager to see you than your cub and me.*

Shifting in my chair, my arthritic limbs aching, I reflect on how much of my letter came to pass; Harry devoted to the cause, the *Women's Journal* flourishing for over twenty years as the true sentinel of our movement, the house I bought here in Dorchester remaining our beloved home. It's almost as if I willed the future simply by declaring it so.

I fold the letters in my lap and turn my attention to the fireplace. The logs in the grate have settled into a smoky glow, but there is still plenty of fire to be coaxed from the char to burn these papers from memory. I consider the finality of erasing the past in that way. Is it the wise course? By unspoken agreement, Harry and I never discussed the episode after he came home—there was no point. He devoted himself to our family and to the cause entirely. Sometimes I thought this dedication might have come from a sense of obligation, some combination of guilt and shame that gave him no choice but to do my bidding, to be the husband and reform partner I had demanded he be. At other times, especially when I watch him at work or at play with Alice—he still reads books aloud to her in the evenings, and he remains the first reader of every poem she writes—I understand that this is where he wanted to be all along. Of late, I have begun to realize there is very little difference between the two.

But do I have the right to smudge out this part of our lives? Would it be any different than how Elizabeth and Susan decided to erase from history their shameful moments, choosing instead to write their *History* without mention of Train or their opposition to the Fifteenth Amendment?

Is it even possible to change the true imprint of the past? The challenge isn't so much in erasing one fact, or one moment from memory. That is done easily enough by extinguishing it from all conversation or inner thought until it ceases to exist, like a flame deprived of air. The real difficulty is in wiping away all the footprints leading up to and walking away from those moments. The wagon wheel is still part of the tracks it leaves behind on a dusty trail. Even if you destroy the wheel, aren't the tracks still obvious to the travelers that come after us?

I finger the letters in my hands, the paper yellowed and brittle, like so many fallen leaves. I never did like the signs of impending winter, the reminder that the earth so frequently becomes cold and inhospitable, the trees standing bare, with no protection from the elements. Nature offers us no way to gather up the leaves and sew them into a coat for the tree. It must stand unashamed in the face of the harsh season. Only then will it be rewarded by spring, a kind of forgiveness, a celebration of having survived.

Perhaps I should leave these letters, then, put them in my drawer to be discovered as fate allows. Let them speak for themselves if ever they are found, evidence at some level that love's winter can be thawed, that renewal is possible.

A quiet knock and cracking open of my door reveal Harry, his white beard leaning beyond the doorjamb. When he sees me sitting by the fire, he opens the door fully and enters.

"I saw the smoke from your chimney on my way up the road. Are you not too warm in here?" A different level of concern then crosses his face. "Are you feeling chilled?"

"Alice indulged my mood for a fire." I refrain from fanning my face with the letters. "Is everything all right at the office?"

It is early for him to be home.

"I have come with the most extraordinary news. I came right upstairs. I didn't even stop to find Alice."

He looks like a boy just given his first bag of caramels, enough to eat his fill and keep some in reserve.

"New Zealand passed women's suffrage! Kate Sheppard has done it!" He rushes in toward me, kisses me on the cheek, and then spins in place. "Alice!" he yells. "She really must be here." He runs back into the hall. "Alice! Come quickly."

"What is it? What's wrong?" Alice calls from the stairwell.

I hear her bounding down the narrow stairs so fast I worry she will injure herself. She practically falls into my room, relief instantaneously replacing the concern on her face when she sees me sitting by the fire.

"I didn't mean to frighten you," Harry says, "but you had to be with us for this."

He tells her the news, and they begin to dance a little jig. Happiness swells inside me. Anne Whitney's poem comes to mind again, about the aloe that blossoms only once every one hundred years. The news from New Zealand is proof that the ground we are tilling is not fallow, even though it is a separate country, even though our weather systems are different, this fight will yield fruit.

"Mother, isn't it incredible?" Alice says, and then to her father, "Are we able to get the headline in place for this Saturday?"

"It's being set right now. And I already dispatched a message to Miss Sheppard to send all possible details. I told her we will devote a full issue to their success as soon as we can."

"Maybe all our syndicators can solicit reactions from their readers, and we'll publish their letters. Isn't it incredible?" she asks again.

"And I thought this week's poem on the front should be swapped out for your 'All Rise' poem. Doesn't that capture the moment well?"

"Wonderful, Papa! I'll rewrite this week's column. I should probably get to the office."

They both turn to me.

"Do you mind if we are a bit late this evening?" Harry says. "I hate to rush off . . ."

I wave my hands. "Go, go. I'm more than fine. Thank you for coming home to tell me."

Harry presses his lips to the top of my head. "You may not have campaigned in New Zealand, but you own part of this victory."

Alice kisses my cheek, and they hurry out of my room and down the stairs, leaving me with a smile I cannot contain. As the house quiets again, I replay the scene in my mind and find watching the two of them celebrate as gratifying as hearing the news itself. They will fare well after I am gone, as long as they have each other. He is still the man who can do no wrong, and she his doting daughter. It is the one thing I have no right to disrupt.

I pick up the letters again. The parchment now looks blemished by the words the ink has left behind. I drop them onto the logs one by one and watch them catch fire.

26

It is a bright October day, and I see more yellow and orange out my window now than green and blue, the brazen colors ready to engulf a whole season just before reducing it to ash. I rarely leave my bed now, my body too weak to make it all the way down the stairs, the prospect of climbing back up an impossible hurdle.

I am attended to every minute, by Alice, Harry, Marguerite, or a visitor, something I have learned to accept. It's terrible to feel so useless, but I do my best to stay in a good humor—my failure is not the fault of those kind enough to care for me. My relative immobility, however, leaves me no choice but to receive visitors in my bedroom. And there have been droves of them. Word of my illness trickled through Boston at the end of the summer, instigating several visits a week from various friends and colleagues. But ever since the notice appeared in *The Women's Journal*, each day brings a new cluster of people to my door. I am blessed by well-wishes of friends and overwhelmed with the kindness of complete strangers.

Just yesterday, my great friends Mary Campbell, Julia Ward Howe, and Mary Livermore all arrived on the same day. The day before, two of Alice's Boston University classmates came by to thank me for boarding them in their first year, and then our first maid here practically ran into the room. She insisted that Alice hear the story about the day I demanded she work to prepare a lavish Fourth of July picnic even though I had promised her the day off, and how I surprised her by inviting no guests but her family to enjoy the feast. I had forgotten all about that day.

I particularly enjoyed the visit of an Amanda Guernsey, whom I hadn't remembered meeting before. She recounted in great detail the day in 1879 when we both arrived at the Massachusetts statehouse in Boston on what was to be a wonderous day. Massachusetts had passed a partial-suffrage law. While women were not given full access to the polls, we would be able to vote for school committee candidates, the state conceding that mothers, deeply involved in their children's schooling, were well-equipped to vote on such matters. I would finally cast a proper ballot.

With my two-dollar poll tax in hand, I joined at least a dozen other women pushing through the doors of the statehouse at opening time. Situated in the basement, the registrar's office was hardly a grand affair, musty cold air permeating a space devoid of sunlight, but it felt to me as though I was visiting the private sanctuary of a royal.

I presented my fee and took time to sign my name as legibly as possible, each letter an indelible marker of my new right. I smiled as Mr. Wightman turned the ledger around to verify my signature and certify my status. He had come to several of my lectures in the upper halls of the building, and we knew each other in passing.

He pushed his glasses up on his nose and tugged on his tie. His mustache and beard were perfectly trimmed, his crisp white shirt newly laundered and pressed.

"I'm sorry. You must sign this as Mrs. Blackwell."

"But that is not my name. My name is Lucy Stone."

"I understand what you call yourself, but to vote you must sign your married name."

"Mr. Wightman," I said, trying not to let this squabble mar the moment, "I pay my taxes under the name Lucy Stone. I own property here under that name. Surely I can vote under that name."

"Mrs. Stone—" he started.

I interrupted. "Precisely, Mr. Wightman. When have you ever called me anything else?"

He sighed. "This law was put in place so mothers could vote on behalf of their children's education. Mothers are married. Married women have a married name. If you'd like to vote today, you must register under your husband's name."

"I'd like to speak to your superior."

"Ma'am. I already spoke to the solicitor this morning. He knew you'd be coming and explained the rule to me quite clearly. I'm afraid this decision is final."

I leaned against the cold counter, stunned. They had designed an impossible choice. If I insisted on registering under my maiden name, I would give up my chance to vote. If I followed their rules, I would be giving up something else entirely. On top of it, this rule had been made specifically for me—there were no other married women in the entire state, as far as I knew, who would face this same dilemma.

I turned my back on Mr. Wightman and walked out of the statehouse, leaving behind my first, and given my current state, likely only chance to vote.

"I was standing behind you in line that day," Amanda said from the chair beside my bed. "There must have been twenty or thirty of us waiting while you argued your point."

I did walk past a long column of women when I left the hall, many of them no doubt wondering why I looked so aggrieved on such a joyous day.

"I signed my name, *Mrs. George Guernsey, born Amanda White*. All the women behind me did the same."

I had never before heard that part of the story. I thanked her profusely for sharing it with me.

There have been so many visitors, each conversation its own small gift to me, a pleasure to unwrap, all different in shape and size. Until it is time to say good-bye. At that moment, they all have the same face, the same glossy eyes, the same droop to their mouths. I try to send each of them off on a cheery note, for there really is no cause for heartache.

There is one visitor who hasn't come. I sense I will need to accept that our friendship ended long ago. I cannot let it weigh on me. There are so many others to be received and comforted.

I watch Harry and Alice closely and worry for them, particularly Harry. He looks wilted, his gaiety and mischievousness gone. I remind him I'm not afraid of where I'm headed, even though it may be unfamiliar. He shakes his head and says any new place sounds better than this place without me in it. He is such a dear.

Dr. Greer stands at my bedside now, with Alice and Harry seated at the foot of the bed, hanging on his every word. I assure them I'm no longer in any great pain but explain as best I can that I am sometimes disoriented, finding myself in a state of middle-of-the-night wakefulness, no matter the time of day. I am neither fully alert nor yearning for sleep, but at times my mind won't engage in either territory. At other times I'm entirely lucid and feel almost well. I can't ever predict which the day will bring.

The doctor nods his head in understanding, telling me this is perfectly normal.

"There is no need to be alarmed," he says.

"I don't know why I would be. Dying is as natural as being born."

His smug smile suggests that he knows more about this than I do, which strikes me as absurd. He looks to Harry and Alice.

"You might want to consider limiting visitors. You cannot underestimate how tiring they can be."

"Then perhaps we should end this visit. Thank you, Doctor," I say.

He raises his eyebrows and excuses himself with a "very well."

"Really, Mother. I do worry all these visits are too much for you."

"Until I cannot talk. I will not turn away those who have taken the time to come."

"Perhaps we could agree on a schedule," Harry says. "Some days visitors can come; some days it can be just the three of us. Wouldn't that be lovely?"

"All three of us? What about the paper?" They have expertly handled the burden of putting up the *Journal* each week with one of them almost always home with me. Having both of them out of the office regularly simply wouldn't work.

Harry and Alice look at each other and exchange a knowing expression. "We've decided to suspend publication for a couple of weeks."

I must truly be near the end.

"That won't do," I say.

"Mother, no one would blame us."

I close my eyes for a moment. Fatigue makes my voice quaver sometimes now, and I want to be sure I can command my calmest tone.

"We have never missed a week since we began publication in 1870. Not one. In the face of disappointment, women need a steady accounting of the progress being made in small towns or in faraway countries. For each state campaign that fails, we publish hundreds of stories of the good work women are doing outside the domestic sphere. For every reformer who passes on, we need news of the next leaders. People need this."

I struggle to catch my breath. I realize now how generous my visitors have been with their words, forcing me to do very little of the talking.

"Surely a few weeks won't make a difference," Harry says.

"No pause. It cannot be."

He sighs. "May I propose this: Visitors can come in the morning, as long as you are feeling up to it. The afternoons will be for rest and for family."

He might be right. The need for absolute quiet suddenly hits me.

"And the paper goes on?"

"Without pause."

I close my eyes and let the darkness envelope me.

❧

I have begun to look forward to my afternoons now. Harry and Alice often read to me, Harry from old books or from letters sent by friends too distant to visit. Alice reads me poetry, much of it lines I love from Whittier and Lowell, Bryant and Whitney. Today she is reading me Petros Durian's poems, several of which she translated herself.

"Tell me. How much of your work is translation, and how much of it is poetry?" How have I never asked her this before?

"That's a bit like asking how much of a speech is the words and how much of it is the delivery."

"Indeed. Thought without action leaves too much undone."

I jerk up as a cough wracks my chest. Alice rushes to me with a bowl and handkerchief. She has become too used to catching my blood before it hits the bedsheets. After I wipe my mouth, we sit quietly for a bit, so my breathing can resume its normal pace. I try to send gratitude to her through my eyes. She fidgets in her chair, and I notice a folded paper in her hands. She looks unsure what to do with it. Panic engulfs me. Was there another letter about the messy business with Harry that Nette didn't rescue? I wrack my brain in search of discarded memories and forgotten correspondence.

"What is it?" I finally ask, unable to let the silence grow any further between us.

"I found the speech you wrote for the World's Fair when I was cleaning up your desk the other day." She looks up at me shyly, like she did as a girl when asking me to review her homework. "Do you really think I can do the job?"

I smile. The only speech I've ever fully written in advance, and yet I still managed to go off script, the biggest news of the day left unspoken.

"Oh, sweet pea, of course you can. You've been doing it for months. And truth be told, you were ready for it a long time ago. I just didn't know how to let go of the reins."

Tears spill over her lashes, and she places her hand over her mouth.

"Why didn't you tell me before?" She pushes past a crack in her voice.

"I didn't want you to feel pushed. I wanted you to be able to make your own decision about Johannes. Just like I had the chance to do."

She nods her head.

"I can't possibly leave Papa," she says after a moment. This is as close as she's come to admitting that it will soon be just the two of them. I smooth a stray hair off her face, as if my touch could erase the pain I see there.

"You're not here to live your parents' lives. You must live your own."

"But this is my life. I'm proud of *The Women's Journal*. And there's still so much work to be done."

I smile and reach for her hand. She is so much like me.

"Then the paper is yours if you want it."

"Thank you for your faith in me." She squeezes my hand tightly.

"What about Johannes?"

She looks to the ceiling, her lip quivering faintly. "I've yet to imagine a way to have both things in my life."

I want to tell her to try, to do whatever it takes not to let her career limit her ability to love, and not to let love squash her professional dreams. But before I can say more, a clatter coming from the front of the house interrupts us. Alice wipes her eyes and goes to the window.

"There is a carriage outside."

It's after three. No one should be visiting at this hour.

"I'll be just a moment," she says, and leaves the room.

Like so much about these past few months, it is both a comfort and a frustration to be this well protected. But there are no two people who know me as well as Harry and Alice, who know just when I need company and just when I need rest. Of all the blessings in my life, I realize how rare is the opportunity to be known so well and to be loved anyway.

It has been a long day already. My arms are heavy, and my head is swimming again with the need for darkness. I trust Alice will send the visitor away. I settle more deeply into my pillows, sleep clawing at me. Just as I am about to doze off, she is back at my side.

"There is someone here I think you will want to see."

I turn my head to see Susan standing in the door.

She is wearing her usual black dress, her hair pulled back in a bun, her wire-rimmed glasses accentuating the point of her nose. No red shawl today. That is reserved for public appearances.

"Why didn't you send word for me when we were both in Chicago?" She comes to the chair on my side of the bed, but I think I see a moment's hesitation.

I push myself back up to a more respectable sitting position.

"I didn't know then. Or at least I wasn't sure."

We remain quiet for a moment, even after Alice leaves us. I think back to standing on the stage at the World's Fair. A mere five months ago I wouldn't have known what to say to Susan. It has been in the retelling of the past that I see it more clearly.

"Thank you for coming," I finally say.

"I think it's fair to say I was summoned."

"Your trip was a success?"

She tells me about the various cities and towns she visited, about the friendly crowds in Wichita and the rowdy opponents she experienced in Shawnee.

"And you wouldn't recognize Topeka. It has grown four times over since the campaign in '68."

The mention of that time is like inviting George Francis Train himself into the room, and we both grow silent.

"Your letter said there were things you wanted to discuss," she eventually says, folding her hands on her lap, more like a student readying for an oral exam than one old friend visiting another. Is there no lingering fondness for me in her heart?

I look over her shoulder and through the window. Where the wind once rippled through the branches as harmlessly as it might play in the strands of a young girl's hair, each gust now threatens to pull the last brittle leaf to the ground.

"You know I've always thought the writing of your *History* a foolish task. Initially because it struck me as premature." *As premature as if a slave had written a* History of Emancipation *from inside the walls of the plantation*, I think, but don't want to expend more words than necessary.

"Haven't we been through all this?"

Retelling the events leading up to the AERA convention helped me see just how clever it was for her to write the story the way she wanted it to be remembered: without Train, without mention of our disagreement over the Fifteenth Amendment, without acknowledging the need for two competing women's associations. I assumed readers at the time would see the nonsense of it, but she knew they would take it all as fact. Even after *The Revolution* folded, two years into its existence, leaving Susan saddled with ten thousand dollars' worth of debt she has spent the rest of her life trying to repay, the story she and Elizabeth decided to tell has become the dominant story of our movement. It will be the only one people remember.

"There is a poem I have been reading frequently lately. Is there a newspaper clipping over on my desk?" I ask, pointing across the room. "A narrow column with a poem?"

She rustles though a few papers and holds up a section of newsprint, the ink smudged on the edges. Her movements are still quick and strong. She will be holding the reins of this fight for years after I am gone.

"'Up and Away'? Is that the one?"

"Yes, that's it. Read it if you would."

She sits, and I watch her eyes move from line to line. I've read it so many times in the last several weeks that I can hear its rhythm in my head as she silently absorbs each phrase, the words easy to recall.

Up and away like the dew of the morning,
That soars from the earth to its home in the sun,
So let me steal away, gently and lovingly,
Only remembered by what I have done.

The second stanza is my favorite.

My name and my place and my tomb all forgotten,
The brief race of time well and patiently run,
So let me pass away, peacefully, silently,
Only remembered by what I have done.

I watch her as she reads the rest, the refrain of the last line repeating in each of six stanzas: *only remembered by what I have done.* She lowers the page to her lap as she finishes.

"This is how we are different, you and I," I say. "You told me long ago that you were inspired by my relic speech, by my refusal to be remembered on my tombstone as the property of someone else, as merely someone's wife."

"Nor will you be."

"But it was never about getting my own name etched in stone. It was only ever about women having the chance to accomplish something meaningful, to be known for having ministered to the ill, or worn the robes of a judge, or run a railroad if she so chooses."

"And you think I have dedicated my life to this cause for recognition?"

"I think the cause needs it. These past few months, I've come to realize that people need a way to make sense of all that has come before. Stories matter. And every great moment in history comes with the story of one person in particular who is integral to it. It is you who will forever be associated with the efforts to elevate our sex."

"You and I both know there is never one individual who can claim responsibility for that kind of progress," she says.

"Of course not, but history needs one person to serve as the symbol, one name to act as the threshold between before and after. Lincoln, Douglass, Washington. For suffrage, it will be you."

"And you think it should be you?"

"The *History* is already written. It is the standing record."

"And you asked me here to register your disapproval of that."

"I asked you here to offer you my advice."

She raises her eyebrows and sits back.

"How generous of you," she says, her voice thick with sarcasm. "You do know that I haven't rested for a moment since I took up this fight. I think I know how it's done."

"I raised a family, Susan."

"Not just that. You should have stood with us in '69. I never understood how you allowed our abolitionist friends to toss us aside so easily in favor of the negro vote. It wasn't right."

I am amazed that she still sees me as the one who made the mistake on that day.

"I could not have lived with myself if I didn't support the amendment. Never did I regret that choice."

"Elizabeth was right. She always said you were too high-minded for politics," she says, matter-of-factly. "The Fifteenth was going to be ratified whether it had our support or not. It was about making a statement."

"You don't know that."

"Wendell Phillips knew it. So did Douglass. In fact, he knew he had wronged us by pushing us to the side but decided it was what he had to do to win. We were trying to win, too."

"As I recall you were furious with him for that," I say.

"Of course. But we reconciled. And he has continued to be one of our greatest champions."

I wonder if Douglass truly forgave her or if this is another story she tells herself. Douglass always was smart enough to keep influencers close, and he and Susan are both politicians at heart, ready to make public concessions in service to their ultimate goals. But true reconciliation, including forgiving her association with Train? I doubt it.

"Has it ever occurred to you how difficult it was for me to take that stance? To stand in front of all those friends and suggest not supporting the Fifteenth? It nearly broke me. But it was what had to be done. We had to make clear that being left behind was not acceptable, that we didn't believe the Fifteenth came anywhere close to the principle of universal suffrage we had all agreed to fight for. But you gave in."

"Has it ever occurred to you to apologize for that stance? I assume you recognize how damaging the entire episode was to our movement? It pitted white and black women against each other," I say.

"But the Fifteenth didn't include them either."

"You know as well as I do that educated suffrage, as you proposed, would have given most white women, a select few negro men, and absolutely no negro women the vote, with no prospects of it any time soon. Even worse, the battle cry you took up, that if Sambo—I think was the favored word—if Sambo were allowed the vote ahead of white women, he would begin to perpetrate outrageous acts of violence against white women. How could you?"

"Those were Elizabeth's words, not mine," she says, defiant.

"And when have you ever disavowed her words?"

She adjusts herself in her chair and says nothing to this.

"It's not too late, Susan. You have enormous influence. You must use it more wisely. This was never supposed to be a white woman's fight."

Her cheeks turn slightly pink. Her spine remains as straight as ever, but this is causing her some distress.

"I think you're more interested in legacy than you pretend," she says. "I was ready to have the crowds boo me if it meant winning what was rightfully ours. You're so determined not to sully your good name that you can't see the strategy of the thing, the course that might have given us a chance to win back then. You gave in."

"The only thing I gave in to was principle. I had learned my lesson well at the Musical Fund Hall. I never wanted to be schooled in that manner again. While I'm certain I did further our cause in some small way that night, change some important minds, it was at the expense of what was right. I never should have stepped foot inside. I could not make the same mistake twice."

As I look at her, I realize there's something else, something even more fundamental to our friendship that has long weighed me down, like pieces of granite tied about my petticoats. Something I've been loath to call out, maybe even afraid to admit. But the process of unspooling my life and knitting it back together for Alice has made it impossible to ignore. All this looking back reminded me how insufficient I have felt for much of my life. My devotion to my daughter came at a price for the cause, and my devotion to the cause came at a price to her. And that doesn't even account for how lacking I was as a wife at times, as the loving companion I had promised to be.

"It was you who abandoned me," I say, practically a whisper, finally putting voice to the puncture in my heart I have been nursing for more than twenty years.

"Pardon?"

"Trying to be a good mother and wife while doing the work of our cause was harder than you may imagine."

"You chose that course."

"So did Elizabeth."

"No, Elizabeth had no choice. She was already wedded, already a mother several times over before she understood the power she had within her for this work. But motherhood limited her. You saw it with your own eyes."

Her words are tinged with resentment still, with renewed anger at me for willingly walking into a matrimonial bond, knowing what I knew, and despite the responsibilities to the cause I had already taken on. She knew firsthand how lonely the road could be. Did she not ever long for a companion? Did she ever consider that a man might be worthy of her, could be considered her equal?

"You know, I've told myself for years that I lost your friendship because of our disagreement over the Fifteenth Amendment. But I lost your support the day I became a mother."

Now that I've said it, I see the truth in it. She never accepted that the work of a mother is as sacred as the work of reform.

"I don't begrudge you your family." She is clearly offended. "Harry has turned out to be a better advocate for us than I initially gave him credit for. And Alice, well, you have raised an exceptional young woman in her. You are to be congratulated."

"The right or wrong of it have nothing to do with who Harry and Alice turned out to be. They are my family. My choice to marry splintered something between us. Your creation of the NWSA was as much a response to that as it was to the Fifteenth."

"Don't be ridiculous."

"Then why purposely exclude me from it?"

"You are a stubborn soul, Lucy Stone. Forever anchored to your version of what is right."

"That we have in common," I say.

We stay quiet for a moment. I watch her face. Something shifts. She grows quieter, less severe in her posture.

"Everyone in this cause is either a lieutenant of mine or one of yours. We allowed ourselves to be at odds for too long," she says. "It may have cost us decades in this fight."

"And I've run out of time."

She puts her hand on mine.

"Surely you didn't ask me here to quarrel. We will eventually win. You must not doubt that."

She will always be about winning in the end. I remind myself that she has only the cause. Whether she agreed with my choices or not, I am grateful for all of them.

"The only victory is true, universal equality. I hope you will work for it," I say.

A cough jumps from my chest to my mouth, catching me by surprise. I reach for the bowl on the nightstand and grab my handkerchief, realizing too late that I'm holding the edge of my bedsheet to my bloody lips.

Susan doesn't flinch. She retrieves the handkerchief from the floor and hands it to me. Once she is satisfied that the coughing has subsided, she puts the bowl aside and expertly folds back the sheet, tucking the soiled section safely beneath my blanket.

"Too much talking," I say.

She sits back down and adjusts the wire rims on her nose, her gaze soft, almost motherly.

"I will miss your voice," she says. "I didn't think I would ever be able to hold a crowd the way you could. Words like music."

I have always gotten such credit for my melodic voice, *like a gentle stream in an angry world*, someone once called it. Like the female eagle, fierce without sounding it, I like to think.

"And you have offered our country a wonderful model of what being a wife and mother and professional can look like. That it is possible. There is no other like you."

I know this statement costs her dearly. If there is any belief behind her words, the admission eliminates the easiest justification she has for her own choices, choices that left her alone in the world.

"I made a mess of it at times, believe me."

She smiles, and a warmth spreads through me, thawing the bitterness and anger that had become a frozen obelisk in my heart, replacing it with a tenderness for my friend I haven't felt in a very long time.

"You're truly not afraid?"

"I only worry for Harry and Alice. Leaving them will be difficult."

She nods. She's been on the other side of that, losing family members while on the road. She has made enormous personal sacrifices for this work, choices that surely wounded her at times, each one placing a different scar on her heart. I know because I have them too.

"How long can you stay with us?" I ask.

"This was an unscheduled stop. I have to catch a train later this afternoon."

"Still counting your miles?"

We both smile at the memory. I feel the door of time pressing on me, threatening to close. There is one more thing I must say.

"Despite our differences, sharing this work with you has been a privilege. Parallel tracks."

She leans onto the bed and takes my hand again.

"I would never have found my voice without you, Lucy Stone."

It's a generous statement, and I decide to accept the gift of it. I'm too tired to protest.

"I should take care not to miss my train. And give you some rest," she says, but makes no move to leave.

I don't know how long she sits with me after I drift off, but when I next open my eyes, darkness has fallen and the chair beside my bed is empty once more.

27

After Susan's visit, time stretches like dough and then contracts without warning. I am unsure for how long I doze and have a hard time tracking the length of time I am awake. Several days slip by as I travel between wakefulness and fitful sleep, never staying in one or the other for long.

When it is light, I watch more leaves take flight from the tree out my window and wonder how much longer it will be before it is completely stripped of life. Alice or Harry are by my side whenever I open my eyes now, even in the dark, a kerosene lamp turned down very low on the table beside the bed. Others come and go, or maybe I am simply remembering snippets of faces and conversations that have wandered through this room over the last few weeks. I don't often hear the sound of my own voice and wonder if it has given way. I test it once, forming my mouth into an "O" and pushing out a small noise. Alice jumps to my side, asking if something is wrong. I shake my head no and hope the smile I attempt actually registers on my face.

As time ebbs and flows, I run through all the stories I shared with Alice in my mind, moving backward, each one a stepping-stone in the babbling brook of my life. Some are soft and smooth, some slippery with moss, others dry and safe, all of them taking me further back. I can almost touch the contours of my mother's face, an image I haven't been able to see clearly for years. I hear my father's deep voice and Luther's laugh. Distant memories come back in sparks, like reignited embers from a dying fire. Coy's Hill is frequently the backdrop of these waking dreams. A mixture of comfort and fear permeates the air, longing and frustration, anger and a resounding peace in the woods surrounded by all those trees.

Another memory flickers.

Even though I began my story with Alice on Abigail's wedding day, I know that many other moments had already been piled on my cairn by then, all pointing me in the same direction. It is in looking fully downstream that the route between here and there becomes ever more obvious, as engrained in my life as the immovable crags of Coy's Hill.

Finally, I am able to see all the way back to the day that just might have been the beginning of it all, a day even more awful than Abigail's wedding day. I try not to let the memory overtake me, but it is one I have never forgotten.

❦

Father gave me permission to drive out the cows for the first time on my ninth birthday, and it didn't take me long to learn their movements, understand when they needed a nudge on the rump with a stick, and when I could stop moving long enough to watch the sun rise over the crags of rock in the distance. One morning, as I listened to the last howls of a distant coyote, I heard a different, breathless cry coming from somewhere behind me. I wheeled around to see Annie Cavanaugh running across the meadow toward our house. She was still in her bedclothes, and her hair trailed behind her like a wild flag. I raced down the back of the hill, losing my footing on a rocky outcropping and righting myself as I hurried toward her. She was one year younger than me, but faster, and she reached our porch before she saw me. Mama, who had a sense for trouble as fine-tuned as any mare, was already at the door, wrapping her arms around Annie and ushering her inside.

When I banged through the door, my mother held up her hand, silently telling me to slow down. I tried to quiet the noise of my own breathing as I watched her lower Annie into a chair in front of the hearth and kneel before her, stroking her hair. Blood trickled from Annie's nose, and her nightgown was torn at the knee. She'd run almost a mile to get to us.

"What is it, child? Is your mother all right?" Mama asked. Annie shook her head no. "Is it the baby?"

Mrs. Cavanaugh was due any time now. Deliveries of calves and infants went wrong every day. But Annie wagged her head again. No.

Mama's back stiffened, and her expression moved from concern to something closer to fear.

"Where is your father?"

Annie shrugged and started to cry harder. Mama pulled her in close.

"Lucy, please go get your father."

My legs wouldn't quite obey my intentions at first, and I almost tripped down the porch stairs. The look on Mama's face and Annie's sobs scared me.

Father was in the field, pulling the plow while Sarah dropped seeds in the newly tilled earth behind him. I didn't call out until I was close enough for him to hear me, and until I was certain I wouldn't start to cry when I used my voice.

"Father, Mama needs you."

"There are two more rows to do here. Breakfast can wait until the work is done."

"She needs you now."

He looked at me then, his ruffled brow showing his displeasure. He didn't abide anyone giving him orders.

I tried again. "It's the Cavanaughs. There's been trouble."

My father grumbled something before lowering the handles of the plow to the earth. He pulled his hat off and scratched behind his ear before taking long, slow strides back toward the house.

Sarah held her apron up, still full of seeds, and looked to me for clues.

"Let's go collect some eggs. I bet the chickens will like those seeds." Luther would have to gather wood for Mama's stove without me.

As I led Sarah toward the chicken coop, I couldn't help imagining what had happened that morning to send Annie running to us. We all knew Mr. Cavanaugh drank too much, and that drink made men mean. I hated the nights my father would ask Luther to bring up an extra quart of cider from the cellar. It made him short with Mama and too quick to use the switch on me. And I particularly dreaded when Joe Kramer would come visiting with his homemade whiskey, looking for a meal. He leered at me in a way that made me squirm. Luther never left my side when he was within ten feet of our house.

When Mr. Cavanaugh took to the bottle, he was known to disappear, sometimes for a day, sometimes for weeks. Despite the disrepair of their farm and the lack of food come harvesttime, there was a lightness I could sense in Annie's voice when he was gone. She would tell me funny stories about a spot she found for hide-and-seek that kept her younger brothers busy searching for almost an hour, or the time they ate what she called pancake bread for supper because her mother forgot to add the yeast. It was when Annie got quiet that I knew her father had come home.

By the time Sarah and I had checked every hen twice and filled our basket with seven fresh new eggs, Father had hitched up the wagon and headed toward the Cavanaughs' farm. Luther had saddled up Nugget and ridden in the other direction to get Dr. Morrison. Annie looked small in the chair by the hearth. She huddled under a wool blanket despite the warmth of the fire and the mild temperature of the day.

My sister Rhoda brought her a mug of warm milk.

"Let's bring those eggs to Mama," Rhoda said to Sarah. "You can help us with the biscuits for breakfast." Sarah proudly trotted toward the kitchen, leaving Annie and me alone. I sat by the chair at her feet.

"Are William and Samuel all right?"

Annie's brothers were a bit younger than Sarah, sweet boys who loved to climb our apple trees and knock the red orbs to the ground.

"They are still asleep, I think. I shouldn't have left them there. I shouldn't have left Ma there, but I didn't know what else to do," she said, her lip quivering as she spoke.

I waited for her to say more. I didn't know what to ask.

"Ma told me Grandpa was coming for us. She wrote him a letter last night to ask him to come for us. But Pa came home this morning and found the letter on the table. It was just his yelling that woke me up at first, but then—" She lowered her head as a stream of tears ran down her face. "By the time I got downstairs he was gone, and Ma was on the floor. There was blood on her face."

Mama stood up then and told me it was time to get to school. I'd never left the house without eating breakfast before, but Mama's eyes told me I had no choice.

I couldn't concentrate that day, with Annie's empty desk a constant reminder of the morning's events. I made it up to the blackboard only once to attempt a problem. The puzzles of weights and measures couldn't compete with the imprint on my mind of Annie's face, stricken with fear and anguish. Once Luther finally arrived at school, he had no news beyond having successfully summoned the doctor, and then being shooed out of the house. I could think of nothing else until the dismissal bell startled me out of my wandering thoughts.

As Luther and I walked home I fingered a small piece of rock candy in my pocket, a special treat from my teacher I had been saving in my desk. I hoped Annie was still at our house, so I could give it to her. Sugar had a way of making people smile.

I was relieved to see the keeping room brimming with activity when we arrived. On the hooked rug in front of the fire, Annie's little brothers, Samuel and William, played pick-up sticks with Sarah, their little giggles suggesting a level of normalcy that quieted my anxious mood. On the far side of the room, Annie and Rhoda worked the loom set up near the back window to take advantage of the afternoon light. I gave a small wave hello to Annie, and she smiled, her eyes still a little glassy but no longer rimmed in red. I was pleased to see a bag of clothes by the door, a sure sign they would all be staying for a bit. Sarah and I could easily share our bed with her, and there was plenty of space in Luther's room for the boys.

In search of Mama, I turned toward the kitchen. That's when I saw Mrs. Cavanaugh. She sat back from the large butcher block in the center of the room to make space for her extended belly, absentmindedly slicing a cucumber. She seemed worn out by the task, as if she'd been at it for hours. Her lower lip was swollen around the dark line of a cut. A scarf covered her hair and the sides of her face, but I could see a patch of purplish blue that swirled down from her left eyebrow to the edge of her jaw, transforming her normally friendly face into something raw and rough. I looked away, instinctively wanting to give her some privacy, or at least not let her know I could see her injuries so clearly.

My mother stood at the sink, her back to us, scrubbing potatoes.

"Is there wash that needs to be hung, Mama?" I asked, hoping my voice sounded normal.

Mrs. Cavanaugh looked up at me but immediately cast her eyes back down and pulled at the edge of her scarf.

"Oh good, you're home," Mama said. "Could you please make some cucumber sandwiches? The bread should be ready to come out. I want to be sure the kids get something to eat before they leave."

"Leave?" I took a tub of butter from the larder and pulled a spreader from the canister on the counter.

"The Cavanaughs are going to stay with Annie's grandparents for a while. Given Mrs. Cavanaugh's condition—" Mama glanced at Mrs. Cavanaugh and then started again. "The baby will be coming very soon, a good time to be under the care of one's mother. Remember that when it comes your time one day, Lucy."

I took the bread from the oven and transferred it to the counter, careful not to let it slip from the long tongs.

"Your father has gone to get Annie's grandfather and should be back with him any time now."

Annie's grandparents lived far away. They would have a long ride ahead.

I kept at the sandwiches even when I heard two carriages pull up, expecting Father to show Annie's grandfather inside. Instead, Annie's father burst through the front door, and in one swift motion had Mrs. Cavanaugh out of her chair and in his grip. He wore no hat, and the skin on his face looked too tight, like it had been stretched over something bulbous, with a thatch print of tiny veins pushing through his cheeks and nose. Mrs. Cavanaugh's arm hung at an uncomfortable angle under her husband's grip, her other hand protectively cupping her belly.

Next through the door was an older man I had met only once or twice before but recognized as Annie's grandfather, Mr. Norwell. He was stout and had soft wrinkles around his kind eyes. I remember him playing the fiddle at a church fair one time. He played happy songs.

"You can't be taking my woman," Mr. Cavanaugh snarled.

"She could have the baby any day," Mr. Norwell said gently. "Just let me take her home to her mother."

"You think I don't see what you're trying to do here? Who's going to cook for me if she's three counties away? This is my wife. She has responsibilities."

"Then let me bring the other children home with me for a little while," Mr. Norwell said. Mrs. Cavanaugh began to shake, half hanging, half standing there. "It will make it easier on both of you when the baby comes."

This comment seemed to remind Mr. Cavanaugh about his other charges. "Get on into the wagon, all of you. Now, or you'll get a whupping!"

Mrs. Cavanaugh began to sputter, water and snot sliding down her face. Her two little boys scurried over to her and clung to her skirts.

"Get," Mr. Cavanaugh said, swiping at them and pulling his wife toward the door.

"Annabelle, get moving or your mother will pay for it!" he yelled over his shoulder, pushing past his father-in-law and storming outside.

I waited for my father to come through the door. He would put a stop to this. He was strong and could hold Mr. Cavanaugh off, even if he grew angrier. Mrs. Cavanaugh and her children could go home to her parents' house, to a safe place for them and for the new baby. Where was he?

Annie walked toward the door, her arms wrapped around her body. I tried to send her a message of courage and hope somehow, but she looked down at the floor, much like I had upon seeing her mother's injuries.

I followed her out onto the porch and stood next to Luther. He put his arm around me, as if he could protect me from the moment. I watched in disbelief as the Cavanaughs climbed into the wagon, the two little boys now huddled on either side of Annie, Mrs. Cavanaugh up front with her husband still holding her arm. He jerked the reins with his other hand and pulled the horses around. The carriage lurched away from our house.

Mr. Norwell dropped into the rocking chair on our porch, his head in his hands. It was then that I saw Father sitting on his horse, not moving. He had seen it all and done nothing.

I broke away from Luther to find Mama.

"I don't understand," I said, running back inside. "Why did you let them go?"

I knelt on the floor at my mother's feet and cried into her skirt. She stroked my hair but didn't respond.

"He is perfectly within his rights," Father said. I hadn't noticed him enter.

"His rights?" I picked my head up. "How does he have that right?"

I never talked back to Father, but the world was shifting beneath me. Father always taught us, "Fair is what is right, and right is what is fair." He would gather us around the hearth and speak proudly of our ancestors, men like Gregory Stone, who gathered signatures in 1664 to protest Great Britain's attempt to govern the Massachusetts Bay Colonies, and my grandfather Francis, who fought in the American Revolution and later became a leader of Shay's Rebellion because he still wasn't satisfied with the rules and those making them. Why hadn't my father stopped the injustice happening on his own front porch?

"Get this child under control, Hannah," Father said. He put a hand on Luther's shoulder as he walked past him and up the stairs.

I sat up on my knees and swiped at my face with my sleeve. "Mama, help me understand."

I couldn't remember a time when my mother didn't look tired and pale, but she was usually quick to smile whenever she caught me staring. Now she didn't bother trying. She caressed the side of my face before letting her hand drop back into her lap.

"Your father did what he could, Lucy. He brought the Cavanaughs here this morning. He rode out to ask Mr. Norwell to come. That is all far beyond his place. We hoped they would be long gone before Mr. Cavanaugh came back, but it wasn't to be."

"But it didn't change anything," I said.

"It is up to the husband to make the rules. And his rules must be obeyed."

"But even with a man like that? Why can't we help her?"

"It's the way it's always been, Lucy."

"But it's not right."

"The sooner you can accept the way the world works, the happier you will be."

"No!" I yelled, and ran for the back door. "I will never accept that. Never!"

I sprinted across our backyard and into the barn. My favorite sheep, Top, stood up like he'd been waiting for me. When I threw myself into a pile of hay, he came and nuzzled my neck, then lay down in the crook of my body. I buried my face in his wooly coat and let it absorb my tears but could not find a way to get settled. My heart would not stop pounding, and every time I moved, I felt something poke into my leg. Shifting, I found the piece of rock candy languishing in my pocket. I held it out for Top. I had no use for sugar anymore.

I feel Harry's hand in mine before I see him, perched on the bed by my side. I force my eyes open and blink. It seems a tremendous effort. The pale, yellow light tells me it must be day again. My mouth is as dry as boiled wool, and I long for the sugar candy of my memory, wondering if I can form the words to ask for the childish comfort.

Harry smiles and rubs my hand.

"William?" My voice is husky.

"He is honored."

I had made a list a week or so ago of people I hoped might be willing to speak at my funeral. Harry had gone to visit William Lloyd Garrison's son this morning.

I nod my thanks.

"You still manage to get more done from this bed than most people in their prime." The light drains from his eyes. "I think of how much more you might have been able to accomplish had I not convinced you to marry me. Do you ever think about that?" he asks.

I shake my head no and try to squeeze his hand, but I'm not sure the pressure is enough for him to notice.

"I was so sure I would make your life better, but I fear I've been wholly inadequate, my love. I slowed you down, I held you back in ways I didn't even realize at the time. Can you forgive me?"

"Please," I say.

"I have been so lucky to call you wife."

I sense he is trying to say good-bye. Is it time to say good-bye?

"You've done so much," I say, my words not quite working. "Husband."

I see him now as his former self, the gallant young man with dangerous curls and mischievous eyes, climbing up Coy's Hill by my side, already making his case for marriage. I picture him standing at the doorway of the sitting room in Pittsburgh and feel the relief of knowing I hadn't lost him. Then Alice sits on his knee, mesmerized by his stories, the love between them palpable and soft, so unlike the charged tension between my father and me.

We shared a good life together, he and I. We formed the most authentic partnership we knew how. And we raised a beautiful daughter, our crowning achievement. I wish I had been softer at times, gentler with him on my dark days. But we found a way to forgive each other our shortcomings, and with forgiveness came a new blossoming of love. How lucky I was to have found him, a man who understood my need to be useful in the world without expecting me to ask him permission for any of it.

Did I thank Harry for all that? I can't remember.

I don't know how much time passes, but when I next open my eyes, Alice is beside me. She is crying.

"Sweet pea," I say.

The boiled wool is back on my tongue, and I have a hard time swallowing.

"Yes, what is it?" She leans down to me and turns her ear toward my mouth.

There is so much I want to say to her, to warn her about, to encourage her toward, to remind her not to forget, but I don't know if I'll be able to speak it all aloud. I want to tell her what a wonderful daughter she is. She is the light in the house, the spirit that gives Harry and me purpose. I want to tell her how much I regret that I didn't do more, didn't win for her all the rights a woman like her deserves. I want to tell her not to choose between love and work, between family and progress. The mixture of it all, the messiness, the challenges, are what enriches the soul. She is so much like me that I know she won't be content unless she's doing all she can to right what is wrong. Whatever form that takes for her, it is how she will live her life, and I want her to know how proud I am of her for her desire to make the world better.

Most of all, I hope she knows the deep joy she has brought me, an unconditional love like no other. Without her my place in the world would have been void of its glory, like a tree that never blossoms. I hope she will stay flung open to the world, open to possibility.

I'm not sure how many of these thoughts turn into actual words. But I feel her nodding. A tear spills from her cheek onto mine.

"Poem?" I ask.

She knows all my favorite poems and begins to recite one by Whittier. My own breathing is very loud in my head. I want to make it stop so I can hear the words, hear her voice.

"'Not on a blind and aimless way, the spirit goeth,'" I hear her whisper.

As Alice's voice washes over me, I take tentative steps across a broad green field and into an orchard. Craggy outcroppings spring from my peripheral vision, and I'm sure I must be back at beloved Coy's Hill, the rocks that used to be our castle to my left, the farmhouse with its wide porch behind me, the trees towering above. I come to the laughing brook of my childhood days and know immediately that I must cross. Beyond the stream is a land that looks familiar but at the same time is unlike anywhere I have been before. It is verdant, with mountains in the distance and wildflowers strewn across the landscape, acres of new territory I have yet to explore. And there is Old Bogue, wagging his tail in the distance, eager for our reunion. I smile, my body suddenly as light and agile as the twelve-year-old's that used to skip across these lands with him. He doesn't come any closer, instead waiting for me to make my own way across.

I look up to the sky one last time, to the clouds rushing by on the wind. My eye catches something moving at a different speed, swooping down out of the blue. A bald eagle. It dips to the stream and snatches a fish in its talons. Flapping up again it steadies, circles, and then settles high in a nest as big as a wagon wheel, several nestlings eager for a meal. My father was wrong those many years ago. Eagles have nested here all along.

I step into the water without hesitation, its temperature as warm as a summer's day. I was right not to be afraid, and I am ready to climb the next hill, no matter how steep.

AUTHOR'S NOTE

This is a work of fiction. I have tried to stay as close to historical record as possible while taking the liberty of changing some locations and condensing or telescoping time in service to the story. Several characters are entirely my invention, but the major players in this book are real historical figures. I have done my best to do them justice based on my research, all while speculating as to each individual's true intentions and imagining the words they may have spoken to one another.

It is true that Lucy Stone seldom wrote down her speeches, and while a few were transcribed and printed in newspapers of the day, the speeches you read here are of my own making. The exception is her famous words at the 1869 American Equal Rights Association convention, when she stated, "There are two great oceans, in the one is the black man, and in the other is the woman." Most of that speech is quoted verbatim.

Additionally, the excerpt from the 1855 *New York Times* article declaring that Lucy Stone had "come under the yoke" due to marriage is directly quoted, as is the letter Lucy writes to Harry from Philadelphia to attempt to break off all ties with him.

In my attempt to understand how these characters expressed themselves, I am forever indebted to the troves of letters written between Lucy and Henry B. Blackwell, many of which were compiled in *Loving Warriors: A Revealing Portrait of an Unprecedented Marriage*, edited by Leslie Wheeler, and the scores of letters written between Lucy and her friend and sister-in-law, Nette Brown, published in *Friends & Sisters: Letters between Lucy Stone and Antoinette Brown Blackwell, 1846–93*, edited by Carol Lasser and Marlene Deahl Merrill. Additional letters, diaries, and family papers were made available to me through the Blackwell Family collection at the Schlesinger Library at the Radcliffe Institute for Advance Study at Harvard University. All of these helped me understand the inner workings of Lucy's heart and mind and of those closest to her. While I occasionally borrowed a snippet from these historical documents for a piece of dialogue or turn of phrase in a letter, the words given to the characters of this novel are otherwise mine.

There are three books to which I am particularly indebted for my understanding of Lucy Stone's life: *Lucy Stone: An Unapologetic Life*, by Sally G. McMillen, which introduced me to this incredible woman; *Lucy Stone: Speaking Out for Equality*, by Andrea Moore Kerr; and *Lucy Stone: Pioneer of Woman's Rights*, by Alice Stone Blackwell. Yes, Alice did in fact write a biography of her mother, finally publishing it in 1930, thirty-seven years after her mother's death. Among other things, it was this book that led me to the various poems Lucy enjoyed throughout her life, including the poem I have Lucy ask Susan B. Anthony to read at her bedside. Lucy enjoyed this poem during her illness, but the author is unfortunately unknown.

Other resources integral to my research include:

My Bondage and My Freedom, Frederick Douglass
Fighting Chance: The Struggle over Woman Suffrage and Black Suffrage in Reconstruction America, Faye E. Dudden
The Solitude of Self: Thinking about Elizabeth Cady Stanton, Vivian Gornick
In Her Own Right: The Life of Elizabeth Cady Stanton, Elisabeth Griffith

The Life and Work of Susan B. Anthony, Including Public Addresses, Her Own Letters, and Many from Her Contemporaries during Fifty Years, volume 1, Ida Husted Harper
Morning Star: A Biography of Lucy Stone, 1818–1893, Elinor Rice Hays
Frederick Douglass, William S. McFeely
Growing Up in Boston's Gilded Age: The Journal of Alice Stone Blackwell, 1872–1874, edited by Marlene Deahl Merrill
Failure Is Impossible: Susan B. Anthony in Her Own Words, Lynn Sherr
Solitude of Self, Elizabeth Cady Stanton
History of Woman Suffrage, edited by Elizabeth Cady Stanton, Susan B. Anthony, Matilda Joslyn Gage, and Ida Husted Harper

ACKNOWLEDGMENTS

Writing a book and getting it out in the world can feel a bit like trying to put together a puzzle with a pile of endlessly changing pieces, a task that would have proved futile for me without the creative, emotional and professional support I received from so many.

My first thanks must go to Jessica Case for her excitement about this book and immediate understanding of its current relevance. You are a joy to work with, and I consider myself enormously lucky to have you as my Editor and Publisher. It is a privilege to be part of the Pegasus family. My thanks also to Jen Rivera, Maria Fernandez, Derek Thornton for the gorgeous cover, and Andrea Monagle—your thorough work to confirm historical details was impressive and much appreciated.

To Michael Carlisle of Inkwell Management for your belief in the potential of my writing career those many years ago. And to Michael Mungiello for your grace and persistence.

As always, I am indebted to trusted readers willing to provide feedback on early manuscripts. To Nora Speer for your enthusiasm about Lucy Stone from the get-go and your steady check-ins on the book (for years on end!). To Deborah Plummer for lending your keen eye to my treatment of racial issues in this story. I have learned so much from you over the years on this topic in general, and your editorial suggestions helped make this a better book. And buckets of gratitude to my sister, Lynn Tetrault, who often believes in me more than I do in myself. That walk on the beach in Nantucket just might have changed everything! I'm so lucky to count you as a sister and friend.

There aren't enough words of thanks for the Four Points Writers—Susan Bernhard, Michele Ferrari and Jessie Manchester Lubitz. Having a consistent place to turn for detailed writing critiques, brainstorming sessions, pep talks and just plain fun has been a godsend. As we stumble through this writing journey together without shelter or supplies, you each offer sustenance just when it is needed most.

To friends and family who read this book at various stages and pulled out your pompoms to cheer me on: Brendan and Sinead O'Connor, John and Deb Apruzzese, Kathleen Sherbrooke, Vincent Apruzzese and Nan Bewlay. Your praise for the book and encouragement means the world to me.

To Pam Loring and the Salty Quill 2018 writer's retreat. Your enthusiastic reception of Lucy that night by the fire sustained me in times of uncertainty more than you can possibly know, and the space to write in communion with other authors was a true gift.

To Caroline Leavitt for your savvy editorial eye and the many ways you helped me better animate Lucy on the page. And to Mitch Zuckoff for generously taking the time to help me see for myself that I needed to write Lucy's story as a novel.

As always, to GrubStreet, a place that made me feel from day one that I belonged. To Eve Bridburg for your continued friendship and encouragement, Chris Castellani for always being at the ready to offer advice, and to the incredible ecosystem of writers, instructors, board members and staff that make it such a warm home for all of us. My life is richer for all of you.

There are two statues without which I would not likely have discovered Lucy Stone nor developed the curiosity to research her further. The first is The Women's Memorial on Commonwealth Avenue in Boston. Sculpted by Meredith Bergman, it is dedicated to "three women who helped shape the City's history:" Lucy Stone, Phillis Wheatley and Abigail Adams. While Adams was well known to me, I had never before heard of Phillis Wheatley, a former slave whose 1773 volume of poems was the first book published by an African American writer in America, nor Lucy Stone. My curiosity was piqued.

The second statue, the Portrait Monument, sculpted by Adelaide Johnson, was unveiled in the Capitol in 1921, six months after suffrage was ratified, and depicts Lucretia Mott, Elizabeth Cady Stanton and Susan B. Anthony, three women who (per the inscription) "stand unique and peerless" in the fight for a woman's right to vote. The fact that the statue was shut away in a broom closet the day after its unveiling (not to be returned to its rightful place in the Rotunda until 1995) is a worthy story in its own right. But what really struck me was the "astonishment" of Sally G. McMillian—as stated in the introduction to her Stone biography—that a statue anointing the foremothers of suffrage could possibly omit Lucy Stone. McMillian's claim that Lucy deserved to be chiseled there set me on a quest to understand what she had achieved, and why she had been so badly overlooked by history.

Those twin experiences of inclusion and omission served as an important reminder to me that marble statues, published histories and broadcasted accounts of events have a way of cementing narratives and enshrining individuals into the foundation of our shared history while belittling or ignoring others. I'm grateful for the current debate across our country about which statues and stories deserve to remain and which need to be reconsidered, removed or told anew.

Lastly, and most importantly, the opportunity to sit in my chair every day to write, and the ability to face the terror of trying to get my work out in the world, would not be possible without the love and support of my family. To my sons, Henry and George, your willingness to challenge me, coupled with your good humor and steadfast affection remind me every day that there is life beyond the page, and a great one at that. I hope you will always keep your minds and hearts open to new ideas. I'll try to do the same. And to Patrick, I know how much you shoulder every day so that I can burrow into my fictional worlds for hours on end. Your support and encouragement are everything. Having the chance to walk through this thing called life with you is a blessing I count every day.